ISLAND WITCH

ALSO BY AMANDA JAYATISSA

My Sweet Girl

You're Invited

ISLAND WITCH

AMANDA JAYATISSA

BERKLEY
NEW YORK

BERKLEY
An imprint of Penguin Random House LLC
penguinrandomhouse.com

Copyright © 2024 by Amanda Jayatissa
Penguin Random House supports copyright. Copyright fuels creativity, encourages diverse voices, promotes free speech, and creates a vibrant culture. Thank you for buying an authorized edition of this book and for complying with copyright laws by not reproducing, scanning, or distributing any part of it in any form without permission. You are supporting writers and allowing Penguin Random House to continue to publish books for every reader.

BERKLEY and the BERKLEY & B colophon are registered trademarks of Penguin Random House LLC.

Library of Congress Cataloging-in-Publication Data

Names: Jayatissa, Amanda, author.
Title: Island witch / Amanda Jayatissa.
Description: New York: Berkley, 2024.
Identifiers: LCCN 2023026675 (print) | LCCN 2023026676 (ebook) |
ISBN 9780593549261 (hardcover) | ISBN 9780593549285 (ebook)
Subjects: LCGFT: Novels.
Classification: LCC PR9440.9.J36 I85 2024 (print) |
LCC PR9440.9.J36 (ebook) | DDC 813/.6—dc23/eng/20230616
LC record available at https://lccn.loc.gov/2023026675
LC ebook record available at https://lccn.loc.gov/2023026676

Printed in the United States of America
1st Printing

Book design by Alison Cnockaert

This is a work of fiction. Names, characters, places, and incidents either are the product of the author's imagination or are used fictitiously, and any resemblance to actual persons, living or dead, business establishments, events, or locales is entirely coincidental.

I've always said that I'm phenomenally lucky to be
surrounded and supported by a group of strong women.
From my grandmothers to my mother, mother-in-law, family,
best friends, and the amazing women I've met in publishing,
they've raised me up, encouraged me to chase my dreams,
and taught me to never give up on what I believe in.

This book is dedicated to them, and to all women
who stand by one another.

In the long fifty-year night,
these are the words that crawl out of the wall:
Suffer. Monster. Burn in Hell.
When morning comes,
I will finally tell.
Amen.

—Carol Ann Duffy,
"The Devil's Wife"

AUTHOR'S NOTE

My beautiful island has been called many names throughout history. It was known as Taprobane by the Greeks, Serendib by the Arabs, Ceylon by the British—which is when this story takes place—amongst many others.

We've been colonised by the Portuguese, the Dutch, and the British respectively, followed by a horrific, thirty-year-long civil war. We are no strangers to atrocities—those committed against us, and also those we have committed against one another.

This story touches on some of those atrocities. The impact of colonialism, the clash of religious beliefs, and violence against women are themes that are prevalent in my novel. The decision to include them was not one I took lightly, but I also felt it would be a disservice to erase these realities, especially as now, about a hundred and fifty years later, much of these issues continue to haunt us.

But while this novel takes place in a historical setting, this is by no means a history lesson. It's simply a story, as many dark tales go, of fear and desperation, and of the limitless boundaries of female rage.

ISLAND WITCH

PROLOGUE

BLOOD COURSED THROUGH him like a rich nectar I wanted to lap up. He moved through the jungle by himself, unbothered, perfectly confident in the way that only a man could be. Like he never had to worry about danger. Like he never had reason to be fearful for his life. Like the thought never even crossed his mind. It was the gift of his birth.

Fear is a woman's burden. We are entrenched in it from the time we are born. Told to protect ourselves, especially our bodies. Heaven knows we've been told to value them more than our minds. We've been told to keep safe. Caution becomes our second nature from the time we are young girls, only blossoming deeper as we grow older. Our fathers, our neighbours, our villagers rally around to protect us, lest we, delicate little things, are unable to fend for ourselves. Be careful of strangers, they warned. Be careful of the jungle. Be careful even of your own thoughts. They say this, even though the fathers, the neighbours, the villagers are often the very ones we need protecting from.

But this man, walking through the lush jungle that was perfumed with wet earth and beads of dew and bodies that lay rotting in the ground, had never thought about protection. He was at home, he thought, making the same mistake as so many before him. Amongst the trees that towered over him, afoot on the springy moss that carpeted his walk, oblivious to the animals who cried out their warnings, he thought he was king.

Little did he know that the jungle never bowed down to any man. Little did he know that I, the jungle's most loyal servant, lay in wait for him.

I licked my lips. It wouldn't be long until his blood ran like sweet wine down my mangled throat.

As noiseless as a shadow, I slunk after him. My breath whispered across the back of his neck. I reached out a finger and traced the air outlining the ridge of his ear. I almost licked the vein that throbbed under his jaw. He must have felt me, then, because he glanced over his shoulder, the small hairs on his arms rising.

Of course, he didn't pay heed to his instincts. A lifetime of never being wary made him believe he was untouchable. He continued on, not realising that I was less than a step behind him. I breathed in his scent. He was no different from the rest of them.

Unable to help myself, I gave the lightest chuckle. So soft, he wasn't even sure he heard it.

But he paused, all the same.

"Who's there?" he asked. His voice was even. There was not the slightest hint of tremble in it. Yet.

But that was enough jest for now. It was time to begin.

Leaving him, I took a shortcut through the jungle and positioned myself at a clearing.

While I was all rotten flesh, cruel gashes and gaping wounds covering my body, he would see only beauty. A woman in white, smiling shyly at him under the moonlight, her black hair floating like silk about her shoulders.

"Will you help me, sir?" I asked, my voice gentle and clear and not relaying even a hint of the fury that churned within me.

I spoke of how fearlessness was the gift of his birth. As it turned out, it was also his curse.

"Of course, madam," he replied without even a moment's hesitation.

I smiled. A real smile that would have shown my rotten teeth and putrid, blackened gums, except his ignorance didn't allow him to see that.

I led him deeper into the jungle, so deep that I was certain no one could hear the screams that would soon come. He followed me readily, a puppy who had just found a new bone. He grinned at me when I turned to face him, his eyes sparkling with expectation.

And in a flash of anger that shot through me, I revealed my true self.

Gone was the lustrous hair, replaced with chunks that fell away from my scalp, a tangled, stinking mess. Gone were the soft lips that he undoubtedly imagined grazing his own, my own ripped to shreds that were bloodied and foul. Gone were the soft hands, now turned to claws of a beast ready to hack at his pitiful face.

I saw the grin melt off his face, replaced, first, by hesitation—were his eyes playing tricks on him in the darkness? And then, finally, *finally* by fear. A shiver of pleasure hummed through me as his pupils grew and his mouth opened in a silent gasp. Blood was delicious, of course, but the look of dread in a man who was unspoiled by the horrors of the world was what led me to the jungle in the first place. It was what kept me here.

Some men screamed when they first saw the real me. Others cowered, frozen in place. But not him.

He turned around and fled.

So, he wanted to play. Wonderful.

He wove through the trees, jumping over protruding roots and ducking past low-hanging branches, nimble and quick. But he could never be a match for me.

I gave him a head start before I pounced forward on all fours, a creature birthed from the darkest depths of vengeance. I caught up to him in a matter of moments, using my nails to slash the backs of his ankles so he couldn't run any further.

I crawled over him, trapping him under me. Extending the claw on my index finger, I traced a line down his collarbone, enjoying the way his heart was pounding, the way his breath came out in desperate gasps, the way he trembled.

He whimpered in horror as I widened my jaw all the way down to my chest and lunged at him, taking a large bite out of his chest. I clawed at the soft flesh of his belly, ripping him open, revelling in the splatter of blood that sprayed on me as one relishes the rain on a warm day.

And as he lay blubbering on the jungle floor, his innards spilling out of him, I leaned over, extended my rancid tongue, and licked the decadent blood off his cheek.

"You're mine now," I rasped into his ear, relishing the desperation that flooded through him. Savouring that it was me who finally made him feel afraid. Luxuriating in the power I now had.

He would suffer as I once did. Suffer for everything he had done. Suffer for the wrongs that were committed before him and those that would no doubt come after him. That was all I wanted. For them to all suffer as I had.

1

THE DEMON-DRUMS STARTED and the little girl's face contorted like a blood-soaked rag being twisted dry. Her tongue hung out, purple and almost to her chest, a dribble of spit leaving a dark, wet mark on the loose nightdress she wore. The thick smoke from the perfumed incense made everything look like it was enveloped inside a dark cloud. I craned my neck out further from behind the curtain that separated the main room from the rest of the house, where I was hiding, hoping that no one would notice me.

My father sat in front of the girl. I knew she was ten years old, but she looked much younger as she thrashed around on the mat that had been laid on the floor. Almost like an animal about to be taken to the slaughter. I noticed that her white cotton nightdress was embroidered with little yellow ducks. I'd had a similar nightgown when I was that age.

The light of the small clay lamp that my father held in his palms cast strange shadows on his face as he chanted pirith. He was blessing her, and most importantly, blessing what was about to happen next. They had passed around pirith nool to everyone who was in attendance a while back—the protective thread that was meant to be tied around our wrists—so that meant things were about to begin.

May the blessings of the triple gem be with you, I silently mouthed, my own prayer for my father. Words I had uttered countless times, but still, today, they wilted on my tongue like sleeping grass when you touched it. Exorcisms were never cheerful events, but there was a certain hardness clinging to the air this evening, leaving everyone clenching their fists and shortening their breath, rigid and strained.

Three young men lined up, waiting for my father to say the word. They had on colourfully painted wooden devil masks. The same kind that hung in our hut—bad spirits to scare away worse spirits. I was thankful that these men hadn't abandoned him. Most people in the village had, though my father, Thaththa to me, would never blame them.

"People have a right to believe in what they choose to," he'd said, the finality in his voice conjuring rocks in my chest. There was a time we'd talk about anything and everything, but not any-more.

A tiny voice cut through my thoughts. "Aren't you scared, Amara Akki?" Siyath Malli asked me. Our parents were friends, and I'd been there the day Siyath was born. That was six years ago, and I was eighteen now. His eyes were wider than the possessed girl's and his lips quivered. Even though he threatened my hiding spot, I couldn't help but laugh at his expression. I put a finger to my mouth and ushered him to join me behind the curtain.

"Why?" I whispered. "Are you afraid of men in masks?"

We had a funny relationship with spirits on this island. We respected them, but we didn't fear them in the same way the British did, or the Dutch before them, or the nuns who taught me back when I used to attend school. We used them to help us, often against other spirits. I suppose you could say it was fighting fire with fire—although the only real fire here was from the torches my father had ordered lit around the property.

"No matter what, don't ever let the torches die out," he had said to his assistants. The same men who wore the wooden devil masks and had tied gejji—bells—around their ankles, waiting to dance a tovil on my father's orders. The devil dance was meant to draw out the evil spirit that had wedged itself inside the poor girl.

The De Silva family had come to see my father five days before. Clifford De Silva had brought home some beef, freshly slaughtered at the market, but when his wife had opened the parcel to make a curry for dinner, the meat had been rotten. Crawling with maggots, he'd said, and the stench had caused his daughter to vomit. It was definitely a hooniyama, Clifford had cried, a curse, cast by his neighbours, who had recently argued with him about a fence put up at the edge of his property. The neighbours claimed it was on five yards of their own land, but Clifford said they'd have to take it up with the British, who had gifted the property to his family for their support.

My father had narrowed his eyes at that, but had not said anything. Support for the British meant that the De Silva family would have joined the Christian church. Or perhaps they had already converted many years ago—their new name certainly suggested so, as did eating beef, which Buddhists never did. And my father made it very clear to me and my mother how he felt about that.

But most importantly, my father didn't like to deal with demons—yakku, as we called them here. My father was a Capuwa, he liked to clarify, and this profession required him to appeal to deviyo—the gods. He was mostly called upon to bless houses, cut limes to ward off the evil eye, administer tonics. Not to be confused with a Cattadiya, who used the dark powers of yakku.

He had given Clifford De Silva some blessed talismans—prayers inscribed and rolled into small clay pots—to hang in the four corners of his house for protection, and suggested he speak to the priest at the Christian church if his troubles continued.

But he didn't have the heart to refuse Clifford when he visited our home for the second time two days later, at the very crack of dawn, hair dishevelled and eyes bloodshot, trembling like a leaf. His daughter, Lalitha, had started speaking in a different tongue, he sobbed. What little they could understand was all profanity. Curse words that the girl had never once uttered in her life—words that she had not even heard before, he claimed. She would lie on her mat, her body bending and contorting while she hissed and spit and snarled. She had tried to bite the Christian priest who came to bless her. She'd been possessed by a yaka, Clifford cried.

His face grim, my father simply nodded and started to make preparations. This was no job for a foreign god. We had to deal with our demons the traditional way.

"It's not the masks I'm afraid of," Siyath Malli said, curling his small body into mine. "It's the yaka."

My father preferred not to deal with yakku, but I had grown up watching him perform these rituals when it was absolutely necessary. I'd usually help him—gathering the objects he needed, making sure everything was ready, though he never let me participate in the exorcism itself. I was still too young, he said, until a few weeks ago when he appeared to have changed his mind completely and declared I wasn't allowed to be involved at all.

I'll claw out your tongue if you tell. No one can find out what happened.

A chill ran through me, but not because of the scene in front of us. Since the last full moon, I'd been having dreams. They started in the same place every time. In a small hut, at the very edge of the world. It was made of mud, like most huts, but it had no sleeping mat, no shelves or baskets to store things in. All it had were old, tattered curtains in a surprising, startling red.

And every time I stepped out of the hut, my surroundings would be different. Sometimes I would be deep in the heart of the jungle. Sometimes on the ocean shore. But each time, without fail, one thing was constant.

Her.

I didn't know her name. I didn't know what she wanted. She was a monster. Demoness. A yakshaniya. Every time I dreamt of her, her image would get clearer in my mind.

I pushed the dream to the back of my mind and looked down at the small boy in front of me. "No, Malli, I'm not scared. And you shouldn't be either. Shall we shout some insults at the yaka?"

But he just shook his head.

"This yaka is useless. He's as weak as a worm," I cried, and Siyath Malli giggled. Closer to the exorcism, others were hurling insults too, as a group of older men and women, maybe the family of the possessed, were reciting pirith. This was the first step—taunting the demon. To shame it into submission. The tovil dancers would come out in a while too, pretending to be devils themselves, pantomiming the most ridiculous scenarios. When the yaka couldn't bear the humiliation anymore, it would speak out, and that's when my father would get to work. He'd transfer it to another object—a bottle, perhaps, or a small pot—before tying it with blessed string and burying it somewhere far, far away where it couldn't find its way back to torment anyone else.

"Come on, let's go outside," I said, taking Siyath Malli's hand. When he was a baby, I'd mixed a spoon of soot with water and put a large black dot on his forehead to ward off the evil eye—as vaha, kata vaha, we called it. *Poison from the eyes, poison from the mouth.* Nobody ever spoke about poison that would leak out of a heart, the way that Clifford De Silva's neighbour's supposedly did. But still, everyone knew that if you made a deal with a devil, it wouldn't be long before the devil came to claim its dues.

It was time for me to leave anyway. The truth was that Thaththa would be furious if he found out that I was here tonight, when he had specifically told me not to come. He'd been teaching me about his craft, and I'd even been taking on the duties of his apprentice after I'd finished with school. It was what he'd been grooming me for ever since I was a little girl, letting me accompany him to all these rituals, and teaching me about the old ways.

But all that changed about a month ago. I'd been ill, I think. The kind of sick that leaves your body feeling like it was on fire and your head was being dashed on the waves. I'd drifted in and out of consciousness until I finally recovered, only to be told by my parents that they didn't want me participating in my father's practices anymore. And I had more than a little trouble accepting their reasons why.

"You're a young woman now, awaiting a suitable marriage," my mother had interjected, and I bit my tongue so I wouldn't say anything to anger her. She had a much shorter temper than my father, and the last thing I wanted was to provoke her. "It's not proper to be out and about, away from home in the middle of the night. It'll ruin your reputation, diminish your chances. Another year and it'll be too late for you to wed at all. No, from now on, you will assist me with my sewing work."

I knew, deep down where the truth always managed to make itself heard, that she did have a point. That I was probably one of the last of the girls from my class at school to be married. That the whispers didn't have to reach my ears for me to know what everyone was saying.

2

WE'D JUST STEPPED outside the De Silvas' home when Siyath Malli tugged on my arm.

"Amara Akki, what's happening over there?"

He was pointing to a small crowd that had gathered just outside the torch line that Thaththa had set up. I had an inkling from the expressions on their faces that this wasn't going to end well, and when I saw who led the group, I knew for certain.

Aloysius Peiris, my father's staunchest adversary, was arguing emphatically with some of Clifford De Silva's relations. He stood almost a head above the other men, skin glowing pale in the light of the flames. He was younger than his counterparts, but most of the men flocked to him like it was the most natural thing in the world.

"These attacks in the jungle," Aloysius boomed while I edged close enough to listen to what was happening. "What are they, if not sorcery? And now all of you are casting your lot with the demon worshipper and all this talk of black magic."

My pulse quickened. This wasn't the first time someone had

tried to link Thaththa to the attacks, but it was certainly the first time I'd heard it done so blatantly.

A few short months ago, villagers would loiter outside well after sunset—chatting to their friends, visiting with loved ones. Children would climb the banyan trees, spying on the teenagers gossiping in the shadows. But not anymore. The stale smell of worry hung in the air, and everyone retreated inside their homes as if their lives depended on it. I supposed they did. Tonight was an exception, because of the tovil, but that was perhaps why Aloysius and his cronies decided to cause a scene.

"Aloysius, we don't want trouble. We just need to rid the poor girl of this demon and then things can go back to normal." I knew the man was just trying to pacify the situation, but I couldn't help but snort. What was normal? Everyone cowering in fear, blaming my father for something he was not involved in. All while they still begged for his help when things got out of their control.

But my snort drew more attention than I'd hoped for. The men from the crowd, the welcome and the unwelcome, whipped in my direction. Eyes were narrowed. I heard a sharp intake of breath from a few of them.

"Looks like the demon worshipper brought his daughter to help with his moneymaking venture." Aloysius's voice was slippery like slime.

"Excuse me?" My voice came out haughty, and surprisingly like my mother's.

"Good thing Clifford's daughter was *possessed*." I heard a small snicker run through the group. "I got word your family has fallen on hard times. How very convenient that your father was called on."

"He's just trying to help her." I made sure that my voice was steady.

"I'm sure he is," Aloysius replied with a smirk.

"If you came inside and saw the girl . . ." I tried to explain. "Lalitha was—"

"My niece and her are in the same class," Aloysius interrupted. "They had their midterm tests this week. Guess who was able to conveniently miss it because of her theatrics?"

"What?"

"And I heard that it wasn't the first time she did something like this either. She fell down with convulsions on her cousin's wedding day last year. They said she was jealous that the bride was getting all the attention."

I thought back to the girl inside, writhing on the floor. If it was all just pretend, she was more convincing than any of the actresses at the Nativity plays put on by the church.

"We are not blaming the girl, of course," Aloysius continued, looking straight at me. "Women, especially young women, cannot be held accountable for their hysterics. It's simply in their nature. But to extort the family at a delicate time like this, now, that is the true crime."

Some of the men he was with cheered.

My body trembled, a traitor to the indifferent image I was trying to maintain. My father had been accused of many things, especially since Aloysius had become one of the aides to the Mudaliyar—the village headman. It felt like he had a personal axe to grind against Thaththa. It didn't help that everyone in this town revered him like he was some sort of prophet. But surely, the townsfolk were smarter than to believe a charismatic man spewing hate over the truth that lay right in front of their eyes?

"I know you are loyal to your father, Amara. But you are young and there's hope for you yet. Rebuke these demon-worshipping ways and come to the light!"

I glared at him.

"Your allegations are preposterous. If you have any real evidence against my father then I'm sure we'd all love to hear it."

Aloysius held his arms wide in a false surrender. "I'm only beseeching everyone to use their heads. From what we see, it's awfully convenient for your father if the people in our town have to be afraid of some makeshift demon, herding everyone away from the church." Sarcasm dripped from his voice like bile.

And then a cough from someone else in the group that sounded suspiciously like *witch*.

That was a new word over here. We have Capuwas like my father who work with deviyo, we have Cattadiyas who work with yakku, we have astrologers who look to the stars and the planets for answers, and all of these jobs could be done by either a man or a woman. A witch—exclusively a woman who is thought to have magical powers—is a new term brought over by the British. It was one of the many new ideas that had started to take root.

Just then, a bloodcurdling scream shot its way through the night air. The yaka had made its entrance sooner than we'd expected.

The men paled. Some of them clutched one another. No matter what they said about not believing in demons, no one could deny how horrific it sounded.

I looked right at Aloysius and gave him a little smile. "This is the best part. Do you want to go inside? You have nothing to be afraid of since she's just pretending."

He managed a half smile. "The two frauds can settle their

business without me," he said, but his voice had lost some of its bravado.

I should have left. I should have continued out and made my way home, especially now that I'd been spotted. But I hadn't lied. This *was* the best part, and surely I could spare just a few more moments to see it?

Leaving the men cowering amongst themselves, I snuck back in and peered towards Lalitha De Silva as she let out another scream. The exorcism had to be working. You could tell because in between the screams and the drool spilling out like snakes from her mouth, there were glimpses of the real Lalitha. The little girl sobbed, her eyes wide and fearful, and she kept trying to curl into a fetal position and suck her thumb—even as her relatives did their best to keep her pinned down to the mat.

There was no way she was simply acting, was there?

Aloysius was right about one thing, as much as I did hate to admit it—there was no way to be sure. But wasn't that the way faith in anything worked?

I wondered what it must feel like to be possessed. Did you know if there was an evil inside you? Were you able to control it? There were times, especially since my nightmares began, that I would sleepwalk. When I'd go to sleep on my mat in my room but wake up somewhere completely different. Somewhere I had no memory of walking to. Maybe being possessed was like that? Maybe you just felt like you were asleep?

The chanting grew louder and louder, until it reverberated in the air like a swarm of bees. The girl screamed and pulled and spat, her movements speeding up as the chanting reached its crescendo.

And then it stopped.

A moment of silence hung in the air.

The girl's mouth opened, but the demon did not speak. Instead, her lips stretched in a wide grin, even though there was no smile in her eyes, which stared blankly at something in the distance. Then her body shook. A loud guffaw from deep inside her belly in a voice that was too deep, too cruel to be her own.

I gasped.

I shot a look at my father, but he didn't seem particularly fazed. He leaned towards one of his assistants, who mumbled something in his ear. Thaththa nodded and reached to his side, looking in my direction.

I ducked behind an older woman.

He hadn't seen me, had he?

I felt my heart sink into my chest.

Lalitha guffawed again, her saliva spluttering around her.

"Umbala hithuwe maava yawaganna leisiwey kiyala, neda?" *You fools thought it would be easy to get rid of me, didn't you?* She spoke in the voice of a man much older than her—low and menacing, breathing raggedly. Those standing next to me gasped.

But something felt wrong to me. I frowned, trying to think why. Those were the same words that the yaka had said at an exorcism about half a year ago. An exorcism that Lalitha De Silva had attended. I remembered it clearly, because she wasn't supposed to be there that night, and her mother came searching for her, questioning all the children until she found her. The De Silvas attended the Christian church, after all, where all talk of yakku and tovils was frowned on. It felt a little strange that these were the same exact words that the yaka uttered now.

But even if Aloysius was right about Lalitha, that didn't make my father a fraud.

Around me, the pirith started up again. The ringing of the

prayers was more important now than ever to keep the demon at bay.

Thaththa turned back towards Lalitha, and I took the moment to slip away. The yaka's voice seeping like poison out of the small girl was chilling, but nothing scared me more than disappointing my father.

3

THE MOON WAS high in the sky as I walked home from the exorcism—a luminous disk casting a ring on the clouds that surrounded it. We'd have a full moon in a few days again, and full moons were always auspicious.

The trees swayed gently in the night breeze, their leaves silver in the moonlight. If I closed my eyes and really listened, I could hear the gentle hum of the wind competing with the light chirp of the odd cicada. It throbbed with familiarity. Normally, this would put me at peace. Tonight it made the hairs on my arms stand up. My dream kept returning, unwelcome, to my thoughts. It was like someone was speaking to me.

She's brought this on herself. No one can help her now.

My eyes fluttered open.

I heard a sound. A rustling. Footsteps, maybe. The strange sensation that I was being watched. Or followed. My dreams came flooding back to me and I held my breath, listening hard.

I hadn't taken a torch of my own. I'd been far too distracted by the exorcism and Aloysius's accusations. But I felt silly now. It might have come in useful for protection if I needed it. I should have known better than to wander by myself like this, especially since the attacks. Most mothers wouldn't dream of letting their daughters out even to their back gardens. Mine was the same, except she had no clue that I wasn't safely tucked away in my sleeping mat.

I felt for my suray, the talisman that dangled around my neck. My father had given it to me a month before, around the same time he told me that I wouldn't be able to accompany him during his practice anymore. The talisman was made of brass and shaped into a small tube. It held a prayer inscribed on a rolled sheet of copper. It was meant to protect me, but I never understood from what.

"Please stop with all the questions, duwa. Just promise me you will never take it off, do you hear?" he had said, tying it around my neck. He had been sad, and a part of me was glad that he was. There was an ache that started within me that day, and it had yet to stop.

The suray was warm between my fingers as I listened again for the footsteps, cursing myself for being so foolish and being out here alone.

But I heard only the wind rattling between the trees.

Taking a deep breath, I continued forward.

"I am safe," I muttered to myself. "This jungle is my home."

I settled into a quick rhythm, my feet easily navigating their way across the soft, mossy floor. I had nothing to fear, I kept reminding myself.

That's when a pair of arms grabbed me from behind, pulling me off the path and behind a large tree, pressing my back against its trunk as a hand clamped down on my mouth.

I'd been wrong to ignore the whisperings of the attacks when the entire village had been warning me for weeks. I'd been so stupid for ignoring my dreams. My eyes tried to focus as my body froze in fear. If I could see the yaka, then maybe I could save myself somehow. I braced, expecting the worst.

"Shh!" A familiar voice, behind a beautiful, wide smile.

"Raam!" I gasped. "You scared me." I wanted to frown. To show him that I wasn't happy. That he shouldn't shock me like this. But my lips betrayed me as they curled into a grin of my own, even as my heart showed no sign of slowing down.

"I'm sorry." The moonlight highlighted the dimples on his cheeks as the remaining droplets of my fear dissolved away. I was still breathless, only now it was breathlessness of a different kind.

He leaned over, his lips brushing my forehead before he pulled away, releasing me from the tree. He smelled of sea salt and coconut, and I wished he had held me there just a while longer.

"What are you doing here?"

"I knew you'd come for the tovil, so I thought I'd wait. See if I could catch you on the way home. I've been missing you." His hand reached for mine, entwining our fingers together while my heart glowed brighter than the stars.

"I've missed you too." I felt heat on my cheeks. I hoped he wouldn't notice. I don't think I could really put into words how much I had longed for him. Not just that I wished he was with me, but that an entire piece of me was gone whenever we were apart.

"So? How are you? Are you still having those dreams?"

I shrugged. It felt wrong to give him details. How I had seen the yakshaniya's face so clearly last night. How the taste of blood felt lush and satisfying on my tongue. How I was waking up further and further from home. It would only make him worry.

"How is work with your mother?" he tried again.

"Work with her is, you know—" I shrugged for the second time. He had been far more enthusiastic than I was when I told him about the turn of events at home. A cruel, ugly voice in my ear whispered that it was probably easier to explain to his family that he hoped to marry a seamstress rather than a Capuwa's daughter, but, again, I shook it off. Raam was supportive and kind. An eternal optimist, searching unabashedly for the brighter side to things.

"I know." He smiled back. That smile again. I forced myself to take another breath.

Still holding my hand, he led me back to the path.

"Come on. Let me walk you back."

"It's too dangerous, Raam. What if someone sees?" Like every other girl in my position, I had to keep Raam a secret. After all, while we had spoken about marriage, Raam hadn't exactly committed yet.

"More dangerous than you being by yourself in the jungle at night?"

It didn't matter that it wasn't. My weak protest was halfhearted, and he knew it. I wasn't ready to say goodbye so soon.

We'd been together for over two years now, though it had become more serious these last few months. Once we became formally betrothed, we'd finally be able to interact with each other in public. There was something exciting about meeting in the jungle, slipping out of my hut in the middle of the night, racing back before my parents awoke. But the last few times I went to meet Raam at night, I couldn't shake the feeling of being followed.

Raam was waiting for the right time to speak to his father—a man he feared far more than anything that happened in the jungle. It upset me that he'd been delaying it for so long, even though Raam had patiently explained it to me many times. I supposed, if I tried hard enough, I could understand. I knew what it felt like to disappoint your family, even if, in my case, I wasn't quite sure why. I didn't want that for him. But Raam's father had recently been appointed to a senior position at the harbour, a role that came with more than just a significant pay raise. His whole family had recently converted to Christianity, for one. And everyone, especially Raam, his eldest son, was expected to support the British and be exemplary townsfolk. His father had even secured a junior clerk position for Raam, and even though he claimed to hate it, I could tell that this was a significant achievement for his family.

As soon as things settled down, Raam promised, he would speak to his father, and mine. I just had to be patient a few more months.

And more importantly, my mother, who had actively started seeking proposals for me since my eighteenth birthday, needed to be patient too. Even then, Raam and I would have to pretend that we weren't already devoted to each other, that he'd simply noticed me at the market or at the temple, or some other socially acceptable location, and that he wanted my hand in marriage.

A lump rose in my throat. I wished that I could talk to Neha, my oldest friend, about this now, but she barely even looked at me when we passed in town. We'd once giggled about boys we thought were handsome, not that there were particularly many of them, but Neha had chosen a different life. Now she spoke of sin.

Sin. We'd used the term to pity someone. "Sin for him," we'd say, "he didn't catch enough fish at sea this morning." Or if we accumulated enough sins, we might be reborn as something bad in our next life—perhaps a dog, or a person from a lower caste. The nuns in my old school, however, used it to talk about the burning fires of hell. Sin was something dirty. A disease we might catch, that would damn us for eternity with no chance to ever redeem ourselves. I often wondered if Neha shared this belief now.

Because there was nothing sinful in the way Raam's body felt next to mine as we walked. Or if there was, I didn't care.

"So, did you ask them?" Raam's voice was low in the fresh jungle air, sucking me back to reality.

"Ask them what?"

"About going to the Devinuwara perahera? It's happening in a little over a week. You said you'd ask your mother if you could go? So that we could meet?"

"Umm . . ." I frowned. I didn't remember this. But then, I often did get a little too caught up in Raam when I was with him. Like his presence alone was intoxicating—making me forget the rest of the world. Making me forget myself.

"You got scared and didn't ask, did you?" Raam's words jibed at me. He grinned. "Don't worry. There's still plenty of time."

I wanted to ask him then if he'd decided when he was going to speak to his family. I'd been nervous about it ever since I heard about their conversion to Christianity. There was little doubt in my mind that they would approve of my father's profession. But my mother had told me that you shouldn't ask questions unless you were truly prepared to hear the reply, because it might not be the answer you want. And I didn't want to ruin the moment. The night was too beautiful.

We walked silently. I was increasingly aware of my palm getting sweaty in his, the way his breath traversed in and out of him—slow and lazy, unlike mine.

He stopped for a moment, holding me back. My heart hammered in my chest. He was going to kiss me. I took a deep breath to steady myself. There was an ache in me that only deepened the longer I spent time with him.

"Hang on," he murmured.

"What is it?" I whispered. I gave him a small smile.

"Shh."

A small rabbit hopped onto the path in front of us. Its white fur shone brightly as it stopped and sniffed at some weeds on the jungle floor. It didn't pay us the slightest bit of attention.

"Sweet, isn't it?" Raam asked.

"Yes," I said, my mind still on the kiss I hadn't gotten yet.

"I wonder if—" But he was interrupted.

A mongoose darted out from the shadows, grabbing the rabbit's neck in its jaws before disappearing again.

A small scream found its way out of my throat.

"Shh," Raam said, pulling me close.

"Oh, Raam, can't you stop it?"

His smile was different this time. More sympathetic.

"This is why I love you, Amara. You're so kind. So innocent."

"Like the rabbit who just got killed?"

"Don't be silly," he said. His face was just inches from mine. I could feel his breath fan against me. "I'll never let anything happen to you."

And then his lips met mine, and the rabbit and the mongoose and the demons that preyed in the jungle all evaporated into the night sky.

4

I CONVINCED RAAM to let me walk the last bit of the way home alone. If I had to weigh out being attacked or having to deal with my mother's wrath if she found I'd been seeing him, well, I'd choose a demon any day.

Most girls were close to their mothers, but mine never appeared particularly interested in me. And so, my father kept me by his side. Our relationship was rare—I'd been aware of that since I was a child.

He wasn't well-read, nor had he ever attended school, but the jungle was his kingdom. He taught me where I could find trees tall enough, with branches so wide that I could sit on them for hours. He showed me how to extract honey from a beehive without getting stung. He pointed to the sky and told me how the stars could point my way home if I ever got lost, just not to let my mother know that I'd been out wandering the jungle at night. He showed me what leaves were needed for his rituals, and the best times they should be plucked.

But he also insisted that I go to school, and that was the first time I'd been aware of how different I truly was. How much of an oddity my family was considered now that the British had established themselves and the church in our town had blossomed and gathered and laid down the rules.

My vast knowledge of the jungle did little to prepare me for what awaited me at school. The girls' class was hardly even a school, unlike the boys'. It was just a simple classroom run by nuns, where they taught us Bible verses and English.

"The witch is here. Be careful, she might put a spell on you," Daphne Perera had said in a loud, meant-to-be-heard whisper as I walked into my class a few minutes late. Her cheeks dimpled in a wicked smile, even though she was the picture of innocence with her lighter skin and thick, sleek braid. I'd only been attending school for a week by then, but that was all it took for her to single me out.

The old chapel had been divided into four quadrants with movable boards, and they were removed whenever there was a service. Otherwise, we sat on hard wooden benches that the sisters called pews, and stared at the blackboard at the front of class. It was extremely uncomfortable to sit on these pews, and I'd gotten into trouble for pulling my legs up on the bench and sitting cross-legged, like I was used to at home. The edge of the chapel held a cluster of wooden cubbies, where we were allowed to keep our books and ink.

"I think she put a love spell on Vasanth," Daphne had continued. She really was the worst of them. "He couldn't stop staring at her yesterday. Or maybe it was just at her tight—"

"Good morning, class," Sister Agatha interrupted, and I made my way over to my cubby quickly.

Sister Agatha started on the day's lesson, so I had opened my cubby to pull out my books before she noticed I wasn't at my seat.

I pushed my hand in, feeling around, when my fingers closed around something wet and hairy. That was when the stench hit me square in the face—of rust and rot and something vile, causing vomit to rise in my mouth. I pulled my hand back in shock, still holding on to the furry, palm-sized thing, a small scream bursting out of my lips.

It must have only been a few seconds, but it felt like it took me an hour to finally understand what it was—the head of a chicken, hacked off from its body. Its beady, dead eyes glared out, unfocused, as it dripped blood from my palm onto the chapel floor. My breath caught in my chest. I couldn't tear my gaze away from it.

From somewhere a million miles away, I heard a giggle.

"What on earth is it, Amara?" Sister Agatha's voice drifted over to me. "Why aren't you in your seat?"

But I was transfixed. Horrified by the way a single drop of blood ran down the chicken's beak.

Sister Agatha stormed her way over to me and gasped herself, her wrinkly fingers covering her mouth.

"What is this, Amara?" she asked.

I just gaped at her stupidly.

"Amara?" She sounded angry.

I heard Daphne Perera answer.

"I bet it's something she uses for her witchcraft, Sister."

A chorus of giggles broke out through the classroom.

I wanted to scream again. Or cry. Or take that chicken head and shove it down one of the girls' throats. Watch her choke on it.

But I stayed frozen. As still as a statue. Unable to say anything. Unable to defend myself.

Sister Agatha acted like the whole ordeal was somehow my fault. She made me go out back and bury the chicken head, and kept me at the chapel for ages as she questioned me about whether I was truly trying to put a curse on one of my classmates. It's true that some Cattadiyas sacrifice chicken blood to demons—Thaththa had told me that demons themselves crave blood over everything else, but are forever cursed not to be able to taste it.

I tried explaining this to Sister Agatha, but she directed me to kneel in the chapel and recite the Lord's Prayer one hundred times. The deep lines around her mouth puckering in disgust, she said that demons were trying to steal my soul and trap it in hell, and that I must be strong in my faith if I wanted to be free of them.

I tried to tell her about the stories of demons on our island. They caused maladies, illnesses of the body and sometimes of the mind, but they'd never kill. The king of demons, Wessamoony, had ordered it so. To ignore his wishes was a grave sin, even for demons. That's what Thaththa said, and he was an expert. Yakku couldn't steal our souls. Our souls belong to us and us only, and it's only after many rebirths and transmigrations that we receive the blessing of nirvana. The words spilled out of me like they had a mind of their own—things I'd grown up believing. I knew they were just stories, but still, if only Sister Agatha could understand them, then she'd understand that I had nothing to do with the bleeding animal head in my cubby.

But my efforts were futile, of course. I'd been warned by Amma not to talk about my father's beliefs at school. Only those who had adopted the religion of the British were allowed to attend. And so, I silently held out my hand and bit my lip while Sister Agatha gave me twenty stripes with her cane.

I cried and begged not to have to go back. And while I expected my mother to be unrelenting, I was surprised when Thaththa also insisted that it was for the best. He even walked me there himself for the next few weeks, just to make sure that I didn't run off to the jungle instead.

"Look for the good, even when it might be hard to find," he said, his voice kind and gentle in a way I'd missed so much these last few weeks.

And he was right—the good did come just a few days later. Neha leaned over while I was gathering my books.

"Don't let that stick in the mud Daphne worry you," she whispered. "She just doesn't like it when someone else gets any attention." The relief that flooded through me was bright and intense. Finally, a friend.

But all that was in the past. Thaththa and Neha had both drifted away from me, and the harder I tried to hold on, the further away they floated.

Why was love so burdensome? Wasn't it supposed to uplift, and nurture, and make you smile? Why instead did it make my heart ache? How come it just made me more aware of how much I had lost?

5

I WOKE UP on the beach again, my toes buried in the sand as water lapped around my ankles, finally jolting me to my feet. The sleepwalking had gotten out of hand lately. I'd moved an old wooden beam next to the mat I slept on so that it would block my path, but I must have found a way to get around it. I should use something bigger the next time. My mother had been so angry with me when she found me out here last week, curled up near a fishing boat with absolutely no recollection of how I got there. Or was that the week before?

I'll kill everyone myself if I have to. This cannot get out.

There was that voice again, burrowing itself in my mind, spreading rot through my thoughts. Was it Amma talking about my sleepwalking? Did the voice belong to her? I could never be sure.

"Sleepwalking means your soul is restless," I'd heard the nuns at school say. "And a restless soul is the devil's playground." Well, if Amma wanted this kept a secret, I could hardly blame her.

Aloysius was already out to accuse Thaththa for anything bad happening in the village, and the last thing I wanted was to stoke that fire.

Our small, mud-walled, whitewashed hut with its thatched roof lay squat just a stone's throw away from the beach—the bougainvillea bushes my mother wrestled with enveloping it like a hug. The garden edged its way right down to the golden sand, the coconut trees standing sentinel, giants against the brilliant blue sky. On the opposite end of our garden lay my second home, the jungle, where the monkeys and deer and my heart ran wild and free.

Our hut was further away from the village centre, if you could call the small smattering of similar mud-walled homes that huddled together a village, about an hour's walk from the main town itself. My father's ancestors, already from a low caste, hadn't changed their names when the foreigners first came to the island, and there was no way Thaththa would set foot inside a church, so he didn't have a land allotment that was considered to be very desirable. Not that I was complaining—I loved the calm of being away from everyone else. The only person who ever seemed to mind was my mother.

I grabbed my clothes off the clothesline and splashed some water on my face from the kaley—the earthen pot—outside. As with all water stored in these pots with narrow lips, it smelled of soil and rain. I could always say that I'd been bathing at the well we had at the corner of the garden if Amma asked why I was outdoors.

As quick as a cat, as silent as a shadow, I managed to slink through to the corner of the hut where I slept. No one saw me, honda velawata. *Thank goodness*. I rushed to dress. Rubbing some coconut oil onto my hair, I pulled it tight into a single braid and put on my clothes. It was a simple white cotton hattey, which was a blouse with gathered sleeves, and a long floral-printed reddha—similar to a sarong, but what women wore. I winced as I pleated the reddha, noticing a bruise on my leg. I must have hurt myself scrambling through the jungle last night.

But it wasn't the bruise that took up my attention. My blouse had gotten tight across my chest and Amma had only just sewed it for me. I sighed, tugging at the gap that had formed between the two clasps. I should go get a pin from the sewing basket. I could just hear Amma's voice chastising me—how could people trust us to sew their clothes for them when our own were ill fitting?

Lajja nadda? she would probably ask. *Aren't you ashamed?* It was a phrase she used often. It was a phrase I wore as unwillingly as this tight hattey. Shame had permeated me for as long as I could remember. It was planted by the nuns at school, and cultivated by the girls in my class. It only grew as I got older, even as I started to understand that I didn't have anything to be shameful for.

Thaththa's father had been a Capuwa before him, and my grandfather had learned the craft from his mother before that. They were gifts from deviyo themselves, Thaththa had explained. It was a reward for all the virtues they had performed in their past lives. He had carried on his family's craft even after both his parents passed away from malaria when he was just a young man.

Back when Thaththa was a child, no one had batted an eye. It was just a profession, same as a fisherman or a brick burner. But then the Christian church started being more vocal, the new Mudaliyar was appointed, with men like Aloysius along with him, and those who had known my father ever since he was a little boy started treating us with suspicion. Almost everyone in our village, and even a few villages over, had needed him at some point or another, but that didn't stop the hushed whispers, the soft jeers, the dirty looks that were often thrown our way, only made worse by these unexplained attacks. It wasn't easy being a Capuwa in these changed times. And it wasn't easy being the Capuwa's daughter either.

I folded my discarded nightclothes, storing them in a round wicker basket, and made sure I had dusted off my sleeping mat.

Amma's sewing machine gleamed in the corner—the one beautiful possession in our house. It was black with a gold pattern decorating its gleaming body, the company name, Singer, boldly emblazoned on its side. The machine was mounted on a polished wooden table and operated by a foot pedal. Amma had been trying to teach me to make stitches as small and neat as hers, but with very little luck. I was far better use helping her take measurements and making deliveries, rather than destroying expensive fabric and wasting precious thread with my lopsided needlework.

Satisfied that my mother wouldn't be angry at the state of my corner of our hut, I started to make my way outside when a gecko chirped. Annoyed, I stuck my tongue out at the pale house-lizard. Its chirp was unlucky. A warning, I was told, that my journey was ill-fated and should be postponed.

I stuck my head out from behind the curtain that separated my corner from the rest of the hut. It was just an old sheet, mended so many times that the pattern was barely discernible, but I welcomed the privacy it gave me. I was lucky that I didn't have to share my tiny section with anyone, like most unwed girls in the village had to with their sisters or grandmothers. My mother slept deeply at the opposite side of the hut, and it was the only way I could escape out into the jungle at night, when the world had gone to sleep.

I'd like to avoid my mother if I could. She'd started insisting that I drink a tonic every morning, saying that it was good for my health. It was probably another attempt at making my skin lighter like hers so I could be deemed more "marriageable," but it tasted disgusting and always made my mind foggy. Especially since I was meant to be taking measurements today, I didn't need anything interfering with my ability to count or remember things.

I could hear Amma talking to someone in the verandah. Who could it be this early, when my father was still fast asleep after returning home past dawn? I inched towards the voices, taking care not to be seen. Eavesdropping was frowned on in all homes, not just ours.

And it would have been better if I hadn't tried to listen. I recognised the voice of the second person easily.

My mother's brother—Jeevan Maama—was many years younger than her. He rarely visited because their parents had disowned my mother when she ran away to marry my father. Amma's grandfather had been one of the first in the south to pledge his allegiance to the British after the Dutch had left, and had been gifted a cinnamon plantation as a reward. Amma's father, who had managed to successfully triple the family wealth, was very unhappy when his only daughter decided to marry a Capuwa five villages over. He believed, according to my mother, that Thaththa had cast a spell on her.

I've heard many rumours of it too. Vashi karala—a love spell—the gossips would whisper. But carrying out an enchantment like that was never something my father would have done. Not when he'd warned me over and over again the cost it would have on a soul when you practiced the craft this way. You might even be reborn as a yaka yourself.

But if it hadn't been a spell, how did their love run dry so quickly?

Strangely, my grandfather, even though I had never met him, had insisted that they pay for my schooling.

Now my grandparents were offering to pay for my dowry, and this was a whole new topic completely. The pressure to marry was something that plagued any unwed girl my age, and it had only intensified for me in the last few weeks.

But I doubted Jeevan Maama had anything to do with my dowry. He had always been indifferent towards me—something that hurt me as a child who longed for the love of her extended family.

If Jeevan Maama ever did come to see us, he did it discreetly when he was certain he wouldn't run into Thaththa. My father wasn't too fond of him, which was understandable, but I think he especially disliked Jeevan Maama because of his business. Jeevan Maama owned several taverns, even though my parents liked to pretend such things didn't exist. My father said it was a paapaya—a sin that would carry over into his next life. I thought it wasn't good of him to judge someone by their occupation—after all, that's what my grandfather did to him.

But Jeevan Maama had been visiting Amma more frequently these last weeks. Once or twice a year was the norm, but three times in about a month was definitely odd.

I peered out from the front doorway to see Jeevan Maama sitting on our only bankuwa, the low bench we used for special visitors. He was handing over a pouch to Amma. My heart softened a little at that. Perhaps the reason he was visiting was to give Amma some help. With the villagers developing this disdain towards my family, we were certainly starting to struggle. While we were never considered wealthy, we had always gotten by. Now, our rice stocks were dwindling, and more than once I'd noticed that Amma and

Thaththa had been having only one meal a day. Any help, even from Jeevan Maama, would be much appreciated, especially as the roof had started leaking again, and the cost of rice had only increased since the tensions with the central country had worsened. The last king had fallen about seven decades ago, and the central part of the island had not been as accepting of the new rulers as those of us on the coast, who had already lived under foreign rule—first the Portuguese, then the Dutch, and now the British—for centuries. Not that it mattered who ruled when our staple became too expensive to eat.

My mother had asked me to go to the village maduwa and see if anyone had left any excess paddy. Sometimes, a kindly wife would leave some out for those less fortunate, and fortune had not been on our side for a while now.

I snuck out as quietly as I could, making sure to avoid the front garden and instead climbing the slender wooden side fence and following the narrow path that led to the village. I reckoned it would make my mother happy if I made myself inconspicuous. Amma had been giving me more lectures than usual recently. She told me that since I was a young lady seeking marriage it was inappropriate for me to be seen associating with men. I was to stay inside when we had anyone calling at the house. She was starting to sound more and more like the nuns every day.

"And so what if I do?" she'd barked when I pointed it out to her. "Goodness knows we could use some piety in this house."

IT DIDN'T TAKE me too long to reach the village maduwa, the unwalled platform with a thatched roof held up by four wooden beams, usually found in the centre of every village. Women would pound paddy here or weave mats together or sometimes even entertain visiting newcomers. I checked every corner, looked behind every bankuwa, for some extra rice, but it appeared the villagers were not feeling particularly charitable this week. We'd have to make do with what little we had for now.

I was just making my way back home, my thoughts occupied again by whatever beast must be revelling in the jungle, when I almost crashed into Jeevan Maama. He'd finished his visit with my mother, and of course this was the only path for him to make his way back home. I was silly for not thinking to avoid it.

"Good morning, Maama," I said, politely. My mother would not forgive me if she found out that I was anything but.

I hadn't seen my uncle up close for a while and I was surprised at how tired he looked. His hair was thinner than I remembered, and his tummy protruded, straining on his short morning jacket and hanging over the trousers he wore. Jeevan Maama had long since given up wearing traditional dress in favour of western clothing—no sarong or hair comb for him. He even styled his moustache in the way of the British, while men like my father sported long sideburns that framed their jaw. It was another reason for my father to hate him.

Jeevan Maama was chewing betel leaves with areca nut, which turned his whole mouth as red as blood, like he was a demon feasting on human flesh.

"Amara, hello." The smell of the crushed betel leaves wafted over to me, and I felt a sudden, inexplicable urge to retch. I've heard mumblings from some of the girls in town that betel leaves and areca nuts were chewed only by low-class Sinhalese. I shook myself. If I wasn't careful, I'd accidentally find myself agreeing with the foreigners.

"You must have come to see Amma." I stated the obvious, because the silence between us was heavy and awkward.

"Yes."

"Thank you," I said, and when he looked puzzled I added, "for your help. It's been essential to us in these difficult times."

Jeevan Maama's face turned as red as his teeth, and he stared down at his woven leather shoes that probably cost more than our entire house.

I internally kicked myself for mentioning the money. I shouldn't have let him know that I saw it and now he was embarrassed.

"You should go back home. Your mother will be upset if she sees you out like this."

I bit my lip, admonished. I was only trying to be cordial.

I bent down and touched his feet—the sign of respect we pay our elders. The wind whipped at my face as I turned around, and I was about to start back when I heard his voice again.

"Amara?" The sun shone directly on his face, highlighting the small birthmark he had on his eyelid.

Jeevan Maama held out three copper coins to me.

"What's this for?" I asked. "You've already given to Amma, no?"

"Just keep this. From me to you, alright?" His eyes glinted with something I couldn't quite understand. Maybe he had heard the rumours too. Perhaps he knew that we were running out of rice, and that our roof needed mending.

"Thank you, Jeevan Maama."

"And Amara?"

"Yes?"

"Let this be our secret, okay?"

His hand grazed mine as he dropped the coins into my palm. A sudden shiver ran through me, even though the morning sun was warm on my back. The smell of his betel leaves grew stronger as I started to feel like the ground was tilting.

I have you now, you little bitch, the voice whispered in my ear, insidious and ugly.

What was coming over me?

I took the coins and slipped them into the fold of my reddha before I rushed back home, hurrying so he wouldn't see the confusion or panic etched onto my face.

6

I'VE ALWAYS HATED the opinion that women are overly emotional. We saw it in all our stories—women beating their chests and crying to the heavens while the men remained stoic and subdued. Men like Aloysius claiming that we were subject to flights of fancy and wild imaginations. Neha had told me that it was because women are more tenderhearted. That this was a good thing. That softness wasn't weakness. But I didn't want to be soft or delicate. I wanted to be strong and in control. That's why Thaththa shunning me hurt as much as it did. That's why it was getting increasingly difficult for me to ignore the dreams and the voices. Who could I tell without being cast into the same lot as all melodramatic women?

No. I needed to gather my wits and get on with my day. There was nothing else to it.

I kept a small hambiliya—a purse woven out of reeds—at the very bottom of my clothes basket, and I dug it out to deposit Jeevan Maama's coins. I didn't have much in the purse to begin with, and I'd usually find a way to sneak whatever made a brief appearance into Amma's own hambiliya when I got the chance. I was tucking it back in when my fingers brushed against a small hymn book.

I frowned. This was from a few years ago. I'd most likely just put it away and forgotten about it. I leafed through the pages and found a note inscribed on the inner cover.

My dearest Amara, though life may take us down differing paths, a piece of my heart will always stay with you. Your best friend, Neha.

I dropped the book, remembering now where I got it from, and why it was tucked out of sight. Why I could never bring myself to throw it away.

I also remembered—a dark cloud settling uneasily above my head—which house I was meant to visit today. With the dreams and the attacks and the tovil last night, I'd pushed it so far back in my mind that I'd forgotten about it completely until now.

Things were different when Neha was my friend. Even the animosity from the people in our village was easier to bear. But we'd started to drift apart during our last few years of school, around the same time I had met Raam. Her family converted to Christianity years before, but had started embracing the religion with more intensity after Neha's father got a chief post in the governor's administration department.

First, they started attending Sunday mass, then prayer circles during the week. But it wasn't just for her family's advancement that Neha embraced this new religion—she ended up truly believing in what the nuns taught us in school. It made sense to her, she said. Like she had found a piece of a puzzle that she never knew was missing. She'd asked me to pray with her, and I had. But all my puzzles remained unsolved. I was lost out at sea and no god saw fit to guide me back.

AMMA HAD INSTRUCTED me to visit Neha's house and take her measurements this morning, and though I'd protested, I had little choice. And now I needed to hurry or I'd be late, and my mother would have more reasons to be disappointed in me. Lately it felt like everything I did annoyed her in some way. She'd click her tongue and mutter under her breath—I never dared ask her what she was saying.

I took my usual shortcut through a small paddy field, so it was easy to keep my mind busy by concentrating on balancing on the ridges that divided the field into neat, square sections. A mist rolled lightly over my path this morning, and I was halfway through when I thought I felt someone behind me.

I peeked over my shoulder a few times, making sure I didn't lose my footing. Nothing. But still the small hairs on the back of my neck prickled, like someone was just a little too close, like their breath was teasing my skin. I thought of my dreams again.

Were those footsteps?

But it couldn't be. I was alone.

And then, just as I reached the end of the paddy field, I heard a giggle right next to my ear, taunting and mean, like the way the girls in my school made fun of me.

I whipped back, as quick as the gust that fanned around me, but I couldn't see anyone. Had I imagined it? It was easy to think so, with the delicate green spears of paddy grass swaying lightly in the morning breeze.

My father used to say that the tovil ritual coaxed other spirits out into the open as well. Especially kaadharayas—the greedy spirits—the unwelcome guests who would hover in the village for a few days after. I touched my suray and took a deep breath.

I'll claw out your tongue if you tell.

A vision of my mother screaming. Snakes of blood wound their way down her arms.

Stop it, Amara. Pull yourself together.

The air felt heavy with intruders and demons as I hurried to the town. I turned back three more times, but there was still no one following me.

Slowing down when I saw the Dutch fort and the smattering of buildings, I tried to catch my breath. Neha's family would be aghast if I turned up on their doorstep panting and drenched in sweat.

The Star Fort was nearby, just a stone's throw away from the main fort itself, so I wandered close to the large archway that marked its entrance. The height of the arch itself never ceased to amaze me, and I longed to see what was inside, but the British now used it as an administrative building for the public works department.

From the outside, all I knew was that it was built by the Dutch in the shape of a six-pointed star, with space for twelve cannons to cover the approaches from all sides. It's strange when I think about it now—how much blood had been shed here, at this picturesque coastal town, and how our entire island changed its course because of it.

I was turning to leave when I felt something sharp wrap around my wrist.

A yaka, I thought, flailing stupidly. The demoness from my dream had followed me here somehow. I gasped, spinning around, trying to pull my arm free. I knew that whatever stalked me this morning would eventually catch up.

"Koheda yanne, duwe?" *Where are you going, daughter?*

It wasn't a yaka—of course it wasn't a yaka, I tried laughing to myself—it was just Heen Achchi, whose real name was lost in the sands of time long before I was even born. She was as much a fixture of Matara town as the Star Fort was, though unlike the fort, we avoided her as much as we could.

Barely four feet tall, Heen Achchi lost another half foot because she was hunched over. Her white hair clung like wisps of seafoam to her skull; the two teeth that remained on her gums looked like lonely, abandoned seashells. But the thing that scared me, the thing that made me want to put as much distance as I could between me and this tiny, old woman, was her eyes.

Coated with a milky glaze, Heen Achchi's eyes had a way of looking at you, of seeing directly into your soul. And it wasn't just that. She had a penume—a second sight—Thaththa explained to me. She was able to look beyond this world, right into the one of the deviyo and yakku. The girls in the village had whispered that she could tell you things. She would declare things about yourself, about your family, that no one ought to know.

"Mata oyawa penawa, hondey." *I see you, you know,* she rasped in a singsong voice. She still hadn't let go of my wrist, and her nails dug into me painfully.

"Atha arinna, Achchi." *Let me go, Achchi,* I said, trying to twist free. I wanted to run away from her. I didn't want her to know my secrets, even if I wasn't sure what they were myself.

"Mata dannawa oyata wechcha dey. Oyage yahaluwa kowuda?" *I know what happened to you. Who's your friend?*

"Mona yahaluwada, Achchi? Mama mey wadata yanney." *What friend, Achchi? I'm just going to work.*

"Oyagey karey ellila inney kawuda?" *Who's that hanging on to your back?*

She really was losing her mind, but I couldn't help glancing over my shoulder, a shudder going through me just the same.

"Kawuruth naha, Achchi." *There's no one.* I managed to wrangle my arm back from her.

"Boru karaya!" *Liar,* she hissed, lunging for me again, but I side-stepped her and hurried away.

"Inna, inna, ithing!" *Wait, wait, will you,* she called after me, but I ignored her.

"Mama dannawa Thaththa monawade karey kiyala." *I know what your father did.*

I paused for a second.

"Mata loku andurak penawa. Oyawe watakaragena thiyenney. Parissamen." *I see a terrible darkness. It's surrounding you. Be careful,* she spat, her words bitter as they trailed after me, leaving a taste at the back of my throat.

I made it through the main fort and onto Neha's street just as the bells in the church started to ring. I paused to look behind my shoulder again. I rubbed the back of my neck. Of course no one was following me. Of course I was alone. Heen Achchi was long gone.

7

BACK WHEN WE were still in school, Neha had invited me to her sister's wedding. I still remembered the day that beautiful Catharine married Dandris, the son of a wealthy coffee plantation owner. I was just fourteen then and it was the first time I'd been invited to Neha's home.

I'd started the day not knowing what to expect, but it certainly hadn't been what I saw. Neha's house wasn't mud walled, like mine, but made with kabook, which the Englishmen called iron-stone clay. I couldn't help running my hands over it—it was as smooth as the paper we wrote on—even though Neha's mother clicked her tongue at me and told me not to leave dirty handprints on the whitewashing.

But that hadn't been the only difference between my home and hers. The one new thing we had in our entire hut was Amma's prized sewing machine, and no one was to go near it without her strict supervision. Neha's home had furniture—real, wooden furniture, and she'd explained what everything was to me. I couldn't imagine sitting at a table and eating with something other than your hands.

"So, do you wash the forks and knives first? Before you eat?"

"They are washed before we lay the table," Neha had replied, giggling slightly.

"So how long do they sit there? What if flies land on it?"

She just shrugged.

"What about how clean your tablecloth is? Won't there be dust?"

"It's not that dirty, Amara!" She laughed. "It took me some getting used to as well, when my father started insisting. But it's fine now, really."

Not *that* dirty. I remembered shuddering. We washed our hands thoroughly before and after our meals, taking care not to touch anything between cleaning ourselves and eating. I didn't think I could ever get used to putting a piece of metal that had touched the table, and flies, and who knew what else, into my mouth.

But everything was absolutely pristine for the wedding. Flowers decorated every surface, and Catharine, the bride, looked resplendent.

She was styled in the manner of brides from the central hill country—since Catharine's father as well as her groom came from there—dressed in a heavily worked sari jacket with frills at the neck, long sleeves that were puffed at the shoulder and the wrist, many beaded necklaces, and a sari that held a beautifully draped frill at the waist. This last feature was never worn in the low country where we lived, and I had made a mental note to insist on one when my own wedding day came. Amma had spent weeks on Catharine's bridal outfit and declared her the most beautiful bride she'd ever seen.

Catharine presented the groom with betel leaves and touched

his feet when he arrived, repeating the action on his parents. They had technically already been married in the church, as both families were staunch Christians, but they were both also Sinhalese, after all, and no marriage ceremony was complete without a procession.

The groom would walk from his home, accompanied by his family, friends, tom-tom players, and a few men chanting blessings. Amidst the sounds of drums and brass cymbals, the groom would then collect his new wife, who was usually perched on a cart drawn by a young bull, and make his way back to his own home, where the newlyweds would take up residence and embark on their lives together. The bride's family and friends would also join the returning procession, and the families would then partake in celebrations at the groom's home.

Dandris, Catharine's groom, was a large man with an even larger smile. He was dressed in the typical Mudaliyar's outfit, as was customary for grooms to wear—a long, dark velvet coat over a printed kambaya, similar to a sarong, with a wide sash, merging western styles with our own local costumes. The velvet coat, I was told, was brought into fashion by the Dutch, and I wasn't surprised because it was ill-suited for the island heat.

The procession had only been walking a few minutes to the groom's house when Neha and I heard a commotion from the front, where Catharine's new husband and his family were.

"What is it? Neha, please go check," Catharine called out from the cart, worry etched onto her beautiful face.

The two of us hurried towards the noise, where we saw Dandris collapsed into the arms of four of his friends, perspiration dripping down his face. One of them was removing his velvet jacket, while the other was loosening the buttons on his shirt.

"Amara," an older woman I didn't know called out, spotting me. "This is the work of an Angam charm, I'm sure of it. I told him to be careful. Run, fetch your father at once."

Luckily for Dandris, our village was small and I could run like the wind. Thaththa, understanding the urgency of the situation, didn't waste a moment. Angam charms caused instantaneous damage, unlike hooniyam, which inflicted weeks, even months, of drawn-out pain.

We returned to the scene, where the groom was now seated on the side of the road, and my father set to work. First he started chanting over a lock of Dandris's hair, which he then tied into a knot. Then he directed his chants over a cup of water that one of the family members had managed to produce. After a minute or two, Thaththa sprinkled some water over the groom's face and then poured the rest of it down the man's throat.

I held my breath.

In less than a minute, Dandris appeared to be recovering. Shakily, he got back onto his feet, the redness in his cheeks paling, and gave everyone a sheepish grin.

"Looks like the heat of the south impaired me more than I like to admit," he announced.

My father frowned. Of course they would explain away his charms. But the woman who'd asked me to fetch Thaththa had drawn him aside.

"Pay him no heed," she was saying in a low voice. "He thinks he's so modern, not believing in the old ways, but I'm certain it was an Angam charm. I live next door to his family, and my housemaid saw someone burying a small vessel near his doorstep. This poor man would have certainly stepped over it this morning, as he was leaving to collect his new bride."

My father nodded gravely.

"If the family requires a protection charm, please ask them to contact me," he replied. No one asked Thaththa to join the wedding party, just like Amma had been politely ushered out after dressing Catharine.

Two girls had loitered a few feet away, obviously listening in on the conversation with twisted smiles.

One of them met my eye.

"Witch," she mouthed at me, while her friend emitted a high-pitched giggle.

"I'm going to walk back with my father," I'd told Neha. If they wouldn't have my father as a guest, even after he helped them, then why should I remain at the party?

8

YEARS AGO, MY father spoke to me about water.

The sun had been a ripe mango about to explode out of the sky. The heat smothered us with an unrelenting viciousness. Not a single shadow flung itself down from a treetop to give us any relief as Thaththa and I walked along the beach to the temple.

It would have been easier, and certainly cooler, to cut through the jungle, but this was faster, he had said. He didn't have much time—the tovil started at sundown and he'd only realised late in the morning that his pot of pirith pan had run dry. Pirith pan, or blessed water, was an essential protection against demons. The Buddhist monks would chant over earthen pots of water, and villagers were encouraged to take them home. We sprinkled it over our front steps and all corners of the house, we anointed ourselves with it when we were ill, and when conducting an exorcism, my father made sure a pot of pirith pan was kept next to the yaka's victim.

"Why is it so important, Thaththa? Aren't your chants enough?" I remember asking him, perhaps as a distraction from the heat.

"Pirith pan is far more effective in keeping malevolent spirits away, duwa. I've taught you that already, haven't I?" He didn't say it to chide me. His eyes, which had been trained up the coastline, searched my face. I wouldn't have usually joined him at that time. If I didn't have school, my mother usually insisted that I help her cook. There was paddy to be pounded and fish to be descaled. Besides, she'd argue, being out in the harsh sun only made me darker than I already was.

But she'd been especially unbearable that morning, as if my presence chafed against her far worse than the heat did. She found fault in the way I held the scaling knife, the way my hair was tied, that I hadn't yet swept the hut. And so my father had insisted that I accompany him to the temple. I didn't need to go. We both knew that, even though my mother didn't.

Who needed the shade of a tree when I had him to protect me?

I smiled at him, so my next question wouldn't sound argumentative.

"But why is it more effective? Why water? Why not bless some roti and have the possessed girl eat it or something?"

A frown appeared on his already weathered, brown forehead. He was searching for his words. Words didn't come as easily to him as they did to me, certainly not as easily as they came to my mother. When he explained things to me, especially about his craft, he approached it with the same cautiousness that made him the best Capuwa on the southern coast.

"Water is special, duwa. When you pray over it, when you speak over it even, it remembers. Just like how we pour water into a pot to contain it, water can act like a vessel itself. A vessel for our thoughts and our feelings and our wishes."

I nodded, but I must have looked confused because he continued.

"You know, it's not just us Sinhalese who believe in this? Even the Christians pray over their water. They baptise their infants. The power of water runs deeper than you think."

"I understand, Thaththa," I said, because I did.

"The water remembers, duwa, even though we might forget."

There were accusatory looks thrown our way when we finally reached the temple, but no more than normal. And the chief monk, when my father approached him and touched his feet, smiled at us serenely. There was rarely any conflict with our local beliefs and my father's practice. Buddhism is a philosophy, not a religion, we were proud of saying on the island. The temple was pungent with fresh flowers brought for offerings and coconut-oil lamps that burned cheerfully, a signpost of devotion. The monks' saffron robes contrasted brightly against the pure white sthoopa—a large white dome that housed a relic of the Buddha himself.

I lurked behind my father while he spoke in a low, respectful tone with the monk. After a while, a vessel of water was handed over to him, covered with a clean, white cloth. My father touched the feet of the monk again before taking his leave.

"Hold this carefully, duwa," he said to me, giving me the clay pot. I wrapped my arms around it and nodded. There was no way I would let him down. If water held our prayers and wishes, then this pot could bear one more—"Keep my father safe," I whispered, as I felt it swish against my chest.

The water remembered.

So perhaps it was all the tears I cried for Neha that never let me forget how much I missed her.

We'd been thick as thieves when we first became friends—when Neha had rolled her eyes with me at Daphne's snide remarks, and giggled as I did when Sister Agatha nodded asleep sometimes in the afternoon heat.

But this was before Neha was asked to tea parties thrown by the families of the very same girls who'd bullied me for years. It was only a matter of time until she replaced our walks in the jungle with watching cricket matches dressed in her Sunday best. In a few weeks she went from being puzzled by the teachings of the nuns to attending church, swearing that something had shifted within her. That she believed now.

And even still, to add insult to injury, Neha's family insisted that Amma sew all their dresses. Her workmanship was not matched by anyone in the town, and Amma wasn't in a position to turn down hard-earned business.

Neha was staying with Catharine while her father and mother travelled to Colombo, I was told. I had managed to avoid talking to her for about a year now. It was easier once we left school. I had refused when Thaththa asked me to accompany him for a protection charm of Catharine and Dandris's new home, and carefully pivoted around Amma's requests when she asked me to deliver some finished jackets, but finally my time ran out.

NEHA'S SISTER'S HOME was even more grand than her childhood one. I know it's absurd to believe that the walls actually sparkled, but perhaps they were a special shade of white that I had not seen elsewhere.

One of the maids greeted me and took me in through the back door to the kitchen.

"Inna." *Wait,* she said curtly, her eyes a fraction more narrowed than I would have cared for, before disappearing.

Neha bustled in not a moment later.

"Oh, Amara, it's you." Neha looked taken aback. She'd clearly been expecting Amma.

"My mother sends her apologies. She is terribly busy today so she wanted me to take your measurements."

Neha nodded and then turned towards the housemaid.

"Ay mey madam-wa pitipassen athulata gaththey?" *Why did you bring this madam in through the back entrance?* she chided, her face pink, though her maid looked unbothered and resumed cleaning the kitchen. Guests were brought in through the front door. The back was for the help. It only solidified our relationship further.

My body flushed hot and I bit my lip. I was here for a job, I reminded myself. Not to dwell on childish grievances.

"Come this way, Amara. We can do the measuring in Catharine's dressing room. She's out with the ladies' circle right now." She looked over her shoulder at the maid who'd escorted me inside.

"Apita téy genna." *Bring us some tea.* "Honda coppawala, ahunaadhe?" *In the good cups, did you hear?*

"I'm really very sorry about that, Amara. But you can't blame them, really," Neha said, her voice apologetic as she swept through the spacious house in an ethereal cream lace dress that I'd only seen worn by Englishwomen. Neha had always been a neat, clean child—much unlike her friend who roamed barefoot through the jungle, her hair loose and flying behind her. But Neha looked different now. More composed. Not a hair out of place. Not a wrinkle in her clothes.

"Everyone has been so on edge since these attacks started. You should see Dandris's mother and sister. They are barely allowing anyone into the house. They want us all to stay locked in, even in broad daylight."

I wasn't sure how to respond, so I just nodded. The ripples of fear that started out small had now grown to engulf the entire town. I only hoped Neha and her family didn't believe the rumours that my father was behind it. I wouldn't put it past them, given Neha's treatment of me. But then again, I was here today, wasn't I?

Mama dannawa Thaththa monawade karey kiyala. *I know what your father did.* The words from Heen Achchi replayed in my mind. Except Thaththa had never done anything. All this was stemming from irrational fear from the townsfolk, fanned by men like Aloysius. Driving people to be suspicious of my father only strengthened the presence of the church, and the position of the Mudaliyar's office along with it. All Thaththa had ever tried to do was help people.

But things have changed with him. The thought came unbidden. He'd distanced himself from me. Had stopped teaching me his craft. Surely, he must be hiding something? I shook my head. No. I mustn't start thinking this way just because of what an eccentric old woman said.

A vision of Thaththa burst into my mind. He was splattered in blood as his eyes rained down tears. He rocked back and forth mumbling the same thing over and over again.

It's all my fault. It's all my fault.

I had no idea where these thoughts came from, but they had to stop. I swatted at my head the way someone would swat at a fly.

Neha looked at me curiously.

"I—I thought I felt a mosquito," I said, feebly.

We'd reached the dressing room and I forced myself not to stare at the almirahs stuffed to the brim with expensive dresses and saris and silks. Were these all Catharine's or had Neha suddenly taken an interest in fancy gowns? She had never seemed like the kind of girl who wanted this sort of life, but then, she had never seemed like the type of friend who would cast me aside so easily either. I worked quickly, opening a small notebook where I would write down her details and asking Neha to stand tall, to spread her arms wide, to turn around so I could measure her shoulders.

It pained me to be so close to her that my hands trembled as I worked. I hoped she didn't notice.

"How have you been?" she asked, her voice tentative.

"Fine," I responded, even though I'd been far from it and I was desperate to talk to her about everything that had been happening. "And you?"

She shrugged and then quickly repositioned herself. "Well, my parents have started—"

"Ah, Neha, I didn't know you had company." A high-pitched voice cut her off, as another woman, Dandris's sister, I assumed, floated into the room.

"Yes, Jacyntha, I do." There was a hint of exasperation in Neha's voice, even though she was smiling at her amiably.

Jacyntha looked over at what we were doing. I saw the way her eyes glazed over me. I was just the help, after all. Neha noticed it too.

"This is Amara. She's my friend from school, and her mother has been tailoring my clothes for as long as I can remember. You know that jacket with the gold lace trim you were asking after? That was made by her."

I felt my cheeks redden. I had once been Neha's confidant and she had been my protector. Now I was just a friend from school who did her sewing.

Jacyntha's eyes travelled up and down my body, taking in my

old-fashioned chintz reddha and the suray from my father that hung around my neck.

"Amara," she said. And then a moment later she made the connection. I could see it in the way her eyes widened and her jaw dropped just a fraction.

"Neha." Jacyntha's voice rose even higher. "May I have a word with you, please? In the other room. Now."

"Excuse us just a moment, Amara," Neha apologised before following Catharine's sister-in-law out. I thought I even saw a hint of an eye roll, though I didn't know why it made me so happy. They went to the next room, but the walls in these larger houses never reached the ceilings in order to encourage ventilation and keep the rooms cool. As a result, they provided little to no privacy, and I could hear every word the two women spoke.

"You must be out of your mind, inviting a witch into our house," Jacyntha screeched.

"Jacyntha, please don't be ridiculous. I've known her for years. She's no more a witch than you or I."

"It's all over town, Neha. That girl's father is the reason these attacks are happening. Aloysius told everyone in the congregation this morning. Apparently, they are going to make an arrest if the attacks continue."

"Well, no arrests have been made so far, and until they have been, I suggest we leave the law enforcement to the proper authorities, shall we?"

"I thought you were smarter than this, Neha. A good Christian woman like yourself. Your family would have better sense, I'm sure, if I were to ask them."

"I'd be much obliged if you guarded your tongue, Jacyntha. If you take issue with any of my guests, I suggest you speak to

Dandris about it directly." And with that, she came back to where I was waiting.

"We are all finished here," I said, trying my utmost to keep my voice bright, like I hadn't heard a thing.

Neha nodded, her face redder than I'd ever seen it.

"Tell your mother that I have a proposal visit next week, and would be very grateful if I could have it before then."

A proposal visit? Again, my heart ached to know the details.

Instead I just agreed, bid her farewell, and made my way down her driveway before I let myself unpack what I'd heard Jacyntha say. They were thinking of arresting my father? Surely that couldn't be true.

I thought back to the nightmares that had been plaguing me. How I'd licked the blood off my lips and enjoyed it.

No.

No.

It was just a dream. Nothing more. A nightmare. Nothing connected to the attacks—how could they be?

But there was someone attacking the people from my village. And if I didn't find out who it was, Thaththa might be arrested.

9

EVEN THOUGH IT was midday, the usual buzz of the town was replaced with something else. While people usually chatted at the town square, pausing near the market to examine wares, bargaining with various salesmen—some who had even travelled from as far as the hill country—today felt different. People still spoke, but it was with hushed voices and gritted teeth. Fear permeated everything like the smell of decay and rot.

And a lot of that fear, I realised, was directed at me. Same as Catharine's sister-in-law, they all probably thought my family was responsible for the attacks.

"This is ridiculous," I muttered to myself. Even though the number of families converting to Christianity had continued to grow on our island since the invasion of the British, our Sinhalese traditions had coexisted harmoniously till now. Couples would get married in the church, but check with an astrologer to see if their horoscopes were compatible first. They would build new houses with money earned from British government jobs, but ask a

Capuwa to perform the mull gala ceremony, the first stone laid in the foundation.

It was never as bad as this.

I loitered by the main junction, dodging a few dirty looks that were cast my way. I was quite close to the convent where the nuns lived, and where Neha visited frequently, though I tried not to think about it too much. There was a girl with long hair selling woven cane baskets, and though she gave me a smile, she stayed firmly on the other side of the road, watching me. I gave her a little smile back.

For a moment, the gossip from everyone rose in sound, like a wave, and I thought I saw fire burst from the girl's eyes, but I blinked and she was back to normal. I really needed to get some proper sleep. My mind was starting to play tricks on me.

I didn't really want to be lurking around the town, especially now, but Raam sometimes took this route on his way home during lunchtime, and it would be nice to see him, even though we wouldn't dare speak to each other in public.

Raam was a year older than me, and we met when he attended the boys' school next to mine. We weren't allowed to speak to each other at school, of course, but the girls' convent shared a low wall with the bigger building where the boys' classes were. He'd already been in his last year, and now that I'd left school too, the possibility of meeting each other was restricted mostly to the jungle, where there was less chance of us getting caught. I wished he'd just speak to my father and get it over with. It would certainly make things easier, especially with the way my parents were behaving lately.

I sat on a low wall and waited, making sure my eyes were cast down. I couldn't stop thinking about what I'd overheard at Neha's, about Thaththa possibly being arrested. I made a mental list of the men who had been attacked—there was Loku Banda, who owned a shop in town; Siripala, a fisherman; and Upali, whose family tapped toddy. Upali was the last to be attacked. It happened just a week ago and there hadn't been one since.

The villagers, as well as the Mudaliyar's aides, had questioned all three men extensively about what they could recollect, but all the men answered the same—they were walking back home after sunset when they were knocked unconscious. The next thing they remembered was waking up with their body in pain so severe that they thought they were burning from within, with gashes that festered angrily, leaking rotten fluids.

Upali the toddy tapper, who had his ear gruesomely torn off during the attack, had claimed it was a demon, but the Mudaliyar's aide had been annoyed at this and asked him why he thought so.

"No man could sneak up on me that easily," he had replied, according to the stories circulating in the village. Nothing was stolen from the victims either. But still, the men would wake up every night, screaming and drenched in sweat, the villagers said in hushed whispers. Perhaps they never saw their attacker, but it was like the assault on them continued every time they went to sleep.

"WHAT ARE YOU doing here?" It was a woman I'd never seen before. She was older than my mother, and looked a great deal more annoyed with me. Her hands sat on her hips and her chest heaved as if she'd been running.

"Um—excuse me?" I was confused.

"What are you doing here, sitting across from our shop? Are you casting a hooniyama on us?"

"I—what? No!"

"Don't lie. I could see it in your eyes. And the way your lips were muttering something. Tell me the truth, once and for all. Who is it you are casting a spell on? Is it my son? Is he going to be next?"

Her voice grew louder with every question.

"I don't know who you are, and I don't know your son, but neither I nor my father have anything to do with these attacks!"

"Liar! We all know your father held a grudge against that fisherman, Siripala. That he didn't pay your father what he owed him. No wonder he was the first!"

I frowned. The part about the fisherman was true. He did indeed owe my father money. It was one of the last times I'd been allowed to accompany Thaththa, so I remembered it well.

Siripala didn't ask my father to perform an exorcism, but rather a blessing to drive any evil spirits away. He had recently built a new hut, and it was customary to perform certain rituals before they started living there. Siripala's wife and young son watched on as Thaththa had walked the perimeter of their walls, chanting pirith as he cut limes using his brass areca nut cutter. He then submerged the halved limes in a basin of water and they all floated cut side up, signalling that the house was free from the evil eye or any malevolent spirits. Satisfied and tired, my father had packed up his things and then turned to Siripala, expecting his payment.

Siripala had looked down, embarrassed, and asked if he could pay him in a few days. The catch had been poor these last weeks, and with the building expenses and the rising grain tax, he didn't have much to spare for the blessing. He offered to pay for the price of the limes, but my father had waved him away.

"When you can manage it," he had said.

Siripala's wife gave Thaththa a small parcel of dried fish as a token. She looked much younger than Siripala, and was quite beautiful. She wore a gold necklace that looked out of place with her demure reddha and hattey. Her eyes had been downcast the entire time, and Thaththa accepted the dried fish as gratefully as if she had given him a bag full of gold. She blushed deeply as he thanked her, retreating into the house as soon as it was polite for her to leave.

But Siripala never visited our house to pay Thaththa back. I knew because Amma would mention it often. My father was forgiving, but it was my mother who had to make the rice stretch an extra week. And there had been chatter around the village that the fisherman had thrown a large feast to celebrate his new home, to which my father was not invited.

Thaththa would never hurt him, though.

"You are wrong," I said, climbing down from the wall. I should leave. The woman took a few steps back, tripping over herself and losing her footing, landing with a thud on her behind.

"Aney!" *Oh, dear,* she screamed.

"What did you do to her?" A young man, perhaps her son, ran up, trying to help her to her feet.

"What? Nothing. She tripped." Surely they didn't think I had something to do with that as well?

"Stay away from us, witch!" he shouted. I looked around helplessly, noticing that many passersby were staring at me fearfully.

The girl with the cane baskets stood a few feet away, her face twisted in anger.

This was just too much.

I knew I was supposed to stay away from the jungle, what with the attacks and all, but it had to be safer than being out in the town like this. Turning on my heel, I hurried away; an anger that had started to burn within me these last few weeks fanned brighter, hotter. Someone needed to put a stop to this soon.

10

MY PARENTS HAD been fighting again. I could tell from the way the air simmered, heavy with tension, tightening the space between the blades of my shoulders from the moment I crossed the fence into our garden. My mother was pounding paddy using the large mortar and pestle we kept outside, which removes the husk and prepares it for cooking, while my father had clearly just stopped chopping firewood. Both their faces were twisted and sullen.

"This is all because you haven't repented for your sins," my mother was spitting.

"Don't bring that cursed talk from your parents' mouths here. This is all your fault. Inviting a devil into our house."

"If it's a devil, then why can't you take care of it? Because you're a fraud, that's why. Lying to people for years. You might have this village fooled, but don't think I don't know. You can't even take care of what happened."

"You're the one who let it happen," my father bellowed. "You're the one who put her at risk."

"All this will be water under the bridge if you'd just accept my parents' generosity. A good dowry will—"

"I told you once, I told you a hundred times: I will not take another cent from your family. Do you actually think that throwing money at this can simply—"

"Shoosh!" my mother said, noticing me there. Her jaw set stubbornly, but she looked nervous.

"Get inside, Amara. I've told you not to loiter around, eavesdropping on us like this." That was a new accusation, I wanted to tell her, but kept my mouth shut. Her anger bubbled away, souring everything that came near it. My mother has never been an easy woman. I know she must believe she made a mistake by running away to live with my father. I'd heard her talk many times of the happy life she lived when she was a girl. But surely, it couldn't have been that wonderful if she was willing to give all of it up? She had chosen Thaththa, hadn't she? She must have loved him once.

One of my earliest memories was of accompanying my mother to the market at the town. Amma worked her way through the various stalls quickly, her smile as tight as the grip she kept on my hand. I noticed everyone staring at us, and at first I just thought it was because my mother was so beautiful.

"Kumari, haven't seen you in a while, no?" a woman called out to her, drawing a few looks herself.

"Yes, Renu. How are you?" My mother's voice was polite but clipped, like she couldn't wait to get out of there.

"We are fine, dear. It's good to see you after so long. Is this her?" The woman looked at me curiously, as my mother took a step forward, shielding me.

"This is my daughter. Yes." There was something defiant in the way she said it. Like she was challenging the woman to say more.

But Renu merely smiled.

"Daughters are good luck. Let's hope yours will bring you good fortune. You've certainly had a few difficult years."

I felt my mother stiffen.

"What do you mean by that, Renu?"

The woman's face reddened. "Oh, no, I just meant, it must be difficult for you. Leaving your parents' house to live with, well, your husband is from a different sort of life, is he not?"

"A different sort?"

"I didn't mean anything by it. Just that it must be a change for you."

"It was nice seeing you, Renu. Do give my regards to your mother," was all Amma said, as she turned around and walked away. I saw more people whispering about her, but then I understood. They weren't staring at her because of the way she looked. They were staring at her because of who she was. The woman who left her wealthy family to marry a man who revelled with demons. And here she was, with the child who tied her to him irrevocably.

My mother made no secret of the fact that she was disappointed with me. After she had given up on her family's riches, she focused on the one thing she had left from them—her fair skin. Not tradable for food, but valuable in its own right. I could imagine how disappointed she must have been, then, when her daughter took after her husband's mahogany complexion instead. She'd tried various potions and balms when I was younger, but of course nothing worked. The tonic she kept forcing me to drink in the mornings was new, but her actions had been the same since I was born.

My parents had always fought, for as long as I could remember, but this last month had felt like the worst it had ever been—amongst each other, but also with me. I was just thankful that I had Raam to lean on.

I supposed the true fragility of love is that everyone believes their own to be special. My parents must have thought theirs was, once. They must have once exchanged love notes, cast glances at each other from across the market square. They must have found comfort in each other's arms, and breathed in the smell of each other's hair, and savoured every tiny moment that the other smiled.

Until one day, they didn't. I always wondered whether it was a gradual thing, like the ocean shaping sea glass, or whether it felt more like a wave cracking down onshore, sudden and hard, just to retreat away into nothingness.

But more than anything, their love scared me. Because if it was true once, if it was possible that they indeed couldn't live without each other, and now they were the way they were, where did it leave my own love? Would Raam and I end up the same way?

No, mumbled a voice in my head that sounded too much like my own for me to take truly seriously. Raam and I were different. Our love was real.

Amma kept mentioning that my grandparents wanted to pay my dowry. She waved it like a flag. I supposed having an unwed woman in the family looked bad on everyone. I loved Raam, of course. I just wished he'd hurry up. The last thing I wanted was to be forced into a betrothal of my parents' or grandparents' choosing just because he didn't speak to his father quickly enough.

I TRIED TO stay out of my mother's way, but she directed every drop of anger she had towards my father at me instead. The fabric I had cut wasn't neat enough. I wasn't to go gallivanting—her word, not mine—through the jungle like some wild woman anymore. My jacket was too tight. I was giving men in the town the wrong impression.

I kept my mouth shut and my head down, not wanting to add fuel to her fire. Usually, when she was like this, I would find refuge in Thaththa. He would make an excuse about how he needed my indispensable help and usher me into the jungle with him. But today he simply escaped by himself.

"I'm going for a swim," I heard him say to Amma, his voice still gruff and clipped.

"Can I join you?" I asked.

When he looked at me, it was like staring into the eyes of a stranger.

"Help your mother," he said, like I hadn't been doing just that all evening.

I ate the small quantity of boiled sweet potatoes and chilli sambol left in the kitchen, trying not to think about how it was less than half my usual portion, trying harder not to think about the way Thaththa looked at me, and crawled onto my mat. There would be no adventures in the jungle for me tonight. It would do me well to get a good night's sleep. I made sure that the ocean was behind me, so my head wasn't towards the south. The south was the abode of Yama, the god of death, and it wasn't wise to sleep in that direction, or so my father had told me.

But even though I could hear the song of the cicadas and the lullaby of the waves, I tossed and turned, waiting for sleep to take me. This was when unwelcome thoughts often crept into my mind—intruders making themselves at home. What if Thaththa was arrested for the attacks? What did my dreams mean? Why were my parents acting so differently toward me?

All the while, the ocean sang, and after some time, my mother's snores joined in the symphony. She always drank a special tea to help her sleep, and help it did, because without it I was sure I couldn't keep sneaking off in the night. I asked her once what it was for. "To keep my demons at bay," she had said, and I was never certain if she said it in jest, or whether she struggled alone in the still of the night, just like I did at times. In another life, I would have found the courage to ask her.

In that narrow corridor between sleep and wake, I heard the voice again.

I'll claw out your tongue if you tell.

Thunderbolts of pain bursting out from within me. My father weeping while looking at me, horrified, like I was a demon. This time, it was his mouth that dripped with blood.

A MOSQUITO BUZZED next to my ear, jerking me back to reality. Had I been dreaming?

I heard a rustling from near the doorway at the back of the house and sat up, but it was so dark that I could barely see my father storming off. He didn't even take a gini-mala, one of the torches we made out of burning coconut leaves, with him. I had no idea where he was going, and even though I itched to follow him—he was hiding something from me, I just knew it—it would be useless. He'd already had too much of a head start. I looked out many times after that, hoping to at least see the light from his small clay lamp twinkle from the verandah, but sleep finally crept up on me.

That night my dreams—my real dreams, at least I hoped they were—were the worst they had ever been.

Once again I was in the hut at the edge of the world. But this time the bloodred curtain that hung at the front door did not open as I tugged on it. It stayed frozen as I pulled, pushed, and tore at it with my nails.

I tried screaming for help. I had to get out. I knew deep in my gut that I had to leave. That it was dangerous for me in here, though I didn't know why.

I had almost given up when I felt it. A gust of wind, enough to drive me back away from the curtain. The fabric swept open, as innocent as a cobweb.

That was when I saw the woman.

This was no demoness. She beckoned to me, breathtakingly beautiful, wearing a flowing white dress. Her hair was loose and floated around her in the breeze, the fireflies that danced around her head giving her a halo of her own. She smelled of fresh rain and the tuberose that bloomed at night. The jungle wasn't a hunting ground tonight. I had nothing to fear.

She walked barefoot and I followed her, calling out to her, asking her to stay. We made our way out from the jungle down to the beach. And though I tried my best, I couldn't catch up to her, even though I was hurrying so fast that I was out of breath and she glided along at the same speed as me. I didn't mean her any harm, I told myself. I just wanted to be close to her.

She stopped at the line where the waves hit the sand, as if she understood what I craved. As if she were some sort of extension of me.

I could hear my breath come out in gasps. My body felt like it was on fire. And still, as I drew closer to her, my initial urgency gave way to dread.

Sensing my hesitation, she turned to look at me. It was when she met my eyes that I felt it—a stab of pain, starting from my navel and shooting down my legs, so blindingly agonising that I cried out.

She didn't look beautiful anymore. She was as wild as the ocean that rose in front of us. The fireflies that once circled her head now turned into bursts of flames. Anger emanated out of her with such force that I staggered back, my feet sinking into the soft, wet sand.

Where she was once resplendent, now she was vicious. Her anger made her skin rotten, and her fingers gnarled, and her body rancid.

It had been her all along. The yakshaniya tricked me. She pretended to be my saviour, but all she wanted was me. How foolish I had been to think otherwise.

There was something at her feet. A sack, I thought at first, but then I noticed it tremble. A moan reached my ears, guttural and ugly. It was a person, I realised with a start. Another woman. Her hair spilled over her face, obscuring it from my view.

I couldn't help it—I knelt down and brushed the hair aside, longing, needing to know who this was.

But this wasn't just any woman. It was my mother. Her face had been clawed to ribbons, chunks of skin hanging off her jaw. There was a deep gash in her throat, gurgling out crimson blood. Her eyes had spun back in her head, like someone possessed, as she wailed.

"I should have known you'd be the end of me," Amma cried, blood splattering from her lips and landing on my face.

I found myself overcome by an inexplicable rage. I wanted to explode. I had come to save her, and this was how she was treating me, yet again?

But no. I was different from the yakshaniya. I was not wicked. I was not cruel.

The water was a relief from the heat that radiated out of the demoness. I had to get away from her and her fire.

Refusing to look at either of them, I waded out to sea and kicked off, swimming as fast as my arms and legs would allow me. I had to get away. I couldn't allow her to take me too.

That's when I felt something wrap around my foot. I thought it might be seaweed at first. I thought I could kick it away.

But seaweed didn't tug. Seaweed didn't pull me back to shore. I was powerless as I felt myself drift right back to where I started. I rolled over in the sand, the salt water stinging my eyes. She was standing above me now, smiling.

"There's no use running," she murmured. "No use at all. You're mine now. This is where you belong." And with that, she knelt down on the sand next to me and wrapped her arms around my body. The pain that started when I first saw her burned brighter. I felt wetness starting to seep down my legs, as the metallic smell of blood mixed with the salty breeze from the ocean.

And as I opened my mouth to scream, she forced her fingers into my mouth, digging her nails into my tongue, trying to force it out of me.

I woke up gasping, choking on my own saliva.

I'll claw out your tongue if you tell.

I should have known that she would always find me, I thought, panicked and dazed. It was just a matter of time.

11

"AMARA, I ASKED you yesterday to sweep the front of the house. Your mind is like a sieve. How can we ever give you off in marriage in this state? Honestly, I don't know what to do with you," Amma scolded me. There was no point claiming that she was mistaken. She'd never asked me to do any such thing. But still I grabbed the ilpotha—a bundle of coconut leaf fronds—and started sweeping.

The dream with Amma last night confused me. I'd been having nightmares for weeks now, but this was the first time I had dreamt about someone I knew. It made little sense to me, even though it drenched me in a type of trepidation I couldn't really understand. I'd checked on my mother as soon as I woke up, touching her face, examining if she'd been hurt, only to be swatted away and scolded for waking her.

Still growing frustrated, I tried to talk to Thaththa, but he brushed me off.

"Where did you go last night?" I asked. "If you went to collect burulla leaves, I could have come with you."

"I've told you already. You are not to get involved with my work anymore. Help your mother. That is all." His voice was gruff and clipped—so different from the love and warmth I was used to.

Thinking about him gathering burulla leaves without me turned the day grey. Like a storm cloud suddenly blocked out the sun. I used to go with him into the jungle when he picked the lush, medicinal leaves for his ceremonies.

I thought back to one of the times we went together, many years ago, combing it over in my mind, savouring when things were different.

"Do you remember what these leaves are used for?" Thaththa had asked. He liked to quiz me. To check whether I'd been paying attention to him. But I'd been going into the jungle with him since I was a child. These weren't things I remembered learning, but things that I had always known.

"They purify, Thaththa. That's why they are worn around the waist during a tovil. And why it's kept next to those who have been possessed. Yakku usually shy away from things that are clean and pure. They are drawn to filth and pain and suffering."

"Good. And what else can you use burulla leaves for?"

"Fevers. Wounds. Body pains. Burns. Ringworm. There's a long list, do you want me to go on?"

He laughed at me then. "You're getting too smart for your own good, duwa. You'll know far more than me soon."

I laughed back. "Never. But I'm going to try!"

We plucked leaves from the shrub-like trees, making sure to break them from the stem so the leaves would stay fresh for longer.

"You know," Thaththa said, after a few minutes had passed, his voice quiet, "you don't have to do this, duwa."

I studied his weathered face, but he wasn't meeting my eye.

"You know I'd rather do this than help Amma cook. She's always scolding me about not putting enough goraka in my fish curry."

His lips twitched, but his smile hadn't reached his eyes like it usually did.

"I don't mean about domestic skills, duwa. I mean *this*." He gestured towards the leaves we'd been plucking. "I've always loved taking you with me, loved that you seem to enjoy learning about all of this."

"So then what's the problem?"

"There's no problem, duwa. I just want it to be your choice, you know. This is my life. My parents were from a caste where we had few options—I knew I was to be a Capuwa from the time I was a young boy. But things are different now. You're going to school. Your mother is from a noble family—they can help you, you know. Help you to study, or marry well, or do whatever it is you choose."

"But I choose this," I replied simply. Like I said, this craft wasn't something I learned. It was as much a part of me as my frizzy hair or the pimples that splattered around my chin.

"You don't have to, Amara."

"I choose this," I repeated, dropping the leaves that were in my hands and wrapping my arms around Thaththa. "I choose this, and I choose you."

He patted my back with a small smile. A real smile this time.

I hadn't seen that smile in weeks now. It made me homesick, even when I didn't leave my hut.

Why had he gotten so secretive? The murmurings from the village crept their way into my mind, but it was becoming harder to shake them off.

I drank some water from our well and splashed what was left of it on my face. My mind was foggy again, like I was only half-awake. I'd barely slept after my dream.

The icy cold water jerked some sense into me. If both Amma and Thaththa were keeping secrets from me, and neither of them would tell me what had changed, I had to find some answers on my own.

AMMA WAS DOWN in the back garden, probably plucking some karapincha leaves to use for today's curry, so I slunk back into the hut, as quiet as a thief. Thaththa kept all his things in a corner of the hut opposite from where I slept and across from Amma's sewing machine.

I rifled through his clothes basket. It was made from wicker, same as mine, although it contained only a few shirts and sarongs folded neatly. I looked through the leather satchel he took with him when he went into town. Here, I had a little more luck. A piece of paper, scribbled on in Thaththa's handwriting.

It was in Sinhala, of course, because Thaththa could hardly read English, but it only took me a few seconds to realise that it was a list of some sort.

It appeared to outline some of the steps to create a yanthraya—a charm used only by Cattadiyas, not Capuwas. A yanthraya, which typically translates to a *tool* in Sinhala, means something very different in demonology. It's an object that is created to bring about great harm to a particular person. The list itself included a few oils and a copper wire, and mentioned sacrificing a chicken.

Thaththa usually had a fixed repertoire of charms he would use, and live chickens weren't used in any of them. They weren't used in exorcisms either, although it's commonly known that sacrificing a live chicken was one of the ways to appeal to a yaka. A yanthraya was a type of dark magic. I couldn't imagine why Thaththa would have something like this. I committed as much of the list to my memory as I could and tucked it back in the bag.

And then when I was hanging the bag back onto its hook, I noticed a small box wedged between the shelf and the wall. Glancing outside to make sure Amma was still in the back garden, I slowly prised it out. The box was wooden, about the size of my palm, and opened without complaint as I lifted the lid. The light caught on the object inside, glinting brightly.

I lifted out a gold pendant, hanging on a matching golden chain. The pendant was a traditional hansa puttuwa—two entwined swans. Commonly known to signify unity and prosperity, it was typical for this symbol to be used in weddings, and for necklaces such as these to be given as a gift from the groom to the bride during a marriage ceremony. This hansa puttuwa was decorated with tiny red stones that shone, sparking something in my memory. I had seen this necklace before.

I heard Amma return and start to putter around the kitchen, so I slipped the necklace back in the box, and the box back into the gap in the shelf.

My heart started to beat a little harder. Drops of perspiration rainbowed their way on my upper lip. There was a tremble in my hands that was certainly not there before.

I knew exactly who that necklace belonged to. I had seen it, myself, when I accompanied Thaththa to Siripala the fisherman's house. It belonged to his wife. So why was it hidden away at our house?

12

I COULD FEEL my heartbeat all the way to my fingertips as I snuck out of our hut. It's not like I wasn't used to stealing away, but this was different. This time my intentions were rooted in suspicion, and it made me feel uneasy.

All I could think about was why Thaththa was acting differently towards me, but seeing the necklace gave me a fresh idea. Was there a different reason for his behaviour? One that didn't involve me directly?

Of course, there could be a perfectly good reason why that necklace was hidden away. Perhaps Siripala had given it to Thaththa as payment for carrying out the protection charm?

But that would be an absolutely gross overpayment. The necklace was worth far more than that. And why would it be hidden away? Thaththa would have exchanged it, surely, especially since we'd been struggling to make ends meet these last weeks.

Another thought slithered its way in—would Thaththa need something that belonged to Siripala to carry out some sort of curse on him? A yanthraya, perhaps? The necklace did technically belong to Siripala's family. The entwined swans signified both the masculine and the feminine energy in a marriage, meaning that the fisherman himself was represented in the necklace. Or was I simply overthinking this?

And finally, the list with the live chicken. I couldn't believe, even for a moment, that Thaththa would carry out a hooniyama like that. There was no way. But then why have a list like that in his own handwriting?

Could it have something to do with the attacks? The voice was soft and ugly and uninvited.

But even as I whacked down on my thoughts like they were elephant grass, they kept springing up. The truth was I'd been taunted and bullied and cast aside for so long, that if there was even a morsel of truth in what the villagers were saying, I needed to know. I'd spent my whole life defending my father, and I needed to be sure that the way he'd been acting had something to do with me, rather than a betrayal of everything he'd taught me.

I had to speak to Siripala's wife. Perhaps she could give me a rational explanation why my father had her necklace.

FISHING WAS A common occupation in our village, although every few years the Buddhist monks talked about how we shouldn't be killing. The whole village would stir, then, with arguments both for and against the truths of survival, only for it to die down after a while with very little changing. Fishing was a way of life on this island, after all. One of our main means of sustenance.

Still, the fishermen weren't wealthy folk. Most of them lived in a small cluster of mud huts close to where my home was, though their huts were considerably smaller than ours, and certainly not whitewashed. The smell of dried fish stained the air around their dwellings, a special type of death and rot, flies buzzing all around—another reason why many villagers tended to avoid that side of the village.

Siripala's new home, the one he had yet to pay Thaththa for blessing, stood a little taller, and a little further out than the rest of the huts.

There was no one in the front garden. My initial plan, weak as it was, was to walk right up and ask to speak to Siripala's wife. Perhaps she would come to the door herself. Then I would ask her how my father came to be in possession of her pendant. Except now, in the heat of the afternoon, I found my will wilting away.

What if I was mistaken? What if the necklace wasn't hers at all? Would I arouse more suspicion on my family by lurking around here, giving Siripala and everyone else more reason to suspect my father of the attacks?

Perhaps it would be better to look around first, see if I could catch a glimpse of Siripala's wife, and check if she was actually wearing the pendant? If she was and I had been, in fact, mistaken, then it would be silly to stir the pot, especially given my reputation.

I made my way back to the front fence and turned down the path that led to the beach. If I was lucky, I could get a direct line of sight into the back garden.

I'd give myself a quarter of an hour. If, within that time, Siripala's wife didn't come outside or I couldn't check if she was wearing the necklace, I would find a way to speak to her. It's always better to take the cautious route first, after all.

There was an overturned boat that gave me the perfect vantage point into their house, and I needn't have worried about setting a time limit for myself. Everything I needed was in full view.

Siripala's wife was descaling some fish, sitting on the back step of the house with a small, sharp knife and three large seerfish, which she would probably salt and dry out in the sun, preserving it for the months to come. Most fishermen's wives would do this with whatever their husbands couldn't sell at the morning market. Usually, some of the wives would bring a leftover fish or two to my mother as gratitude for my father's help. We hadn't gotten any fish since the attacks started.

The woman had a wide, open face. Two locks of her hair had come undone from the knot that lay low on her neck, and her dark forehead was a maze of worry. Her eyes were large, like a startled doe's. Something about her felt misplaced. Like I shouldn't be seeing her here, hunched over a seerfish. Like she belonged somewhere else, far away.

She wore no necklace.

A small boy, Siripala's son, whom I also remembered from the blessing, played a few feet away from the hut. He was filling a small clay pot with damp sand, packing it in tightly, and turning it over. He'd made an entire wall of these little castles, and was starting to decorate them with leaves, when he accidentally knocked one over.

"Ammaaaaaa," he wailed, as dramatic as a toddler that age could be.

"Haiyyo, putha, ochchara anddanna tharam deyak nah ney?" *Oh, no, son, there's no need to cry over something so small, is there?* she called out, her hands slick with fish. But the boy kept wailing.

"Puthey oka navaththanna. Thaththa nagittoth keinthi yahy." *Stop that now. If your father wakes up, he'll be very angry.*

It felt wrong to be here, lurking on the outside, watching them.

Like a beast that stalked its prey—the thought flashed into my mind abruptly. I was spying on her, on her family. People were allowed to have private moments. If I was going to speak to her, I had to do it now.

I started to stand up from behind the boat, but I heard a sound from inside the house.

"May mona magulak the mey?" *What the hell is this?* It looked like Siripala had woken up after all.

The woman stood up then, setting the fish aside, as her husband emerged from within the hut, wearing just a stained sarong. It was the first time I'd seen Siripala since the attack. His wounds had scabbed over, now settling as deep burgundy stripes down his face and chest. There were deep puncture marks surrounded by bruising on his shoulders. His left hand was bandaged, weeping yellow pus. His wounds looked vicious, but nowhere near as livid as Siripala's face, which was twisted into an ugly scowl. He was unrecognisable as the man who'd spoken so politely with Thaththa.

His wife didn't answer him, but I could see even from where I hid that her face was as white as a sheet.

"Leelawathi, mama kiwwa neda, mey dharuwawa hada ganna barinam mama honda paadamak umbala dennatama kiyadenawa kiyala?" *Leelawathi, haven't I told you that if you can't raise this child right, I'm going to teach the both of you a lesson?*

And with that he grabbed a handful of his wife's hair with his good hand, dragging her towards where his son screamed.

"Kata vahapiya!" *Shut up!* he hollered at the boy, reaching down and trying to grab him with his arm that was bandaged. The child screamed louder and tried to swat him away.

Siripala dropped his wife and, reaching back, slapped his son across the face.

"Aney, puthata gahanna epa. Gahanna onanam mata gahanna." *Please don't hit him,* his wife cried. *If you really want to hit someone, hit me instead.*

I was frozen, my body as cold as if someone had drenched me with a pot of icy water from the well.

He managed to pull the both of them back inside the hut where his words were muffled, but I could still hear his wife's pleas and his son's screams. There was a loud whipping sound, like the whistle of something cutting through air, and more shouts. More screams. Wailing that made my head feel light and heart weak.

It wasn't like I could rush inside and save them, could I? I'd never felt so helpless. The injustice of what was happening made my breath come out in hot gasps, my fists curled into balls so tight my nails hurt my skin. I've known what it felt like to be bullied. This was worse than the time Daphne Perera put a chicken head in my cubby. There was no word for what went through me, but I felt it rumble through my body like thunder looking for release. Looking for a chance to erupt.

And as I thought of Daphne, I heard a crack so loud I thought I had broken a tooth from clenching my jaw so tightly. The shock of the sound was enough to make me jump to my feet.

The sound of something rolling, and then a dull thud, as a coconut hit the ground in Siripala's back garden. It must have fallen onto the roof from a nearby tree.

It was enough of a sound to interrupt what was happening inside.

Siripala himself came out to inspect the damage. The gashes on his chest and face looked darker, except now they matched the ugliness that I'd just seen churn within him.

It was only when he eyed me warily that I realised I had exposed myself too.

"Moko?" *What?* he asked. The acidity with which he spoke to his wife was replaced with something else. Was it fear? I must have looked a sight, my fists balled and breathing as if I'd run all the way here.

"I was sent to ask if you needed any sewing work done," I replied, blurting out the first thing that came to mind. "We do curtains, as well as sarongs, jackets, and anything else you might need."

His eyes narrowed.

"Not today," he said, simply. But I couldn't help but notice the wind had disappeared from his sails. Maybe that meant he'd leave his wife alone, at least for now. My anger felt vindicated, somehow. At least he'd stopped.

I was still shaking as I made my way back home.

Whoever was carrying out the attacks, they surely picked a worthy candidate. I couldn't think of anyone who deserved it more.

Thaththa was a big believer in karma. What goes around, comes around, he'd say. The universe has a way of correcting itself. Bad things happened to those who deserved it. Like the attacks. Perhaps Siripala deserved to be attacked? Maybe he was just getting back what he gave out?

But then I remembered the look of fear on his wife's face. If people got only what they deserved, what had she done that was so terrible?

13

THIS TIME WHEN I stepped out of the hut at the end of the world, I was on the beach at dusk. Only a sliver of orange bled into the inky blue sky; the stars had not yet made an appearance, making it hard to see. Everything was still. Even the waves felt too quiet.

But I didn't need my sight or my hearing. I was guided by something red and raw and angry that burned through me, pushing me forward. She was behind me this time. I couldn't see her, but I knew she was there. She had me marked from weeks ago and now she followed me as I made my way down the beach, searching for cover, for some way to protect myself.

I could sense her trailing me, mirroring my actions. I took a step, she took a step. I paused, she paused. I turned around and she had vanished. Poof. Just gone.

If it weren't for the putrid breath that wafted over to me, smelling of death and decay, causing bile to sting the back of my throat and all my small hairs to rise, I might have thought I'd imagined her.

The yakshaniya had me marked and so I knew, if I let her, she would continue to hunt me until I was in her grasp. Until she could dig her talons deep into my belly and feast on the flesh of the soft part of my neck. Until I belonged to her completely.

And so I forced my feet to stop moving forward. I made myself still. She was with me before the next wave smothered the shore. She had only been biding her time. The yakshaniya bared her teeth at me, sharp and dark, like the fangs of a wild beast. She didn't have teeth the last time I saw her in my dream. I knew she was getting stronger.

"You're mine now," the yakshaniya rasped.

My fingers were locked around my small blade. It was now or never. I steeled myself and in one swift motion I twisted my arm, driving my knife squarely into her chest. I felt the metal connect with her flesh. With her bones. I heard the soft groan that escaped her lips.

She staggered before me, collapsing into the sticky, wet sand. That was almost too easy.

But the blood that poured out of the yakshaniya was bright red, not the blackened tar I was expecting. And when she raised her head to cry out, the eyes that stared back at me, wild with fear, were not hollow and black, but dark brown, and so very familiar. The birthmark near the eyelid was soon covered in blood. The flesh was soft.

Human.

As he breathed his last breath, his final words leaked out.

I have you now, you little bitch.

I knew that voice just like I knew those eyes. I'd seen that birthmark many times before. It filled me with rage I could barely comprehend, piercing through me like acid. I thought I understood, then, what the voices were trying to tell me. But the more I grasped at it, the faster it slithered away from me, like a water snake in a stream.

And when I pulled the knife out of the body and lifted it back up, it was with a mangled, rotten arm that didn't belong to me. I moved the blade to tattered lips that weren't mine, only to realise that it wasn't a blade at all, but gnarled talons that grew from my own fingers. And when I licked them, savouring the blood, relishing how sweet it was, that enjoyment belonged not to the yakshaniya, but only to me.

"AMARA, WATCH THE fire! Make sure it doesn't go out or the curry will be ruined," Amma barked. Our kitchen was a small shed a few feet away from the rest of our hut. Three large stones sat at one corner, a pile of sticks between them burning brightly. We'd balance a pot between these rocks to cook, and today a fish ambul thiyal bubbled away, smelling of garcinia and pepper and chilli. Normally, we'd have fat chunks of fish swimming in the gravy, but today was mostly bones. The smell was heavy, making me nauseous. It was all the anger that swirled within me—the villagers who were treating my family like criminals, my father who had suddenly cast me aside, men like Siripala who were so indescribably cruel to their wives, and worst of all my dreams, which made little sense to me—it heaved and groaned, making it difficult to focus on much else, making it impossible even to eat.

I was just stoking the flames with a large stick when I heard a bicycle bell ring at the front of our house.

My mother frowned, scraping the flour for the roti she was

making off the back of a clay bowl. Hardly anyone from the village visited us anymore, and we weren't expecting company.

"Could you go and check, please?" Amma sighed. "Behave yourself. No small talk, do you hear? And for God's sake tie your hair back without parading around like some sort of harlot. I'd thought you would have learned by now."

I bit my tongue and quickly pulled my hair into a bun. I'd left it down to dry after swimming in the ocean that morning. I'd woken up from my dream feeling like my body was alight with fever. Amma had been snoring in her corner, but Thaththa's mat was empty again. I'd tossed and turned, trying to go back to sleep in vain. My thoughts muddled around me, murky and tangled, trying to make sense of something, of anything, Once again, I'd had a dream where I was hunting. Where I'd killed. Again, the taste of blood on my tongue.

I'd abandoned my sleeping mat at sunrise, stealing away to the beach. I waded out into the water and held myself under the waves, trying to drown out what it felt like when I drove my talons into a man while he whimpered and begged for mercy. How powerful I'd felt, for the first time in my life. How my rage finally had some release. The salt water didn't help erase the ripple of satisfaction that hummed through me, but the mundane tasks Amma had me do in the kitchen did. Like every bad dream, this too settled into the dark crevices of my mind, moving from light to shadow, until it would return to me once again.

There was a man standing next to a bicycle near our fence. He was dressed as the English do, in trousers and a jacket. Something about him sent a stab of dread into my heart, even though I didn't know why.

My pulse racing, I stepped out onto our verandah.

"Yes, sir?"

"I'm from the Mudaliyar's office. Where is your father?" His voice was gruff and unfriendly. If he was from the Mudaliyar's office, then he worked with Aloysius. Could that mean they were coming to arrest Thaththa, like Catharine's sister-in-law had said? I wanted him to leave with every bone in my body.

"He's not home right now," I replied.

His eyes narrowed. "I asked where he was." His lips were turned down and his eyes kept peering into our hut behind me, like he was expecting to see a yaka jump out any moment.

"I'm afraid I don't know."

"Is anything the matter?" my mother asked. She had come up behind me and made me jolt. But she sounded nervous also. Like she could sense it too.

"You must be Kumari Van Court?" he asked, as my mother nodded. He had pointedly used her maiden name.

"Your brother was found in the early hours of this morning. He was attacked last night by the same assailant who has been terrorising this town." He spoke quickly, savagely, watching her face as he said it.

It took a moment, and then another, for the weight of what he said to sink in.

"Is—is he—?" She stumbled back and made to lean against the mud wall of our hut.

I stood as still as a statue, unable to will any part of me to move. I tasted blood on my tongue. Was I biting it, or was it from my dream?

My dream.

My body went cold, like an icy wave had washed over me.

I knew who those eyes belonged to. I had recognised that voice.

I clutched at my chest. The world swam before me. I needed to sit down.

I took two steps back and collapsed on the steps of our verandah.

"Yes, yes. He's still alive. You women." He sighed. "There's no need for theatrics." The aide's voice was hard. "He's with the village vedha mahaththaya."

"Attacked by whom?" The words slipped out of me before I could stop myself. I looked over to my mother, knowing she'd be displeased, but she was too upset to care. My dream from last night bounced through my thoughts like an echo.

"Attacked by whom?" He was mocking me now. "That's exactly why I'm here. Tell me, *madam*"—he addressed Amma again, his stress on the word making it anything but respectful—"do you have any idea who could be responsible for this?"

A stricken look fluttered over Amma's face, but she took a deep breath and met the aide's eye.

"I'm sure you are aware of my brother's line of work, sir? I don't think he could have managed to set up his business without collecting a few rivals over the years."

My heart continued to race, but I forced myself to focus on what was happening in front of me.

The aide raised an eyebrow.

"A convenient explanation, isn't it?"

"Surely you don't think we could hurt our own family?" The question popped out, while both my mother and the aide turned to me sharply. What was I doing? Was I just trying to absolve myself of guilt? I had nothing to do with the attack, I tried to convince myself. Nothing.

"Looks like you haven't taken enough time out of your demon worship to raise your daughter with manners."

It was like a slap across my cheek. He comes to our house, accuses us of hurting my uncle, and expects me to be silent? I took a breath to reply, but I met my mother's eye first. Disappointment flashed through them, and so I swallowed my anger. The last thing I wanted was for her to look bad in front of the Mudaliyar's aide.

"Listen"—the aide dismissed my outburst with a wave of his hand—"it's a known fact that your husband held a grudge against your brother. Possibly your whole family."

My mother's face went stone-cold.

"Perhaps, given the circumstances of me leaving my home, it would be more practical to believe that my family holds a grudge against him, and not the other way around." I had never known my mother to defend my father, but I was glad she did.

"Do we have any other information? What were his injuries?"

"Amara, that's enough—" Amma started.

"Curious you should ask," he snarled. "Most of the injuries are the same as the other attacks. Slashes across the chest, puncture wounds on his neck, except for one interesting thing. His teeth were pulled out. All of them."

Tears ran down Amma's face at this, and I felt tiny pinpricks of darkness cloud my sight. I couldn't believe it.

"Where was he attacked?" I asked, my voice weak.

"I'll be asking the questions, you hear?" the aide growled. "As you must know, we don't believe these attacks are isolated by nature. And our office recently came into possession of some interesting knowledge. Would you like to hear what it is?"

I knew from the way he asked that we wouldn't like to hear it at all.

"Siripala, the fisherman who was harmed a few weeks ago—is it true that he owed your husband money?"

"Half this village owes my husband money," my mother retorted, her tone shifting. "He never goes back to collect. Perhaps if he did, we wouldn't be living in this dilapidated house out in the middle of nowhere."

"What's all this, now?" We were interrupted by Thaththa walking up the path to our home, returning with a small sack of vegetables. He smiled politely at our visitor.

The aide gave a small start when he realised who it was.

"Your brother-in-law, Jeevan Van Court, was attacked last night." The words fell out of him too fast. He took a step back as my father approached.

Thaththa frowned and looked at Amma.

"I see. What terrible news. Kumari, have you offered this gentleman a drink? Let me bring you a seat, sir. Tell me how I can help in any way."

"There's no need for that," the aide retorted. "I just need to know where you were last night."

"I was at home, with my family," Thaththa replied, his voice calm, the unspoken accusation rolling off him like morning dew on a leaf.

"Anyone else who can corroborate that?"

What a ridiculous question. He'd just said that he was with us. This aide was just trying to pin the blame on him under the guise of an investigation. Except—well, Thaththa wasn't at home with us. I'd woken up after the dream where . . . I couldn't even bear to think about it now. But when I'd woken up, shivering and afraid,

Thaththa hadn't been there. I assumed he'd gone out like the night before.

Thaththa just smiled pleasantly at the man, whose frown had deepened as beads of perspiration started to dot his forehead.

"I'm sure my wife and daughter will happily swear to it."

"Just your wife and daughter, then? How convenient." But his voice had lost the edge it had when he was speaking to just Amma and me. Thaththa's reputation, no matter how falsely it was earned, had some benefits.

But all the while my father expertly smoothed over the aide's questions, my mind kept getting dragged back to my dream.

Did it somehow predict the attacks that were going to happen? That was ridiculous. None of the other men who were attacked appeared in my dreams.

I never thought about the woman if I could help it—at least, not during daylight. The way she beckoned to me. The way I could feel her, deep inside that part of me where I knew things to be true.

"Listen, I'll be honest with you." The aide took a deep breath, forcing his chest to puff out like that would somehow be intimidating to Thaththa. "It's all starting to look very suspicious, you hear? I was sent simply to question you, but very soon, the Mudaliyar's office will need to make an arrest. And I think we all know who the guilty party here is."

"It certainly does sound like an arrest needs to be made, sir. But I can assure you that I have no part in this. Neither, I'm afraid, is there any evidence tying me to an involvement in these attacks. And so I must ask that you do not trouble my family until you have any further proof." Thaththa took a small step closer to the aide, who took a fairly large one away from him.

"Let's see about that, shall we?" The aide turned around and tried to feign a smooth exit, but he tripped over his bicycle twice before he could ride away.

Thaththa walked up to our fence to watch him leave, and it was then that I noticed that Amma was trembling like a leaf.

Something in my heart gave way. It hurt me to see her so sad. I touched her arm lightly, even though she wouldn't meet my eye.

"I'm sure he'll be alright soon, Amma. Don't worry. I'll say a prayer for him."

Amma claimed to have converted to Buddhism when she married Thaththa, but I knew she still prayed when she could. Shaking off a god you grew up worshipping wasn't as easy as leaving your family, after all.

She just shrugged my hand off and looked at me—her eyes ablaze with resentment so potent I wondered what I'd ever done to deserve it.

And then she turned her attention to Thaththa.

"This is all your fault! We are treated like monsters in our own home all because of you!" She descended on him the moment he was close enough.

"What do you mean, it's my fault? Jeevan had many enemies. Countless men he'd cheated. I'm sure he just got what was coming to him." He spoke calmly, proceeding to unpack the vegetables from his sack.

"Oh, enough of this! I know it was you who hurt him. You wanted to take revenge, didn't you? Even though it wasn't his fault. He couldn't help it if—"

"Can you listen to yourself, Kumari? You are losing your mind!" My father's voice rose. I took a step back. I knew what would come next.

More shouting. More fighting. I could hardly take it anymore.

"You ungrateful son of a bitch. You talk about him like this even now when he's keeping this family afloat. Even when you pretend you are too good for his money."

"I never wanted anything to do with that man or his money. All that was your idea." His voice was even louder, reverberating off the walls in our small house. "This is karma, Kumari. What goes around comes back around. Karma, do you hear?"

My mother released a laugh so cruel it stung my ears. "Oh, this is karma, alright. The sins of the father, after all. Only it can't end in marriage this time, will it?"

I hated when they fought like this. I just wanted to leave. But through all the shouting, another realisation descended on me—did Amma also think that Thaththa had something to do with the attacks? She was often upset with him, yes. Often angry and disappointed. But she'd never accused him of harming anyone else before. What had changed?

14

I BARELY TOUCHED my roti and fish curry. The dread that set in when I first heard about Jeevan Maama's attack soaked through me like I was a rag, leaving me bloated, heavy, unable to breathe. It seemed inevitable that Thaththa would be arrested soon, and yet there was nothing I could do about it.

I had tried to slip away, but Amma kept giving me more tasks around the house, as if inundating me with work distracted her from her own pain.

I waited until the sun was low in the sky and the world turned tangerine.

"I brought in the chilli that was drying in the sun, and removed the husk from all the coconuts. I'm very tired. I think I'm going to sleep," I announced, pretending to yawn. I needn't have bothered. My parents both glowered from opposite ends of our garden, too preoccupied with their own anger to pay any attention to me.

I pulled my curtain shut, and moved the wicker basket where I stored my clothes. From behind it, I retrieved two old gunnysacks, left over from buying rice during better days. I had filled them both halfway with dry sea sand, which I then moulded into the shape of a sleeping body. Laying them on my mat, I patted them into position and covered it with a sheet. There were no windows in our hut, and the darkness allowed me my freedom.

I kept low as I crept out of our gate, but I needn't have worried. It was just me and the jungle now, exactly the way I liked it. The sounds of the cicadas rose around me, punctured only by the occasional call of an owl. Even the air felt different out here—rich and thick and deep, perfumed by damp earth and the whispers of the trees.

The horrors of the day had taken on a surreal quality—dreamlike, almost. Like I was floating on a wave. Just a piece of driftwood, rather than a sailor manning my boat. No matter how much I tried to make sense of it, everything felt out of my reach. My fingertips would just graze what I was searching for before it was lost to the white foam of the ocean again.

The trees blocked out what little light was left. The jungle had turned quiet. Oddly so. I could hear the leaves crunch under my feet as I walked, echoing around me. Or were those the voices in my head?

His teeth were pulled out. All of them.

Looks like you haven't taken enough time out of your demon worship to raise your daughter with manners.

The fisherman who was harmed a few weeks ago—is it true that he owed your husband money?

The Mudaliyar's office will need to make an arrest. And I think we all know who the guilty party here is.

Thaththa never dabbled with yakku—and deviyo can't be called upon to hurt someone. Thaththa had strict rules about that. Strict rules that he never broke.

So why had he written down a spell that clearly used demonology?

No, I thought to myself. No. There was no way my father would harm a fly. Not Siripala the fisherman, not any of the other men from the village, and certainly not his wife's own brother, no matter how much he disliked him. There had to be some other explanation.

Perhaps he's not responsible for the attacks because you are, you little bitch.

I thought of how real it felt when I tasted Jeevan Maama's blood. The rage I felt at Amma, the way it coursed through me like fire. My body broke out in goose bumps.

What was this voice that always stole itself into my ear? Always taunting me with fears so deep I wouldn't dare think of them on my own.

THE DEEPER I walked into the jungle, the more I felt it again. I was being followed.

I took a deep breath and tried to shake it off. There was sweat trickling down my back, but I was shivering. Now that I was truly alone, my body felt like a pile of dried leaves—the slightest gust or movement, and I'd be swept away. I was barely holding things together from the fear and worry.

Steadying myself, I continued to the usual clearing where I met Raam. This had been our spot for a while now, deep enough that we didn't have to worry about our voices carrying or being caught by anyone else.

I wondered how prudent it was to meet him today, with my head and my emotions running amok. I didn't want to be the type of woman who was upset all the time, like my mother was. Where navigating her moods was as difficult as rowing a fishing boat out to sea in the middle of a storm.

But I was not my mother, I reminded myself. I was not bitter. I didn't move through life like it was some kind of broken promise. And Raam would never be like my father. He was never cold, or withdrawn. If anything, he was the only constant in my life.

I couldn't see the sky to be sure, but I knew I must be late. I always felt guilty if I kept him waiting, not that he ever said a thing to hurt me.

I needn't have worried.

"There you are," Raam said, wrapping his arms around me. He wore a white, spun-cotton shirt that was a size or two too big for him. It made him look even more boyish and mischievous than usual. His hair was shorter too, more in the style of the British than a hair knot adorned with a tortoiseshell comb like my father wore his. Raam used to wear a sarong, but he stopped shortly after his father got his new position. But he was barefoot and his trousers were at least a few inches too short for him, even though they hung low on his hips. He was almost enough to make me forget the dreams and the voices and the attacks and absolutely everything else.

"Hello," I said. My voice had a tremble to it, betraying everything I was doing to hold myself together. The dam inside me was paper-thin, about to tear open.

"What's wrong?" Raam asked, leaning back to study my face. He tucked a strand of hair behind my ear and it was enough to burst the fragile facade holding everything together.

My tears were sudden and ferocious. I buried my face in his

white shirt as I heaved, steadying myself when I felt his palm on the small of my back.

"Tell me, what happened?"

How could I ever tell him everything? How could I tell him that my entire world was getting swept away by the tide while I watched, helpless, from the shore?

"It's Jeevan Maama," I managed between sobs. "He's been attacked."

"Attacked! Do you mean by . . . ?"

I nodded. "The Mudaliyar's aide came by our house today." I couldn't tell him my doubts about Thaththa. Or about my dreams. They were too outrageous. And besides, I didn't want him thinking the worst of Thaththa before he even got to know him.

"Poor darling. You must have been so afraid." I wasn't afraid of the Mudaliyar. I was afraid that my dream might have had something to do with it. Or worse yet, that my own father was involved in some way. But Raam was rubbing my back as he hugged me and it felt so nice to finally be comforted.

"I just hope he'll be okay. They said—they said the attacker had pulled out all of his teeth."

Raam gave a small shudder at that, but continued to comfort me.

"Amara, this is your uncle who owns the tavern, right?"

His voice was gentle and yet I pulled away slightly. That was always the first thing everyone saw in Jeevan Maama. It didn't seem fair.

"Yes." My voice was guarded.

"Look, these things happen in the tavern business, okay? It's not just the drink, you know. It's the cards, and the women."

"The women? What do you mean?"

Raam just gave me a small smile.

"You know how so many people see it. They call it a papayak. You know, a *sin*?"

"Do you think it's a sin?" My voice was harder now that I'd stopped crying.

"You know I don't believe in all that. Surely, we've evolved past believing in fantasies. I just think that some people need to be realistic about the risks they take, that's all. Like you, sneaking out here to see me."

He was smiling again, his fingers grazing at the gap between my blouse and my reddha that I hadn't noticed before.

"Raam." There was warning in my voice. We'd been here before.

"Alright, alright, I'm sorry." He let go of me, holding his hands up. I didn't want him to let go. Not completely. He gave me an apologetic smile, going over to where the root of a nuga tree jutted out of the ground and sitting down.

I followed him over.

"I'm sorry," I said. I'd been keeping him waiting. I knew he wished I wasn't so particular. But without a proposal I had no safety net.

Raam gave me a good-natured shrug, but that only made me feel worse.

"What time is it, anyway? Shouldn't you head back?"

"I guess I should." I hesitated, smiling at him. "Will you walk me back like you usually do?"

"I think I'm going to stay here a while. My father's been in an exceptionally foul mood today. Probably best that I kept clear of him." He put his palms behind his head, elbows splayed, and leaned back against the tree.

"Raam."

"What?"

But what could I say to him? I was the one pulling away.

"You know I love you, right?"

He smiled. "Of course I do. I'm sorry for pushing this. It just, well, it gets difficult for me sometimes. You're so beautiful, and so special to me. I just wish you would trust me, you know?"

"I do trust you, Raam."

His eyes said he didn't believe me, though he never spoke the words.

"It's alright. I'll speak to my father soon. As soon as his probation period is cleared and he's confirmed at his post. Things will be different then, I promise."

I sighed. "Raam, I hate doing this, you must know that. I don't want to pressure you, but I'm eighteen. I've been dodging my mother's proposals for two years now." I hunched down so my face was level with his and touched his cheek. He didn't move away.

I knew I would give in to it eventually. Raam had been asking for a while. I'd just hoped we would at least be officially betrothed by now. Back when I would speak to Neha I had mentioned it to her, phrasing it more like an abstract question, and she looked absolutely horrified.

"Amara, you can't do it before you are married, or engaged to be married at least. What if someone finds out? Or what if he leaves you? You will never be able to marry anyone else. No one wants to marry a used woman. Besides, it's a sin." There was that word again.

But it wasn't sin that bothered me. I knew very, very little about the relations between a man and a woman. It took me a while to even understand what Raam was asking of me. But I'd also learned, through unclear whispers and hushed talk, that this was how women got pregnant, and one thing I knew, even if the mechanics of pregnancy were never quite explained to me, was that an unwed pregnancy was one of the worst things to happen to a woman.

Raam wouldn't ever leave me. Would he? He was so sweet and caring. I was so lucky that he had chosen me. There were so many girls who admired him, who thought him exceedingly handsome—I'd heard the gossip around town. I never understood what he saw in me, a dark-skinned Capuwa's daughter, who everyone believed was a witch. Raam didn't care what people said, though. He told me I was beautiful, that he admired my free spirit. It didn't matter if we had to keep things a secret, so long as we knew we belonged to each other. We didn't need a wedding vow to affirm it. His heart was mine.

I STILL REMEMBER when I first saw him, back when I was in school. Daphne and her friends had been exceptionally horrid to me that day, so much so that I snuck out before the final bell rang and hid behind my usual kottamba tree. I just couldn't chance them taunting me on my way back from school again, especially since things between me and Neha had started to get tense. I stayed put until I heard the gaggle of girls leave, their shrill laughter puncturing the humid afternoon air. I was peering from my hiding place, wondering whether the coast was clear, when I saw him, perched on the low wall, chewing on a piece of mango and watching me.

"What are you hiding from?" he'd asked, his dimple absorbing his cheek and engulfing my heart.

The day grew hot in an instant, as if all the breeze had been swallowed by the sea.

"What makes you think I'm hiding?" I replied. A question to answer a question, hoping it made me sound interesting, rather than timid and fearful, which I undoubtedly was.

"Fair point. I guess you could say that I was *hoping* you were hiding." There was a mischievous twinkle in his eye then, one I had grown to love in the two years we'd been seeing each other.

"And why's that?" I was trying to keep my voice light. I didn't want this beautiful boy to think I was some sort of strange recluse, with no friends and no one to talk to. I certainly didn't want him noticing the sweat that was now soaking into the armpits of my blouse.

"Because I know a fantastic hiding place. Much better than this one."

"Oh?"

"It's in the jungle. I can show you, if you like?"

I was hesitant. He could tell.

"Don't tell me you wouldn't like to see a new hiding place. I've seen you out here every day this week, during the interval."

I'd looked down then, shame washing over me. He knew. He knew the other girls hated me. He knew I was an outcast who preferred to hide during break time rather than make friends.

"Hey, I didn't mean to upset you. I'm sorry. I just wanted to tell you that, well, I've noticed you before, that's all. I've noticed you and was waiting for a chance to talk to you."

"Daphne put you up to this, didn't she?" The words tumbled out of me, everything suddenly falling into place. This had to be another one of her cruel tricks.

"Daphne? She's the one who always looks like she's stepped in cow dung, right?" He wrinkled his nose in a pretty good imitation of her.

I gave a small snort, but still looked at him suspiciously.

"You don't trust me enough to go into the jungle with me yet. That's fine. That's good, actually. But until then, can I meet you here again tomorrow?"

Despite my best efforts, I found myself nodding.

I told Neha about him the very next day and her eyebrows shot up so far I thought they'd get lost in her forehead.

"Raam?" she asked. "I've heard the girls whisper about him. He's the handsome one, right? I think Daphne was sweet on him a while back, though I don't think he paid her any attention. He hasn't paid any of the girls much attention, from what I've heard."

I felt a small warmth in me then. Though I would be careful not to mention him too often. Things with Neha hadn't been the same and I didn't want her judgement.

He met me at my tree again the next afternoon, and the next, and I let him show me the jungle the week after. Of course, there wasn't much for him to introduce me to—I knew these trees and these paths like the back of my hand. But still, I marvelled at everything he showed me like it was brand-new, because in a way, it was brand-new. It was the first time I'd truly felt wanted, and that was new enough for me.

But still, something always held me back whenever he asked for more. I loved him, truly. I just didn't feel like it was the right time yet. We had the rest of our lives ahead of us. What was the rush? It wasn't that I didn't love him, or trust him. I loved him completely. But it was possible, wasn't it? To love someone with your entire being and yet still want to keep a little part of you for yourself?

But what if he thought I didn't love him anymore?

"Listen, it's not just the marriage thing, alright?" I said, an idea, albeit a weak one, springing to mind. "It's just—it's just this suray, that's all." I pointed to the copper tube that hung around my neck.

"Your talisman?" He looked puzzled. He'd never been one to pay much attention to protection charms, even before his family converted religions.

"Y-yes. You know, you're not supposed to do, um, things like that when you wear one."

"Things like *that*?"

"Yes. I'm not supposed to eat red meat either, you know. No beef. Or pork." That bit was true, even though we never brought red meat into our house anyway. My father said red meat was filthy and attracted yakku, who were drawn to the smell of flesh.

But Raam just gave me a little chuckle.

"You are so sweet, you know? So innocent." He leaned over and gave me a light kiss. It was enough to make me melt.

"If this is what's holding you back, then let's just get rid of it." I noticed only then that he was lifting the suray over my head.

"Raam, no!" I cried out. My father had said wearing it was important. He'd given me a whole speech when he put it on me, just a few weeks ago. *Under no circumstances are you supposed to take this off. Only to bathe, that is all, do you understand me, Amara?*

And then a flash of something else—of feeling powerless, of being in pain, of silent screams that just couldn't manage to break free of my body. Of blood sinking into the sand.

"Oh, come on, you don't really believe in all this stuff, do you? Where's my smart, intelligent girl? If you get any more superstitious, you'll end up like Heen Achchi—you know, the old woman with the cloudy eyes who scares everyone that goes by the Star Fort?"

"My father will be so upset with me," I tried.

"I think your father is busy enough these days not to notice," he said, half jokingly. What was that supposed to mean? I was suddenly alert. Did Raam also think that Thaththa had something to do with the attacks?

The thought was enough to push my worries about the suray out of my mind.

I let Raam slip it off me and put it into his pocket.

"You don't mind if I hold on to it, do you?" He breathed into my ear, making me feel like my knees would give way from under me. "It'll be nice to have something to remember you by. To remind me that you're mine."

He started kissing my neck and I found myself saying alright, even though I didn't really agree with him. He told me this often—that I was his. And while I knew he only said it because he cared, there was something about his words that didn't quite fit. Did he have to possess me to love me? I wasn't an object to be owned. You could love something without staking a claim on it, couldn't you? Like I did the jungle, like I loved the sea.

But Raam loved me, and that was what was most important.

"Now you better get going, before your mother loses her temper and tells you that you can never leave the house again or something," he said.

I was so relieved that I just kissed him on the cheek and turned to leave. I thought he'd want to do it immediately and I'd have to come up with a whole new set of excuses.

"Oh, and Amara?"

I paused, holding my breath.

"I know you probably still haven't asked, but don't forget about permission to go to the perahera?"

I nodded, giving him a small smile.

"Well, I'm going," I said, the typical goodbye.

"Yes, go and come," he replied. To not mention coming back was bad luck. And with my suray gone, I needed all the luck I could get.

"Raam, please be careful in the jungle. There've been so many attacks lately. I don't know what I'd do if something happened to you."

His smile eclipsed the moon.

"Don't worry about me, Amara. I'm not afraid of any beast, from this world or any other."

15

I USUALLY CUT straight through the jungle to get back home, but a dull throb had started murmuring in the pit of my stomach. All this talk about the attacks had left me uneasy.

I stuck to the shadows and took the more open route that hugged Nilawala Ganga—the river that snaked its way from the deeper rainforests in the central country to kiss the sea less than a mile away from the town fort.

There was a tiny island on this river, Kiralapana Doowa, that no one ever visited because of the crocodiles that surrounded it. One of them had snatched a young child from the riverbank just a year earlier. I kept a close eye on the path as I scurried forward. The Doowa was a hulking mass on the shimmering waters, looking like the head of a beast about to swallow any innocent being that crossed its path.

I'd only been walking a few minutes when I heard rustling behind me. I was being followed, there was no doubt about it. I muttered a small gaatha under my breath—a chant to keep me safe—and tried to keep my mind off it. I just had to make my way home as quickly as possible.

I reached for my suray out of habit, but of course my fingers just grazed at the bare skin below my collarbone. I winced as I touched a small wound that had scabbed over. I hadn't noticed it before. Had I scratched myself while I was sleepwalking? How foolish I had been, letting Raam take the suray. My father would be livid when he found out. Maybe that's why he gave it to me, realisation dawned—my mother had definitely complained to him about the sleepwalking.

I'll kill everyone myself if I have to. This cannot get out.

Had I done something while I was wandering, half-asleep? My mother must have been worried about the neighbours finding out, and having to deal with even more rumours and gossip about our family. She wasn't a foolish woman—she definitely knew about everyone calling me a witch. Maybe the suray was a guard against this nightly curse. To keep me safe.

Taking a deep breath, I squared my shoulders. Where was this voice coming from? It wasn't like me to doubt Thaththa. I just missed him, that's all. Again, I wished I could just find out who was truly responsible for the attacks. Vindicate our family once and for all.

But the footsteps behind me didn't go away. As I was hurrying by the riverbank, a putrid smell reached my nostrils—of rotting fish, or decay. Or death. I gave myself a little shake. Fishermen often disposed of their excess haul by the river. Dozens of fish, lying on their sides, their eyes unfocused towards the heavens. Some flapped around, trying to save themselves, as if they still had hope.

Finally, suffocated, they would rot in the sun. That was probably what I smelled. There was no need to be so frightened, I just needed to get home.

But my arms broke out in goose bumps and cold sweat started to bead down my back. A yaka had found its way out of my dreams and into reality, I thought, my fear starting to grow irrational.

"Who's there?" I called out in a voice that didn't quite sound like mine.

More rustling. Closer, this time.

I didn't wait to see what it was. I broke into a run, forcing a path through the reeds and shrubs underfoot.

And then the moon dipped behind a cloud, throwing the entire world into darkness, just as I stumbled, perhaps on an exposed root of a tree, perhaps on a sleeping crocodile, and went sprawling face-first into the soft mud of the bank.

The rustling behind me grew closer as I flailed around, trying to stand up in the sludge. It was reaching me. Any moment now the attacker would wrap his hands around my feet and I'd never be seen again. I was going to have the same fate as Siripala the fisherman and Jeevan Maama. I wasn't like the fish that flapped on the shore—all my hope dissolved into the mud beneath me. I squeezed my eyes shut and prayed.

"Are you alright?" a voice called out from in front of me—a soft, gentle voice, belonging to a woman. The rustling behind me was gone.

I opened my eyes and looked up.

It wasn't a woman, but a girl who gazed down at me in concern, her brow furrowed. This was no yakshaniya. Not from my dreams nor otherwise. She crouched down in the mud next to me and offered her hand. Something about her felt familiar.

"Need some help?"

"I—I thought I was being followed," I said, my breath coming in gasps and splutters.

"Followed?" She peered out behind us. There was a lit torch in her hand that cast mile-long shadows onto the riverbank, and though the shadows looked like monsters themselves, we were quite alone.

She gave me her hand again and I accepted this time. Making sure I didn't get any mud on her, I struggled to my feet.

"We should move away from the bank," she said, her voice low. "The tree line is safer if you think there's someone else out here."

She believed me. Even when it was clear there was no one there, she didn't doubt me. Something stirred in my chest. Something I hadn't felt in a very long time.

Wordlessly, I followed her back to the trees. She walked so gracefully it looked like she was gliding. Her reddha, much too long for her, dragged softly in the mud, and she carried a small sack in her right hand. There was a wide, low-hanging tree branch a few feet away. Sticking the end of the torch in the soft earth and leaving her small sack on the ground, she hoisted herself onto it and sat like it was a bench, inviting me to do the same.

I hesitated. I was already late. My mother would have my head if she noticed me missing.

But something kept me back. How could I walk away from the first stranger who'd shown me kindness in weeks?

I pushed myself up and sat, angling my body to face her. Our feet swung a few inches over the ground. The light from the girl's torch cast a warm, orange glow on her. Her long black hair was neatly braided and hung down her back. Her small, heart-shaped face looked delicate and kind.

Something slipped into place. "I've seen you, haven't I? The other day, in town. You were selling those woven cane baskets."

I guarded myself, then, remembering the way her face had flashed with anger. She was probably one of the townsfolk who believed I was a witch, who blamed me and my family for all the horrible things that had been happening lately.

But she nodded, smiling. "Yes, I saw you too. I'm sorry those people in town were so horrid to you. It made me really angry. I wanted to come forward and say something, but, well, I'm new here, and I was a bit nervous."

This admission filled my heart. How often are others' motives coloured by our own view of the world? I'd always been so resentful that I'd been judged prematurely by everyone who met me, only to do the same to this girl. She saw how unfairly they were treating me. Somehow, it gave me strength. Made me feel a fraction less alone.

"So what brings you to the jungle at night?" she asked.

There was something about her that made me not want to lie. Like it would have been pointless not to be honest with her anyway. That she could already see beyond me, deep down into my soul.

"I was meeting somebody," I replied.

"In the jungle, at this time of night? That sounds very romantic." There wasn't a shred of judgement on her face. She really must not be from these parts.

"It is, I suppose."

"And you think there's someone out there following you tonight?" she asked.

"I'm not sure. I—I know there was no one when you looked.

Perhaps because I've been worried about the attacks, but it's just this feeling I've been getting."

"Like when the hairs at the back of your neck start to prickle?" she asked, matter-of-factly.

I studied her face to see if she was making fun of me, but she was solemn.

"Yes, exactly like that. How did you know?"

"I get that feeling sometimes too, especially when I'm in the jungle. I think the moon and the wind form an alliance to try and trick us. Maybe that's the jungle's way of protecting itself."

She spoke of the jungle tenderly. Like it was alive. Like she loved it as much as I did. There was a certain comfort in knowing that the very thing you loved mattered to someone else as much as it did to you. A bond between us started to grow like a vine.

"Do you come out here a lot?" Trees stretched on for miles where the Dutch and the British hadn't made clearings for farmland, so it was easy to lose yourself out here if you didn't know your way. Unless, of course, getting lost was your purpose.

She cast her eyes down, her cheeks reddening slightly.

"Yes, I suppose I do. But please don't tell anyone? I'll get into so much trouble if I'm found out."

I almost laughed.

"Deal. As long as you do the same."

"Of course." She pinched her lips together with her index finger and thumb for a moment. "Your secret is safe with me."

I loved the sound of that.

"These attacks really have everyone at their wit's end, don't they?" she asked, changing the subject.

I nodded.

"Do they have any idea who it could be?"

"Not yet, I'm afraid," I replied, even though I felt the tips of my ears on fire. There was no way I could tell my new friend my suspicions. Especially when I wasn't even sure what I was so worried about to begin with.

Her eyes bored into mine. "You know, I worry so much at times like this. No good ever comes from panic. With fear comes the abandonment of reason, and that's when things become dangerous."

"What do you mean?"

"I mean that people start pointing fingers. Blaming others without enough evidence. I've seen it happen before too." Once again, I felt humbled by her. Here I was believing that I was as alone as a boat out at sea, when there was someone else who saw things so similarly to the way I did.

"So you're not from here, then?" I asked, remembering what she'd said about being new in town. That was probably why I hadn't seen her before.

"No, I've not been here too long. Certainly not long enough to make any friends."

"Well, some people live in one place their whole life and don't have any friends." The words slipped out before I could give them any thought. Like she drew them out of me.

"The people here aren't too welcoming, then?"

"To my family, no."

"And why is that?"

"You've probably not heard yet, but my father is a Capuwa."

She frowned. "The Capuwa in my old village might not have been widely embraced, but he was certainly not regarded with any hostility."

"Unfortunately, it appears that most of the townsfolk blame my father for the attacks."

She gave a small sigh at this, and shook her head.

"And what about you? Do they avoid you because of this as well?"

"Everyone has considered me a witch for the longest time now. It's just gotten worse since the attacks."

"A witch, eh? How very . . . colonial of them."

A short laugh burst out of me, my mind going back to the woman in town who tripped while asking me to leave. It's funny how rumours take root—funnier still how they grow and flourish. I'd experienced it firsthand back at school, a week after I found the chicken head in my cubby.

It had been our interval and I was leaving the chapel when Daphne bumped into my shoulder.

"Excuse me," I apologised, quietly. I was a fast learner and didn't want any trouble.

Daphne just smirked, but as she turned her back to me, I heard her voice ring clear.

"Cluck cluck."

Her friends burst out laughing, and I was about to reply when I was interrupted by a short scream. Daphne slipped on the chapel steps and landed badly, sprawling on the mud below.

"My ankle," she gasped. It was already starting to swell. I could see so even from where I stood.

"She did this!" Daphne's friends said, pointing to me.

If I'd had the power to do that, I wouldn't have stopped at just Daphne's ankle, I remember thinking. But ridiculous as these allegations were, my reputation was sealed. I was a witch.

From then on, every time someone tripped on the playground,

it was my fault. If it thundered too loud, the girls would whisper that I was angry. One time Sister Agatha got ill with a sore throat, and I heard Daphne vehemently tell everyone that I took the nun's voice away with black magic.

"So how are you liking this part of the island?" It was my turn to change the subject. "Whereabouts do you stay?"

"Punchi's house is at the edge of the jungle, you know, close to—do you know that lady with the milky eyes? I think everyone here calls her Heen Achchi? It's close to where her hut is."

"You stay with your punchi, then? Why did you move?"

She looked down. "I had—" She hesitated. "I had an incident where I used to live. It was a few villages over. There was a man—" She rubbed her face. "He—"

"You know, it's fine," I interrupted. "I'm sorry I pried. We don't need to talk about this now." She spoke with such a sadness to her. Whatever happened must have been truly terrible.

"Anyway," I continued, "don't you wish things could go back to the way they were, you know? When we were younger and everything felt . . ."

"Simpler?" the girl offered.

"Definitely simpler. Before these attacks. Before my uncle got hurt."

"Your uncle was one of the men who were attacked?"

"Y-yes." I realised that the anxiety over my dream had taken a brief respite while we'd been talking, but now it clamoured back to me. "We just got word of it today."

"The man who owns the taverns?"

I nodded, again wary of judgement.

She looked unsettled.

"What is it?" There was an edge of defiance in my voice.

"Oh, no, it's nothing. It's just that, well, I've—I've heard of him, from before." She had gone pale.

"You've heard of him?"

"Um, yes." I could sense reluctance in her voice, but she carried on. "I'm sorry, I shouldn't even be talking about it."

"No, tell me." I was curious now. I'd only ever known Jeevan Maama as my mother's brother, and I'd only ever heard what Thaththa had to say about him. Had he been right to loathe him? Or was Thaththa overreacting?

"It's just, there's—there's a rumour. That he—well, that he forced himself on a girl. Or so I heard. She was young. He got her pregnant. All the blame fell on her, of course. She was too forward. She should have been at home. She was ostracized, forced to make the worst choices." A cloud passed over her face.

It was something about the way she said it—the anger and sadness that swirled just under the surface of her words. The way an angry tear made its way down her cheek.

Was she talking about another girl in her village, or was she talking about herself? Jeevan Maama had taverns in many towns down the southern coast. He could easily have met her during visits to his businesses.

But was he truly that terrible? Was Thaththa right about him all along?

I thought about Siripala the fisherman, and the way he treated his wife. Did Jeevan Maama also deserve to be hurt for the things he had done?

"I'm sorry I'm making you talk about the absolute worst topics on a night like this," I apologised. Even if this girl had been, in fact, accosted by my uncle, the last thing I should be making her do was relive anything.

"It's fine. Really. Can I tell you something and you'll promise you won't judge me?"

How could I possibly judge her, the one person who finally understood me?

"Of course," I replied.

"It actually makes me feel better talking to you. Like I'm not the only girl in the world with problems. It makes me feel less like I'm on my own."

If I could have thrown my arms around her right then without scaring her I would have. If only she knew.

"And to hell with the attacks! The world has taken away so much from us women already, why should it take away the jungle as well?"

I nodded. She was right. I envied her power, her perseverance through difficult times. If she had the courage and strength to fight back against the world, then what was stopping me?

"If you need remembering that the jungle is your home," she said, as if she read my thoughts, "here—" She picked a leaf from the tree we were sitting on and pressed it into my hand.

"What's this?"

"My mother always kept one with her. It's a talisman of sorts, I suppose. We believe in harnessing the power of nature. The jungle is soft and lush and beautiful, but it houses strength beyond our wildest dreams."

"Thank you," I said, slipping the leaf into the waistband of my reddha and climbing from the tree.

She followed me and picked up the sack.

"My aunt wanted these coconuts to make a sambol for tomorrow," she said, opening the bag and pulling out the brown fruit covered in a husk. She tossed one over to me.

"Think fast!"

I giggled and caught it.

"I should get these home soon. I'm already in enough trouble."

She held her arms out so I threw the coconut back at her, but she made little effort to catch it. Instead, it sailed through the air and landed with a crack on the jungle floor, bursting open into two halves.

"Oh, no! I'm so sorry," I tried apologising, but she waved me away.

"It's fine. I'll just scrape these as soon as I get back. No harm done." She smiled at me warmly. "We really should get going now."

"Wait!" Something in me ached to stay there with her. "What's your name?" I couldn't believe I hadn't asked sooner.

She laughed, realising it too. "You can call me Bhagya."

"I'm Amara."

"Amara," she repeated. My name sounded different on her lips. Richer, more luxuriant.

And with that we said our goodbyes.

It was only when I slipped back into my corner of the hut and lay down that I realised the footsteps had not followed me back home. Perhaps the jungle would protect me after all.

16

I'D BEEN SLEEPING for perhaps an hour when the voices outside jerked me awake. I stuck my head out from behind my curtain—not too far out because I was still in my nightgown—and peered out. There were three men in our garden, and it looked like they were threatening Thaththa as my mother looked fearfully on. One of them held a large hunting knife and another a sickle—a moon-shaped blade usually used to cut paddy.

"We know you did it," the man with the knife was saying.

"Admit it now and perhaps we'll let you live," the larger man behind him growled.

"I told you gentlemen already." My father spoke confidently and quietly. "I had nothing to do with Jeevan's attack. That's not the way my craft works. If that were the case then all my enemies would be in their graves. All those who have wronged me would have been brought to justice. But here I am, simply trying to provide for my wife and child."

"Then where were you the night he was attacked?"

"I was right here, at home with my family."

One of the men reached out and backhanded Thaththa across the face.

"No!" I cried out. I couldn't help it.

"Stop! Please stop." My feet had found their way to the verandah without me even realising it. "My father would never hurt anyone, please leave him alone."

The man who hit my father took a step back. I don't think he expected to see me.

"You!" the one with the knife exclaimed. He looked me up and down as I stood trembling in my thin nightdress. "So you're *his daughter*? I didn't think I'd be seeing you again." I didn't know what he meant. I had never met this man before in my life.

"Get back inside," my mother hissed, crossing over to where I stood and pulling me back.

"As you can see, you've troubled my family enough for one day," Thaththa said. "I am as upset about Jeevan's attack as everyone else."

The man with the sickle raised it above his head, as I screamed out.

"Enough!" Thaththa bellowed. "I have been more than reasonable—bearing your taunts and jeers. But I will not be threatened like this in my own home. If the Mudaliyar has enough evidence, then let him arrest me. But I will not be tried in the court of public opinion."

I was sobbing, fear and anger thundering through me like a storm. How dare they threaten him like this? How dare they?

The men gave each other a look that I couldn't understand. The one with the sickle lowered his weapon.

"This isn't the end of it," the growly man said, turning towards the fence. The other followed, but the man with the knife who'd spoken to me just stood there. When I met his gaze, he licked his lips and smiled.

My mother yanked my arm and dragged me inside the hut.

"Aren't you ashamed? Parading yourself around like that in front of those men? You're just asking for trouble, aren't you?"

"So I was just supposed to stay here while Thaththa was beaten? Doing nothing like you?"

My mother slapped me.

"Kumari, that's enough." My father had also come indoors.

Seeing him broke something in me and I felt tears pool in my eyes.

"Thaththa, I was so scared."

"It's okay now, Amara. This is just a misunderstanding, that's all." His voice was kinder than it had been in weeks and it only made me cry harder. I moved towards him, trying to wrap my arms around his body like I used to just a few short weeks ago.

But he stepped back from me. It was just a foot, but it might as well have been an entire ocean.

"Where's your suray?" he asked.

I swallowed. I hated having to lie to him. Hated myself for being silly enough to let Raam take it off me.

"Oh, it's with my things. I was just about to wash."

"Make sure you put it back on. And don't worry about these men. Everyone is on edge right now, and it makes people unreasonable. I'll speak to the Mudaliyar about it myself if things keep getting out of hand."

I had my doubts whether the Mudaliyar would ever take our concerns seriously, especially with men like Aloysius at his side, but still I took a deep breath and tried to calm down.

Amma had started sweeping the hut, her emotions as displaced as ever. Seeing those men must have been scary for her too, but instead she chose to focus only on what she could control.

"She needs to be given in marriage," Amma complained and for once the topic didn't bother me as much. "It's improper for a girl her age to be unwed. It's what's making her run amok like this."

Thaththa just nodded and stepped out of the house, his face ashen.

"Get dressed, we need to go into town. You've been sleeping later and later these days. How do you suppose you'll find a husband like that?" Amma said, her voice deadpan. "And don't forget to take your tonic."

But I could only stare at Thaththa, who walked out of the gate without so much as a glance back at us. At me.

"No need to be in such a mood. Are you on your menses or something?" my mother asked. I turned away from her so she couldn't see me roll my eyes.

I went to the well and splashed some water on my face, willing my heart to stop pounding, forcing my breath to be calm. I couldn't tell what was worse—my fear and rage at the men who were threatening Thaththa, or the way it was so easy for him to dismiss me afterwards. It was getting harder to navigate my anger, perhaps even more so than my pain. At times it felt like my hands were bound—I wasn't allowed to confront those who tormented me and my family. I had to keep my head down, choke back any outrage, and learn to make peace with it. Amma used to say that it was every woman's burden. But surely they didn't all have it as badly as I did?

And her question about my menses kept rattling around in my mind, nagging me. If being a woman was such a curse, then why did women themselves help perpetuate this injustice?

I thought back to when I had my first blood. My mother had never spoken to me about what to expect, but Neha had been through the ritual earlier in the year, and she, thankfully, spared me no detail.

The ceremonial process had been the same as always. A small, leafy shed—kola-maduwa—was erected at the bottom of our garden, separate from the rest of the house, and I was segregated for fourteen days, not allowed to see any men. It was believed that the start of a girl's menses left her most vulnerable to demons and other evil spirits, so an elderly woman was to keep me company. That should normally have been my mother and grandmother, as it was for Neha, but Amma busied herself with cleaning the hut and preparing for guests instead, and, well, I had no delusions about my grandparents suddenly materialising. Some of the women from the village took turns, but most barely spoke to me, using the time to snooze, probably enjoying their brief reprieve from household tasks.

Neha did visit me with her sister, Catharine, and I was glad, even when Catharine chided me for offering Neha some water. I was not supposed to touch any cooking utensils or water vessels at the time. This period was known as kili—taboo—where women were thought to be unclean. We weren't allowed at religious places of worship either.

But still, Neha and I giggled in the light of the lamp that burned with seven wicks about silly things she told me about school, and I showed her the iron sickle my mother had left near me to ward off evil spirits. Catharine looked at us disapprovingly, but broke into laughter herself when I did my impression of Sister Agatha, clamping her fingers over her mouth as my mother shot her a sharp look from inside the house. We were supposed to be subdued and pious.

My father wasn't allowed near me, as was customary, but every morning when I woke up there were cut fruits next to the kola-maduwa, and I knew he was thinking of me.

He and my mother had consulted the village astrologer, my mother told me. Neha spoke of her own horoscope—the astrologer had said that the stars were particularly lucky for her.

"Were they lucky for me?" I asked Amma, but she pursed her lips as usual.

"We didn't check all that. Just when the auspicious time was for you to bathe."

My bathing indicated the end of my kili period. It was officiated by a washerwoman I had never seen before in my life. She led me to a secluded part of the garden with my face covered, and had me face north as the astrologer had prescribed. I was to stand on a special mat, surrounded by jackfruit twigs and leaves, and a pot of coconut flowers known as a punkalasa.

The washerwoman herself stood on a vee goda—a heap of unhusked rice—and poured water on my head from a clay pot. She caught me by surprise—Neha had forgotten to tell me this—when she dashed the clay pot against the nearby jack tree after she bathed me.

Dressed in a clean, new reddha, I was handed a sickle and told to go to the same jack tree and stab it several times. I still remember the chant I recited dutifully—

"If I attained puberty under an unlucky star, let the effects of it pass on to this milk-bearing tree. May no danger befall my father, my mother, the man who is to marry me, or me because of it."

A jackfruit fell, then, narrowly missing the washerwoman's head. She looked at me with her eyes narrowed, like it was my fault, and clicked her tongue.

But there was a feast inside our hut, laid out just for me, and I could see my father for the first time in days. I remember when he saw me after—hair still wet but braided neatly, flowers woven into the plait, and wearing my new clothes. I smiled at him, suddenly shy, and he smiled back. He'd missed me too.

But he didn't miss me anymore. What had changed? Was it him, or was it me?

17

THE CHURCH BELLS thundered as we reached the town centre. It was Sunday, so the square was busier than usual. Families of the girls I had known from school streamed out of the looming, arched building, their eyebrows arching even higher than the steeple when they noticed my mother and me.

My body felt tightly wound since those men had threatened Thaththa that morning. I'd been carrying my anxiety with me for weeks now—ever since I'd heard Thaththa was being blamed for the attacks—but lately it felt harder to bear. My breath was shorter, and my stomach ached. I tugged at my blouse. It had ridden up at the waist, showing about three inches of bare skin. My mother noticed me adjusting it and clicked her tongue.

"Why didn't you drape your reddha over your shoulder?" she asked. She wore hers like that—a sari. It kept all the essential parts hidden, but was never very convenient to move around in. "You're older now, Amara. It's high time you started behaving like a lady. No wonder the Englishmen think we are savages."

"They are the savages, not us," I mumbled.

"Excuse me?" Amma asked. But the way her lips almost disappeared into her face told me that I shouldn't repeat myself.

Amma couldn't help it. She was raised by parents who revered the foreigners, and why shouldn't they? Their allegiance to these newcomers guaranteed them land and wealth and status. A place in society. A place she had renounced by marrying my father, and a place that he could never have.

Not that he wanted it, of course.

I had once asked him why he never carried out exorcisms on Englishmen. They were rich, after all, and could probably pay a lot more than the villagers, who barely honoured their agreements to begin with.

"Because there's no need to," he replied.

"What do you mean, Thaththa?"

"They don't require my services because yakku never possess them, duwa."

I knew they were more powerful than us, but I never thought they were more powerful than demons too.

"How lucky they are, the Englishmen."

My father snorted.

"It's hardly luck, duwa. Even the yakku won't go anywhere near them. Though they crave human blood and carcasses, even demons possess certain ideas of cleanliness and decency. They won't go near those who don't cleanse themselves with water after they . . . you know."

"After they what, Thaththa?"

"After they, ah, after they pass bodily fluids," he replied, red in the face.

"Oh."

But when I confided this information to Neha the next day, she looked horrified.

"Amara, no. You mustn't say such things," she gasped.

"And why not? I know your father has started working for them, Neha, but that doesn't change the fact that they are strange."

"Amara, did you ever stop to think that maybe the *yakku*"—she inflected the word like it was alien to her—"leave the Englishmen alone because yakku don't really exist to begin with? That they're something we Ceylonese believe in so much that we've convinced ourselves they are real?"

We had stopped talking soon after that. Perhaps this conversation played a part in it.

I was tugged back to reality when I heard a small scream. Whipping around, I looked to see where it came from. Was someone else being attacked?

Eyes wide and lips trembling, a small boy pointed at Amma and me. His mother was trying to get him to lower his hand, but he was too upset. I couldn't hear what he was saying, but I guessed it had something to do with demons or witchcraft.

A few people crossed the road to the other side as we approached them, as if our presence alone would be enough to unleash a yaka.

Near the centre, a group of townsfolk clutched their pamphlets. They eyed us with suspicion, mumbling amongst themselves, their voices carrying over to us like bees.

. . . Attacks . . .

. . . Witches . . .

. . . Demons . . .

Any smear one could think of, cast our way, worse than a bee-sting.

"Rejoice in the Lord," a voice boomed and every inch of my body recoiled. "For He is our saviour. His love knows no bounds." Aloysius smiled wide, showing us all his teeth. He was holding some pamphlets in his arm.

"Kumari Van Court, I'm surprised to see you out on a Sunday. Did you come for mass?" His words were pleasant but his tone jeered. The group behind him looked fearful, clutching one another, like my mother would suddenly transform into some sort of demonic beast.

"Aloysius Peiris." My mother nodded. "Good day." It looked like Amma was already acquainted with him. But how?

"Hardly a good day when there are devil worshippers running rampant in our town," a woman who stood with the group behind Aloysius hissed, and a few women in the crowd gasped, while others gave nervous giggles.

Even my mother's eyes widened at that. She'd heard the whispered taunts—we all had—but no one had openly spoken to her like this in public before. The tides were definitely turning in this town, and it wouldn't be long before my family were cast out at sea.

"Take a pamphlet, dear sister. Remember, there's hope for you yet, even though there isn't much even the Lord Himself can do for your husband's soul." Aloysius made a swooping gesture of handing Amma one of the sheets he was holding, but Amma squarely turned away.

"Come along," she scolded me instead. "Let's not dally here. We have business to do."

I noticed her look over her shoulder more than a few times as we walked away.

"Do you know him? Aloysius, I mean," I asked.

"What absurdities are you speaking of, child? I was acquainted with his family, once, long ago. But that was before I met your father."

Regardless of whether Amma knew him or not, or what Aloysius said, one thing was abundantly clear—the church was packed with worshippers. There were more people attending Sunday mass than ever before. Whatever rumours were being spread around town, fear of the attacks was certainly driving people to be more religious.

We walked further towards the market and Amma paused, craning her neck down a lane we were passing.

"Mary asked me to stop by and note down her measurements," she said, looking undecided. "I wonder whether it'll be unseemly to visit now. It being a Sunday and all."

I didn't care about whether it was a Sunday, but Mary was the wife of Loku Banda, the local shopkeeper who had been attacked about two weeks ago. My curiosity was immediately piqued. What was she like? I thought back to Siripala the fisherman's wife—would the woman be similar? It seemed ridiculous to think so, but yet, a part of me roused. The visit from the thugs this morning had only made me more anxious to solve the attacks.

"Shall we see if she's in first?" I asked.

I could tell that Amma was of two minds. But we both knew that we needed the payment, and delayed measurements meant delayed bills.

We walked quickly down the lane and had almost reached Mary and Loku Banda's house, when we saw someone step out of their garden and make their way towards us.

"Good day," a British officer said, his tan uniform standing out against the usual dress we locals wore. He wore a wide hat with one side of the brim pinned up, as officers in the army usually did, and his polished brass buttons glinted in the sunlight.

My mother just nodded at him, gripping my wrist and tugging me behind her. We rarely had any interactions with the British army, even though we saw them often enough in town. They oversaw the guarding of trade routes and ports, and I had absolutely no reason to ever speak to one. It was rather strange that one of them would be visiting Loku Banda.

I eyed this man curiously. His blond moustache and lighter skin looked almost otherworldly to me, though he was red in the face and sweating through the collar of his uniform.

But he seemed to be in a rush, and Amma pushed me through the gate that led to Mary's garden. Their hut was built in a similar style to ours, but considerably larger. Loku Banda's shop was very successful, even though he had only started running it a few years ago.

"Mary Haminey?" she called out, her voice demure.

"Who is it?" Mary came to the front of the house. She looked rather ill. Her hair was undone and her reddha was draped messily around her, the pleats not quite tucked into the waist.

"I came to take your measurements. But I can come later if this is a bad time." Amma's voice sounded strange too. She worried far too much about propriety sometimes.

"Kumari Haminey, it's Sunday. It certainly isn't a good time for me. Would you mind please coming on another day?"

Amma's face reddened, as did mine. Perhaps Mary didn't want to use our services anymore either. It wouldn't be the first time since the attacks started.

"My apologies, Mary Haminey. I'll return sometime this week." Amma bowed her head and turned to leave.

"Yes, you do that," Mary replied, but she was looking up the lane, not at Amma, who had already made her way down the garden.

I gave Mary Haminey a small smile, but she just frowned at me.

"She did look rather ill, Amma. It was most likely just that." I tried to console my mother when I caught up to her.

But she just shook her head, her lips tight.

"Come along. We've wasted enough time as it is."

18

WE REACHED THE further side of town, and Amma stopped in front of a large, whitewashed mud hut. It was obvious that whoever lived there was wealthy since they had two cattle grazing outside, along with multiple coconut trees.

My mother hesitated again. Her shoulders, usually pushed back proudly, appeared to sag a fraction of an inch. They perked back up the moment she noticed me looking at her. I really couldn't blame her for worrying after our last encounter, but then, I didn't recognise this place, and something told me we weren't here to take measurements.

Pushing open the small fence, she continued towards the house with me trailing after her.

"Sanchi Haminey?" she called out.

A lady stepped onto the verandah with her arms crossed. She was dressed in a stylish chintz reddha, and her jacket was made of cutwork fabric, with large, decadent sleeves gathered at the shoulder and elbow. I had begged and pleaded for Amma to sew me a jacket like that, even in simple fabric, even using an old sheet, but she had refused, saying it would be an extravagance.

"Ah, Kumari. I wasn't expecting to see you." The tone of her voice rose and fell dramatically. She wasn't acting afraid of us, which was a welcome relief after the display at the town square.

"I know it's been a long time, Sanchi Haminey. Have you been well?"

"I suppose as well as can be. You heard that my Joronis received another promotion? He's now an assistant clerk at the port authority. How is your husband doing? Still running around chasing the devil?" She laughed heartily at this while my mother gave her a strained smile.

"We are well."

"That's good to hear, indeed. I've been hearing all this nonsense about blaming your husband for the attacks, but you know Joronis and I don't pay any heed to idle gossip."

"Thank you, Sanchi Haminey."

"I would offer you a drink, Kumari, but we have to make it to town. Joronis has been invited to lunch at Julius Peiris's house, you see." She paused, and then clasped her hands over her mouth in an exaggerated gesture. "Oh, how silly of me to mention Julius. Especially after your engagement to him."

I tried not to show my surprise as I stared at my mother. She had been engaged to Julius Peiris? That was Aloysius's uncle. They were one of the wealthiest families in town—mostly through gifts from the British for their support.

Was that why Aloysius had such a disdain for my father? Because my mother hadn't married his uncle?

"All that is water under the bridge, Sanchi Haminey. Long-forgotten history. I am much happier now, with my husband."

"If you say so, Kumari. If you say so. Now tell me, what brings you here? Not a social visit after so long, surely?"

"Actually, Sanchi Haminey, I'm here on some small business."

Sanchi Haminey's darkened eyebrows met each other in the middle of her wide forehead.

"Business, you say?"

"Yes, I happened to meet Nowroos the other day at the market, and he told me that you were inquiring about a pair of earrings. He told me that you were unable to find anything to your liking."

"Well, yes," Sanchi Haminey replied, her voice uncertain. "Nowroos has a lot of big talk, but his craftsmanship doesn't come anywhere close to his father's, may he rest in peace."

"I happen to have a pair, made by his father, in fact. I could sell them to you, if you wish."

A heavy pause hung in the air as Sanchi Haminey's eyes widened like saucers.

"I couldn't," she replied, in a voice that heavily implied that she most certainly could.

"They have only been worn a handful of times, and are still in perfect condition. I'll give you a much better price for them than Nowroos would, I assure you."

"Hmm. I don't usually buy things secondhand, Kumari. My Joronis wouldn't hear of it."

"These aren't secondhand, Sanchi Haminey. They are exquisite antiques. Only two pairs were made in this design, and the other, I heard, is worn by the governor's wife herself."

Sanchi Haminey's eyes looked like they would fall out of her skull.

"Can I see them?"

My mother produced a small hambiliya—a purse made out of

woven, coloured reeds—from the folds of her sari. Sanchi Haminey practically ripped it from her hands.

"My . . ." she said, examining the small gold studs. "Why would you part with them? Have things been so difficult since you married?"

"All these lies about my husband's involvement in the attacks have certainly had their impact. And there's been some unexpected expenses this past month." My mother's tone was neutral, but it still wrenched my heart. Of course, things had worsened since everyone had started shunning Thaththa. And now that Jeevan Maama was attacked, he wouldn't be helping us either. Were things so bad that Amma had to sell the few nice things she had? My mind flew back to the necklace I had found—the hansa puttuwa—and I felt a small spark of anger. Why was she the one having to make the sacrifice? But Amma continued on, oblivious to the chaos in my mind.

"I hardly have use for these anymore. And I'd much rather they be worn by someone of your stature."

"Hmph, flattery will get you nowhere, my dear. How much for them?"

Sanchi Haminey smiled at the earrings, greed dripping off her like sap from a mango tree, as my mother named her price.

AMMA WAS QUIET as we walked back to town. Those earrings were the last thing she had from her family, she had told me once, when I caught her pulling them out of the box and admiring them. I'd never seen her wear them, only look at them.

"They are beautiful," I had told her, then.

"Yes, they are, aren't they."

"Why don't you ever put them on?"

She snatched the earrings away from me. "To do what? To cook and clean and look after you? Why would I need gold earrings for that?"

"You could wear them when we go to town?" I had offered.

"No point in getting dressed up to be the village laughingstock," she replied, her tone defeated.

"Can I have them, since you're not wearing them? I mean, when I'm older."

She looked at me with an expression that was difficult to read.

"No," she said, simply. "No. These are the only things I have left that are mine."

I hadn't understood then, and I wasn't sure I understood now, but I could feel her pain thrum in the air between us.

"I'm sorry, Amma," I said.

"Are you, now?" she replied, bitterness curdling her voice. I kept quiet. I didn't want to upset her further.

She turned right, towards the market.

"Aren't we going home?" I asked.

"I have to make a payment to Jayasiri's shop," she replied. "Then we can go. Hurry up, now. Stop dawdling."

"Jayasiri?" I asked. Jayasiri was notorious for selling items used in Cattadi rituals with yakku, as well as potions he brewed himself to cure various ailments. As far as I knew, my father regarded him with much suspicion. Besides, shouldn't we be using this money to buy some paddy?

"I thought Thaththa only bought his items from Loku Banda? When did he start buying things from Jayasiri?"

"How your father chooses to conduct things is none of your business, do you hear?"

She looked wistfully at the coins that had replaced the earrings in her hambiliya.

"Let's get this over with. We need to get home and make dinner."

I agreed, even though doubts about Thaththa had started to run rampant in my mind once more. The items on the note I had found in his bag could be purchased from Jayasiri's shop. And if he had bought the objects, then he must have conducted the ritual—must have created a yanthraya.

Who was he trying to curse? How many were there?

19

"I BREWED YOU some beli maal," I said, trying to hand Thath-tha the coconut shell he used as a cup.

"I already had some today," he said, turning his back on me. I pretended to act like I wasn't stung. I waited a few minutes while he fixed some thatching on our roof that had come loose. I didn't know what happened after I got ill a few weeks ago, but something had shifted. It coloured things the way smoke from a bonfire tarnished the air. My parents had never been so secretive. I had never felt so uneasy.

"Thaththa, we haven't gone to the temple at all this month. I was wondering if you'd like to go with me?" That usually pleased him.

He didn't even respond. Not a single word as he continued to work on the roof.

I bit my lip. I had to put my hurt aside for now. It wouldn't do to dwell on it. What I needed to do was find some answers. If only there was someone else who knew about yakku and their powers like Thaththa did. Anyone else who could talk to me about yanthra or the list I had found.

I was poorly hemming some sheets when a solution sprang into my mind, as sudden as a wave that knocks you off your feet. There *was* someone who might know more about the dark practices that went into working with yakku. She was here, in our very town, even though talking to her would certainly not be an easy task.

Most people, including myself, thought Heen Achchi was losing her senses, but that didn't mean I couldn't try and get some information out of her. I had to do something, before everything that raced through my mind forced me to disintegrate.

I told Amma I was delivering some finished curtains to a customer in town and made my escape as soon as I could.

I hesitated at the edge of the jungle. The main road took so much longer, and I was anxious to get some answers soon. But looking at the jewelled leaves of the trees put my heart at ease. The new friend I made last night was right. There was power in the jungle. It was up to me to use it, not to shy away from it.

Pushing my chest out and my shoulders back, I made my way in.

But I had walked only a few feet when that old feeling came back, more vicious than ever. The feeling that a million claws were just out of my line of sight, hiding in the shadows, waiting for the right time to plunge into me.

I thought I heard a rustling in the leaves above me and stopped. I had managed to get only as far as the tall banyan tree, less than twenty feet away from the jungle edge. This tree was so tall that I couldn't see too far past its lower branches. No one let banyan trees grow this tall anymore, especially close to the village, because they said it attracted yakku, who sought to live in them. But at the same time, no one dared chop down fully grown trees either, lest they angered a yaka who'd already taken up residence there. The rustling stopped as I squinted up, wondering if a demon was waiting for me, fangs extended, tongue hanging down in greed all the way to its chest. If I hesitated under the tree just a moment longer, perhaps it would scoop me up in its talons, sinking its teeth into my flesh as I . . .

I shook myself firmly. I had more important matters at hand without getting distracted by childish fears. Really, I was becoming as bad as the people in town. But just in case, I turned around and took the main road. Who was I to think I was any more special than everyone else? If a yaka had set its sights on me, no amount of courage or bravado would help.

I had to make a quick stop before I spoke to Heen Achchi, because Amma would have my head if I didn't actually deliver the curtains, especially now that we needed every cent we could get. The order had been placed by Malkanthi Haminey, who'd had the fabric especially brought down from Colombo to hang in her brand-new rest stop for travellers. Previously, the town only had an ambalama, a shed built from clay, that anyone could sleep in if they got tired while travelling. But Malkanthi Haminey and her husband had started serving travellers food and drink for a fee, and were well received by anyone passing through Matara town.

The rest stop was well constructed, much more like a British-style house than the small huts we lived in in the village. Amma had been asked to sew the curtains that hung in the doorways between the various rooms. The front part of the house served cool drinks and fruit for anyone, traveller or not, while the back areas were reserved for sleeping.

I rapped on the doorframe, hoping Malkanthi Haminey was in. It would be extremely annoying to carry the sack of curtains all the way back home, much less take them with me to see Heen Achchi.

"Malkanthi Haminey?" I called out.

"What do you want?" A man, sharper and older than the pleasant owner of the rest stop, appeared, his arms crossed.

"Is Malkanthi Haminey here?" I asked.

"We aren't open."

I looked around to where plates of baked goods and baskets of fruit were laid out for anyone who wanted to buy them. They certainly weren't closed. My body tensed. This man just wanted to get rid of me. He probably believed the rumours, just like everyone else.

"I have a delivery for her," I said, gesturing to the sack that held the curtains. "She put this order in a few weeks ago and it's ready now."

"You get those cursed goods out of here right now!" His voice rose and he took a step towards me.

I felt my legs tremble. This man was much bigger than me, and with his face scowling in anger, he looked like he could be a yaka himself.

"She gave us the fabric herself. My mother has been sewing for her for many years now," I tried explaining.

"Do I look like I give a damn? I want you out of this house, witch!" Flecks of spittle sprayed out from his mouth.

"There's a balance to be paid to us." I held my ground, not because I was brave, but because I knew there was no way Amma could make the rice stretch any further.

"Get out!"

"Do you want it to be known that you owe money to a witch? Do you want to see what happens when you have a debt to pay to my family?" I didn't know where this shot out from. I didn't know how I made my voice sound authoritative and confident when I said it. I just stood there, glaring, as the man's face twisted and grimaced while he fought a battle in his mind, weighing out his options.

Finally, he pulled out some coins and tossed them onto the floor.

"Take this and get out. Don't ever come here again, you hear me?"

I dropped the curtains in the corner of the room. Let him get rid of them. Let him burn them, for all I cared. I took my time gathering the coins. I didn't want to taunt him, but my head felt light and my body felt like it was not my own.

Malkanthi Haminey was a long-standing client, and it would pain my mother to learn we wouldn't be getting her business anymore. The injustice of what kept happening sent a shudder of anger through me. It wasn't fair. None of this was fair.

But then, if my father did have something, anything at all, to do with these attacks, were the people in the town wrong? I needed to speak to Heen Achchi. She may not have all the answers, but perhaps she could point me in the right direction.

I WAS ALMOST at town when I saw Neha. She was going into the nunnery, carrying a large basket. It was probably food for the nuns. She spent more time with them now. I ducked behind a tree before she could see me—I couldn't take another awkward meeting with her. Not now. When someone once knew you better than you knew yourself, how could you ever learn to understand them changing?

I pushed everything that had happened that morning out of my mind and hurried to see Heen Achchi. She was exactly where she always was, at the Star Fort, sitting on a small bench in the shade, chewing betel, gazing up at the sky like it held every answer anyone had ever searched for. The sun was low, casting everything in a saffron light. It was beautiful now, but it also meant nightfall would be upon us soon.

"Adha yahaluwa koh?" *Where's your friend today?* she asked, before I could even introduce myself. She didn't turn to face me.

"Mama witharay, Achchi." *It's just me, Achchi.* I was treading carefully. The last thing I wanted to do was offend her.

"Ay achchiwa mathak wunaiy?" *Why did you remember me?*

"Achchigen podi uddawwak illanne avey." *I came to ask a small favour from you.*

She turned her head a fraction of an inch in my direction. I had piqued her curiosity. Not many took her gift seriously anymore. She wasn't regarded with danger and suspicion like my father was, but her old age and senseless rambling did not leave much room for her to be respected.

"Monavada danaganna oney?" *What do you want to know?*

My eyes darted around the entrance of the fort, unsure where to start. It wasn't like I could just come out and say it. I'd never voiced my doubts and suspicions aloud before.

"Ochchara hithate barak dhe, lamayo?" *Is it such a burden on your head, child?* she asked. "Enna, mekha leysi wadak nemey waagey." *Come, this doesn't look like an easy job.*

And with that, she shuffled to her feet and started to walk away. I supposed I was meant to follow, and even though I didn't quite want to, I did. She pottered forward with no cane, her feet nimbly skimming the path, her chin always pointed up. It was like she was being guided by something else.

"Koheda yanney, Achchi?" *Where are we going, Achchi?* I asked.

It wasn't difficult to keep up with her, but I was very aware of the looks we were getting from everyone we passed. It was certainly doing nothing for my reputation being seen with her—another mystical outcast, a wrong turn away from being called a witch herself. We weren't so different, Heen Achchi and I. Perhaps, many years from now, when I was old and grey, I'd be treated the same way she was.

"Enna koh." *Come, will you,* was all she answered as she hobbled along, leading me a few streets over to a quiet part of town at the very edge of the jungle. There was a tiny mud hut there, hardly visible if you didn't know to look for it, and I supposed that was where Heen Achchi lived when she wasn't sitting outside the Star Fort.

We followed the small, pebbled path that led us to the hut, comfortably nestled under a canopy of trees. I hesitated as Heen Achchi stepped inside and bustled around, digging out a small clay lamp and filling it with oil, making sure the wick was drenched and hanging out the side.

"Koh, ithing? Indaganna." *Come, now? Sit down.*

It was dark inside the hut—a startling change from the evening light outside. I could barely see my hands in front of me, let alone what hid in the shadows. Why did she bring me here? I started to feel nervous, but then, I could leave anytime I wanted. I came to get answers, and I couldn't do that if I panicked.

"Magey yahluwek methana langa inney. Kalaawa langa." *One of my friends lives close by. Near the jungle.* I don't know why I said it. Perhaps to let her know that I wasn't completely alone. That I had a friend who was just a scream away. Like that would even help. Like I even knew exactly where Bhagya lived.

"Mama dhannawa, lamayo. Eya mageth yahaluwek thamai." *I know, child. She's my friend too.*

I wasn't sure if she meant Bhagya or her aunt, but it hardly seemed to matter.

Heen Achchi took a seat on a small bankuwa, with the clay lamp on a box in front of her. She was gesturing for me to sit opposite, so the flame from the lamp danced between us, illuminating her creased, papery skin.

She rubbed her hands together and stared into the flame, the milky film on her eyes glowing bright. Was it just my imagination or could I see the white cast swirl? She started to mutter something under her breath, but I couldn't make out any of it.

This was different from when I would accompany Thaththa. The shadows on the walls danced from side to side, even though neither of us was moving. The temperature in the hut dropped sharply, and I started to shiver.

"Thaththa ganadhe prashna thiyenney?" *The questions you have, are they to do with your father?*

I nodded.

"Kathakaranna, lamayo." *Speak up, child.*

"O-owu, Achchi." *Y-yes, Achchi.*

"Mmm, mama danagaththa. Thaththagen karadara goday. Thaththage hitha venas wela. Ekay, oyagey waradeemak nemey." *Mmm, I knew it. You have a lot of issues with your father. His feelings have changed, but that is not your fault.*

"Ay ehema wela thiyenney, Achchi?" *But why has that happened, Achchi?*

"Eka nam Thaththama karagaththa loku weradeemak. Eya dhan samawa illuwe nathnam thawa godak karadara ey." *That's a big mistake that your father made. If he doesn't seek forgiveness now, there will be many problems to come.*

"Monawada Thaththa karey, Achchi?" *But what did my father do, Achchi?*

"Thaththa deviyota loku agawrawayak karala thiyenney." *Your father has greatly disrespected the deviyo.*

I knew it. I knew he had been doing something wrong.

"Heen Achchi, aththatama danaganna oney, yanthra walin balapaam monawada?" *Heen Achchi, what I actually need to know is, what harm can one do with a yanthraya?*

At the mention of this question, Heen Achchi started shuddering. Her voice rose an octave as she answered, her milky eyes reflecting my fear back at me. A gust of wind picked up in the hut, making the light of the lamp flicker, making my hair flutter around me.

"Mey lamaya nam panditha wadiy. Ekem kisima hondak labenney naha, therunada? Yanthra kiyanney godak bayanaka deyak. Vadhina kenata haniyak wenna puluwan, marenna puluwan, hithey thiyenna dhey nathikaranna puluwan. Deviyo wath lang venney naha yanthrayakata." *This child is far too smart for her own good. No good could ever come of this, do you understand? A yanthraya is very dangerous. It can hurt people, it can kill people, it can alter their memory. Even deviyo won't come anywhere close to a yanthraya.*

It can kill people? Could it even harness the powers of yakku to carry out attacks?

"Thaththata parissamen inna kiyanna. Deviyo vadi kalak mehema asaadharanakam daragena inney naha." *Tell your father to be careful. The gods don't bear injustices like this for too long.* My body went cold.

"Thawa deyak thiyenawa." *There's another thing,* Heen Achchi said. I held my breath. The light from her lamp glowed brighter and the flame suddenly got very still.

"Lamaya vatey loku andurak thiyenawa. Wishwasayen inna.

Devi maniyota pooja dhenna. Api sthreeyin ekathukaragath pawu walin leysiyen beyrenna baha." *I see a darkness surrounding you. Stay in faith. Make offerings and pray to the goddesses. We women can't easily absolve ourselves from the sins we are entrenched in.*

"Eh kiyanne, Achchi—" *What does that mean, Achchi,* I started to ask—but Heen Achchi suddenly shoved the table away from her, causing the lamp to slide off and smash onto the floor. My eyes struggled to adjust as Heen Achchi pushed herself to her feet, her breath coming out in rasps.

"Achchi?" I asked, tentatively, my heart racing.

Heen Achchi made a choking sound and froze, her body completely rigid. Her lips twisted apart crookedly, as if they were being prised open against her will.

And then she released a guttural scream, loud and shrill and echoing through the tiny hut as her eyes rolled back deep into her skull. I slid back and pressed myself against the wall, every part of me trembling.

It was then I noticed Heen Achchi's feet. They were twisted completely on their ankles so that the tops of her feet were folded over, touching the ground. She took one step forward, and then another, screaming every time.

"Athi than prashna kara. Palayang than methaning." *Enough questions. Get out of here,* she rasped, in a voice very different from her own.

I didn't need asking twice. I pulled myself up and fled, despite the fear that flooded through me making it difficult to breathe.

20

THE WALK HOME wasn't easy. I kept reaching for my suray, berating myself each time I realised it wasn't there. Heen Achchi's contorted body had wedged itself into my mind. Her screams echoed through my very being. Thaththa always said that practicing this craft came at a cost. But still, it took a while for my heart to stop feeling like it would explode.

When it did, her words came rushing back.

Tell your father to be careful. The gods don't bear injustices like this for too long. She had to be referring to the attacks. What else could Thaththa want with a yanthraya?

And there was the other thing she said.

We women can't easily absolve ourselves from the sins we are entrenched in.

She might as well have sung me a riddle. I came for answers, but only had more questions.

I was too afraid of the demons to go back into the jungle, and too afraid of the angry townsfolk to go back into town, and so I walked down the ocean shore all the way back home.

I rarely took this route because it was far too hot in the daytime, and left me feeling oddly vulnerable at night. The path passed by a smattering of taverns, the largest one owned by Jeevan Maama, where men would gather to drink toddy, leaving them red-faced and rambunctious. I took my hair down from the knot at the nape of my neck. It wasn't much, but I felt like it cloaked me, kept me safe. Amma would call it indecent, but she wasn't here right now to lecture me.

I kept my head down as I hurried past the busiest tavern, hoping not to draw any attention to myself. These drinking rooms were more like open huts, and I could see clearly into them, which meant the men who were patronising them could see out clearly too. Luckily for me, the men appeared to be engaged in an exuberant drinking song, one of them even drumming on a bankuwa to the beat of the music.

I was almost past them when something made me look over, like my neck was connected to an invisible puppeteer's string. My eyes went to it immediately, even though it took a few more moments for my mind to catch up.

To the cowlicked hair on the tall boy who stood at the very centre of the room, one arm flung around another man, a mug in the other, as he belted out the song.

My breath quickened. My stomach churned. I'd joked that my heart would always find Raam, no matter where he was. I just didn't think where he would be was a tavern, especially when he seemed so critical of Jeevan Maama, who owned it. He'd never told me about these visits.

A small ember lit within me, not yet a fire, but angry just the same. How dare he be so judgemental of my uncle when he had no problem patronising his tavern? And if he kept this from me, what else did he hide?

I was so preoccupied from seeing Raam that I grew careless. Two steps later, my neck still arched towards the tavern, I crashed into a man. I could tell from his breath that he'd been drinking—the stench rose off him in waves, mixed with the smell of betel leaves that had turned his teeth and lips red.

"Where are you going, all by yourself, pretty thing?" he slurred, reaching for my arm.

I don't know if it was my anger at seeing Raam that made me do it, or maybe I was just tired of always being pushed around by the men in this town, but I bared my teeth and snarled. My hair hung in front of my face, obscuring much of it from view. I knew exactly how it made me look.

If they wanted something to be afraid of, I'd give them something to fear.

The man's eyes widened as he gave a high-pitched yelp. Luckily for me, his friends were much too interested in their song to hear him. Fearing for his life, the man hitched his sarong up and ran.

I marched the rest of the way home, my head held high. I knew it wasn't much, but for the first time since my father stopped me from learning about his craft, I felt a small semblance of power.

It was almost enough to withstand Thaththa's cold gaze when I got back home.

"You took quite a while to make those deliveries. You know you're supposed to stay indoors after dark," Thaththa said, mistrust oozing out of the both of us like pus from an infected wound.

"I've been taking the long route on the main road, like you asked. It makes everything slower." I ignored the stab of hurt and answered him, feigning aloofness.

What Heen Achchi had said about him snaked through my mind again.

Like I had a million times over these last few weeks, I tried to untangle my thoughts. To find the thread that would lead me back to some answer. If Thaththa was responsible for the attacks, then why was he doing it? I was distracted as I tried to re-pin my reddha—the pleats had come loose during my walk along the beach—and pricked myself on the soft flesh of my waist.

Something stirred in my mind.

A few weeks ago, when I had taken ill, and it felt like I was burning from the inside, my father had given me some herbs, brewed into a tea, that made me sleep. I'd woken up from time to time to see Thaththa chanting pirith over me, giving me more potions and tonics, fat tears rolling down his face. But Amma's face twisted red with anger, spitting—

I'll claw out your tongue if you tell.

It was my mother's voice. Recoiling from her harsh words, I'd stared at the red curtains that blocked out the sun, every part of me hurting, wondering how I had gotten so much blood under my nails.

But there were no red curtains in our hut. That had to have been a part of my dream; maybe all of it was. I was no closer to getting any answers than I was weeks ago. It suddenly felt like a swarm of flies had descended on me, making everything foggy.

Thaththa shuffled around the hut, not even looking at me as he grabbed his bag and headed towards the door. "Well, your mother has gone to visit the neighbours, she should be home in a while, and I'm going into the jungle to collect some burulla leaves."

He didn't need to collect burulla leaves. There was a whole sack of them sitting in our maduwa. He was lying to me.

I wanted to call to him, demand to know what had changed. As if hearing my thoughts, Thaththa paused at the door.

"Amara," he said, his eyebrows knitting together the way they did when I was little and came home crying after someone called me a witch—or worse. He'd sit me down on his knee and rub coconut oil into my hair, knowing that it always soothed me, as he told me that words didn't mean anything. That no one could harm me. That he would never let them. Then he would take me for a walk in the jungle, which he knew was the best balm for any wound.

I looked at him expectantly. The time for oiling my hair had passed, but perhaps he'd ask me to walk with him? Perhaps I could tuck my hand in his arm, and we could lose ourselves in the giant trees, listening to the way the wind whistled through them like we used to.

But he turned his back on me, sighing heavily. "Make sure you stay home until your mother comes back, you hear?"

I nodded, as he walked out without saying goodbye.

Tell your father to be careful. The gods don't bear injustices like this for too long.

No, my father was a good man.

But what did good men have to hide?

MY BODY MOVED of its own accord as I crept out of the hut after Thaththa. I kept my distance as he took the path through the jungle. I noticed he was wearing his best sarong, and the tortoiseshell hair comb that he wore only for special occasions. He must have thought I was a fool for believing that he was going out to pluck some leaves off a tree.

And he was whistling.

It felt like a punch directly to my stomach when I heard that, bouncing off the emerald leaves as the tune made its way back to me, letting me know that I was on his trail. My father only whistled or hummed or sang when he was happy. It was usually as we took walks together through this very jungle. The little tune echoed through the cracks in my heart.

If there were demons in the jungle tonight, either they stayed away or my mind was too busy to notice them.

Thaththa walked for the better part of an hour, almost to the opposite end of the jungle. We'd left the seashore far behind, and I had started to feel hot and sweaty by the time he made his way to a small hut by a large jackfruit tree. I'd never seen it before, but then, I'd never wandered so deep into this part of the jungle before either.

I made sure I stayed hidden while I looked around. There was washing hung up on a line—an old sheet that women wrapped around their bodies as they bathed at the well, and a woman's blouse. There was a pot hanging over some firewood in front of the hut—the fire had been put out even though no one had cleared away the soot or charred wood.

Thaththa wordlessly removed his woven sandals at the doorstep and made his way inside. He didn't announce himself. He didn't wait to be invited in.

Whose hut was this? Why was my father here? Surely, if he'd been called to perform a protection charm, or some other enchantment, the family would have met him outside? No, he had to be doing something wrong. Perhaps this was where he went to carry out spells he didn't want anyone to know about. Maybe this had something to do with the attacks.

I had to get a closer look. Not daring to go directly into the clearing, I circled my way around to the back of the hut, still making sure that I was within the tree line. The cloth that hung over the back entrance was pulled to one side and offered me a view into the single room housed within the crude mud walls. It was dark inside, and I strained to get a better look.

It took me a while to make it out. There was a grunt, and then a groan. And then a cry—not one of pain.

That's when the moon peeped out from behind a cloud and I made out the two bodies lying on the mat in the room, clothes cast aside, completely lost to their passion.

I felt a wave of nausea wash over me. Was this my parents' secret hideaway that they came to when they needed to get away from me? I could understand it, I supposed, even if it did make my skin crawl. Our house was small, and the cloth we used to separate my sleeping corner from theirs did little to muffle any sound that passed through. But indelicacy aside, they were always so angry. It was hard to imagine that they could be intimate or romantic or loving towards each other.

And then the woman sat up, tossing back her long black hair that had come undone.

It didn't take much to see that she wasn't my mother.

She was younger than her, for one, I could see that even from where I hid, and darker. I knew her from somewhere—

The realisation hit me like a bolt of lightning. This was Siripala's wife, Leelawathi. I had watched her just the other day when I spied on the fisherman's hut.

Disgust erupted through me as I backed away. I could hardly believe my own two eyes. Suddenly, I understood exactly what people meant about sin. How it was disgusting. How it doomed your soul to hell.

The urge to find out my father's secrets was replaced by the urge to get as far away from him as possible.

21

I RAN SO hard and so fast through the jungle that my feet were scratched and bleeding. But still I relished the pain.

Outrage and shock stormed through me like a current, and the wave of nausea I felt earlier rose up in me like a tidal wave. I couldn't help it—I leaned over and vomited. My throat burned and my eyes stung and that made it easier somehow. Holding on to a tree for support, I tried to steady myself. My breath caught in my throat as I attempted to make sense of what I'd just seen.

I had thought the necklace might have been used in the spell for the yanthraya that I had found in Thaththa's bag, but she most likely just gave it to him as a gift. He probably wanted something to remember her by, the same way I had given Raam my suray. And maybe the yanthraya was something he cast on my mother. That's how he was able to keep sneaking off unquestioned.

Back when I was at school, Sister Agatha told us that adultery was a sin. It was such a grave sin that it was in the Ten Commandments. Thou shalt not commit adultery. Along with thou shalt not lie. How many commandments had my father broken today? Even if he wasn't a Christian, even if he didn't practice the new religion of the British, it was still wrong. It was wrong in Buddhism, it was wrong in Hinduism, it was wrong in every religion. It had to be. I knew that my mother wasn't an easy woman, but what he was doing was much, much worse.

My mind went to what the Mudaliyar's aide had said, about Siripala the fisherman owing my father money. What if my father had hurt him because of something else? Like being involved with Siripala's wife and wanting her all to himself?

But my father would never hurt anyone. Perhaps it was this new woman. Perhaps she was poisoning him, controlling him to do what she wanted. Was this why he was acting differently towards me? That must be why my father had suddenly changed. That had to be why he didn't love me anymore.

The confusion inside me turned to rage. It burned bright within me, that first ember now a roaring fire that didn't want to be put out.

I hated her. I hated what she had done to my father. What she had done to our family.

"I curse you," I spluttered. "I curse your existence. I call on every demon to wreak havoc on your life. To destroy you like you've destroyed what's dear to me. I call on every demon—"

"Amara?" The voice pulled me out of my tirade, though my body still trembled with the gust of my anger.

I looked around to see who it was. I'd thought I was all alone in the jungle.

"Are you alright?"

It was Bhagya.

"How—what are you doing here?" I looked around me. I was

close to the river where we had met before, even though I hadn't paid attention to where I was running.

"I was out here like usual when I heard you," she explained, not unkindly. She laid an arm on my shoulder.

"What's the matter? It sounds like you're upset."

The sob that shot out of me caught me by surprise, and I turned away, not wanting Bhagya to see me cry. Her arm never left my shoulder.

"Hey, it's alright." Her voice was soft as she rubbed my back, making me cry harder. She gently led me towards the same tree we had sat on just last night, even though it felt like a hundred years ago. I crawled onto a branch and she climbed on after, settling down so our knees touched and her arms were wrapped around me. The comfort and tenderness sent a new ache through my body. It'd been such a long time since I'd had a friend.

Finally, when my tears stopped flowing and my heart had quietened down, I took a deep breath.

"A vile, wicked woman has ruined my father's heart," I announced.

It sounded dramatic, juvenile, now that I'd spoken the words out loud, but I didn't care. I looked defiantly at Bhagya, daring her to say something, to make fun of me. All this time I had thought it was my fault. I thought I had done something wrong, something irrecoverable that made my father not want to have anything to do with me. I even thought . . . I even went so far as to think that he was responsible for the attacks taking place in the village. It turned out that the answer to everything that'd been plaguing me was laughably simple.

Tell your father to be careful, Heen Achchi had said. *The gods don't bear injustices like this for too long.*

Of course the gods couldn't bear it. Neither could I.

Bhagya's eyebrows drew together in concern.

"That sounds horrible," she said. "But tell me from the beginning, won't you?"

And so I did. I told her about how my father had grown distant from me, and how he was refusing to teach me his craft. About how he hardly looked me in the eye anymore, and how his temper had gotten worse, especially around my mother. I told her how he lied to me and how I'd finally followed him into the jungle, and what I'd just seen.

"So you can see . . ." The bitterness in my voice made me sound unrecognisable. Like my voice and my mind and my body and my heart were all separate objects—fractured and waiting for the final blow to reduce them to little fragments. "So, you can see, all this is her fault. I hate her."

Bhagya rubbed my back.

"What a terrible thing for you to go through," she said.

I nodded, biting my lip. It felt good to give my feelings a voice for the first time, instead of holding it all in and wondering why things had changed. It felt like I was throwing everything to the wind. Like I was setting all my pain free.

"Do you know how long this has been going on for?" she asked.

"No, this is the first time I've seen him with her."

"And your mother? Does she know?"

"I don't think so." If Amma knew she would have exploded. She wasn't exactly subtle—it would have made its way into one of their arguments. I would have heard.

"Do you know who the woman is? I'm guessing she's the one you were trying to curse when I found you."

"She's married to the fisherman, Siripala," I replied. "You know, he beats her. The fisherman, I mean. Perhaps he knows about this affair with my father."

"Or perhaps that's why she's sought comfort in someone else."

Something about Bhagya's tone made me hesitate. Did she have a point?

"Do you think she knows that your father is married, and has a family?"

I frowned. Why was she asking me these questions? "I'm absolutely certain. Not just that it would be impossible not to know in a village as small as ours, but I've visited their home with my father. He cast a protection charm on their hut when it was built."

"Well, what if she was mistaken? What if she was new, like me? I didn't know anything about you until we met last night. I didn't know anything about your family except your father's profession until just now."

"She wasn't mistaken." My voice was flat. Bhagya needed to learn when to stop.

"And you know this for certain?"

"No—I mean, she had to know." I edged away from Bhagya and crossed my arms.

"What makes you say that?"

"I just—are you defending her?" My voice rose just a little bit.

"No, no. I don't know anything about her to defend her. But try to think about this clearly. Why is it you've put all the blame on her?"

"Because it's her fault!" It had to be. Thaththa was honest and good and kind. He was the perfect father to me while I was growing up. And he'd changed. Something had made him change. It had to be her.

"Amara . . ." Bhagya's voice was gentle, even though there was something firm in the way her lips were set. "All your life you've been upset that people have judged you before they got to know you. Why are you treating this woman the same way?"

That cut deeper than what I had just seen in the hut.

All the relief I had felt from confiding in Bhagya vanished like footprints being washed away from the shore.

"You have no idea what you're speaking of," I replied, my voice shaking.

"Amara, I didn't mean to upset you. I just think—"

"Just because some man hurt you and you were sent away from your home, that doesn't mean every man is terrible, Bhagya. It doesn't mean my father is the villain here. You're just as bad as the people in the village, accusing him of everything!" The words burst out of me, as vicious as acid.

She looked like I had slapped her.

"You don't know what you're saying." She said it more to herself than to me.

"I should go," I said, sliding off the tree branch. I couldn't bring myself to look her in the face. "My mother will be upset if I'm not at home."

I half expected her to say something, but she was silent as I started to make my way back. I was so stupid for thinking that I had a friend, even though what she said nagged at me like a thorn stuck to the bottom of my foot.

Of course, it took two people to . . . do whatever it was Thaththa and Leelawathi were doing in that hut. I wasn't delusional enough to believe that he wasn't a willing participant. But I knew him. I'd known his heart before I even knew myself. How was it possible that someone so good to me, someone with so much love, could have a side to him that was so ugly?

THERE WAS NO torch lit in front of my house, which meant my mother hadn't returned home yet. Good, I could sneak back in and start boiling the sweet potato for dinner. Hopefully that would put me on her good side long enough that she wouldn't notice when I snuck out again later tonight to meet Raam.

Raam.

I'd almost forgotten about seeing him at the tavern earlier this evening. It hardly seemed as preposterous now, in light of what my father was up to, but that didn't mean he was off the hook yet. But still, my irritation with Bhagya had dulled the anger I felt towards him. I was so silly to think I'd made a new friend. Raam was all I'd had all along.

I was just entering through our verandah when I stepped on something soft. The moon had disappeared again and the sky was an inky, bruised purple that yielded no light. I bent down to see what it was.

It was yellow, and long—a bunch of bananas, I realised.

That was strange. Perhaps it was left for my father, though if it was a gift to the family, it was usually dried fish or paddy.

Something rippled through me. A shiver of a phrase I'd heard my father repeat many times. Bananas were what we offered demons during a poojawa. We couldn't give them what they really wanted, which was human blood, but ripe bananas smelled strong enough that it gave yakku some small satisfaction in receiving them.

So why was this offering left on our doorstep?

22

"YOU WERE SUPPOSED to boil the jackfruit! Don't you remember? Haiyyo, the sweet potato was for next week, and now the jackfruit will spoil and go to waste. And we can't afford to waste anything, don't you understand?"

"I—" I didn't remember her saying anything about jackfruit.

"For goodness' sake, Amara, when did you become so forgetful? Now what will we do next week? You'll have to eat air."

I didn't reply. It was useless trying to argue with my mother. She'd never accept that she was in the wrong. I kept quiet while I ate and cleared up, and then went to lie down on my mat.

Thaththa returned home and went straight to sleep on the verandah without dinner. I'd normally try to speak with him, but I felt far too disgusted. My visit to Heen Achchi had left me shaken and afraid for him. How stupid I had been.

It wasn't long until I heard Amma's snores echo through the hut as well.

I arranged my sacks of sand and slunk out through the back

entrance as usual. I was just starting to make my way towards the jungle when I heard a sound.

"Amara . . ." It came from the beach, high-pitched and raspy.

My body went cold. Had the yaka that followed me through the jungle finally caught up to me? I felt for my suray, but my fingers only brushed against the fabric of my blouse.

"Amara . . ." I heard the whisper again.

I thought about running back inside the hut. Anywhere to get away from her.

And still, I was drawn to the sound. Goose bumps breaking out over my arms and every part of me trembling, I took one step towards the voice, and then another.

My heart was racing so hard in my chest that I thought I would faint. Still my feet moved forward, almost with a mind of their own. What hold did the yaka have over me? What did it want from me?

It stood at the very end of the garden, behind a coconut tree. I could barely see it, but I knew it was there. The night sky was blanketed in clouds, making it impossible to see further than soft edges and looming shadows. What was real and what wasn't blurred into the darkness, smudged out of the corners of what I could make out.

"Amara!" The voice, barely more than a scratch, was excited now. It knew I was coming. It knew I had no choice. I was almost at the tree. It could reach me any moment now.

And then, the tiniest laugh, familiar even though it was hastily muffled, and Raam peered out.

"Raam!" I exclaimed a little louder than I would have liked.

"Shh!" He held his finger up to his lips and beckoned for me to follow him down the shore.

Out of view from my home, he grabbed my arm and pulled me into him.

"I didn't scare you, did I? I'm sorry I had to whisper. I just didn't want your parents to hear me," he murmured into my hair as I wrapped my arms around him, still shaking in fear. Or was it relief? Comfort that it was just him, and not the yakshaniya who haunted my dreams. I must have absorbed the fear that swirled through the village. I needed to get a tighter hold on myself.

"What are you doing here?" I managed. I kept my voice low. We were walking down the shore and were very much alone, but sound had a way of carrying in the night, especially if helped along by the ocean breeze. Besides, I hadn't fully decided if I had forgiven him yet. I tried to discreetly give him a sniff, to see if I could catch a whiff of the toddy I'd seen him drink earlier.

"It's a surprise." He sounded excited.

"Well," I said, pulling away and crossing my arms, "I'm surprised you even made it, given how you were singing along at my uncle's tavern earlier this evening."

He stopped walking and turned to face me.

"You were by the tavern?"

"I took that route on my way home. I thought you said taverns are places of trouble. That nothing good comes from drinking."

Raam clicked his tongue and shook his head.

"I wasn't drinking, Amara."

I frowned. I had seen a mug in his hand. Although I couldn't smell anything on his breath now, and he certainly wasn't behaving the way the inebriated men at the tavern did.

"Then what were you doing there?"

Raam gave me a little laugh that I usually adored but today it grated on me.

"I was celebrating."

"Celebrating what?" My voice rose a little. I was tired of always having to ask so many questions.

He sighed. "Look, I don't want to ruin your surprise. Just come with me, please?" He smiled his usual smile and, while I took a moment longer to thaw, I knew I could never refuse him.

He kissed my forehead gently, making me melt like seafoam sinks into the sand.

"Come on, then."

"Where?"

"Well, you'll have to follow me."

He wrapped his arm around me again and led us further down the shore. We were well and truly alone now—where the jungle met the beach and not another soul, not even a night owl, dared to swoop by. Even the clouds parted, as if just for us. The stars glittered down cheerfully, our only audience, as the moon conducted its orchestra of ocean waves to rise and fall like the breath of a giant beast.

There was a ruined, abandoned old fishing boat that lay on its side on the sand. A vine from the jungle had found its way over the wooden frame, half covering the boat's hull with soft leaves that quivered in the ocean breeze. Raam led me around it, where I saw that he'd laid out a large straw mat, lit a few small clay lamps, and decorated it with pichcha mal—jasmine flowers—which were my favourite.

"Raam!" I exclaimed again. I could barely keep the glee out of my voice. He'd been so preoccupied with his father's new position and his new job that it had been months since he'd made a sweet gesture like this.

"Why don't you take a seat, my lady?"

I giggled as he helped me onto the mat.

"These are for you," he said, handing me something wrapped in a banana leaf.

"Athirasa!" They were my favourite sweet—deep-fried cakes made of jaggery and rice flour. I'd only mentioned it to him once. I couldn't believe he remembered.

"I know you really like them." There was something bashful in his smile that I hadn't seen before. "You thought I'd forgotten, no?"

"I—well, you have managed to surprise me, that's for certain." I reached out and gave him a kiss. How could I stay angry with him when he treated me like this?

There was something chaste in the way he returned it. He didn't lean into me like he usually did, closing the space between us. And then he pulled away much sooner than usual, sitting back and settling against the old boat.

"Is everything okay?" I asked.

"Why wouldn't it be?" His smile was warm. But still—

"So, how was your day?" It was innocent, the way he asked it. He couldn't have known what kind of day I'd had. How it had shaken me to my very core. The way it had made me question everything.

"It was alright," I replied. I didn't want to think about today. Not under this perfect night sky, on this beautiful mat while I held on to my favourite treat.

I lifted the athirasa to my lips and took a little nibble. It tasted off, like the coconut oil it had been fried in had gone bad, but I'd never say that to Raam.

"I actually wanted to share some news with you, Amara."

I set the athirasa down and looked at him, the pace of my heart starting to pick up slightly. I knew all of this effort he had made had to be for something. Perhaps he was going away. Perhaps he was going to end things with me. Maybe this was his way of letting me down easy. I knew Raam—his heart was soft. He would always try to pad his blows.

"Listen, Amara, I know that I've kept you waiting a long time. I understand that you've been eighteen for a few months now, and that it's not proper that you are yet unmarried. This is why I wanted to talk to you. Look, I can't ask for your hand right now. Not without my family's blessing. And you know how things have been at home. But my father got word today that they will be confirming his position soon. Perhaps in another three months or so. You think you could give me three months? The first thing I'll do as soon as he's confirmed is speak to him. I promise."

I was dumbfounded. All these days hoping and waiting—what were three months when we had the rest of our lives?

"Oh, Raam, that's—I don't know what to say."

"You don't need to say anything, Amara. I'm sorry for making you wait. I know it can be difficult—waiting for something you really want."

I nodded, leaning into him and feeling his arms wrap around me. That was all the comfort I needed.

"So this is what you were celebrating at the tavern? This news from your father?"

"Yes, Amara. I was overjoyed and knew I had to wait at least a few more hours until I could see you. So I met with my friends instead. Please don't be angry with me."

But how could I be angry with him when he'd just told me that we could be betrothed before the year was out?

"Raam, thank you," I said finally. "I'm sure I can avoid my parents' proposals for a few more months. Goodness knows my father's been preoccupied enough." The good news wasn't enough to dissolve the bitterness that flooded through me whenever I thought back to what I'd seen Thaththa do.

Raam tilted my chin to his face. I knew he could sense my anguish.

"What is it, Amara?"

"No, it's alright, really." I didn't know if I wanted to tell him everything. It felt like a line that was drawn in the sand—once I crossed it, there would be no return. Raam would lose respect for Thaththa. It didn't matter that I already had.

Raam looked away, a cloud passing over his face.

"Oh, I see. Well, if you don't want to share with me—"

"No, Raam, it's not that. It's just—"

He took my hand.

"You can tell me, Amara. You know I'm always here for you."

I took a deep breath, willing my voice to be steady. I didn't want to be the girlfriend who cried all the time. I didn't want to be a wife who couldn't share things with her husband. I certainly didn't want to be my mother. I'd already lost Neha's friendship. I couldn't lose Raam too.

He was asking, and that meant he cared.

"I saw my father today with another woman." The words were clipped and taut. I braced myself for what Raam would say.

"Another woman?"

My silence drove the point home.

"Oh, no." He shifted closer and put both his arms around me. "When you say *another woman*, do you mean—?"

"Yes. I mean he was with another woman in the worst possible way."

"Oh, dear. I'm so sorry, Amara. What a horrible thing to find out. Who was she?"

"You know Siripala, the fisherman? Well, his wife."

"Oh, her. Well, I can't say that I'm too surprised."

"What do you mean? What have you heard about her?"

"Just about the type of woman she is, you know?"

"What do you mean by *type*, Raam?"

He pulled on my arm gently, so I sat back against him, leaning into his chest.

"Well, I don't exactly know how to explain it to you, Amara. There are certain types of women, you know. They want things from men. They prey on them, I think."

"You think she preyed on my father?"

"Perhaps. I wouldn't put it past her."

"So, you think it's her doing, then? Not my father's?" I felt a little triumphant, even though I couldn't quite explain why.

"Your father is a man, Amara. From what you've told me about your life at home, I take it that your parents aren't very happy together. Perhaps your mother hasn't been giving him the, you know, the care he needs. It makes a man an easy target for women who don't have the best morals."

A sudden worry flittered around me.

"What? Does this type of thing happen often?"

He traced his fingers over my arms.

"All men have needs, Amara. It's just the way they are made. And if those needs aren't being met by their wife or partner, well, it leaves them vulnerable. And then, these loose women can come in, show them the smallest bit of attention, and have them wrapped around their little finger."

Was that what was happening with my father? I couldn't remember the last time my parents smiled at each other, let alone showed each other any affection. Was that why the fisherman's wife decided to prey on him?

But surely, my father had been a willing participant, hadn't he? It couldn't be all the woman's fault. It irritated me that this thought crept into my mind again. I was starting to sound like Bhagya. Did she have a point? Was my father also to blame?

"You know," Raam continued, "I heard in the village that Siripala never paid your father his debt. Perhaps his wife thought she could pay for it another way. Who knows how these women's minds work?"

I remembered the way Siripala had spoken to her. The sound of his abuse cutting through the air that day as I hid outside their hut. The thought felt obscene, unwelcome in my head, so I shooed it away.

And then a different kind of worry started to pour into me.

"Raam, when you say *all men*, do you mean yourself too?"

Would Raam be the victim of a loose woman, like my father was? Would he find comfort in someone else if I didn't give him what he wanted?

He tucked his chin on my shoulder.

"I love you, Amara. You have to believe me when I say that. And to answer your question—no. I'm not like them. I would never dream of pushing you into anything, even though I do wish you would trust me a little more."

My breath was catching in my throat.

I nodded.

"As soon as we are engaged, Raam. I promise."

He kissed my cheek.

"Anyway, we have little to worry about. After all, you're mine. I don't need a formal engagement to know that."

You're mine now. The words from the woman in my dream echoed, sending a shudder through me.

I just nodded.

23

THIS TIME WHEN I left the hut at the edge of the world, I was swallowed deep into the belly of the jungle. Leaves crunched underfoot as I pushed forward, moss-coloured shadows cast down by the lush canopy of leaves shimmering in front of me. The peace I had once known in the jungle had long since withered away. My heart was not still. Something was wrong.

My body felt like it was on fire, burning up from the inside. It made me want to claw at myself. Something insidious had found its way within me. This fire wasn't welcome. I wanted it gone. I needed it snuffed out. But the feeling wouldn't go away, and so I ran, praying for release. Branches from the trees groped at my face and arms and chest, and thorns pressed themselves wickedly into my wrists and sides, but they hardly mattered to me—I just needed to escape.

And just when I thought this inferno within me was subsiding, the yakshaniya was before me.

Something about her was different. The rotten skin on the left side of her face was replaced by skin that was grey and smooth. It had been cruelly sewn in with a hand far from delicate, the short, bloodied stitches trailing down from her forehead, past her eye, and down her cheek. She snarled at me. While I was weakness, she was strength. I feared her, but she revelled in our meeting. I was what she wanted, what she had been waiting for. I could run, I knew, but I'd only ever be running towards her, never away.

Her long, scraggly black hair roped down her back like a knot of snakes; crescent moons of rust caked under her long, curved fingernails. There were dark, wet drops of blood that dripped from her arms and legs to her bare feet.

And yet, her cruel face wasn't one of a stranger. There was a part of me—a part buried so deep that I'd have to swim into the crevices of the ocean to retrieve it—this part of me knew her. And just like that, it also knew that I was right to be afraid. That everyone should be afraid.

She took a step closer to me, her limbs like spider legs, her body clicking and disjointed as she moved.

"Stay away from me!" I screamed, except no sound left my throat.

"Leave me alone!" Still nothing.

Her lips spread wide, revealing a rotten smile drenched in fresh blood.

She was taunting me. She knew I was powerless against her.

But I wasn't here for her to play games with me—like a beast toying with its food before devouring it. I turned on my heel, trying to run away. Just then, the root of a tree pulsed up, sending me sprawling down onto the jungle floor.

"No!" I screamed, but there was still no sound.

Vines had started snaking their way over to me, wrapping

themselves over my arms and legs, binding me tight. I tried to fight back, but it was no use. I was powerless.

"No! Someone help me!" I cried, voiceless, as the woman threw her head back and laughed with no mirth, just hollow, cruel anger.

I felt the vines press against my lips, pushing their way into my mouth, choking me, making their way down my throat. I could barely breathe, let alone scream. I tried to fight against it, but even in my dreams I knew it was no use. The jungle had claimed me now. The woman had me in her power.

A piercing pain, hot as fire and sharp as the fangs on a cobra, shot through me as I tried to scream once again. I had to protect myself. I had to do whatever it took. To beat her, I had to become her.

The moment that realisation dawned on me, I felt myself change. Become more powerful. Stronger. My hands grew bony, hard. My fingernails became talons before my eyes.

Without thinking, running on nothing but pure instinct, I dug my talons into the vines that were choking me. I slashed at them mercilessly, ripping them out in chunks.

It took a while, but I eventually managed to free myself. I finally stood up, heaving. Victorious.

But the yakshaniya kept laughing. I could hear it, swirling around me, choking me even though the vines were gone.

And when I looked down, I understood why.

I was splattered, not in the sap from the vines I had destroyed, but in blood that ran down me in rivulets. The smell of fresh death clouded the air.

What had I done?

Hesitant, meek, all the fire within me extinguished, I peered down even though every inch of me screamed not to.

There was someone curled at my feet, whimpering on the ground. Vomit rising in my throat, I reached down and tugged on the person's shoulder, turning them over so I could see who it was.

Thaththa writhed in front of me, choking on his own blood. His eyes peered up—wide and helpless. He opened his mouth, perhaps to ask me something, but more blood gurgled out, dripping down his chest and pooling on the jungle floor.

"No! Thaththa!" I screamed. My voice came out, loud and booming, this time. I knelt down next to him, trying in vain to stop the blood as he turned purple, then grey, then lifeless.

"You're mine now," the yakshaniya said, before she laughed and laughed and laughed.

24

"AMARA, THERE'S A stain on your blouse," Amma hissed, hesitating at the tall gate. Iron rods speared their way towards the sky like demon teeth, guarding a large property overshadowed by coconut trees.

The driveway was long, at least a few hundred metres, and I was damp with sweat by the time we neared the house. Dread enveloped me. It stifled me just as much as the humidity of the late morning. The pounding that started in my chest found its way to my ears.

My dream the previous night had left me uneasy and being here did nothing to calm my nerves.

Amma had shaken me awake early in the morning and insisted we leave the house even before the sun rose. I was in a daze, my nightmare still fresh in my mind. At least I hadn't sleepwalked. I looked around for Thaththa, but he wasn't there—perhaps he was with Leelawathi again. I got the feeling that Amma wanted to be out of the house before he got back, and knew I had been right when I realised where we were going.

I tried to take a deep breath, but the air was pungent with the smell of rotting fruit. Mangoes that had fallen from the trees had burst open, covered in flies, waiting to be swept away. The comfort of the ocean's salty tang was a snuffed-out memory here. The wind that coursed its way through the trees whistled us its warnings, bidding us to go home.

I gasped at the house that towered formidably at the end of the drive. A whitewashed arch choked its entryway, while the large verandah that wrapped around the building bristled with circular pillars. The roof was covered in terra-cotta tiles—patterned waves looking like the scales of some yet-undiscovered beast. Latticed wooden panels shielded parts of the verandah from the sun, guarding its secrets, forbidding it life. A rickshaw—a carriage with large wheels, usually used by the Englishmen and pulled by their local servants—lay close to the entrance, a dark-skinned, bare-chested man in a sarong polishing its wheels. He did not greet us.

This was where my mother grew up, and I couldn't imagine a life so different from what we had now, in our tiny, single-room hut. It was no small wonder that she resented my father. And me. I'd always imagined that the jungle was my sanctuary and that the ocean shore was better than any grand palace. Conch shells and exquisite fruit greater than any riches. But I'd never had real wealth. I'd never had anything to give up. My mother had. And she did.

Amma rubbed at the small mark on my sleeve with her handkerchief, and when that didn't do anything she yanked the fall of my sari, the one she had draped on me herself that morning, across my back and over my other shoulder, and laid it so that it hid the offending smudge.

"It's better this way. More modest." She wore her sari covering both shoulders as well. "Why didn't you check if your clothes were clean, child?"

But she didn't care for my answer. She was too busy fretting.

"Why?" I had asked earlier that morning as we bounced in the back of a neighbour's bullock cart. He was transporting sacks of grain to the market at my grandparents' village and had agreed to let us ride with him.

"They've asked for you." Her voice was terse. I recognised the panic. She was dreading this.

"They've asked for me?" I replied, incredulously. This was certainly a development.

"Just keep quiet and remember your manners," she said in reply. I could hear the words she didn't say—*Don't embarrass me.*

The first time I'd been aware of my grandparents' presence was when I was about twelve years old. A letter arrived for my mother one day.

"Who's it from?" I remember asking after the postman left. We never got much mail. Anyone in my village who needed to get word to my father just walked to our hut.

My mother didn't reply, but I noticed that her hands were trembling slightly and a sheen of sweat coated her upper lip.

She pulled out the sheet of paper and read it quickly, her eyes darting over the words like a grasshopper. The contents of the letter did nothing to soothe her, I could tell. She asked me to make dinner and waited for my father to come home, pacing our front garden, agitated and upset.

They spoke in fierce, hushed voices when he did arrive. I was long used to their arguments by then, and didn't think this was any different, except they left me with one of the elders in the village the next day and went somewhere. They didn't tell me where, but Amma was wearing her best sari, and Thaththa had oiled his hair and his beard.

Then it had been my turn to pace. I wouldn't play with the younger children, I wouldn't eat, I wouldn't help the older ladies weave a mat. The family who watched me didn't let me escape into the jungle either. I was frantic. They'd left me, I thought. They'd left me and they weren't coming back. But no, I chided myself. Thaththa would never do that to me. He'd never abandon me.

They didn't come by afternoon, nor by twilight when the sun was flinging itself into the sea. They didn't come when the bats started taking flight, and they remained stubbornly away as an owl started hooting.

The moon swung between the clouds when I finally heard them, their voices travelling faster than their actual selves, and I ran towards them as fast as I could, throwing myself at Thaththa and bursting into sobs.

"She's been like this the whole day," the elderly lady hmphed. "You really should talk to her about her manners."

But Thaththa didn't care. He stroked my head and gave my mother a sharp look. Together we walked home, my arms wrapped around him as Amma walked in front of us, chin up high and resolute, even though I was yet to find out why.

"We have to discuss something with you, duwa," Thaththa said when we were finally inside. There was something in his voice I couldn't understand.

My mother and I sat on the verandah, but my father stood near the steps.

"Tell her," he said, his voice gruff.

"The girls' school in Matara town has an opening. It's not as big as the boys' school, more of a convent, actually. And you are to attend from Monday."

"What?" I asked, not quite understanding. I'd never even considered going. None of the girls in my village went at the time, and barely any boys either. School was for the wealthy. Those who had converted to Christianity and were loyal to the British.

"Your grandparents insisted. They are patrons of the church and have secured you a spot."

"But—"

"No buts," my mother interrupted. "I'll buy the fabric for your uniform tomorrow and stitch it over the weekend. Your father will get the rest of your supplies. That is all."

"Thaththa, how—"

"Listen to your mother, Amara. It has been decided."

My mother had spoken to me in enough English for me to understand, and I had a basic knowledge of reading and writing. My mother had insisted I learn when I was younger, and my father had strangely supported her. It was one of the few things they ever agreed on.

And they both held on to this belief with grim resolution, no matter how much of a disaster school was for me.

But that was the very first time I had given any thought to my grandparents. They'd had minimal contact with Amma over the years—a letter or two, and I think she visited them a handful of times. She'd told me that her father was strict, and her mother went to church every day, but beyond that they were a mystery. I heard they had paid for our larger-than-average hut with its whitewashed walls around the time my mother had me. And they had gifted her the sewing machine.

25

A SHORT, OLDER woman with the same complexion as my mother stood just outside the main house, her hands on her hips. I knew she had to be my grandmother right away. She was dressed similarly to us, even though her fabric was quality chintz and ten times more expensive. Her face was powdered in talc that was too light for her skin, giving her a grey cast, and did nothing to hide her scowl.

"So this is *her*," she said by way of greeting, the crease that deepened on her brow making her look more like Amma than I thought possible.

"Yes," my mother said quietly, in a voice so unrecognisable that I had to glance over at her just to make sure.

My grandmother looked me up and down, not quite meeting my eye. Surveying me like one would inspect a cow being sold at the market. I was glad Amma had adjusted the fall of my sari.

She clicked her tongue, as if my mere existence was annoying to her. I supposed it was.

"Doesn't look a thing like you, you know. She's all *him*, dark skin and all. I certainly have my work cut out for me." What did that mean? What work was she doing with me?

Amma climbed the three short steps to the verandah and touched the woman's feet.

"Hmph," she grunted. And then, looking at me: "You can come in from the back door."

"She's my daughter, Amma."

I took a breath. This must be the first time my mother had ever stood up for me.

"And the reason we are all in this mess. If you'd just seen that physician like I told you, without running to your father instead and getting trapped into—"

"*Amma.*" Her usual edge had snuck its way back in. Was this how all daughters felt around their mothers? Like they were teetering on the edge of a cliff? Like one wrong move, one incorrect word would send you both hurtling down? Like everything was a negotiation, a power swap, an unspoken battle?

My grandmother—my aththamma, though I hardly dared call her that—gave a small shrug. "You can argue with me now, Kumari, but you better stay in line when the De'Fontaine family get here. We already lost the graces of the Peirises when you jilted that poor Julius. I'm not letting that happen again."

Who were the De'Fontaine family? Why were they coming? And what did that have to do with Julius Peiris, Aloysius's uncle? My questions were silent daggers directed at Amma, but she dodged my glances and followed her mother inside. No one commented when I followed them through the front.

I'd been inside a few grand houses in my time, Neha's sister's house being one of them, but even that didn't prepare me for my mother's childhood home.

We entered from the isthoppuwa—the verandah, where my grandmother had met us—directly into the cavernous drawing room. It was crammed with sweeping, upholstered armchairs, and beautifully carved, small ebony tables. I'd never seen that much furniture in a single room. A pair of ivory elephant tusks rainbowed their way over a calamander cabinet inlaid with more ivory, while a breathtaking three-pronged chandelier hung suspended from the ceiling. I tried to stop myself from staring, but it was no use. If I had thought Catharine's house to be grand, well, this was palatial.

In the very centre of the room was an upholstered ebony kavichchiya—a settee—where an older man sat reading a newspaper. *The Colombo Journal*, the large letters printed on the front page spelled out. He was dressed in a white kambaya that reached his ankles, and a matching white jacket. An older generation's compromise between island tradition and upper-class fashion. A particularly large tortoiseshell comb nested in his slicked-back white hair, and a thick hedge of his neatly trimmed sideburns hung from his ears to his jaw. His mouth was curved in displeasure, like he was perpetually disgusted by the world around him. This was most likely my grandfather. I could tell because it was no doubt him who had gifted me my bushy eyebrows.

A large crucifix hung on the wall behind him, almost the same size as the one that hung in my classroom at school. Unlike the one in the chapel, however, the Christ on this cross had his eyes focused not towards the heavens, but straight down at us. He appeared to weep, leaving me more anxious than ever.

Amma went over to her father and touched his feet, but he didn't look up from his paper. She beckoned for me to do the same, and I complied, even though my head and my heart were racing.

I'd just knelt down when I heard the newspaper rustle. I looked up, hesitant. His eyes met mine, just for an instant. I think I felt it then. Some of the pain my mother had been bearing. It nettled through me like a current. I could hear my heartbeat in my ears. My breath was sharp, his was languid, and then he went back to his paper. I stood back up, not trusting my legs to remain steady.

Amma rushed me to a small room at the side of the house, where my grandmother and a maid waited.

"I assumed she would show up improperly dressed, so I took the liberty of laying out some of your old things."

My mother's face reddened, but she nodded.

"You haven't thrown them away?" Amma asked, her voice small.

"We just hadn't gotten around to cleaning out your almirah." My grandmother shrugged, her voice gruff, but I could almost feel Amma soften. Eighteen years was a long time not to clean out a wardrobe.

The maid came up to me and took my elbow, instructing me to sit at the vanity, where she started to undo my braid.

"Err, excuse me, but what is—?"

"Just do as you are told, Amara," my mother snapped as my grandmother raised her eyebrows.

"Amma—" I started again, but she glared at me before turning and leaving the room. My grandmother stayed back a moment, surveying me. Then she clicked her tongue and left too.

The maid raked a comb through my thick, unruly hair. It hurt, but I didn't dare make a sound. I didn't know why, but a sense of foreboding had started to run its way through me. The air around me grew hot. I surveyed the room. It was small and dark, a large almirah taking up most of the space, leaving a dark gap at the corner where it didn't quite meet the wall. It sent a chill through me—like someone was watching me from in there, biding their time.

I was brought back to reality by a particularly hard tug on my head.

"Ow," I said, trying to rub my scalp, but the maid kept combing resolutely.

The mirror in front of me was murky, its brown patches making my reflection look mangled and ill.

I was thankful when the maid decided that my hair wasn't going to get less tangled and pulled it into an updo, with a few curls hanging loose at my temples.

Then she made me stand up and pulled off the reddha I was wearing, her eyes lingering judgementally on the now exposed stain that marred my blouse.

"Mehema inna." *Stay here,* she said, disappearing out of the room, while I stood alone in just my jacket and cotton underskirt.

Again, the feeling of eyes on me. I turned towards the dark corner.

A fly buzzed by.

Then, a low chuckle.

I gasped. Was there someone else here?

I peered at the gap but couldn't see anything. Perhaps if I got a little closer?

Shakily, I put one foot in front of the other and edged nearer.

Only dark shadows.

A gecko cried out.

Another chuckle, deeper this time, making me gasp again.

"Who's there?" I asked, my voice just above a whisper, almost unheard through the blood gushing in my ears.

I reached the gap between the wardrobe and the wall and peered in, but it was empty.

I felt one of the tendrils that hung over my face move, almost like someone was blowing on me.

"Koheyda giyey ithin?" *Where did you go so?*

The maid's voice shocked me so hard that I spun around, my hands flying to my mouth to muffle a scream.

"Eh almaariya lock karala thiyenney." *That almirah is locked.* She sounded suspicious.

"Mata saddayak ahuna." *I heard a sound,* I explained.

"Mey geval wala ehema thamay. Dhan enna." *These houses are like that. Now come.*

She'd brought a freshly laundered white blouse made from some sort of luxurious woven material. It was more beautiful than any blouse I'd ever worn. She helped me into it, and then expertly draped a beautiful sari over me. It was made of green silk and reminded me of the way the light danced off the jungle leaves early in the morning. She secured the fall on my left shoulder with a brooch decorated with dark green stones, and then fixed a matching clip onto my hair.

I looked in the murky mirror and thought I was mistaken. Surely that grown-up woman in its reflection couldn't be me? I even looked, dare I say, elegant.

The maid left me alone again while I admired myself. I'd never thought of myself as a vain person, but this was certainly new. I turned to my side, and then my back, craning my neck over my shoulder, looking at myself from all angles, each one feeling newer than the other.

And then when I was shifting around again, I saw her in the mirror. The yakshaniya from my dream, standing just behind me. Her gruesome lips were pulled back as she chuckled, revealing her rotting teeth. The stitches holding her face together were red and raw. Her putrid breath wafted over to me as she reached a claw-like nail over to one of the curls that hung down my neck.

I spun around, a scream erupting from deep within me.

But she was gone.

"What is the matter, Amara?" Amma rushed into the room, but I couldn't answer her as I stood panting, my eyes wide.

"I—I thought I saw something," I said finally.

"Stop being so dramatic. I need you to behave yourself today, you hear me?"

I nodded, trying to steady my breath. At least I finally had her alone. My mind was still on the yakshaniya, but I also needed to know what was going on.

"Amma, what's happening? Why am I here? Why am I dressed like this?"

At the mention of my new outfit, Amma seemed to be pulled back into the moment. She looked me up and down. The furrow in her brow loosened a fraction.

"That was my favourite sari. It looks nice on you." It was possibly the closest she had ever gotten to giving me a compliment.

"Oh, also, I almost forgot. This was to be given to me as part of my wedding trousseau, but obviously I'd left all that behind. Your grandmother had it sent to me recently, for you to wear today."

She turned me to face the mirror and draped a necklace over my collarbones.

A hansa puttuwa necklace.

The very same hansa puttuwa necklace that I thought belonged to Siripala's wife. The thought left me reeling. My suspicions had been wrong about everything. Of course she would never have given up such a prized possession. Of course the necklace wasn't taken to carry out some sort of evil charm on her husband. Of course Amma had probably just hidden it away—either for safe-keeping or for keeping it a secret from Thaththa.

But no matter how deeply shaken I was by this realisation, I was in no way prepared for what Amma said next.

"Amara, listen. You are here to meet someone today—" She held up her hand, already anticipating my questions and objections. I knew, then, exactly where this was going.

"His name is Desmond, and the De'Fontaine family are from a good stock. We can't have you unmarried and running wild forever, and your father doesn't seem to want to do anything to further your prospects. Your grandparents graciously agreed to make the introduction. Their favour is important. To us, and to me."

"How could you do this?" The words rushed out of me hot and angry. How could she betray me like this? Bring me here with no forewarning, with no indication, simply throwing me to the wolves.

"Don't be ridiculous, Amara. How dare you question me? After everything I've done to raise your position in this world. You and I both know the time has come for a suitable marriage. Things might have been difficult sometimes, but I have always, always put this family first. Whatever my own cost."

"I will not marry a man just because the grandparents I have never even met until today seem to think he's a suitable match, Amma."

"Always with the drama. I'm not asking you to marry him today. Simply meet him. Give him some betel leaves and touch his mother's feet. Show them the manners I've tried my whole life to teach you. That's all." She turned to leave, making it all sound so simple.

"How could you do this?" I asked her again, trying to keep the tremble out of my voice. "You married for love."

"And look at where that got me, and you. Us women need to be smarter than that."

26

THE SAME MAID who dressed me had laid the table with milk rice, kavum, kokis, and a variety of traditional sweetmeats. My grandfather and grandmother—I had been instructed to refer to them as Aththa and Aththamma in front of our guests—had situated themselves at the verandah where they would greet the De'Fontaines, along with my mother. They would invite them inside and exchange pleasantries, and when my grandmother called for me, I was to enter the room.

Until then, I stayed in the same small room where I got dressed, where the whispers of the yakshaniya continued to haunt me, where a million eyes watched me as I tried not to sweat through the beautiful new sari jacket I was wearing. Her face, mutilated and stitched together but still grinning, swirled in front of me, letting me know I'd never be alone.

In a panic, I thought of Raam—how betrayed he'd feel if he found out about this. How upset I would be if the roles were reversed and his family arranged for him to meet another girl instead.

And through all of that, I was also trying fruitlessly to choke down my guilt. I'd seen the necklace and immediately assumed it had something to do with a hooniyama. So much so that it left me questioning my own sanity. I'd been seeing things, hearing voices, sleepwalking, jumping to the worst conclusions . . . surely, any logical person would agree that my mind was running away from me. Perhaps that was what all this was. I was slowly losing my senses. The best I could do now was just keep my head down and get through the afternoon with minimal conflict. I didn't trust myself to do anything else, even if I was uncomfortable.

By the time the maid came to get me, I was in a shambles. My hands shook as she handed me a sheaf of betel leaves and asked me to hurry.

"Sinawenna." *Smile,* she muttered, though my lips felt locked in place.

The De'Fontaines were seated in the drawing room, and they all turned towards me as I entered.

"This is our only granddaughter, Amara," my grandmother said in the voice of a kind and amicable imposter. "She just turned eighteen. She's a serious girl, with a good head on her shoulders, so we never felt the need to rush marriage."

Mrs. De'Fontaine, to her credit, beamed at me.

"Nice to meet you, Amara."

"How do you do, Mrs. De'Fontaine?" I replied in the same tone my mother had taught me to when I was younger.

I handed the betel leaves to both Mr. and Mrs. De'Fontaine and knelt down to touch their feet. I kept my eyes low and my voice demure. I could hear mumblings of approval from everyone. I didn't care for their approval, but I was also losing trust in myself. I'd been mistaken about so many things, and this clearly meant a lot to my mother. I knew no one was keeping score of my wrong-doings, but the guilt that pulsed through me left me wanting to make amends in any way I could. So what if I was introduced to someone? It wasn't like I would ever agree to marry him.

"And this is my son, Desmond."

I finally faced the man I was supposed to meet, and if my grand-parents' wishes were to be fulfilled, the man I was supposed to wed.

He looked up at me, a lopsided smile hanging loosely from his lips. He was stocky and well-built, like he'd never wanted for any-thing in his life. He was dressed in trousers, with his hair combed back neatly. He looked older too—none of the boyish charm that Raam exuded. Yet, he seemed pleasant, his demeanour unharried, which had the effect of putting everyone around him, including myself, at ease.

"My pleasure to meet you, Amara."

"L-likewise," I replied, the words clumsy and heavy in my mouth. "C-could I offer you some tea?" Another wave of mumbled approval.

"That would be wonderful."

I turned, thankful for something to do. The maid had already laid out the tea tray, so all I had to do was bring it over. I took a steadying breath, gathering myself. I just needed to get through this afternoon.

Desmond hesitated a moment when picking up his teacup, his eyes taking in my hair, my sari, lingering on the skin at my neck-line. Blood rushed to my cheeks as I continued to serve tea to my grandparents and mother. Amma gave me the slightest nod of ap-proval. This was a strange day indeed.

"Come, sit with us, Amara," Mrs. De'Fontaine said.

I took the smallest chair that was the furthest away from Desmond, as was proper.

"Your grandmother tells me that you are a very skilled seamstress. Is this true?" I reckoned Amma wouldn't want me talking about her business—it was unseemly for a woman from her background to work, after all—so I simply nodded.

"And do you cook also?"

"Yes, Amara has been helping in the kitchen since she was a child."

"Always a good skill to have as a woman, though I think Desmond will have enough maids for that. Lord knows the house in Colombo is far too large for a single servant to handle."

The thought came unbidden, as sudden as a cloud on a sunny day: Me in a white lace dress, with my hair pulled up in a sophisticated knot. A house as big as Neha's, or even my grandparents', with maids to cook my dinner. Living in Colombo. The new city, rumoured to be far larger and far more developed than Matara was.

With no jungle.

With no ocean.

And no Raam.

I swallowed. It was what my mother wanted. But what about me?

"You attended the convent in the town, didn't you?"

"Yes, all thanks to the kindness of my grandparents," I replied. If they want a docile puppet that's what I will give them, I thought. Just for today. But I won't give up my jungle. I won't give up on my heart.

I snuck a glance over to my grandfather, who was looking at me curiously, as if actually seeing me for the very first time.

The conversation then went on about the town itself, what decisions the governor was making and how it was affecting taxes, and general talk that did not interest me at all. Desmond appeared to be of the belief that the British were making some very positive changes to the local industry.

"They are setting up a railway system to connect the entire island. Think of all the opportunities it will open for business."

"Creating access for the locals is getting increasingly important too," his mother said. "I've heard that some families are planning on leaving Matara because of some demon terrorising locals in the jungle. Have you heard of it?"

My entire family's cheeks grew red. Looked like my mother's marriage wasn't the only dirty secret they kept hidden away. They were obviously not mentioning Jeevan Maama's attack either, probably on account of his occupation. How many secrets could one family keep from the world?

"Oh, Amma, please. Let's not fall into this primitive mumbo jumbo," Desmond proclaimed, rolling his eyes. He addressed the rest of us. "I apologise for my mother. She tends to get caught up in all this fantastical hoo-ha, no matter how much I tell her that it's all nonsense."

Good thing my grandparents had clearly failed to mention my father's occupation. What did they think? That if they found me a suitor from as far away as possible, they could reinvent my reputation as the perfect bride-to-be?

There was a pause in the conversation—heavy and awkward, like a hole that needed filling.

I picked up the empty tray and made to collect everyone's empty teacups. I noticed the grateful nod my grandmother gave me.

Desmond placed his cup and saucer carefully on the tray.

"Thank you, Amara." He smiled warmly, his fingers grazing my knuckles so lightly that no one but I could notice.

His fingernails were blood-soaked talons about to mangle my hands. *I have you now, you little bitch.*

The words were sudden and loud, a clap of thunder in my ear. The vision of his talons shocked me. I jerked the tray back, the cup clanging against the saucer.

Where had the voice come from? It sounded so familiar.

But as I looked around the drawing room everything was as it had been, except that Desmond's cheeks had turned pink and his mother was smiling coyly. My mind was playing tricks on me again. I couldn't keep doing this.

Holding on to the tray so tightly that my fingers were white, I rushed to the kitchen, which hugged the side of the house, and took a moment to gather myself. It was so hot inside. I could feel perspiration trail down my neck and into my blouse. I stood near a window and fanned myself, trying to calm down.

I had a partial view of the back garden from where I stood, and I could see a solitary figure, draped in white, make its way up the path to the house. He looked almost ghostly, floating as he did, somehow not belonging in the manicured garden.

It was only when he got a lot closer that I realised that he was a priest, noticing his collar and the large cross that hung from his neck. Why was he visiting now? And not through the main entrance to the house?

He stopped for a moment, as if he noticed me staring at him, and I moved away from the window.

A new maid I had never seen before materialised in the garden and greeted him, leading him in through a side entrance to the house.

"Athulta yanney naththey ay?" *Why aren't you going back inside?* the maid who'd helped me get ready asked, sticking her head into the kitchen.

"Tikakin ennam." *I'll come in a minute,* I replied, fanning myself rapidly to prove a point. "Father kenek avilla inney madam wah hambuwennada?" *Did the father come to see Madam?* I tried my luck.

The maid gave me a sour look.

"Nah, Jeevan mahaththayata yaathna karanna. Hamadhama enawa. Loku Mahaththa dhanney naha, ithin mokuth kiyanna nam epa, ahunadha?" *No, he comes to pray for Jeevan sir. He comes every day. Your grandfather doesn't know, so don't say anything, do you hear?*

I nodded, and she disappeared again.

I hadn't realised that Jeevan Maama was here, in this very house. The last I heard he had been living on his own, near one of the taverns he owned. My grandparents would certainly have thought his business improper, though not shameful enough to exile him from the family like they did to my mother. Jeevan Maama had probably been brought back here after his attack so that he could be tended to.

Something came over me then. I had to see him. My dream of him, of piercing my talons deep into his chest and then licking off his blood, clawed its way into me—the taste of blood fresher than ever. I had to see him for myself. I needed answers.

Making sure that no one saw me, I slunk out the kitchen door and to the verandah that circled the house. Most of the maids were busy with the guests anyway, so I needn't have worried. Creeping to the side where I'd seen the priest disappear, I peered in through the window.

The priest stood gravely by the side of a small wooden bed.

There was a candle lit in the room, even though it was daylight, and it threw eerie shadows on the wall—demons dancing on my uncle's soul.

The priest was praying, sprinkling water from a thin, long bottle about the room. I pressed my face close to the glass, hands cupping either side of my eyes to cut out the glare from outside.

Jeevan Maama lay on the bed, though I only assumed it was him. The man who was moaning and thrashing about in pain was unrecognisable. A large gash covered his face, which was partially bandaged, and plenty more bandages snaked down his shoulder, arm, and one of his legs. The fabric oozed with something yellow—whether it was pus or a medicated balm was hard to say. Whatever it was that had attacked him, he was lucky to be alive.

He opened his eyes, which were so bloodshot that it was almost impossible to see the irises, and looked around the room, unfocused. He opened his mouth, groaning loudly, and that was when I noticed his gums.

His teeth were pulled out. All of them, the Mudaliyar's aide had said. It had upset me then, but in no way did it prepare me for how truly horrifying it was now—his gums dark and bloody and deeply wounded. Craters where his teeth once were.

The priest turned towards the window, and I ducked down quickly. If he did see me, he made no mention of it. I waited, my heart about to make its escape out my throat, until he finished his prayers, from what little I could hear, and when things became quiet, I peered in again.

The yakshaniya was inside the room, her face right up against the window.

Gnarled, nasty, with a smile twisting her mouth wide, her

tongue rotten and licking the glass a mere inch away from me. Her nails scratched against the windowpane, making me go numb. I was in too much shock to scream out.

It jolted through me like a lightning bolt—hurt and fear and pain. It coursed through my body, choking me, making my insides scream.

I tried to breathe, but it was futile. I couldn't take it. It was too much to bear.

I pulled away from the window and rushed back up the verandah, making it only halfway before I had to stop. I hurriedly jumped off the raised platform, trampled my way over a small flower bed, bent at my waist, and threw up the boiled mung beans Amma had forced me to eat for breakfast before we came here. Everything in me felt vile. Poison coursed through my veins. I shuddered as the look of vicious glee on the woman's face clung on to my mind's eye like a parasite, making me retch over and over again until tears ran down my cheeks.

My beautiful clothes were ruined. Vomit was smeared over the delicate silk of the sari, and my hair had come undone from its elaborate style. Finally feeling able to straighten up, I wiped my mouth and turned back towards the verandah.

My mother and grandmother both stood there, mirror images of each other with their lips pursed and their hands on their hips. Their anger so palpable that I could taste it in the back of my throat, even more acrid than the taste of my vomit.

27

ONE OF THE housemaids brought me a glass of water and fanned me for a few minutes, while another brought a damp cloth and tried to dab off as much of my vomit as possible. My grandmother even gave me some neroli oil to apply behind my ears and on my wrists "to mask that filthy stench," she hissed.

The De'Fontaines left rather quickly after that, citing the distance of travel and exhaustion from the afternoon heat. It was fairly obvious that I'd been retching in the side garden, I supposed. My grandmother had pulled Mrs. De'Fontaine aside and spoken with her, no doubt trying to put my episode down to nerves or something. Desmond did give me a smile as they left, but I didn't think too much of it. I was just glad this day was coming to an end.

I changed back into my old clothes and the maid took the sari I had ruined, shaking her head. I came out of the dressing room to find Amma alone, her face blotched and red. She was angry. I could feel it rise off her like waves, the air around her simmering in heat.

She must have realised that I'd snuck off to see Jeevan Maama, and my antics meant that she didn't get a moment to see him for herself. It was as unforgivable as wrecking the meeting with Desmond.

We left the compound as soon as we could and waited for the bullock cart back for at least an hour on the main road, my mother glaring at me the entire time.

"I really am sorry, Amma," I said, softly, after we'd journeyed in silence for what felt like an eternity, our bodies rocking back and forth by the large wooden cartwheels navigating the recently constructed road network. I'd been to that village once before, years ago before the new roads were built, and it had taken us close to a day for our journey. Our cart had even gotten stuck in the mud, with Thaththa having to rally two more men to push it out. It had taken only a few hours to get there that morning. I supposed Desmond was right about one thing—not all development was terrible.

Amma didn't respond right away, and when I turned to look at her, I noticed her eyes were unexpectedly wet.

"Why must you always make things so difficult, Amara?" she asked. Her voice shook a little, but not in anger, the way it often did when she spoke to me. A single tear broke free and trailed down to her chin. I would have preferred it if she slapped me, or yelled at me like she usually did.

I knew it wasn't a question I was meant to answer. But still, it took me by surprise when she continued, her voice cold and distant, like she wasn't quite there.

"Jeevan never understood why I chose this life either. Why it was my cross to bear. He came to me the night before my wedding and told me he'd help me run away. Let's go to Colombo, he said. We can start fresh there. Forget about Julius, forget about your father. He never forgave me when I said no. Called me the most horrible names. He could never understand a woman's responsibility."

I hesitated, but the question flew out of me.

"Why didn't you go?"

My mother blinked, looking at me like it was for the first time. Like she'd never considered a life different from the one she was tethered to.

"I had already broken my father's heart. I didn't want to stomp on it further."

I paused for a moment, turning what Amma said over in my mind.

"So, Aththa *wanted* you to marry Thaththa? Not Julius Peiris?"

She gave me a smile that mothers have been giving their daughters since the dawn of time. A smile that said I wouldn't understand, that I couldn't, not right now, but that I would soon enough.

"You're lucky you had him. Jeevan Maama, I mean," I offered. I'd wished I had a brother or a sister, especially when I was younger. Someone to take my side when things at home got difficult.

Amma just shrugged.

"Even he's changed these last few years. All men eventually do."

She gazed out of the cart then, her silence stretching like the ocean—both of us lost out at sea, the distance between us, which moments before had given us a brief glimpse of the other, now widening, setting us adrift, leaving us to swim in our own separate directions.

We sat like that for ages, our bodies bumping roughly against the wooden body of the cart, our faces shielded from the heat by the woven coconut leaf cover that stretched above it like a giant, upside-down U.

I thought back to the visions of the yakshaniya I kept seeing. Who was she?

I must have fallen asleep at some point, deep and dreamless, for the first time in days. It was as if the demoness had crossed over from my dreams into this world, at last giving me some reprieve in my sleep.

"Amara." My mother shook me awake.

I opened my eyes, dazed and confused and trying to make sense of everything.

"Amara, you were moaning in your sleep."

My stomach hurt. Not as badly as it did when I saw Jeevan Maama, but a dull ache of discomfort thrummed within me. I could taste blood in my mouth, like when I woke up from my nightmares. I instinctively curled into myself, pressing my legs together and wrapping my arms around my knees.

My mother watched me curiously.

"Are you falling ill?" she asked, the first time she'd checked on whether I was alright since I vomited.

"It's nothing," I said. How could I ever tell her what raced through my mind, not giving me a moment's rest?

"Anyway, we are almost home."

I closed my eyes again and leaned my head back. Thank goodness. If I had time, I'd go for a quick swim in the ocean. I needed its balm to soothe my wounds, even if I didn't even know what part of me was injured.

"I know we left home in a rush, but did you remember to take your tonic this morning?" Amma asked.

I nodded, not meeting her eye. I hadn't taken the tonic in days. A new thought crept into my mind—was that why I was losing my hold on reality?

But the yakshaniya, the attacks, Jeevan Maama, and everything else was about to become as insignificant as a buzzing mosquito.

Amma took a deep breath.

"I spoke with your grandmother before we left. The De'Fontaines liked you. They want you to marry Desmond as soon as possible."

28

THE SKY REFLECTED the chaos in my heart. It started with a darkening. Grey clouds swept over the sun, casting the afternoon into shadow, only to be punctured with bolts of lightning so bright they scorched my eyes. And then, with a howl of thunder, the skies cracked open as they wept, pelting their tears into the hot, thirsty earth.

"There's no way I can marry a man I don't know!" I screamed, with no regard for who could hear me.

"No woman ever truly knows a man until she marries him, Amara. There's no need to be so dramatic."

"Does Thaththa know?"

Amma shrugged. "He'll agree eventually. He coddles you, but even he knows this is for the best."

"I won't do it, Amma."

"You will, Amara. You will be obedient for one time in your life. You will not shame this family any longer."

"What shame have I brought? What wrong have I done?"

Amma pursed her lips at this.

"It's all for the best," she said, her voice hard.

We reached the dirt path that would lead us home, but the rain pelted down with such ferocity that the best the bullock cart driver could do was to give us two old sacks we could throw over our heads to shield us from the weather.

It felt like the sky was assaulting us the moment we stepped out.

"I don't care what you say. Thaththa won't agree to this," I shouted over the unforgiving island rain.

"We'll see," Amma shouted back, though I could barely hear her.

Thaththa wouldn't do this to me. It didn't matter if he was in love with another woman. It didn't matter if he'd changed. If he'd stopped caring about me, even. He wouldn't force me to marry someone. He wouldn't betray me, not when it really mattered.

Trembling, I ran towards our hut, leaving Amma behind, my feet slipping and sliding in the mud. She hurried behind me—I didn't know whether it was to admonish me further or just to get some relief from the rain.

But something shifted as we neared home. My anger started to evaporate, replaced instead with a sense of apprehension that started off with a soft thrum. It bloomed into a full-blown throbbing when I noticed our small gate left open.

Both my parents were very particular about keeping it shut. A wild boar or a porcupine might make its way inside, they insisted, and destroy the vegetable patch my mother carefully tended. We'd definitely shut it when we left this morning, and there was no way Thaththa would have left it open. I threw my mother a look over my shoulder. She looked worried too.

"Haami!" Amma called out, but her voice got lost in the storm.

"Thaththa?" I tried. The ocean wailed against the shore, aggravated and nettled by the rain, its crashing competing with the sky to see who could be louder.

I stayed on the verandah as Amma pushed her way inside. I knew he wouldn't be in there. My father loved to watch the rain—he'd never waste a storm cooped up in the hut. The afternoon was dark, but there was still enough light to see something tucked into the corner of the verandah—another bunch of bananas, along with something else.

It was a small statue, about the size of my hand, carved rudimentarily out of wood. It was a woman with multiple arms, carrying the head of a man in one, and a sickle in another. Her tongue hung out to her chest, and she wore a necklace. The craftsmanship on this statue wasn't intricate, but I knew what her necklace was made of—human skulls. This was Kaali. Mostly worshipped as a Hindu deity, she was known as being a champion for women. It was common for girls on the island to appeal to her when they felt ill-treated, regardless of whether they were Buddhist or Hindu. Like witchcraft and demonology and charms, religion had nothing to do with our practices. Some called Kaali a goddess; others, a demoness; some simply called her Mother. Like any woman, Kaali presented different versions of herself, depending on who called out to her.

But what was a statue of her doing on our doorstep?

"Kumari Haminey! Kumari Haminey!" I heard from the back of the garden, where our kitchen was.

"Amma!" I called, warning her. My dread had evolved into a wild animal, thrashing at my insides.

It was Siyath Malli. I hadn't seen him since the exorcism the week before. He ran towards where I stood.

"Malli, what's wrong?"

"Amara Akki, oh, thank goodness! I've been waiting for you at the back all this time. You need to come quickly!"

"What is it?" Amma appeared next to me, clutching the fall of her now-soaked, most expensive sari.

But Siyath Malli spoke to me only, his eyes wide with terror.

"Amara Akki, please come. It's your father. We found him at the edge of the jungle this morning. He's been attacked."

29

I TRIED TO hold back my sobs. I must be brave for my father.

But when I saw him, lying in the village maduwa, deep gashes on his face and shoulders and body, I thought I would faint. He convulsed in pain, his eyes rolling into the back of his head, his mouth drooling. The skin on the right side of his face had been peeled away, revealing flesh that was shockingly red. I could barely breathe. There was an inexplicable ringing in my ears, and darkness pricked at the corners of my eyes.

I'd seen him lifeless just like this in my dream. The yakshaniya had sewed his skin onto her face.

"I have to sit down," was all I could manage, as I rushed away from the maduwa and collapsed onto the ground. The rain, perhaps taking pity on me, perhaps understanding my fear, eased down to a gentle drizzle. I was grateful it didn't disappear completely—this way I could blame my tears on the raindrops.

No, I told myself. My dream couldn't have had anything to do with it. I dreamt that Amma was attacked too, and she was still fine. There wasn't a connection. There couldn't be. But what about Jeevan Maama? I had dreamt of his attack, hadn't I?

No one knew for how long Thaththa had lain in the jungle, but they assumed that the attack had taken place sometime before dawn.

"What was he doing in the jungle at that time?" they asked, as I thought of Siripala's wife in their clandestine hut and tried not to break into tiny pieces. He should have been more careful. He should have just stayed home. He should have been a million different things, including a faithful husband or a father who didn't cast me aside, but still, there he was, trembling with fever as his cuts oozed crimson blood and my heart shattered for him over and over and over again.

I took a few deep breaths and forced myself to step back towards the maduwa. I couldn't bear seeing Thaththa that way, but I didn't want Amma to deal with this alone either.

Siyath Malli's father had found Thaththa and carried him to the first place of shelter he could find, and summoned the local vedha mahaththaya—the herbal healer—to treat Thaththa. The vedha mahaththaya was still a young man, fresh from his apprenticeship in the hill country, but he was calm and confident, and assured us that my father would live.

"You just have to make sure he keeps sipping from this," he told my mother, giving her a clay jar full of liquid, "and rub this ointment on his wounds daily." He also gave her a bag of herbs with instructions on how to brew them and showed my mother how to change his bandages.

Amma nodded, practical and calm. I'd never seen her so quiet. It was almost as unsettling as seeing my father wounded and unconscious.

The rain eased, and a few men from the village held the corners of the straw mat that Thaththa lay on and carried him back to our house. They were kind to us. Siyath Malli's mother brought us some roti and lunumiris—onion and chilli sambol—she had made. Two more villagers came by, offering their sympathy and support. No dirty looks. No snide remarks. It appeared my father's attack absolved him from the suspicion of carrying them out in the first place. It felt like some sort of wicked joke.

We laid Thaththa on the verandah. It was where he preferred to sleep, and where the ocean breeze would keep him cool and lift his spirits. Amma situated herself next to him, her back against the wall, a woven palm leaf fan in hand ready to chase away errant mosquitoes, and told me to go to sleep.

"I can watch over him," I suggested.

"Just go to sleep, Amara. Please don't argue." She sounded so tired. I didn't want to give her more trouble.

I lay down on my mat, though sleep was the furthest thing from my mind. Jeevan Maama's injuries upset me, yes, but my father's had sent me spinning. Once again I was filled with guilt—there was a time I even suspected that he might've been responsible for the attacks. I was just as bad as the rest of the townsfolk. A hypocrite.

The night air was thick and heavy after the rain. The island itself quiet. There was no chattering from the animals in the jungle, no bats or crickets or owls, and even the ocean waves reduced their volume down to a bare whisper.

That was when I heard the rustling on the roof. I sat straight up on my mat. Had I imagined it?

No, there it was again. The unmistakable sound of the woven coconut fronds swishing, being disturbed. Monkeys got onto our roof sometimes, and civet cats—perhaps it was one of them? But neither of these animals would come out on such a damp night.

The scratching worsened as I felt around for the small oil lamp we kept on a shelf. I wasn't supposed to light it by myself, especially indoors. It was too dangerous, my father had explained to me; it could set fire to the whole hut if I wasn't careful.

Both my parents were asleep on the verandah while I reached for the small tinderbox my mother had brought with her when she eloped. I managed to start a small flame and carefully lit the wick at the base of the lampuwa—the lamp—before setting the delicate glass chimney over it. The immediate relief from darkness gave me some comfort, but it lasted only a second.

I pressed my hands over my mouth to stifle a scream.

The yakshaniya had found me again.

Five times bigger now, she crawled along the wall, her dark spindly legs scampering, reaching for me, here to take from me what she could not take from my father.

She writhed and wriggled, a dark shadow—wait, was it just a shadow?

I looked over at the lamp. A spider was stuck inside the glass chimney, panicking, trying to climb its way out. Its shadow threw itself against the wall of our hut, horrifically magnified.

I let out my breath and laughed. How silly was I? But still, my hands shook as I freed the poor spider and picked up the lampuwa. Stepping outside the hut from the back entryway, I held it out to cast the dim light onto the roof. Except for a few stray leaves that had gotten tangled in the thatching, it was bare. Of course it was. It was most likely a civet cat who'd decided to explore and then realised the roof was too slippery.

"Amara, what are you doing?" my mother called out, her voice thick with sleep.

"Just thought I heard a sound, Amma," I replied, hurrying back inside. My mother stood at the doorway. With dishevelled hair and half-undone sari, she looked like a yakshaniya herself. I braced myself, waiting for her to scold me about the lamp, but her eyes were glazed and unfocused. She held something in her hand.

"I think you left this outside."

It was the wooden statue I'd found earlier. My mother would normally have been upset that I possessed an idol of a god, but she simply handed it to me and went back to the verandah.

I eyed the carved figure again.

Something about it felt wrong. Something about it felt like demon worship.

THE NEXT MORNING felt washed new, especially after the rains, but my heart remained a stormy grey. Thaththa hadn't gotten any better, but then, he hadn't gotten any worse, so I took that as a good sign. My mother put a cold rag on his forehead to cool him down while streams of perspiration ran down his body. They had bandaged the side of his face—a relief for him, and perhaps also a relief for me. Thaththa moaned in his sleep, and occasionally gasped in fear, like a monster had caught up to him in his dreams. He had opened his eyes at dawn, long enough for Amma to convince him to let her spoon some kandha—porridge—into his mouth.

Amma hadn't mentioned Desmond De'Fontaine again, which was some small respite in these times. I would talk to Thaththa after he recovered. Until that, things could wait.

I'd just finished sweeping the front garden when I saw a rustling across from our fence, closer to the jungle boundary. I tensed, wondering who it could be. Fear in the village was at an all-time high, especially after Thaththa's attack, and the only thing brave enough to be in the jungle right now would be a yaka itself.

But a few seconds later, Bhagya's face emerged from behind a tree.

"I came as soon as I heard about your father," she said, no preamble. I was glad. I hadn't seen her since our disagreement, nor did I think she wanted to see me either.

I motioned for her to wait, casting a look towards our hut, but Amma was dozing next to Thaththa and wouldn't miss me for a while. Then I stole away, over the fence and into the jungle, as quick and swift as a beast myself.

Bhagya waited for me under a malaboda tree.

"I'm so sorry," she said, as soon as I joined her. She sounded genuine as she wrapped her arms around me. I was too tired to cry.

"Do they know who was responsible for the attack?"

I pushed the dream that I'd had the very night that Thaththa was attacked out of my mind. I would only sound ridiculous if I confided such a thing to anyone, let alone her.

"It's the same thing. The wounds, I mean. The same as everyone else who was attacked. And it happened in the jungle, just like with the others. Whoever, or whatever, has been attacking all these random people—"

"Men," Bhagya interrupted me. "Haven't you noticed that all the victims have been men?"

"Well . . ." I paused. "But it is usually men who are on their own in the jungle at that time of night, isn't it?"

Bhagya gave me a small smile. "You and I both know that's not exactly true."

She was right. I'd been in the jungle at night more often than I'd been on my sleeping mat. And I'd never been attacked.

"So you think this yaka or whoever is just targeting men?"

"Well, not all men. Maybe—just listen, alright? Maybe the men had something in common? Maybe they are being attacked for a reason?"

30

MY FACE FLUSHED, my whole body lit from within. I didn't even know why, but somehow I felt closer to an answer. I had to keep my voice steady as I sat down on a knotty root. What if there *was* something more? Something no one else was seeing. "But what could my father have in common with these men? Most people in the village even thought that Thaththa was the one responsible for the attacks himself."

"Most people in the village can't tell their heads from their own behinds."

I snorted despite myself, but Bhagya continued, "Loku Banda, your uncle, Siripala. There could be a pattern . . ."

I studied Bhagya's face. Her jaw set firmly, and her eyes looked like they were on fire. There was something about her determination that left me unsettled, even though I couldn't quite understand why. I'd wondered myself if the men who were attacked deserved it. So why did it grate against me when she suggested they were linked in some way?

But then my mind flashed to Siripala grabbing his wife by the hair and beating her inside their hut, and I felt acid hit the back of my throat.

No, it didn't matter that Thaththa had strayed—from Amma or from me. He wasn't anything like Siripala.

I stood up, blood rushing to my head.

"Amara, are you okay?" Bhagya's hand hovered over my shoulder, her eyes wide and a little red around the rims, like she'd been crying.

"Let's go see Loku Banda," I said. I needed to do more than flitter around my hut, my mind turning circles with worry. Besides, if Bhagya was trying to hint that the attacked men were terrible people, Loku Banda would prove her wrong.

Bhagya knitted her brows and nodded. We were quiet as we started our walk to town. Something stewed in the air between us, the chatter of monkeys the only sound puncturing through the jungle morning.

"Ah, mey kawuda mey kalaava assen ringganney?" *Ah, who's this, creeping around through the jungle?* a voice rasped from the shadows, jolting me out of my thoughts.

Heen Achchi peered out from behind a tree—her white eyes as wide as a jungle critter's. She gripped a small sack in her thin, wiry hands.

"Towumata yana gaman." *We are on our way to town.* I slowed down, but didn't stop. After our last encounter, I wanted to put as much distance between us as possible. I shuddered a little, remembering the way her body went rigid and her feet turned over. Her scream still hovered in my mind.

"Ah, mey inney yahaluwa." *Ah, here's your friend,* Heen Achchi said, eyeing Bhagya, who smiled warmly at her.

"Achchi, monawade kalaava maddhey karanney?" *What are you doing in the middle of the jungle, Achchi?* she asked, her voice far friendlier than mine.

"Dhanney naa vaghey." *Like you don't know,* she muttered, holding up her sack, which swung around like a pendulum.

"Bhagya, let her be, she talks in riddles that no one can understand," I muttered, hoping my voice wouldn't carry. I didn't want Heen Achchi to mention our last meeting in front of Bhagya. I didn't want my friend to learn of her warnings about my father angering the gods.

As I spoke, the sack slipped from Heen Achchi's hand, landing with a thud on the jungle floor. I saw some fruits tumble out—a papaya, and a pineapple, and some mangoes and bananas—as the old woman clicked her tongue and set about picking them up. Seeing the bananas reminded me of the fruits and the statue that were left on my verandah. It stilled puzzled me, even though more pressing things had pushed it to the back of my mind. I fleetingly wondered whether Heen Achchi had left them for me, though that would hardly make sense.

"Inna, inna, Achchi." *Wait, wait, Achchi,* Bhagya said, swooping over to help her as Heen Achchi smiled at her appreciatively.

"Ah, meka thiyaganne." *Here, keep this.* Heen Achchi handed Bhagya a small mango, which Bhagya sniffed lightly and tucked away in the fall of her reddha.

"Yana gamana parissamen." *Be careful on your journey,* Heen Achchi said, leaving us and making her way deeper into the jungle.

BHAGYA AND I were across the walkway from the Nupe market, perched on a small tree. A large part of the market was housed in an open-sided, T-shaped building. It was known throughout the island for its woven hambili purses, books composed by ancient poets, textiles, silk umbrellas, and perfumed lamps. It was relatively quiet today, the main hustle and bustle reserved for the weekends, but there were still a handful of women and a few housemaids from British households milling around.

Loku Banda owned a large shop off to the side of the market. He'd been selling his wares for so long that he needed a more permanent structure than the sellers who'd lay their items on straw mats on the floor. He spent most of his days there—starting from early in the morning when the sky was still a deep blue, often till well past sunset. He sold coconuts, and oil, and curry powder. Most of the women in our village knew him well. He was friendly and jovial, giving everyone a good deal and a fair price. He'd slipped my mother some extra turmeric if she left it off the shopping list on months that Thaththa didn't get much work, and usually gave me a few pieces of sukiri—rock sugar—if I accompanied her. He'd returned to his shop as soon as he had been able to after his attack. He said he didn't want to abandon those who needed his groceries. As far as personalities went, I couldn't think of anyone more different from Siripala the fisherman.

"So, what's our plan?" Bhagya asked me.

"Why don't we go talk to him? You'll be able to see what kind of person he is then, won't you? Judge for yourself if he's anything like Siripala?" I wielded the accusation like a weapon. I needed to prove Bhagya wrong. If indeed there was a connection between the attacked men, it must be something else.

"I think it might be better for you to speak to him," Bhagya replied. "He doesn't know me, after all, and might be more comfortable opening up to you. Ask him what he remembers about the attack. We might be able to find a clue."

"A clue?"

"Yes, we're here to find out as much about the attacks as possible, right?"

My cheeks coloured. Yes, that was the original idea. I'd just gotten defensive.

I'd known Loku Banda, even if it wasn't well, since I was a child. It wasn't just Amma who would visit his shop, but Thaththa too. While he usually got the coconut palms and banana leaves for his exorcisms from either the jungle or our garden, he'd visit Loku Banda for incense and food items we'd use to make offerings. And, perhaps most importantly, Loku Banda had never treated my family any differently, even after he had been attacked.

But still, a nagging worry in my mind made me nervous. I had a certain perception of Loku Banda and it felt deeply unsettling to sully it, especially with something unpleasant. It was normal to feel that way, wasn't it? To not want to ruin your impression of someone? To believe what you see because it's far more comfortable to accept than what someone chooses to hide?

I mustn't worry so much, I told myself. Loku Banda was kind and generous, unlike Siripala.

Once we had decided, I climbed down while Bhagya waited for me, still up the tree. It was tucked neatly to the side of the main road, and with enough leaves on its branches to cover her from anyone who was to look up. I was supposed to join her there after I was done.

Loku Banda stood behind a waist-high clay wall while he chatted with customers, the woven coconut frond roof keeping him sheltered from the sun. Most of the other vendors laid their wares on a woven mat, but Loku Banda was far more established. The little hut that served as his shop was well stocked, with shelves of products lining the back wall. He'd been supplying the village with kulu badu—kitchen staples—for as long as I could remember.

Loku Banda's wounds had been similar to Thaththa's. He was found bloody, covered in gashes and bite marks, but instead of losing the skin on his face, he had been scalped. I remember shuddering when I first heard it. Loku Banda was a handsome man, and his long hair had always been pulled into a knot and decorated with a comb. His attacker had prised away the hair from his forehead to the back of his skull. It was bandaged now, healing well, he told everyone. He had a pink scar running down the side of his cheek. Somehow, though, his injuries didn't look as ragged on him as they did on everyone else. Perhaps it was the friendly smile that still hadn't left his face.

"Amara," he greeted me warmly as soon as he noticed me. "I heard about your father. I'm so sorry. Of course you know the same thing happened to me. It took me some time to get back on my feet, but I've been recovering. I'm certain he will too."

"Thank you, Loku Banda. I really appreciate your kind words. I was, actually, wondering if you'd be able to help me."

"Most certainly. Tell me anything you need, it's on the house. I know these next few days will be especially difficult."

He thought I was asking him for wares. And he was just going to give them to me for free. My heart warmed. How could this man possibly deserve to be attacked?

"Actually, Loku Banda, I was hoping you could give me some information. I'm trying to find out more about the attacks."

"Oh, I see. And why is that?"

Bhagya and I had discussed this, and decided it was better to take the more honest route.

"I just feel like I need to do something. Rather than wait around the house hoping he will get better. I was wondering if you could tell me what you remember about that night."

He looked me up and down, his eyebrows gathering together on his scarred forehead, and seemed to decide there would be no harm done.

"Come to the back," he instructed, and I quickly circled my way to where he said.

He handed me a small sack when I got there, filled with odds and ends for the kitchen—some rice, a pumpkin, a little cloth bag with dried pepper, some chillies.

"For your mother," he said, simply, ignoring me when I tried to thank him and gesturing to a small bankuwa, which he placed a respectable distance away. Again, I was touched by his actions.

"I don't know if there's much you will learn from what I say. I was on my daily route back home. I've been taking a shortcut through the jungle since I was a little boy and never had reason to fear it, but this day, something felt wrong. It was like I was being followed. I kept moving forward, hurrying, until I tripped over the root of a tree. Before I could pick myself up off the jungle floor, it was on me like a flash.

"It felt like claws were digging into my back, and the pain was so fierce I thought I must surely die. And when I screamed, it bit me. I don't know for how long we struggled . . ." He touched his head, his voice trembling.

"I apologise. You are young and I don't mean to scare you. The next thing I remember is waking up feeling as though my body was on fire. My wife told me I was in and out of consciousness for at least a few days." His face clouded over as he spoke, his pink cheeks turning ashy. This was obviously painful for him to relive.

"Thank you, Loku Banda, I know this must be difficult for you."

I hesitated, aware of how inconsiderate this question was, but pushing forward nonetheless.

"Do you remember anything about who attacked you?"

He shook his head. "I never got a good look. The fellow from the Mudaliyar's office, you know, Aloysius, scoffed when I told him this, but I swear to you, it was not from this world."

"What makes you say that?"

He took a deep, shuddering breath, refusing to meet my eye. "Every night, I still have dreams about it . . ."

"Dreams?" I asked, my heart starting to beat faster. I'd heard about the dreams through village gossip, but I'd never learned the details of what horrified the men so much.

"Yes, it still visits me, every night while I sleep. These large talons grab ahold of my hair and pull so hard . . ." His voice faded, a stricken look on his face as he clutched his head. "And a woman's voice, but like nothing I've ever heard before, saying, 'You're mine now. This is where you belong.'"

31

I FLOATED BACK to the tree, my thoughts doing somersaults away from my body.

I was so lost in my own world that I almost didn't see Neha across the street from me. She must have noticed me this time. I think she might have started to raise her arm up to wave at me, but I spun around. There was no way I could speak to her now. She would immediately know that something was wrong, and, well, there was no way I could have that conversation with her right then.

I climbed up to where Bhagya sat, and she listened with rapt attention as I told her everything Loku Banda had said. Everything about the attack. But for some reason, I found myself leaving out how the woman who haunted him seemed like the same woman I saw in my own dreams.

I'll claw out your tongue if you tell. No one can find out what happened.

Was that what Amma had meant? Had I been attacked myself and they were just trying to cover it up? But all the men who were attacked were covered in gashes and wounds. I did have a few bruises and scratches that I couldn't explain, but none anywhere close to the injuries of the rest. No, I had just been sick with some sort of fever like they said.

"Amara? Amara?" Bhagya waved her hand in front of my face. She looked concerned. "Are you alright? You looked a little pale. And you've broken out in a sweat."

She was right. Beads of perspiration dotted my forehead and my upper lip.

"Here, eat this." She'd managed to peel the mango that Heen Achchi had given her, and she passed it to me. I took it gratefully. I couldn't even remember the last time I had eaten something.

But I'd only taken one bite when nausea washed over me, my latest suspicion fresh in my mind, and I shook my head, handing it back to her.

"I can't eat now. I feel ill."

She nodded, and took a deep appreciative whiff of the mango—her long lashes forming crescent moons on her cheeks and her shoulders rising up to inhale—before tucking it away.

"Hey, who's that?"

A woman was approaching Loku Banda's shop.

"That's his wife, bringing his lunch. Her name's Mary," I whispered, remembering how she brushed us off when I visited her with Amma a few days ago. Amma went back and got her measurements the next day, she'd told me, and I was glad she hadn't asked me to join.

Now that I could get a clear look at her, I noticed that Loku Banda's wife was very beautiful. Fair and slender, she handed over a parcel of rice wrapped in a banana leaf. He touched her arm appreciatively, and she kept her eyes down—demure, as was customary. We were too far away to hear what they said to each other, but it was worlds away from how I saw Siripala speak to his wife, or, I thought, my heart sinking, the way Thaththa often spoke to Amma. Loku Banda wasn't a terrible husband, that much was obvious. They both sat on the back steps to the shop, the smell of the rice and curry wafting up to where we sat on our tree as he ate with his hand.

I knew we shouldn't have been watching, but it felt comforting, in a way, to see them. To know that not all marriages were doomed. That there were some good men.

He chatted pleasantly to her the entire time. She stayed relatively quiet, but she brought him a small tumbler of water after he finished, which he used to wash his fingers. Then she bundled up the now-empty banana leaf, gave him a small goodbye, and left.

I felt triumphant, even if it was just for a moment. All the attacked men weren't horrid. Bhagya was wrong.

"Should we make our way back now? Amma probably needs my help with things around the house." And while I was relieved about Loku Banda, I needed to make sense of what might or might not have happened to me.

"Let's stay a little while longer," Bhagya replied, but I shook my head.

"No, I should go home."

I suddenly felt exhausted. Like there were answers just out of my grasp and I was tired of reaching for them. I'd been reaching for them for so long that I was wearing myself down to the bone. The sun had grown hotter since morning and I was feeling dizzy. I climbed down from where I sat, and stumbled a little when my feet touched the ground.

"Well, well, well, look who it is," a voice cut through, sharp and hard and familiar. My entire body recoiled at the sound. The voice that had taunted me for years. The same one that had convinced my entire class at school that I was a demon-worshipping deviant. The one that had laughed gleefully when I found a decapitated chicken head in my cubby.

Daphne Perera stood before me, not a hair out of place, fresh and fragrant despite the suffocating afternoon sun.

"What were you doing up that tree, witch? Were you spying on me?"

Spying on her? I never even noticed she was there, but the last thing I needed was to draw attention to who we'd really been watching.

I wanted to retort with something vicious and witty, but my head felt light, like when I'd been holding my breath for too long when I was swimming. Later, I might come up with the perfect reply, but at that moment I just hated myself. I stood there like an imbecile, blinking at her.

"I'm surprised you have the courage to show your face here, after everything your family has done to wreak havoc on this town," she continued.

"My father was attacked too, Daphne," I managed. I hated the way my voice sounded around her—high-pitched and tinny. Like I was just the same little girl back at school. I hadn't seen her in a year, and yet I regressed the moment she bullied me.

She threw back her head and cackled cruelly.

"Isn't that what you Buddhists say about karma? That you finally get what you deserve? I know it a little differently—after all, God does punish those who blemish His name."

My resentment of her had been built brick by brick over many years of torment. It now towered, heavy and tall, ready for me to kick it down. Except I just stood, mute, letting her stomp all over me just like she did for years, quivering in anger.

I was so frozen that I didn't quite notice who came up behind her.

"Is anything the matter, darling?" Aloysius asked, offering his arm to Daphne.

It felt like the wind had been knocked out of me.

He wore his Mudaliyar's office uniform, and the adorned jacket gleamed in the bright sun, matching the sparkle of Daphne's hair.

"Oh, everything is just fine," she replied, and then turned to me. "I trust you've met my fiancé, Aloysius Peiris?"

I needn't have been so shocked. It was impossible to think of two people better suited for each other. Both my tormentors, now to be wed. I'd have laughed if I wasn't so taken aback.

Daphne continued, "The Mudaliyar was very pleased with the report Aloysius handed in about your father. He's even been talking about giving him a senior position, after your father's arrest."

Aloysius had the nerve to look a little embarrassed at this.

"Darling, let's not talk about such unholy things on a beautiful day like this—"

"I already told you—my father was attacked himself. How could he be responsible?"

"The devil always finds a way," Daphne replied, her voice cruel and high. A few people had gathered to watch our exchange, curiosity written all over their faces. Thaththa was just a pawn to them. For Daphne's fiancé to secure a promotion. For the townsfolk to find something to gossip about.

"But we must all remember," Aloysius said, his voice deep and resonant, turning to address the crowd, "that even those who stray from the flock can seek forgiveness, so long as they truly repent."

I shuddered with rage. I had nothing to repent for. I wasn't a vicious bully.

Bhagya laid a cool hand on my shoulder. I'd almost forgotten she was there. Neither Daphne nor Aloysius even looked at her.

"But this isn't the time to discuss sinners. The Lord will deal with them in due course. Come now, darling," he said, addressing Daphne. "Let's take our leave." He escorted her away, smiling and nodding at the crowd that had gathered, leaving me with a deep desire to kick them both, as well as myself.

Why did I always wilt away when Daphne was around? It was so unfair. Anger washed over me as I ignored Bhagya, ignored the people who had started dispersing now that Aloysius had left, and stalked back into the jungle.

Let the demon find me and attack me if it wanted. It couldn't be worse than dealing with Daphne.

32

I WALKED HOME in a sullen daze. Bhagya tried making conversation, but I couldn't find it in me to respond. I was too enraged with myself for how I couldn't react to Daphne, almost enough to lose sight of what Loku Banda had told me. Almost enough to forget what had happened to my father.

Thaththa.

He had slipped from my mind for the briefest of moments, but the reality of it hit me in the chest like a fresh punch. I said a quick goodbye to Bhagya and rushed through the jungle, as fast as my feet could take me. Parts of my dream played in my mind—of him writhing on the floor, of him gasping for air as blood gurgled out of the gashes on his body. I wanted to scream. I wanted to tug my hair out and shout that I had nothing to do with it. That I would never, not in a million years, hurt him.

I was almost home when I was interrupted once again—this time by Raam. It wasn't our usual day to meet, but he was waiting for me at the turn I always took back to my house. He sometimes came out to surprise me on days his shift ended early, and I had always been pleased to see him.

"I can't stay for long, I need to check on my father," I said, making sure we were still swallowed by the trees.

"Oh, I thought we could spend a bit of time together," he said, giving me the smile I usually couldn't resist.

"You know I'd love nothing more." I gave his hand a quick squeeze. "But it's important that I get back soon today."

"But I came out all this way." He smiled as he said it, even though I could hear the disappointment in his voice. "All my friends from work went down to the beach in Talpe, but I stayed back just for you. Because I missed you so much."

My heart hurt. I ached to remain here with him, to get lost in the jungle and his arms, but even thinking about it drove me into a spiral of guilt. I needed to be at home, to help Amma care for Thaththa. She'd be wondering where I was now too.

I reached up onto the tips of my toes and gave him a small kiss.

"I've missed you too. And you know I'd rather stay here with you. But I really need to check on Thaththa."

"What's happened to him? One of his spells backfire?" His smile while he said it told me it was a joke, but it prickled me just the same.

"He was attacked, Raam. He was returning home through the jungle, this jungle, actually, when it happened."

Raam's face fell. He pulled me into his chest.

"I'm so sorry, Amara. I didn't realise. Of course, of course you must go back home. I'm so selfish, I'm sorry."

"It's alright," I said, appeased. "You would have been at work the whole day. You had no way of knowing."

"I'm a fool. I don't even know why you're with me."

I hugged him tight, but he didn't hug me back.

"I feel absolutely terrible." He sounded so dejected. "You deserve better than me."

"Raam, there's no one in this world who will ever be better for me than you. But I really do have to hurry back."

My face was red. I knew I had to tell him about my meeting with Desmond De'Fontaine, and how Amma was insisting I marry him, but I also knew that this wasn't the time. It wasn't something I could mention in passing, without giving Raam an explanation of how it all happened without my knowledge. And right now, I just wanted to get home.

"Yes, yes. You should go," he said, dropping his arms and turning away from me.

"Raam, I love you. Please don't forget. I just have a lot going on right now."

"Yes, yes, of course. I'll go and come, then, Amara."

I should have probably stayed a few more minutes to make sure that he was okay. That he was happy. I should have kissed him a little harder, hugged him a little tighter. But the truth was that I just wanted to get back. Raam would understand.

LUCKILY, A STRING of neighbours and well-wishers and curious town gossips had brought over enough food that Amma had plenty to hold her over.

"Where were you, Amara?" The fight had completely gone out of her voice, petals of bruised mauve blooming under eyes that looked dimmer somehow. Like a lamp extinguished by a sudden wind. It felt cruel to be difficult when she was this forlorn.

"I just had to run some deliveries into town, Amma. I didn't want us to fall behind on business." I hated lying, but I couldn't burden her with any truths right now. "And Loku Banda said to give you this." I handed her the gifts from the shopkeeper.

"Loku Banda? Did you happen to hand him his wife's sari jacket when you were making deliveries?"

"Um, no. I—must have missed it."

"Haiyyo, now we'll seem so rude. It was marked clearly also—Mary. She told me she needed it urgently. Something about going to visit her family. She's already paid in full. Could you rush back and give it to him? They'll think we are terrible, if not. Accepting gifts while in debt to them."

I sighed. The last thing I wanted was to go all the way back to town, but I didn't want to disappoint Amma either.

"Shall I deliver it to their house?" I asked. It was a little closer than walking all the way back to the market.

"No." Amma's voice was forceful. "You saw that she doesn't like to be disturbed. Deliver it to Loku Banda."

I nodded and took the parcel. I was already tired, but I was happy to help in any way I could.

I took the main road this time. There was no need to tempt fate. I kept a steady pace and reached the town again before too long.

Keeping a sharp lookout for Daphne, I found my way back to Loku Banda's shop. The sun was starting to set, and the market was far less busy. Sellers were packing up their wares, and shop owners had started to count their earnings for the day. Long shadows loomed out in front of me, forcing me to be on guard. Anything could be waiting for me in the darkness.

Loku Banda wasn't at the front of his shop, and I cursed myself for coming all the way back here for no reason. Now I'd have to make the long walk again tomorrow. I should check the back of the shop, just in case he was there. Or maybe I could even leave this package for him in a safe place?

I went around to the back, where I had sat with Loku Banda just a few hours earlier.

To my surprise, he was there, talking to a British officer.

I stepped back into the shadows. Something about their expressions made me want to keep my distance. But still, I peered around the wall that shielded me from their view. I'd seen this officer before, I noted, remembering the blond moustache and the way he wore his hat jauntily to the side. He was the same officer who was leaving Loku Banda's house when we went to take Mary's measurements. Loku Banda hadn't been at home that day, had he?

"The delivery from the hill country will be coming tomorrow. I trust you'll make sure it reaches me," Loku Banda said, his voice harder than when he told me about the attack.

The officer smirked. "What you locals do to evade paying your taxes. You know the general has been getting quite suspicious. I don't know if I can keep this up for much longer."

Loku Banda looked annoyed. "What do you mean? We had an agreement."

The officer shrugged. "Things change."

Loku Banda took a step towards him, his face red.

"Listen here, do you know how much I've had to sacrifice for our little agreement?"

"And while your pretty wife has truly sweetened the deal for me, there's only so much I can do when the general gets involved. Now, if I could visit her, perhaps, an extra day of the week . . ."

"You bastard."

"Says the man who is happy to sell his wife to avoid taxes."

Horror—a different type of horror to the one of monsters and demons—engulfed me as understanding slid into place. Why the officer had been leaving Loku Banda's house that day. Why Mary had been upset. Why Amma had ushered me out of there so quickly, why she was adamant I didn't go to Mary's house by myself this evening, and had me go all the way to the market instead. Amma must have known, or at least suspected, after we saw the officer leave Mary's house.

I'd been too quick to think Loku Banda was a good man. He was just as bad as the rest of them.

33

AMMA WANTED ME to stay indoors.

"Please. Now's not the time to be so stubborn, Amara. Just listen to me, for once in your life. Keep inside for now. No going into the jungle. I'll tend to Thaththa. His treatment is complicated, and I don't want you meddling with anything, you hear me?"

I agreed, if only to keep the peace. She had not mentioned the De'Fontaines' proposal again, and while I knew we would have to discuss it eventually, we'd struck a tenuous truce for now. And thank goodness, because I didn't think my heart could handle anything more.

But still, I couldn't do everything she asked. I didn't want to stay away from my father. All the questions I had after visiting Loku Banda dissolved the moment I saw Thaththa's face, slackened by the various herbs he was forced to drink. I just wanted to be near him.

And so I waited until my mother was asleep before shifting next to where Thaththa lay, still on his mat on the verandah.

He slept fitfully, his body making sudden jerking motions. I could see his eyes dart from side to side under their lids, like a creature caught in a trap, trying to spring free. His mouth twisted in pain. Or was it fear?

I laid a hand on his forehead, like he did to me when I was little and not feeling well. His skin burned with the fury of a hundred demons, and I gasped at the heat under my palm. If the wounds from his attack didn't kill him, then this fever certainly would.

I looked over at my mother, asleep even though it was still early, her back resting against the clay wall of our hut while she pulled her knees up to her chest. I couldn't bring myself to wake her. She'd been tending to him without a break ever since we'd brought him home—a mix of guilt and fear and anger tinting her exhaustion.

Taking care not to make a sound, I found a small rag and padded down the garden. The ocean breeze felt fresh against my skin, a much-needed respite from the muggy heat of our hut. I drew a pot of water from our well, glad the sound of the crashing waves drowned out any noise I was making. Our well water was always harder than from those dug inland—the water acrid and salty against my lips. A common curse of wells this close to the sea. But it would do for now. I soaked the rag in the cool liquid. It wouldn't be much, but I hoped a cold compress would grant my father even a grain of relief.

The sky swirled with clouds tonight. The moon hadn't yet risen. I barely made out my father's outline on the verandah as I crouched over him, pressing the cloth to his forehead. He moaned slightly, though I didn't know if it was in pain or in relief.

"It's alright, Thaththa," I whispered. "You'll be alright soon." Empty words, I knew, but these very same words always made me feel better when he used to say them to me.

I was turning the rag over when the stench hit me. Rot and decay and rust. The smell of death. But how? I brought the rag closer to my nose and inhaled, immediately wishing I didn't. I could barely see my hands, but I could tell they were tinged with something thick and dark. What had I applied on my father?

I grabbed the rag and moved to the edge of the verandah, trying to get a better look. There was barely any light, but I knew something was wrong.

The rustle behind me made me whip around.

That was when I saw her. She was on her hands and knees, hair spilling over her face like a cobwebbed curtain, crawling towards Thaththa as he lay helpless on the floor.

"Stay away," I tried to scream, but my voice never made it out of my throat. My feet were rooted to the spot. I was just a powerless statue.

"No!" I tried again as she got closer, her back arched, body contorting, disjointed but fast, like a cockroach scurrying towards a crumb.

My voice was still muted, but she paused, looking up at me and smiling, baring her rotten teeth.

"Get away from him!"

But the yakshaniya leaned her face down next to my father's and, not looking away from me, slithered out her black tongue, licking his cheek in one stroke.

"This is what you want, isn't it?" she hissed.

"No! Stay away from him!" Still no words, only tears spilling down my face.

She held out a claw-like finger and slowly, almost gently, pushed it into his mouth.

"Please!" I pleaded.

At first I thought she had heard me, because she pulled her arm back. That was when I realised that she'd hooked his tongue onto a long, talon-like nail and was drawing it out of his mouth. Thaththa's head lifted off the floor, a pendulum swinging on this grotesque thread.

"Stop it! Leave him alone!"

She grinned at me again and, reaching down, took a bite of his outstretched tongue.

"No! No! Please!"

"None of you will escape me now," she cooed.

I JERKED AWAKE to find myself standing. I didn't feel my sleeping mat under my feet, nor the sand from the seashore. My toes were buried in moss and fallen leaves. I looked around, confused and disoriented. I was swallowed so deep in the jungle that the only sounds around me were the cicadas, the night owls, and my racing heart.

How had I ended up here? Had I sleepwalked?

I must have sleepwalked, I decided.

"It was just a dream." I said the words out loud to reassure myself. I needed reassuring. My dream had felt so real. Too real.

I took a deep breath.

"It was just a dream." I had sleepwalked again. All the way into the jungle this time. It comforted me to repeat myself. Thaththa was safe at home. I had nothing to worry about.

I took another breath and looked around for a familiar tree or a bush or a rock—something to let me know where exactly I was so that I could find my way back.

That was when it started again—the prickling at the back of my neck, the small hairs on my arms standing at attention, the feeling that someone, or something, was just beyond my shoulder.

I shivered, feeling exposed and vulnerable.

I needed to get home. And soon.

I closed my eyes and listened carefully. I wasn't sure where I was, but the ocean would be my guide. I could hear its low rumble from behind me, so I turned, making sure my steps were calculated and quick. Something felt uneasy.

Was someone right behind me?

I stopped a few times, looking back over my shoulder, but as always there was nothing but shadows. The jungle heaved and sighed, and the more I walked, the more I felt something stalking me.

The trees grew thicker, forming a screen that blocked out what little moonlight there was to begin with. The floor was slippery with moss. The jungle was slowly, surely transforming into a trap. The perfect hunting ground. I was defenceless against whatever was after me, keeping to the darkness, blending into the trees.

I could feel the footsteps even before I heard them.

I hurried along as fast as I could. It was too risky to run, not with the occasional roots throwing themselves before me, and the uneven rocks jutting out on the path. If I were to fall, I would be caught for sure. Bhagya wouldn't be there to save me this time.

I skidded on some wet leaves and swore. This was useless. I could never outrun what was following me. I liked to say that the jungle was my home, but deep in my heart I knew the truth—I was merely its guest. An occasional tenant. I could never compare against something the jungle birthed into existence. I would never stand against that which the jungle called its own.

The footsteps were getting closer. There was an urgency to them that foreshadowed my own dread.

I had a better chance if I hid. If I could somehow go unnoticed. The edge of the jungle was still too far for me to reach it safely. But I knew exactly where I could take refuge.

There was a large tree a few strides away from me, with a fairly large beney—a hollow—in its trunk. Glancing behind me once again to make sure, I quickly climbed in.

I could fit if I crouched, wrapping my arms around my legs and keeping my chin tucked away between my chest and my knees. Too late, I prayed that there were no snakes or monitor lizards in here with me. It was common for some animals to make these empty spaces their nests.

My breath echoed around me, amplifying in the enclosed space. I was sure I could hear my heartbeat reverberate off the tree bark. There was a faint chitter-chatter of insects scurrying around. In my crouched position, I could barely see what was outside. Was I safe? Had I managed to trick the yaka?

I waited a minute, an hour, a lifetime, my heart racing every moment, wondering when I would be caught.

Nothing came. No sounds except my own breath and the passive calls of the jungle in the distance.

I shifted my weight, hoping I'd hidden for long enough. I slowly pushed my head and shoulders out from the hollow, blinking into the dim, speckled light.

That was when the rustling started again. The footsteps were nearby.

This was it. It had found me. And here I was, stuck defenceless in the hollow of a tree. I clamped my hands over my mouth to muffle my panicked breathing, pressing back hard against the hollow. I reached for my suray uselessly, knowing it wasn't there, still unable to shake the habit. I cursed myself for giving it to Raam. I should have known better. I should have done more to keep myself safe.

The footsteps grew louder and louder. I could hear them circle the tree.

Any moment now, a claw would reach in and yank me out. Any second now, I would be ripped into like Thaththa and Jeevan Maama and Loku Banda were. Perhaps I wouldn't be so lucky. Perhaps the yaka would simply finish me off rather than just leave me injured.

One step closer, and then another.

I couldn't die like this. Like a rat, hidden in a hole.

If I was going to die, I might as well put up a fight.

Gathering every ounce of bravery that I possessed, I pushed myself out of the tree.

"Stay away!" I screamed.

It took a moment for my eyes to focus on what was in front of me.

I expected to see jaws as wide as a shark's, claws as sharp as a bear's, a beast as hungry as a leopard.

But in front of me was a ripple of white. A ghost—not a demon like I had expected.

It was a woman with long black hair. She'd been haunting me in my dreams. She must be the one attacking everyone in the jungle too. Any second now she'd turn around, and then everything would be lost.

So slow that it felt like a million lifetimes, she spun to face me.

But instead of her cruel, mangled face, all that was in front of me was a scared girl.

"Neha?" I cried out, incredulous.

She was frozen—her eyes wide and shoulders pulled up to her

ears. Her white lace dress glowed in the dim moonlight, and her hair had come undone. She was clutching a small golden cross that hung from her neck.

"Neha, what are you doing here?" I put my hand on her shoulder and shook. It seemed to pull her back into this world.

"Amara," she sighed, a small tremble in her voice. "I'm so sorry. I didn't mean to scare you."

"What do you mean? What are you doing here? Out alone in the middle of the night. It isn't safe."

It was instinctive, the worry I had for her. Years of love and care couldn't be erased that quickly.

She took a deep breath to steady herself and gave me a small smile.

"I know it's not safe, but I had to come as soon as I heard about your father. And it's not that late yet, is it?"

I'd been so tired today that I didn't even know what time it was.

Every bit of fear that circulated through me dissolved, to be replaced with a warmth I couldn't quite understand.

"You really should have waited till dawn, Neha. What if something happened to you?"

She smiled sheepishly.

"I know, I know. But my parents haven't returned from Colombo yet and Dandris's family wouldn't have been overjoyed to learn I was leaving the house unaccompanied. And I couldn't wait. Besides, you were the one who gave me a fright, you know. What are *you* doing out in the jungle?"

I shook my head. "I don't even know."

"What do you mean? You know how dangerous it is these days."

I raised an eyebrow at her, and she gave me a sheepish smile.

"Alright, then. I suppose I've been no better, following you around this past week."

"What? You were following me?"

She looked away. "I didn't mean to keep doing it. I was trying to gather up the courage to come speak to you."

I felt stunned.

"But, why?"

"I was worried about you, Amara," she replied quietly. "Ever since the day when you came to take my measurements. Something in you has changed. It was like a light has gone out or something. I—I wanted to keep an eye on you."

"Keep an eye on me?" I repeated, incredulous.

"Y-yes. I'm sorry. I left presents for you too, hoping you'd realise. Some bananas—I know they are your favourite—and I found this small statue in the market that I thought you might like. Catharine's sister-in-law would have thrown a fit if she'd found it in the house, so I left it on your doorstep."

I took a step back. "That was you!"

She gave the briefest nod. "Like I said, I never meant to alarm you. I just wanted you to know that I was thinking about you, you see."

"So why didn't you just come and speak to me? Rather than following me and scaring me like this?"

"I—I wasn't sure you'd want to talk to me, Amara."

Something in me bristled.

"I wasn't the one who wanted to stop being your friend, Neha." I tried to keep my voice mild. I didn't want her to know how much it hurt. How much I missed her.

"I never said we couldn't be friends, Amara, just that—"

"Just that suddenly I wasn't good enough for you. And those bullies from school were. Look, I know that my father's craft doesn't exactly fall in line with your new beliefs, but you just cast me aside like some sort of worthless rag."

It felt good to say it out loud. Like it gave my sadness a purpose. A direction. It wasn't just me feeling bad for myself. There was a real reason why my heart felt battered.

"I'm sorry, Amara, I really am. But it's not like you embraced my newfound faith either, you know? You were so disappointed with me whenever I tried to talk to you about it."

"How could you blame me? You saw the way the nuns, the way Daphne and the other girls treated me. Calling me a witch? How could you follow a religion that encouraged people to do that? You've seen firsthand what the church has done to my family. We've gone from being a village necessity to being shunned by everyone."

"Amara, I know that the church can be . . . different in its ways. And that many twist its teachings to get what they want, especially with the foreigners ruling over us. But I also know that my reasons for trying to understand it have more to do with a greater sense of purpose. With what feels real to me. It has little to do with anyone else."

"And what does feel real to you?"

"Love, Amara. It's what my faith is built on. It's why I miss you so much." Neha's eyes were wide, pleading with me. But I wasn't quite ready to forgive her just yet. I didn't understand. How could she compartmentalise it so easily? I thought of Sister Agatha. The god she spoke of spewed anger and punishment and floods and fire. Not love. I could never connect the kind face on the painting of Jesus with the one twisted in agony that hung on the cross. I couldn't compare Neha's gentleness with the hateful vitriol spewed by Aloysius.

It was too much for me to understand, standing here in the jungle in the middle of the night.

Neha's eyes were full of tears. "Look, I—I didn't mean to hurt you. Not by any of it. I was just trying my best to balance everything out—"

"How was it *balancing things out* when you just stopped speaking to me, your oldest friend?"

"I never wanted to cut ties with you, Amara! You're the one who called me a hypocrite."

"Because you are a hypocrite!" There was no point trying to sweeten my words. "We spent years avoiding the nuns, dodging all the rules the British made us follow. And now suddenly, you decide to join forces with them? I've seen you, you know, visiting those nuns all the time. You could just move ahead, and I was just a forgotten inconvenience, and for what? All—"

"All because my family needed me to, Amara. My father's business was failing. There was talk of us selling our home and moving to Colombo. So when he got this new job, it was a godsend. And jobs like his, well, they come with added responsibility. We all had a part to play, and I wouldn't let my family's downfall be me."

I stayed quiet. She'd mentioned something about her family falling on hard times, but I never connected it to her change in attitude. I'd been too upset to learn that she'd been invited to Daphne's tea parties.

"And it's not just about my family and making new friends, Amara. My faith—it's like I've finally found something bigger than myself. I understand that it's difficult. That it must have been confusing for you. But finally, I have found something that gives me so much peace and happiness. And it has nothing to do with the British and their ways. It has nothing to do with the nuns or people in the village or the bullies at school. But it has everything to do with how I felt the moment I knelt down and truly gave myself up to a higher purpose. Please try to understand."

I never knew she felt this way.

"I just wish you'd spoken to me about it. That you hadn't just pulled away."

She smiled. "You didn't want to hear it, Amara. You hated the new ways too much, and justly so. But please just try to understand that my experience is a little different from yours."

"That's not fair, Neha."

"Look, I know I didn't handle it the best way when it came to our friendship. But I felt like I was being pulled in a hundred different directions at once. You can understand what that feels like, can't you?"

The fight, the hurt, the bitterness left my body as suddenly as a storm that withered away into nothing. I felt my shoulders sag.

"So, what now?" I asked. I knew I wasn't supposed to ask questions unless I was prepared for the answers, but I was feeling hopeful.

"Well, I've missed you, you know?" She gave me a shy smile. "That's what."

"I've missed you too," I conceded.

"Now tell me about your father. Is he recovering?"

"He's, well, he hasn't woken up yet. He's been burning up with a fever. Amma has had the vedha mahaththaya come in to check him, and he says to be patient."

"Do you know what happened? Is it true about this demon?" She reached for me, putting her arm around me, and I wished she'd never let go. I could barely believe how desperately I had missed her.

"We don't know who did it. There were many who thought my father was responsible for the attacks himself. Maybe this was their way of getting back at him?" I hadn't even thought about this explanation until the words fluttered out of my mouth, but it did ring true.

Neha nodded.

"That's so horrid, Amara. I'm so sorry. It must have been terrible to go through all of this by yourself. When I saw you today, walking alone at the Nupe market, I felt absolutely awful. I hadn't even heard about the attack then. I only learned of it when Aloysius and Daphne came storming in to complain to Dandris at dinnertime."

"So, you are friends with Aloysius?"

"He's a friend of Dandris's family," she said, guarding her words. "I've heard the nuns talk about him when I visit the convent. He and his family are big supporters of the church, you know, but some of the nuns are wary of him. They say he's mixing up his politics a little too much in the faith."

"Anyway . . ." I wanted to change the subject. I didn't want to have the one happy moment I'd had in ages spoiled by talking about Aloysius. "You were mistaken about seeing me alone in the market. I was with my new friend."

There was a look on her face—was it jealousy? Much to my surprise, it felt a little satisfying.

"Oh?" she asked.

"Her name is Bhagya. She hasn't lived in town long."

"Oh, what does she do?"

"She sells baskets. Perhaps you've noticed her. She displays them outside the convent where the nuns stay."

Neha shook her head.

"So you're good friends, then?"

"She's been helping me, actually."

Neha gave me a small smile. "Helping you with what?"

"Well, we've been trying to learn more about the attacks."

"Amara, you must be careful! You don't know who could be behind it. They could be very dangerous."

I laughed. It felt good to be around her. Like the bits and pieces of my life fit together better. Like a part of me that had been missing these few weeks was finally found.

"Not that much more dangerous than wandering around the jungle at night. Come, let me walk you to the main road. You should get back before Catharine notices you're gone."

She nodded. "I'll come visit your father as soon as possible. I have some important news to tell you also, but now is not the time. My parents will be back tomorrow, which will make it much easier for me to visit."

34

MAYBE IT WAS finally reconnecting with Neha, but I slept heavily, waking up feeling rested. The morning blossomed, clean and fresh, the birds announcing a brand-new day. I rolled on my mat and stretched. I was still inside our hut, which meant I hadn't sleepwalked again.

I quickly dressed and made my way outside. Both my parents were still on the verandah, fast asleep. I went to the kitchen and lit a fire, putting some water on to boil. I noticed a sack of paddy near the mortar and pestle, waiting to be pounded, and made a mental note to do it later.

The mortar and pestle reminded me, once again, of happier times, when I used to accompany Thaththa to exorcisms. These basic kitchen utensils, found in any home, were usually kept next to the victim during the ceremony as a means of offsetting Kuveni's curse. They symbolised abundance, Thaththa told me, but I had been far more interested in hearing about Kuveni. It had been one of my favourite stories as a child.

It all started when King Vijaya, the first king of the island, and a few hundred of his followers arrived on these shores.

Soon after they landed here, one of Vijaya's men was captured by Kuveni, a Yaksha princess, the daughter of the leader of the demon sect, who had magic of her own. One by one, she captured all Vijaya's men who came in search of their comrade. Finally, Vijaya himself confronted her, threatening to kill her unless his men were released.

Kuveni did indeed let Vijaya's men go, falling in love with the king instead. Vijaya rewarded Kuveni by taking her as his wife, and convinced her to turn her back on her own people. So strong was the love Kuveni had for Vijaya that she helped him conquer many villages, including her own city, Sirisavatthu, and even bore him a son and a daughter.

Unfortunately, after establishing settlements around the island, Vijaya believed that in order to be a "true royal," he had to marry someone of royal lineage. He banished Kuveni back to her village, with their children. Some believe that Kuveni was killed in her own village, while others think she took her own life by jumping off a cliff. But whatever version of the story, one thing was constant—Kuveni cursed Vijaya and his people for generations to come.

This is why this island has never known peace, many whispered. This is why our kings fought amongst themselves. This is why our rulers were ousted by foreigners in our land. We all come from King Vijaya's bloodline, after all.

And yet, the women would mutter to themselves, and yet the men never learned.

Was this what had happened to Thaththa? Was he also a victim of a curse that had spanned generations? Was Kuveni's wrath enough to impact us, even now? Or was the answer simpler than that? Much closer to home?

But these questions did nothing to ease the worry in my heart.

I BREWED A mug of beli maal in the kitchen and took it to Amma. I lightly touched her shoulder, but she jerked away like I had thrown the drink in her face.

"I'm sorry I startled you, Amma. Here's some beli maal," I said, keeping my voice low so I wouldn't wake Thaththa. He slept restlessly, thrashing in fits of shallow dreams.

"Oh, thank you," Amma said, her voice listless. Her tone left me unsettled.

"Amma, I'm going into town. We are low on a few things for the kitchen, like coconut oil. I thought I'll go and get some."

Guilt bled into my crisp morning, wilting away my good mood. But I had to keep digging. I had to keep trying to solve who was behind the attacks.

Sister Agatha from school often said that the path to sin is a slippery slope. And deception is a sin, so that definitely, certainly, without doubt made me a sinner. And if I were a sinner, was I just as bad as the men who were being attacked? Would that make me one of them?

I tried asking Bhagya about this, after we met in the jungle and walked over to Upali's hut. I'd somewhat unwillingly filled her in on what I saw outside Loku Banda's shop. She didn't say much. Upali was the third and last man on our list, other than Jeevan Maama and Thaththa.

"The way I see it is a little different," Bhagya replied, quietly.

"So you don't think all sins are the same?"

"Well, I think there are things we do that hurt people, and there are things we do that don't. As long as what I do doesn't hurt someone, or put them in harm, then I'd rather not worry about it."

"Even if it's wrong?"

"Who gets to decide what's right and what's wrong? A religion or a philosophy that's been changed and convoluted to fit language and culture and politics? Who gets to set the rules? Tell me, do you think that lying to your parents so you can help your father is just as bad as a grown man beating his wife and child?"

"Um, no," I replied meekly.

"Exactly." She looked triumphant, and I kept quiet. I didn't want to get into an argument with her. She was right—I wasn't hurting anyone. I wasn't the same as the men we were spying on, even though spying on people certainly didn't feel like a good thing to do.

WE APPROACHED THE small hut where Upali lived with his parents, slowing down as we walked past it. We had decided that we would first try to spot Upali before going up to his house, where we would most likely be greeted by his mother. Two unmarried girls calling on a young man was most unseemly, and Amma would have a heart attack if word ever got back to her.

Our eyes darted around as we tried our best to look nonchalant, but it was harder to find a safe vantage point this time around.

Upali's hut lay alone, surrounded by a large, flat land punctured only with coconut trees. The trees themselves were connected by tightly tied ropes at their peak, a spiderweb that zigzagged right through the property. His family didn't own the land. To possess that many coconut trees was a sure sign of wealth. Upali's father had simply leased the land from an Englishman, probably paying him a monthly fee per tree, which Upali would tap for toddy.

Every day, Upali would tuck a heavy mallet and a sharp knife into a basket around his waist, pay his respects to the tree by worshipping it, and ascend fifty feet to the very top. When he found the coconut flower stalks, he would use his knife to slit them open, allowing the sap to ooze into a clay pot. After finishing the first tree, he would move across the tightrope connecting the next one, as though it was an airborne maze, repeating this process until he had moved through all the coconut trees on his land. I'd watched Upali's father speed through on these ropes when I was a child, and it reminded me of how ants would cross a clothesline—nimble, agile, more at home on a rope high up near the sky than on the land.

After allowing the pots to fill overnight, Upali would return the next morning and lower them down to his father, who had given up climbing since he had taken a fall a few years ago. After that, things moved fast. The family would race to transfer the toddy to bottles and transport it to the market. Fresh toddy fermented into alcohol in just a few hours. A few more and it turned into vinegar, mostly used for preserving fruit and vegetables. Some of the women would cook the toddy down, turning it into treacle used in jaggery or sweetmeats.

Perhaps it was the dangers of his job, perhaps it was because he was still rather young, but Upali was unmarried. There was no wife to ill-treat or be unfaithful to.

I gazed at the treetops, wondering if he was already up there, but I couldn't spot him. The coconut trees stood empty, the ropes a bare tangle against the piercing blue morning sky.

"Could he still be recovering from his wounds?" It had been about two weeks now.

Bhagya didn't reply, still looking for a safe hiding place even though there were none to be found. The hut looked empty too—no fire outside, no laundry hanging out to dry, no voices or chatter or anything but the cries of the occasional monkey.

"Have they gone somewhere, do you think?" I asked.

Bhagya was frowning now. She still didn't answer any of my questions, but peered down the road.

"Someone's coming."

"What? Where?"

She pointed. There was indeed someone; it looked like a girl about our age, maybe a little younger, coming towards us.

"We should go," Bhagya whispered. Her voice was low and urgent.

"Go where?" I asked. Upali's house was at the end of the road. The only way back was to pass the girl. We could run towards the coconut trees, but their trunks were far too narrow for us to hide behind.

Bhagya looked upset.

"Look, we're not doing anything wrong," I tried. "We're just walking, right? Come on."

"No, you don't understand. We shouldn't be seen."

"Too late for that now," I said under my breath.

The girl eyed me curiously as she approached us. I smiled back, politely nodding in her direction. I recognised her from around the town, though I'd never spoken to her before. I think she might have been a year younger than I was, though I couldn't be sure. She looked pale and drawn. Her eyes were shadowed and red, and her hair fell out of its plait like she'd never bothered to brush it after she woke up that morning.

"Is this Upali's house?" she asked, pointing down the road. There was so much sadness in her eyes as she looked at me. The kind of sadness that makes your heart weep just by being near it.

"I—I think so," I replied.

"Do you know if he's in? I came yesterday also, but he wasn't there."

"Um, I'm not sure. Maybe you could check?"

"If that really is his house, his parents won't let me see him. They pretend no one's home."

"Oh, I see." I didn't know what else to say. I looked over at Bhagya, but she was staring down at the ground, refusing to meet anyone's eye.

"Well, we should get going." I made to walk past the girl, but she suddenly grabbed my arm.

"Did you come here to see him too?" she snarled, suddenly vicious.

"What?"

"Upali. Were you with him? Now? Is that why he won't speak to me anymore?"

"Of course not!"

"His house is the only one down this road. You must be coming from there now. Did you sleep with him last night?"

"No! I've never met him. I don't know what you're talking about."

"Liar!" Her voice was loud and hoarse. "He's refusing to see me since the attack. I need to speak to him. Please."

I tried pulling my arm away, looking over at Bhagya again,

silently pleading with her to do something, but she stood silent, rooted to the spot.

"Let me go." I kept my voice mild. I didn't want to upset this strange girl further.

"Not unless you give him a message from me. I don't care if you're his new woman. Just tell him—tell him that if he won't see me, I'll kill myself."

"Listen, I really don't—"

"Tell him I'll kill his baby. You do that, you hear? Tell him I'm expecting. And unlike him"—she shot me a look of disgust—"I've only ever had one partner."

"Look, I'm sorry, we really have to go."

She looked a little confused then, like she was searching for something, and I managed to break free.

"I don't know how to help you. I'm sorry, I really am." My words tumbled out of me as I hurried away.

I didn't even look to see if Bhagya was with me, I just ran as fast as I could back down the road and into the jungle. I stopped only when I was certain we were far enough to be safe.

I rested my back on a tree and sank to the ground. I guess Bhagya had followed me after all, because she did the same.

I eyed her as she sat, looking as dejected as the girl we met outside of Upali's house.

"Why didn't you say something?" I asked her.

"What could I have said?" Her voice was laced with sadness.

"Well, she looked like she was about to attack me, but you didn't do anything." Irritation edged its way into my voice. I needed her, and she'd just frozen like a startled deer.

"Amara, why are you upset with me?"

"Because this whole ridiculous plan to find out more about

these men was your idea and the moment someone confronted us, you just left me there."

"I didn't leave you." Her voice was calm and that irritated me more.

"You might as well have!" I shot back.

"Amara, that isn't the real reason you're angry and you know it."

"What? What on earth do you mean?"

"You're upset because all the men who were attacked were terrible people and you're worried that means your father is one of them too."

"No!" It was all I could manage, because she was only partly right. I wasn't just worried that Thaththa was terrible. I was worried that meant I was at fault in some way too.

"You already know that your father was being unfaithful to your mother. Even after she left her family to be with him, and all the sacrifices that she's made."

How dare she?

I didn't need to take this. Of course I was upset that Thaththa was having an affair with Siripala's wife, but that didn't mean he deserved to be attacked, his skin flayed, drowning in pain and horror.

"I need to get home now." I stood up and squared my shoulders. It had been nice to have a new friend for a while, but something about Bhagya left me feeling at odds with myself. The way she was hinting at things she expected me to understand. The way she was fixed on proving her own ideas, rather than searching for what had truly happened.

Bhagya was too extreme. Perhaps it was what happened to her before, perhaps it was just the way she was. At a different point of my life, I would have tried to be more patient. I would have coaxed the truth out of her, perhaps, and tried to soothe her wounds. But right now, I had my own problems to worry about. I had to understand what had happened to me. Sneaking around, trying to learn more about the characters and morals of the attacked men, wouldn't change that.

"You know," I continued, "when we started all this, I thought you were trying to help me find answers about what happened to my father. I thought we were trying to understand more about the attacks. But all you've done is fixate on these men's wrongdoings. How will that change anything?"

"Amara, don't you understand?" Her voice was soft, pleading. It made me want to scream. "It does change things. It changes everything."

"You're wrong. We don't have the right to go around judging people like this. Spying on them. It doesn't help a soul."

"You don't think uncovering the truth helps anyone?"

I took a deep breath, trying to steady myself. There was no need to take my anger out on her. Perhaps if Thaththa wasn't shivering in pain on the floor of our hut, perhaps if I'd been able to shake the feeling that I was tied up in the attacks in some way, perhaps then I'd have been able to go on this fool's journey with her. But I had more important things to do. I didn't care about the attacked men. I needed to find out who was responsible for hurting them.

"I don't think we should meet anymore."

I walked back home, trying not to think about how much my head spun and my heart hurt, but all the same it felt good to speak my mind. At least I hadn't just stood there, stupid and dumbfounded like I had with Daphne and Aloysius.

But as I walked and my head cleared, I started to think about everything I'd witnessed about the men who were attacked. If I put the doubts of my own possible attack aside, and accepted that the men, Thaththa included, were all terrible to women—their wives, their girlfriends, and whoever else—then who would wish them harm?

The women they were hurting?

Or someone else?

35

THE THOUGHT BURROWED its way into my mind and wriggled its way around like a worm seeking release. It wasn't like the women in our town had some sort of assembly where they could air their grievances. I was sure that Siripala's wife and Loku Banda's wife and certainly my mother weren't friends in any way.

But if the men who were hurting them had a common enemy, who could it possibly be?

I racked my brain, trying to think of something Thaththa had told me. While demons sometimes acted of their own accord, especially if they were slighted in some way, the most common occurrence of them hurting someone was if another person used the power of the demon to carry out their bidding. It was why everyone had been so quick to blame Thaththa for the attacks, after all. He had, at least according to the villagers' understanding, the most involvement with demons.

But he'd obviously never attack himself, so who else could it be?

"Did you manage to get everything we needed?" Amma called. Her voice was hoarse, her eyes bloodshot.

"No, Amma. I'll go back again later today," I lied, marvelling at how easily the words rolled off my tongue.

"Premalatha from the village came by earlier. She said she saw you wandering all alone through the market yesterday."

"I wasn't by myself. I was with my friend Bhagya. She needed some things for her aunt so I went with her," I replied.

"Who's Bhagya?"

"She's new. She lives with her punchi."

"In town?"

"Their hut is in the jungle close to town, I think."

Was it me, or did Amma pale a little?

"Isn't that where that woman with the sight lives?"

"She lives close to her, though I've never been to her place."

"You shouldn't go by that way. The jungle is dangerous." Amma always found a way to discourage me from wandering.

"Yes, Amma."

"I don't think I've seen you eat anything for a while now. You need to take care of yourself, you hear?" Her words went straight to my heart. Here she was, worrying about me, running herself ragged caring for Thaththa, and what was I doing instead of helping her? Prancing off with a girl I barely knew, lying through my teeth, trying to solve a mystery that was clearly out of my depth. When did I become so very selfish?

There was nothing I could do right now about the thoughts that whistled through my mind anyway. I just needed to think. And I could certainly do that while trying to make myself useful.

Picking up the ilpotha, I swept the hut, and then the outside kitchen. Some women from the village had brought over dried fish, so I lit a fire and set about making a curry. I scraped some coconut and kneaded some dough for roti as well, flattening it before balancing the flat pan on top of the fire. It soothed me to work, somehow. It kept my mind off the pain and embarrassment of the last few days. It kept my thoughts off Bhagya. It gave me the space to think about this impossible puzzle I'd been trying to solve, when I didn't even have all the pieces.

But still, the smell of the freshly cooked meal left me feeling ill. I served a plate and took it to where my mother sat on the verandah. She had just finished changing Thaththa's bandages again.

"Here, Amma, you should eat this."

She looked in surprise at the plate I handed to her. I was expecting a lecture—something about how I'd salted the curry too much, or burned the roti. No matter what I did it tasted odd to me. But she only gave me a tired smile.

"Thank you, baba." *Baby.* She hadn't called me that since I was a child, and I almost dropped the plate in surprise. Amma really must be exhausted.

I quickly gathered the set of old bandages so she couldn't see my face.

"Let me go wash these," I said, hastily. She gave me another weak smile.

"Would you mind checking on my order list to see if there's anything due this week? I might need you to pay them a visit if so, and let them know there's a delay."

"Of course, Amma."

I went to the drawer in her sewing machine where she kept a small ledger detailing orders from her various customers. I flipped it over to this week and studied the page. We were in luck—there was nothing that needed attention immediately. That was a relief. I checked last week's as well, just to make sure that we were all caught up. Amma had everything under control. She was always so organised, so meticulous. Everything I seemed to lack.

A name at the top of the list did catch my eye—Mary.

I'd dropped her jacket off with Loku Banda yesterday, of course.

But something about seeing her name sparked an idea. I leafed through her book a little more.

Leelawathi. That was Siripala's wife. Amma had sewn her son some shirts about a month ago, before Siripala asked Thaththa to bless his hut.

I didn't know the name of the girl we had met outside Upali's, but I was willing to bet Amma had sewn something for her, or at least for her mother. I was so silly not to have thought about it earlier. Amma was one of the more popular seamstresses in the village, especially for those who couldn't afford the fancy tailor who had his own shop in the town square. Of course she would know most of the women.

But simply knowing them didn't mean she could be responsible for the attacks. That would take knowledge of demonology and would require years of practice.

She *had* been married to my father for eighteen years, a small voice in my head murmured. Surely she could have picked up some things from him?

And then didn't she sell her earrings to make a payment at Jayasiri's shop? The very shop where she could buy everything she needed to carry out such demonic acts? She did say that she was paying it on Thaththa's behalf, but that could easily have been a lie.

But even if she was lying, she wouldn't attack her own brother. She loved Jeevan Maama and he was even helping us financially now. But the last thing she said about him nagged me like a thorn—*Even he's changed these last few years. All men eventually do.*

I walked back over to where Thaththa rested, chest rising and falling softly. He'd look like a child being put down for a nap by his mother if it weren't for the bandages all over his face and limbs. Even though Amma had just changed them, bright red was already blooming on the white fabric. Amma sighed as she put a cold rag over his forehead. She looked so much older than she had just a few days ago, her eyes like hollow cavities. My chest squeezed. I'd been running around like a silly schoolgirl, leaving her to tend to Thaththa without pause.

Tending to him so carefully that she didn't even let me help with his remedies.

A thought shot through me like an arrow, but still I shook it off.

There was no way, no way at all that she would do something like this.

I'll kill everyone myself if I have to. This cannot get out. Her voice rang as clear as a bell. She'd said it while my father sobbed.

I felt dazed. I needed to sit down.

But a voice at our fence pierced my thoughts.

"Amara?"

It was Neha, along with her sister Catharine.

"Neha, Catharine! Hello. This is a surprise!"

"We heard the news about your father, and thought we'd visit to give you our condolences," Catharine explained. "The family is together today since our parents returned. Dandris and our father have arranged for the whole family to go for the perahera, so we thought it would be best to visit before we left."

Neha was holding a small pot in her hand, which she presented to my mother.

"Good afternoon, Kumari Nanda." She'd known my family for so long that she referred to my parents as Aunt and Uncle. "I'm sorry I couldn't visit Maama sooner. I brought this balm made from the bark of the ehela tree. It's supposed to soothe the skin."

My mother smiled pleasantly, despite being so tired. She'd always liked Neha. She probably wished she had a daughter who was more like her—soft and peaceful and sweet and religious. Not one who disappeared into the jungle every chance she got.

"Neha, Catharine, how kind of you both. We've missed seeing you, Neha. I hope you're well?"

Neha exchanged pleasantries with Amma. I fidgeted the whole time, worried that she'd let slip that we'd met earlier in the jungle, but Neha was perfect. They chatted about my father's recovery, about herbal remedies, and whether or not the monsoons would start early this year. Even I was surprised at how well it was going.

"I heard there's a proposal in the works, Neha. Your parents must be very pleased."

A proposal? She had mentioned something about a proposal when I visited to take her measurements. Perhaps that was what she meant when she said she had a lot to tell me.

But Neha just smiled, splotches of pink appearing on her cheeks.

"Would it be alright if I prayed for Maama, Kumari Nanda? I thought it might bring you some comfort."

My mother nodded, her face soft and grateful. She'd left the church behind when she married my father, but I knew she still prayed when things were difficult. Could she stray so far from her beliefs that she'd practice demonology herself? I was surely mistaken in my suspicions. Everything that was happening was causing me to overreact.

Catharine and I closed our eyes and bowed our heads, while Neha knelt down next to my mother.

"Dear Heavenly Father," Neha started, her voice soft and melodious and different somehow from how she usually sounded. "We thank you for bringing your son back to us. During these difficult times we know that you are with us, watching us and guiding us. Please deliver him from his injuries, and please let him know that he is not alone in these trying times. I also pray for Kumari Nanda and my dearest friend, Amara, that they will have the strength to endure these tribulations. That you will continue to grant them your grace, and most importantly, your comfort, while Maama recovers. We ask this in your name, amen."

"Amen," Amma repeated, and I found myself mumbling it too. I had always wished that I could see God the way Neha did—as kind and gentle. Somone who looked down on us with love, not fire and thunder and rage. I envied Neha, then. I envied how she could be so sure of herself, when I was left floundering, uncertain of my parents, uncertain of my faith, uncertain of myself.

"We are just leaving to Devinuwara, Kumari Nanda, so we had best take your leave. Please let me know if the balm helps. I'll be more than happy to bring more."

"Yes, dear, thank you."

Neha got up to leave, but Catharine hesitated.

"Actually, Kumari Nanda, and I apologise if this is forward or insensitive of me, but would Amara perhaps like to join us for the perahera? My father received a special invitation because of his post at the governor's office. We have arranged for a cart to take us, and there is definitely space for her. My family and Dandris's will be there, so she will be accompanied, of course. It might be a welcome break for her. I know these last few days haven't been easy."

"Oh, that's very kind of you, Catharine," I started to explain, "but I don't think—"

"What a wonderful idea, and how generous of you, Catharine," Amma interrupted, much to my surprise. "Amara would certainly enjoy the perahera, I think. A much-needed break for her." Amma had never shown much enthusiasm towards religious festivals like this, and I was surprised to think she'd start now.

"Amma, I couldn't possibly leave you and Thaththa right now."

"You fretting around here and wearing yourself down with worry won't bring anyone any good, child. Go and enjoy yourself."

Who was this intruder and what had she done with my mother?

Neha and Catharine were looking at me in delight, but something felt wrong.

"No, Amma, I really should stay." Why did she want me gone? Was it so she could summon the yakshaniya again? So she could do something to Thaththa without me being in the way?

"Nonsense, child. It makes little difference to me. There's plenty of food, and your father and I will just be resting. Besides, it would be rude to decline an invitation from your oldest friends."

"It's decided, then. Get your things, Amara. The cart leaves from our house in an hour."

This felt like one of my bad dreams all over again, but I had to be logical. If Amma truly wanted to hurt Thaththa, then she had plenty of opportunities to do him harm. She was his wife, for goodness' sake.

I quickly changed into some clean clothes and hurried away with Catharine and Neha, the pressure finally making me give way to my friends' request.

"I know you're worried about your father, Amara, but this will be good for you, you wait and see," Neha whispered as we hurried to the main road. There was a small cart waiting to take us to Catharine's house.

"Thank you, Neha." I firmly pushed my doubts about Amma to the back of my mind. What kind of daughter could ever accuse her own mother of such a thing anyway? I mustn't be so desperate for answers that I'd see evil at every corner. "I really am excited to go. Raam has been asking me about going for a while now, but I never thought I'd get permission. And then it didn't seem quite so important."

I thought I saw Neha's smile drop a little.

"You still see Raam?" she asked. I knew Neha didn't approve. She'd never had a boyfriend and had always said it was wrong to sneak around. It was why I'd never truly confided in her about the extent of our relationship.

I just shrugged, and luckily Catharine interrupted.

"Let's hurry," she said to the driver. "The last thing we want is for everyone to leave without us. You remember Jacyntha, my sister-in-law, don't you? She'd leave us behind in a heartbeat if given the slightest chance."

"Catharine!" chided Neha. "You mustn't say such things. It's highly unbecoming of a woman in your position!"

Catharine burst into laughter and I felt a rare smile curl on my face. Surely, I could have just one night to enjoy myself.

36

DEVINUWARA LITERALLY TRANSLATES to "the kingdom of the gods." The Sri Vishnu Maha Devalaya—the Great Temple of Blessed Vishnu—stood at the centre of the temple compound, painted blue with intricate white trim. Even though a perahera itself was considered a Buddhist tradition, Buddhism and Hinduism were joined together so tightly on this island that to distinguish them separately almost felt like trying to divide the sky and the ocean where they meet at the horizon. The two religions had, for as long as we all knew, coexisted harmoniously. It started with the kings, my father had explained to me when I was younger. Even though the kings were mostly Buddhist, their queens, usually made so by arranged marriages from India, often practiced Hinduism. The kings would devote a section of their temples to their wives' gods, so they could worship in unison.

The Devinuwara temple was no different. We laid pink and white lotuses at the statue of the Buddha under the large boh tree and recited a small prayer as soon as we arrived. The flowers were a symbol, Thaththa explained to me when I was younger, of how fleeting life is. That nothing is supposed to last forever.

I eyed Neha as she placed her flowers in front of the statue as well.

"I thought you don't say these prayers anymore," I couldn't help but ask.

She gave me a small smile.

"Someone told me that I didn't respect other religions, and I'm trying to change that."

And she was right. Religious ideologies aside, a perahera was enjoyed by all. Far more cultural than religious anyway, most of the town had gathered around the Temple of Vishnu to watch the parade. Small clay lamps twinkled, making us feel like the gods themselves anointed this day. Crowds of locals as well as Englishmen milled around—some marvelling at the temple itself, others offering prayers at the smaller altars built on the side for various other gods. A handful of people were breaking coconuts—raising their arms high into the air and smashing the brown fruit onto a stone. It was a special offering to the deviyo. One that demonstrated exceptional devotion.

But there was something different in the air tonight. Glances over shoulders, mothers holding on to their children a little too tightly, groups being warned not to leave anyone behind, especially when walking back home. News of the attacks had spread far and wide, it seemed.

Neha's and Dandris's parents, Dandris, and Catharine were invited to sit beneath a makeshift canopy, along with other businessmen and government servants from town, but Neha whispered animatedly to her father for a few minutes, and then told me we could wander around.

We happily escaped the stuffy tent, and Neha bought us some sweetened, grated coconut, which was served in a betel leaf cone. We must have looked a sight, an elegant, upper-class woman and the island's witch roaming around, hand in hand, nibbling on coconut.

But despite everything around me, I kept thinking of Amma's ledger, of all the women she knew. Perhaps those women had confided in her. Perhaps they'd told her what their husbands or boyfriends had been up to. Or perhaps she'd gathered as much, when she visited them?

I did keep my eyes peeled for Raam. He wasn't expecting me today, but I was hoping I could surprise him.

"Want a bit of the betel leaf?" Neha asked, popping a piece into her mouth.

"Sure," I replied, but I chewed on it only a moment before spitting it out.

I have you now, you little bitch. The words, the very words that I had forgotten about over the last few days, crashed back into my mind. I looked around, inexplicably shuddering. How did this fit into everything that was happening?

"Are you alright?" Neha asked, looking concerned.

"Yes, I'm fine."

"Then come on, the tom-tom drummers have started. It's about to begin!"

She grabbed my hand, and we found a spot where we could watch the procession.

There were dancers dressed up as demons, wearing wooden masks and grass skirts, drawing gasps from the audience. We saw both the up-country as well as low-country dancers, each dressed in red and white, some of them somersaulting. The stilt-walkers made me and Neha clutch each other, afraid they would tumble down, but they simply smiled at us as they danced, their added height as exciting to them as it was to us. There were bands of singers, drummers, and those dressed up in animal costumes. There was even a group doing a comedic skit while dressed up as Englishmen. Neha and I clapped and cheered, and the more we did, the more my doubts about Amma slid out of my mind.

There was a brief break between performances, and Neha grabbed my arm.

"Amara, I need to ask you something." She looked solemn.

"What is it?"

"You mentioned earlier that you were hoping to meet Raam—"

But we were interrupted by a haughty voice from behind us.

"I'm surprised they let a witch onto this sacred land." It was Daphne. I knew it even before I turned around. Of course she'd be here tonight. The entire town usually attended this perahera, and she'd never pass the opportunity to flit around feeling superior to everyone else.

Her hair was curled and piled high on her head, and she wore a beautiful pink dress in the style of the British. She stood a whole foot above me, surrounded by a few of her friends, one of which, to no surprise, was Jacyntha—Catharine's sister-in-law. And she was with her fiancé.

"Amara," Aloysius said, dipping his chin by way of greeting.

"Good evening, Daphne, Aloysius," I said, eyeing Neha, who had gone red in the face. I could tell she was upset, even by the light of all the flames. And of course she would be. Aloysius was a Mudaliyar's aide, and her father worked closely with the governor. It wouldn't do for her to be openly rude to him. Neither would she be forgiven for openly snubbing Jacyntha.

"There's nothing good about this evening with you here, witch!" one of the women in their group, whose name I didn't know, screeched.

"Clarice! Shush!" Daphne said dramatically, giggling. "It's just a joke," she said, addressing Neha, her smirk just as infuriating now as it had always been.

"Ladies," Aloysius said, smiling at them jovially, "perhaps we should go back to our seats. There's really no need to draw any more attention to these un-Christian ways."

"Anything you say, Aloysius," Jacyntha cooed. Did she flutter her eyelashes at him? Then her mouth contorted into a cruel sneer as she eyed me. "The last thing we want is a curse on us too."

"That's enough," Neha said. She kept her voice light, giving everyone a smile. "There's no need to make such jokes, Daphne, Jacyntha, Clarice."

"You're quite right, Neha. I'm bored already," Daphne drawled, turning away, taking Aloysius's arm while looking pointedly at Jacyntha. A few men came up to Aloysius and shook his hand reverently, bowing their heads low.

But Jacyntha wasn't paying attention to them. "Neha, will you join us in our tent?" she asked, a wicked glint in her eye. "I'm sure your father wouldn't want you wandering around like this. It's most improper."

She knew exactly what she was doing.

Neha's eyes widened as she realised what I had known for a very long time—that sooner or later, regardless of her apologies or tearful confessions in the jungle, sooner or later she would have to choose a side. But she was my friend, and I loved her, and I didn't want her to suffer. Not on my account.

"You go with them," I whispered. "I'll catch up to you later."

"No, Amara. I'll stay with you. Don't go."

"It's fine, Neha. I understand, really. I'll meet you later."

"Are you going to meet Raam?" she asked, her voice a fierce whisper.

I knew it. She was still trying to control me with her piety. But she could follow the rules if she wanted; they were never for me.

"You shouldn't insult your in-laws," I ordered. "I will find you later, alright?"

And with that, I turned and left her.

37

I KEPT TO the shadows after I left them. I didn't want any of the town gossips to see me walking around unaccompanied. Things felt different from this angle. The firelight danced off the faces of people, turning them into demons. Monsters lurked in the nooks and crevices, waiting for their next prey. I felt on edge, like even the slightest motion would send me tumbling down.

Thankfully, I found Raam not more than a few minutes after I left Neha. I could have spotted his cowlicked hair from anywhere.

For a brief moment, I thought he saw me too. The firelight danced over his face, illuminating it differently somehow to the others. His eyes widened slightly, then narrowed, before he turned away and started walking towards the direction of the beach.

Surely he must have been mistaken? Perhaps he didn't see me in this dim light.

I wove my way through the crowd, as nimble as a jungle cat. The beach was further away from the temple, and it took a few minutes for me to reach him.

"Raam!" I finally caught up and pulled on his elbow. "Raam, it's me! Wait!"

But when Raam turned around, he looked at me like a stranger—with hurt and anger instead of the love and tenderness I was used to.

"I'm surprised you even remembered me," he replied, his eyes downcast. I looked around. The crowd had thinned significantly where we were, honda velawata. *Thank goodness.*

"Raam, what's that supposed to mean? I came all the way here to see you."

"Oh, did you now?" His voice trembled. "Are you sure it was just me you came to see?"

The tips of my ears felt hot. I didn't know what he was talking about. Why was he being this way?

"I don't understand what you mean, Raam. Who else would I come to see anyway?"

Anger flashed in his eyes then.

"Do you take me for some sort of fool, Amara?"

"Raam, I—"

"You know, everyone warned me about you. The demon worshipper's daughter is bad news, they said. Stay away from her. She's loose. Her parents care more about chasing after yakku than raising her right."

"Raam!" I was shocked. He'd never spoken to me like that before. My voice had gone high-pitched and it attracted the attention of a few festival-goers nearby. "Why are you speaking like this?"

He seemed to notice the attention we were getting also. Wrapping his hand around the upper part of my arm, he led me away towards the shore. He walked fast, and I was tripping over myself in my efforts to keep up, the damp sand kicking out from under me.

"Raam, slow down."

His fingers were digging into the soft flesh of my arm.

"Raam, you're hurting me."

But he didn't stop until we were far away from the crowd. Until there was no one around to hear us. Then, finally, he turned me to face him, letting go of me and crossing his arms over his chest.

"I can't believe you would do this to me, Amara. I've loved you so much."

"What is it, Raam? What have I done?"

"So you deny it, then?"

"Deny what? Tell me what you think I'm so guilty of."

"Do you deny that you're to be betrothed?"

"Betrothed?"

"Yes, betrothed to Desmond De'Fontaine. It's all over town. What a step up this must be for you."

It felt like the wind was knocked out of me.

"What? Oh, no, Raam, that's just—that's just a misunderstanding."

"Oh, please, Amara. You can drop the act. No wonder you've been avoiding me. I've been watching, you know. I've seen you sneaking away from your house. Telling me that you had to take care of your father instead. But you haven't been at home, and you haven't been to see me. And then guess what I got to know?"

"What?" I didn't want to know the answer. I knew it couldn't be anything good.

"I heard you were caught leaving Upali the toddy tapper's house early in the morning today. What do you make of that?"

"Surely, Raam, you can't be serious?"

"First Desmond, and now Upali? All while you swear to love me, and that you want to marry me."

A tear dashed down his cheek and he wiped it away forcefully. I was dumbfounded.

I took a deep breath. I could barely hear the ocean, so loud was the beating of my heart.

"Raam, I promise you, on my life and yours. I'll promise you on anything you ask me to, there never was or never will be anyone else for me but you. I love you. Why would I ever want another?"

"Then why is Desmond De'Fontaine all but yelling it out to the whole west coast that he is to be your husband?"

"I don't know, Raam! I haven't agreed to anything. My mother blindsided me with a meeting, that was all. It was at my grandparents', so I couldn't refuse. I told you, Raam, I told you they were getting anxious about me. That's why I kept asking you to talk to them. There was only so much I could do on my own. Now my mother wants me to marry him, even though I've refused."

"So you're blaming me for all this? It's my fault, is it?"

I sighed. What a disaster. I should have told Raam as soon as it happened, but Desmond De'Fontaine and everything at my grandparents' house fell right out of my head as soon as I'd heard about Thaththa's attack.

"No, Raam, of course it's not your fault. I should have told you sooner that I was tricked into meeting him. But it happened just before Thaththa's attack, and you know how upset I've been about it. I'm just waiting for him to recover so I can talk to him. I know he'll listen to me."

"What if he won't?"

"He will!" I insisted.

"And what about Upali? Do you deny you were at his house?"

I paused, and my silence sent him on another spiral.

"I knew it! I knew I was right. I can't believe you."

"No, no, Raam. Listen. I can explain everything."

A laugh I had never heard escaped his lips. Wicked and hard. Foreign on the soft mouth I used to kiss with so much longing.

"Well, you can try, but I don't know if I'll ever believe you."

It was time to come clean to him. To explain what was going on.

"Listen to me, please. And after you've heard me out then you can decide for yourself. I promise, Raam, I love you and I'd never do anything to hurt you. To hurt what we have."

He raised an eyebrow, and I launched on.

"After my father's attack, I was upset. And I thought, well, we thought—"

"Who's *we*?"

"Me and Bhagya. She's a friend of mine. She's been helping me."

"Helping you do what?"

Helping me with something so ridiculously juvenile that I was embarrassed to speak of it, but I had to tell Raam. He deserved to know the truth. "We thought there might have been some sort of connection between the attacks. We've been studying the other victims, trying to see if there was . . . well, something. Anything to help us understand what was happening."

"And was there?"

I felt heat rise in my cheeks. I shook my head. I couldn't tell him that the only connection was that the men were all terrible people, my father included. About my suspicions about my mother.

"No. We were wrong. I just wanted to, well, I wanted to do something. Something that might help Thaththa, even if it did feel a little far-fetched. That's why we were at Upali's house. We didn't go in or anything. I don't think he was even there. We were just trying to see if we could find anything out about him. About how he was attacked."

"So that's what happened? You're not lying to me?"

"You know I could never lie to you. It was stupid, I know. I was stupid." A quiver had crept into my voice.

"Why didn't you tell me, then? That this is what you've been up to?"

"I—" The words got lost on their way out of my throat. Why didn't I want to tell him?

"Because I knew, deep down, that there was nothing I could do. I just wanted to help. I hated seeing my father hurt."

He gave me a small smile then. Sympathy was starting to take hold of him, I could tell.

"And Desmond? You promise me there's nothing there?"

"Of course not, Raam. It was all a mistake. I didn't even know I was to meet him, and I barely even spoke to him directly."

"You're so innocent, Amara. But also so naive. Come here."

I collapsed into his arms, holding him harder than I ever have.

"I'm sorry, Raam." My voice was wobbling all over the place.

"It's alright. Just don't keep things from me again."

I nodded in his chest, relief flooding through me.

"You do love me, don't you?" His voice was kind again, like I was used to.

I nodded again.

"I love you more than anything, Raam."

He reached down, tilting my chin upwards. His lips brushed mine softly, hesitantly. His next words, when he spoke them, were soft too. So soft that it took me a moment to understand the gravity of what he was saying.

"Then prove it to me."

I felt a beat pass. And then another. The sounds of the perahera had faded into the distance. All I could hear was the waves crashing, close enough that I thought they would knock me over.

"Raam—"

"Show me, Amara. Show me that you love me."

His lips encased mine, his tongue probing its way into my mouth as my heart took flight like a bird.

Every argument why I should and shouldn't do this grappled in my mind.

I loved Raam. I didn't want to lose him. What if he lost interest in me like my father had lost interest in my mother? What if he changed his mind about marrying me?

But I didn't feel ready.

Was I ever supposed to feel ready?

But where would we do it? Here, on the ground?

Would there ever be a perfect moment? Was I searching for something that didn't exist? I thought back to all the women who had been wronged by their husbands. Did waiting for marriage help them in any way?

And all the while my mind raced, Raam kissed me deeper, his hands pushing underneath my good white blouse with the mark on the sleeve that didn't wash off. My mother would be so angry if I ruined this blouse further, I thought stupidly as Raam, his body pressing hard against mine, started leading me behind a large cluster of rocks. Finding one that was low and flat, he put his hands on my shoulders, making me kneel, getting on his knees on the rock alongside me.

"You are so beautiful," he said, his voice just a breath.

"So are you," I said. Or maybe I only thought it. I wasn't sure. I wasn't sure of myself.

"I love you, Amara. You trust me, don't you? You love me, right?"

I nodded. Of course. Of course I loved him and trusted him and wanted to give him everything. So why was my body recoiling at his touch? Why did I want, more than anything, to be back at home in our little hut, curled up on my hard mat and listening to the sounds of the cicadas?

But Raam had undone the clasps on my blouse and the cold air felt sharp against my chest.

"You are so beautiful," he murmured again.

I closed my eyes and leaned back. I should enjoy this. I was supposed to enjoy it. I'd enjoyed it when he kissed me, didn't I? When he held me close and stroked my back and our bodies felt like they fit perfectly into each other.

But something pushed its way into the back of my mind. Something sharp, and cold, and painful. My legs clenched together instinctively, and my body stiffened.

"You like that, don't you?" Raam said with a smile. I didn't realise that he'd started to push my reddha up. The rock felt rough and wet against my bare legs. And then against my bare thighs.

I didn't reply, but he wasn't really waiting for an answer.

Why was I so uneasy? Why was I anticipating the pain even before I felt it? And I certainly felt it, searing, tearing at me from between my legs, shooting up through my navel. I wanted to scream. I wanted to push him off me. But instead I pressed my palms hard against my mouth and remained frozen. Fear and hurt and disgust swept around me, through me, but still I was paralysed.

Raam grunted incoherently, his thrusting stilted. My eyes were closed. I didn't want to look at him.

Flashes of the woman from my dream clawed their way through my thoughts. She'd finally caught up to me, dragging her long, broken fingernails over my exposed skin. I gasped.

"It's good for you too, isn't it?" Raam asked. "I knew you'd like it."

He kept pushing in and out of me. I felt tears prick my eyes, but my hands never left my face. I tried to shut my mind away. This would end soon, I told myself. This would end soon and then I could go home.

And it might have been soon, or it might have been one hundred years, but Raam finally grunted and collapsed on me completely, flattening me against the rock.

"You were wonderful," he said, caressing the side of my face. He kissed me again, as he rolled to his side. I just lay there, limp, exhausted, sore.

He wiped himself off on his sarong and made to adjust my reddha. I sat up, gingerly, pulling the light fabric down, finally feeling some comfort.

"You didn't need to be so coy, you know. Playing hard to get with me. I can appreciate a woman who knows what she wants."

At what point did I want this? I wanted to ask, but I stayed quiet. I looked around—the moon was still shining brightly, a field of stars giving it a scattered audience. The waves still hurled themselves onto the powder-soft, silver sand. The coconut trees still swayed like lonely towers, thin and graceful. Everything was the same, and yet nothing was the same.

Raam held my hand and helped me from the rock. He kept me close, guiding me back towards the perahera like I was a fragile doll about to break.

"I love you, Amara. I love that now you're truly mine." We had started to reach the crowd again and so had to part ways before anyone saw us. "I can't wait till we are married and can do this every day."

I flinched at the thought. But why?

The woman from my nightmares briefly flashed in my mind again, even though it didn't make the slightest sense.

"AMARA!" NEHA CALLED, as Raam melted into the throng of people. "Where have you been? I've been looking for you!"

My face felt rusted shut as I forced my lips into a smile.

"I'm here," I said, in a voice that floated a million miles above me.

"I was starting to worry. Are you alright?"

I certainly didn't feel alright. I hoped she didn't notice how I was dusted in sea sand and how some of my hair had fallen out of its knot.

"They are serving coffee and biscuits at the tent. My father wanted me to ask you to join us."

"That's alright," I said. The last thing I wanted was to be ridiculed again. "I really don't think I should be anywhere I could bump into Daphne."

"What was that, witch? Are you talking about me?"

Daphne was right behind me as both Neha and I whipped around. She was by herself, holding a cone of grated coconut.

I was exhausted. My body ached. My mind was tired of racing from demons to attacks to my parents and now what had happened with Raam. I was at the end of my rope and could not suffer any more of Daphne's wickedness tonight.

"I was just leaving," I said.

"That's right, witch. Run away and tell your demon-worshipping father about me. I'm not afraid. My Aloysius is working to have him arrested as soon as he makes a recovery. We all know that he faked his own attack just to throw suspicion off himself."

"Daphne, that's enough," Neha interjected.

"Don't think your father's job protects you, Neha. When you dally with a witch, your soul is preyed on by the devil himself."

"Stop calling me a witch." The words burst out of me before I could get a handle on my tongue.

Daphne raised her eyebrows, a small smile playing on her lips. I was provoked and it made her happy.

"What did you say?"

"I said, stop calling me a witch." I was fed up. Fed up with her baseless accusations and lies. Fed up with the way she made me feel. Fed up that I never seemed to be able to do anything about it.

"Okay, then, I won't call you a witch. What shall I call you instead? Whore?"

I was stunned.

"Oh, no need to look so wide-eyed and innocent with me. I couldn't help but notice you disappeared off to the beach with Raam." She eyed me up and down. "Look at you. It's no small mystery what you were up to. Did you put a love spell on him too?"

Neha gasped. "Daphne! Stop spreading such horrendous lies!"

"Stop it now, Daphne." I felt all the blood in my body start to boil.

"I'll stop when I very well please, you whoring witch."

"Shut your mouth!" My voice grew louder. I didn't care if those around us could hear. Neha tried to put her hand on my shoulder, but I shrugged it off.

"Or what, you'll put a spell on me?" Daphne giggled. "Listen, you might have all the people in this town shuddering in their boots, but I'm not afraid of you."

"Well, you should be!" The yakshaniya flashed into my mind, and for the first time I wished I was her. What I wouldn't do to dig my claws into Daphne's smug face and rip her into tiny little pieces.

We glared at each other, all the mean, horrible things she'd done to me flashing through my mind. The cruel taunts in school. The chicken head in my cubby. The way she and Aloysius were plotting to have Thaththa arrested. The anger that burst through me only grew, its flame engulfing me as I shuddered in fury.

My eyes bored into Daphne's. She continued to smirk—untouchable—her pink, smooth cheeks dimpling. She looked like one of the cherubs I'd seen painted on the walls of chapels, despite having more evil in her heart than Satan himself.

Anger coursed through me, thicker and more vicious than any poison. I couldn't look away from her. I could barely even move.

And then, as I stared at her with a rage so deep my body hurt, Daphne's eyes started to get glassy and come unfocused. Her skin paled from pink to grey and her face went slack. She gave a small shudder first, and then another, and another before breaking out in complete convulsions. One of the passersby noticed her and started to scream, but Daphne's mind was somewhere else as she slid onto the ground, her head lolling from side to side. She had urinated on herself while her mouth foamed. Her eyes slid back in her head, showing only the whites.

I couldn't move. I couldn't even stop looking at her. Horror replaced rage as I just stood there, dumbfounded about what was happening.

"What's happening here?" Aloysius boomed, pushing his way

through the crowd, noticing his fiancée on the floor. "Daphne? Oh, good Lord, Daphne!" He knelt down next to her, clearly distressed.

Something about seeing him there unfroze Neha.

"Someone please call for help. You—" She pointed at a small boy. "Go to the main tent. Get my father, Thomas De'Almeida. And my sister. Actually, bring them all. We need a carriage to the infirmary at once."

But Aloysius just looked up at me, his eyes wet with tears and his face twisted in rage. "What have you done?" he hollered. "What have you done?"

38

WHEN I OPENED my eyes in the hut at the edge of the world, the curtains were drawn wide. Outside, I could see a crimson sky. It wasn't the colour of a sunset. This was the dark red of retribution. I had done something terrible, and there was no going back now.

I stepped out, wondering where I would find myself this time. Wondering if it was safe, if I was safe. Wondering what the yakshaniya had in store for me today.

I was in a paddy field. Serene and green, it lay undisturbed as I walked on the niyara, wondering when she would join me.

I needn't have worried. A tickle against my neck, a chuckle in my ear—I whipped my head around and there she was. Her nose to her chest was covered in blood. She had been feasting.

But on what?

As if she'd heard me—heard my thoughts even though I hadn't spoken them out loud—she spread her clawed, bloodied arms, inviting me to look into the water where the paddy grew in enclosed liyadi.

The blood red of the sky reflected back to me, along with a pair of eyes, unseeing.

I choked back a scream as a body floated to the surface. It was Aloysius. He was bloated from the water, the dead grey of a corpse, even though his eyes appeared to look directly at me.

The yakshaniya pointed again—this time at another body. Siripala the fisherman.

Then Loku Banda.

Bodies kept popping out of the water like bubbles from a swimming fish. All of them dead. All of them with looks of pain and suffering etched across their faces, their mouths forever locked in silent screams.

"I'll claw out your tongue if you tell," the demoness rasped, a small string of laughter leaking its way out of her.

And then, another body bobbed up, so bloated and rotten that I couldn't recognise it at first.

But I noticed his cowlicked hair and the way his trousers were a few inches too short for him.

Raam stared at me blankly, all the light gone out of his eyes.

"No!" I screamed. I jumped off the niyara and into the water. The mud was slick and slippery and I slid half my way over to him.

"No!" I grabbed his body and held it close to me. This couldn't be happening. Raam couldn't leave me. His head lolled from side to side, a trickle of yellow bile streaming down his mouth. His beautiful, perfect face and his beautiful, perfect body were covered in gashes. There was no saving him now.

I turned to her. "What have you done?"

She laughed her usual laugh, her scraggly hair shaking as she rasped.

“What have I done? What have *you* done?”

That was when I noticed that I was covered in blood myself, from my neck to my chest to my arms. I touched my face and felt the sticky wetness coating it.

“No,” I cried. “I would never hurt him. I would never hurt anyone.”

And then, all the bodies that floated in the liyadi rolled onto their feet. They all turned to look at me at the same time. There were tens, twenties, hundreds of them. All men. Some of them men I had never even seen.

And then, in unison, they all chanted, “I’ll claw out your tongue if you tell.”

The yakshaniya just squealed in delight, her laughter bleeding all the way up to the bloodred sky.

39

DAPHNE'S CONVULSIONS HAD felt like they went on forever, but they must have stopped after a few minutes, thank goodness. She had been rushed to the infirmary in Matara town, where the upper-class Sinhalese and the foreigners were usually treated. The crowd that gathered had all been worried and afraid for her, and Aloysius was screaming at everyone and anyone that it had been my fault.

I stayed silent through his accusations.

Was it my fault?

I knew I hadn't cast any spells on Daphne—Thaththa had taught me better than that—but I was staring right at her, wishing the worst on her, when it happened. I'd been so angry. But simply being angry couldn't cause this, could it? If so, people would be falling down with convulsions all the time.

Neha's father had placated Aloysius and told him, rightfully so, that the most important thing was to have Daphne taken to the infirmary immediately. He had accompanied them himself, instructing Catharine and Dandris to take me and the rest of the family home. I had sat silently next to Neha the whole cart ride back, while everyone else stared at me, wondering if what Aloysius said was true. That I truly was a witch.

Neha looked the most upset of all.

"Amara," she'd leaned in and whispered, "I need to talk to you about something."

"Not now, Neha." I hadn't been able to deal with her piety and her doubts then. If she also wanted to believe I was a witch, well, then let her.

I had lain on my mat the whole night, too afraid to fall asleep. The anger that had once coursed through me had blown out, replaced with something far worse. Something I couldn't even describe, even though it echoed like a cavern within me.

And when I did fall asleep, my dream only made it worse.

I rose with the birds and the sun, pushing myself up off the mat and making my way down to the beach without even thinking about it. I needed to swim. I needed to feel the salty water swirl and crash around me, washing off this feeling. The waves were flat this morning, the sea a steely grey. I waded in until the water was up to my shoulders, not even noticing whether it was cold or warm. A wave started to crest, and I braced myself.

I let it crash over me. I would shatter if I wasn't already broken. And a piece of me was, no matter how hard I tried to deny it.

It was the feeling that had followed me around for the last few weeks, like a stench I couldn't scrub off. Like something was wrong deep inside me, not just in my bones but in my very essence. In all the minuscule, fragmented parts that made me *me.*

Something called out from the water. Was it something, or someone? Or was it just in my head? I could never be sure. I wasn't sure of most things anymore. Days and nights blended into each other like salt had once bled into the sea.

Another wave swelled in the distance. I knew what I had to do.

"You never turn your back on the ocean," Thaththa's words echoed, almost like he was here, next to me, holding my hand, making sure I faced the horizon.

There are two ways to beat a wave. You jump over it—letting the salt water make you lighter than you've ever been, willing your legs to push hard against the pillow-soft sand. Or you dive under it.

"Which will you do?" he would whisper. I could smell the salt on him, on me.

"I'm going to dive, Thaththa." I had been nervous then, but he was proud. His smile was different when he was truly happy. I hadn't seen that smile in so long.

I wasn't going to dive today.

The wave continued to rise—a giant lumbering its way to the shore.

I stood firm.

If you've ever stood at the exact spot that a wave breaks then you know. It feels like you are being crushed. Like you will break every bone in your body, like you will disintegrate into a million pieces.

But as I said, I was already broken.

The water, once a soothing tonic, now stung my eyes, blinding me. I revelled in the feeling. The burning was more cathartic than I could have imagined. And finally, with just the horizon for company, I allowed tears to flow down my face, washing away the salt, washing away the pieces of myself that ached and bled. Setting them adrift at sea.

WHEN I RETURNED home, it was with purpose. I had to know the truth. I had to know what happened to me.

Instead, I saw my mother's worried face.

"Thaththa's fever broke last night, so I thought he was on his way to recovery. But he started shivering again this morning. The vedha mahaththaya will only visit again later in the afternoon, but I really am worried."

This turn for the worse came after I'd left him alone with her last night. I knew, then, that my suspicions had been right. That this was all an act. That she'd done something to him to hurt him further. That she was probably behind my attack as well. My mind might have forgotten, but my body remembered. It had known something was wrong from the very start.

I'll claw out your tongue if you tell. A part of me always knew it was her voice.

I took a deep breath. There was nothing left to lose.

"What did you do to him, Amma?"

"What do you mean? He's been taking his medicine as usual. I applied some of the balm that Neha brought. Oh, goodness, do you think it might have been that? Do you think that made him worse?"

"No, Amma." I kept my voice steady. Rational. "You know it's not Neha's fault that he's like this. Tell me what you did to him."

"What I did to him? Amara, you are surely out of your senses. I've done nothing but look after this man."

"Liar!" The word shot out of me. I didn't even try to stop it. "You did this. I know you did. Tell me the truth!"

"Amara, you've lost your mind."

I was shaking now, my voice raised. There was no need to keep up pretences. No reason left to be diplomatic. There had always been a line drawn in the sand, and I had finally chosen to cross it.

I took a step closer to where she sat.

"You found out, didn't you? You found out about him and Siripala's wife and this is how you thought you'd get your revenge."

Her face went slack at this, her mouth hanging open in disbelief, and so I went on.

"You started with the other men in the village, didn't you? Husbands of your clients. Men who ill-treated their wives. You thought you would teach them a lesson. And then you did the same to Thaththa. Tell me the truth!"

"Amara, I truly—"

"Tell me what you did to *me*!" I rushed over to her and held her shoulders, glaring into her eyes. I couldn't recognise my mother in them. I only saw hurt and anger and fear.

"What do you mean?"

"Tell me what happened a few weeks ago! Tell me what happened for things to suddenly change! Why I'm having the same nightmares as the men who have been attacked. Why I have been seeing things, feeling things, that I can't explain. Why you have been forcing me to drink some horrible tonic every morning. Tell me!"

She turned so white that she looked like a ghost herself.

"I can't tell you that, Amara. I'm sorry. It's not my fault, and it's for your own good that you don't know." I was right. They had been hiding something from me.

"Tell me!" My voice was deep and forceful. I had never heard it like this before.

"Amara, you won't understand—"

"There they are! The witches are here!" Aloysius's voice exploded over Amma's. He marched into our garden with three other men, his face gaunt, but shaking in rage. The men behind him looked grim, their mouths set into hard lines.

"What's all this, Aloysius?" Amma asked.

"Hasn't your daughter told you? She attacked my fiancée last night. Daphne is still in the infirmary. She hasn't woken up."

"What?" Amma turned to look at me.

"I didn't attack her. She fell ill of her own accord."

"You cast a spell on her!" Aloysius hollered.

"I did not!" I retorted, looking helplessly at my mother. At the other three men. I couldn't tell if anyone believed me. I didn't know if I believed it myself.

"Aloysius!" This time it was Neha's father making his way up our garden, a tearful Neha following him.

"Have you come to defend this witch, Thomas? Has your daughter turned your head from the truth that's right in front of your nose?"

"See reason, Aloysius. I know you're upset right now, but—"

"Of course I'm upset, Thomas! I knew it would come to this. All of you are so accepting of these demon worshippers. It was just a matter of time!"

"Aloysius, the doctor himself said Daphne's seizure was probably due to the heat and the excitement of the evening."

"I—" Aloysius started, but Amma cut him off.

"If the doctors have reached a diagnosis, then it would be in your best interest, Aloysius, to leave." Her voice was firm. "There's no need to make a fool of yourself. Don't let this silly feud stirred up by your uncle so many years ago cloud your head like this. Go, be there for your fiancée."

One of the men accompanying him put his hand on Aloysius's arm. He deflated a little, but then squared his shoulders.

"This isn't the end of things, Kumari. I won't rest until you and your demon-worshipping family are arrested or chased from this town."

We all held our breath until he left.

"Thank you for coming, Thomas. Neha," Amma said, gratitude brimming in her eyes. Who knew what might have transpired if they hadn't come? "Can I offer you something to drink?"

"We'd better return home," Neha's father replied, with a small nod. "It's an important week for us. Especially Neha."

Amma smiled. "Does this mean—?"

Thomas De'Almeida beamed. "Yes. We will announce the betrothal on Sunday, but you might as well know. Our Neha is to be engaged to Raam De Zoysa."

I blinked.

The sun fell out of the sky.

The ocean went silent.

Amma was saying something to Neha's father, smiles on both their faces. None of their words made any sense.

Neha and Raam. *My* Raam? I must have been mistaken. I had to have been mistaken.

I had misheard, that was all. Or there must be a different Raam. Or I was so distraught by Aloysius's visit that I was simply imagining things.

But then my eyes met Neha's.

They were wide with guilt.

My heart stopped. Then it shattered.

"Amara," she whispered.

"How—?" I choked, but I couldn't finish my question. Not with Amma there. Not with Neha's father there.

My lips kept quiet even though the shards of my heart dug into my chest, sharp and cruel.

Fury and confusion swirled in me, a scorching liquid about to spill over. About to burn everyone it came in contact with.

And with that, something did boil over within me, but not the way I would have expected.

Nausea took over as I pushed myself out of the way. I stumbled to the garden and vomited, choking as I tried to catch my breath. I held on to a coconut tree for support, trying to steady myself, willing this feeling to pass. It took a few minutes for me to stop heaving.

Neha and her father must have taken their leave, believing me to be sick or shaken from Aloysius's visit. Amma was waiting on the verandah when I made my way back to the hut. She stared at me, her hands on her hips.

"That's the second time I've seen you vomit, Amara," she said, her voice sounding dark.

"That's really the least of my concerns now, Amma." My friend was betrothed to the man I loved. Did anything else matter?

My mother crossed over to where I was standing and brought her face close to mine. She looked upset.

"Did you have your menses this month?" she asked. There was urgency in her voice.

My menses? What was she even talking about? I hadn't really thought about it. My days were irregular at best, and I had so much on my mind these past few weeks.

"I—I'm not sure—"

My mother tsked and looked away. I could tell she was doing a calculation in her head.

"Think, Amara," she said, and when she looked at me this time, her lips were pressed together tightly and her face was red.

"I—I think I'm supposed to have them soon. But you know I'm always late. I didn't think too much of it."

"Didn't think too much," my mother muttered. "That's what's been getting you into trouble to begin with."

"What trouble?" I had no idea what she was talking about.

My mother suddenly grabbed me by the arms and shook me.

"It's all your fault. You always ruin everything."

"Amma!"

"You've really done it now, Amara. Gotten yourself pregnant, haven't you?"

Gotten pregnant? I—I couldn't be pregnant, could I?

I felt blood rush to my face and my body felt cold. There was no way that could be possible, could it?

"No," I replied quietly. "To get pregnant I'd need to have—"

"Sex, Amara."

My face must have given it away because she slapped me, hard.

"I should have known this would happen. How will Desmond De'Fontaine, or anyone else for that matter, marry you now?"

"What?" I felt dazed. "No."

"You've never brought me anything but suffering. Forced me into this life I never wanted, just because of one mistake."

She slapped my face again, and again.

I couldn't fight back. My mind was reeling.

Was I pregnant?

Everything spun around me.

My mother was sobbing now, still making attempts to hit me, but I stepped back.

I needed to get away from here. I needed to see Raam. He could explain what was going on.

I turned around and ran. I could still hear her sobs echo through me, echo through the jungle, as I fled.

40

THE BUDDHIST SCRIPTURES, at least the ones I've been told of, don't talk much about love, choosing instead to focus on detachment. Nothing is permanent, everything is temporary, we are told. Flowers will wilt. Even these scriptures will fade someday.

That wasn't the comfort I needed right now. I needed love. I needed caring. I needed to talk to Raam. I needed him to tell me that there had been a mistake. Some misunderstanding. That he would clear things up and everything could return to the way it was.

Love is patient. Love is kind. One of the nuns at school was fond of reciting this particular verse from the Bible. Love does not envy, or boast. It is not arrogant or rude. That was what I reminded myself as I waited in the jungle. Raam usually finished with his clerical work by afternoon and took this route home. If I waited here, I could intercept him.

I had no way of knowing the time. I was hungry, and thirsty, but still I sat down at the foot of a tree and waited. I didn't care how long I had to stay here. I needed him. I needed him to tell me that things would be okay.

My palm found its way to my belly. Could it be true? Was I really pregnant? I remembered when one of the women in our village got pregnant she said she was vomiting constantly too. My thoughts swirled around me like seafoam, half-formed and barely tangible.

I was dozing off when I heard rustling, and Raam emerged, wearing the trousers and tunic he wore for work.

"Amara, what are you doing here?" He was smiling. He's happy it's me, I thought, my heart lifting, relief pumping through me. He wouldn't be so pleased if he was engaged to Neha after all, would he? Whatever this was, we could face it together.

"I needed to see you." Where could I even start?

"This is wonderful. What a pleasant surprise." Before I could say anything else, he reached down and gave me a deep kiss, his arms encircling my waist, leaning me back against a tree.

"Raam—" I tried feebly.

"I know. I couldn't stop thinking about you too. Last night has not left my mind. Here, let me show you." He took my hand and guided it to the top of his trousers. I could feel him, hard, and tried to pull away. He started kissing my neck.

"Raam—"

"There's no need to be so shy. You've already had me. Can't you see how my body longs for you again?" He thrust his hips into mine, pinning me back to the tree. "You like that, don't you?" He grinned, tugging on the clasps of my blouse.

"Raam, stop!" I pushed lightly against his chest. "What's this I hear about you being engaged to Neha?"

He took a step back from me, all the colour draining from his face.

"Who told you?" he asked. It wasn't a denial. He didn't say it was a mistake.

"Is *that* what matters?" I asked, my voice tight. I could hear my heartbeat in my ears.

"Listen, I know—" He ran his hands through his hair, his eyes darting everywhere without meeting mine. "I know this is so—look, it all happened so quickly. Before I could even wrap my head around it, my father and hers had arranged the whole thing. You know the status her family has, and how hard my father has been working to establish us. We thought—*he* thought—it would give us some security. Solidify his position at the harbour."

"So you've known about this?" My voice barely escaped my throat. How many times could my heart be trampled on? How many times could it be torn out of my chest?

Raam's face, previously pale, was now red.

"I—I mean, I didn't think—I wasn't sure—"

"Did you know about it yesterday? On the beach?"

Raam looked down, refusing to meet my eyes. I had my answer.

"Were you ever planning to speak to your father about us? Did you truly believe you would marry me?"

"Of course, Amara. You must believe me." A tear ran down his cheek. It always hurt me to watch him cry.

"Did you ever love me?" I knew I shouldn't ask questions if I couldn't handle hearing the truth, but I had to know.

"Of course I love you! I just—I just don't know what to do." His voice was breaking. He was a little boy, still trying to find the courage to confront his father.

"Then let's run away together, you and me. We can go right away." I didn't know where the words came from, but as I spoke them I realised that I didn't want anything more. Let us escape this terrible town that was convinced I was a witch. Let us run far away from our parents who plotted and planned and ruined our lives. Let us go where no one knew us. Where we could start afresh. A new family.

"Amara, I—we can't just—"

"And why can't we?"

"I have responsibilities. Obligations to my family. I do love you, but—"

"Raam, please, I'm pregnant." I'd hoped to be more delicate than that, but the words tumbled out.

There was a pause as this news registered, for him and for me.

"What?" He took a step back, his eyes wide.

"I—well, I think—"

"You think you're pregnant or you know?" he asked. His voice was different. The way he looked at me was different.

"I—well, I'm not sure. I've been vomiting. And I haven't had my menses."

He took another step back, running his hands through his hair.

"I can't believe this."

"I can't either. I—that's why I think it's best we just leave, Raam. Leave all this behind and start anew. A family of our own, like we've always wanted."

He paused for a beat. "I should have known."

"Known what?"

But he stayed quiet. He was in shock, I told myself. I was in shock too. But he loved me. There was nothing we couldn't handle as long as we were together.

"Raam, look, I know this is all scary right now. But we'll be okay, you'll see. I know things might be tough for a while, but I'm a hard worker, and you are too. We could make it work. I love you,

Raam. I've always wanted to spend my life with you. Isn't that what you said yesterday also? That you couldn't wait for us to get married so we could be together all the time? Well, looks like the day came sooner than either of us thought. I know it might be scary, but I won't be afraid if I have you by my side."

Raam looked at me, his expression blank for just a moment. And then he threw back his head and laughed.

It confused me. Was he laughing out of happiness? Happiness that we'd spend our lives together? But when he tilted his head back down, I knew. There was no mirth there. His laughter was cruel.

"Amara, Amara. What a little minx you turned out to be."

"What?"

"I can't believe you thought I'd get tricked like this."

"Tricked? No, Raam, you don't understand. I think I'm really pregnant. I'm not trying to trick you to marry me."

"Oh, is that so? So you hear about my engagement and just rush here to say you're pregnant? Maybe you are, maybe you aren't. But I have no doubt that I'm not the father."

"What? Raam, how could you say something so hurtful?"

"How could I be hurtful, Amara? Me? What about you, with your pure, virginal, wide-eyed attitude? Dangling yourself in front of me on a string. Teasing me and making me wait, while you've already been with someone else. Or maybe even many others. How would I know?"

"Someone else? Others? Raam, we made love while you were engaged to my best friend!"

"Oh, please. You hadn't spoken to her in over a year. Stop lying to me, Amara. If you had never been with anyone else before me, then why was there no blood yesterday?"

"No blood?" I asked, feeling stupid.

"I knew you were not what you were pretending to be. I knew you were just a common whore. Fit for a good time until something better came along. But I could have never guessed how cunning you were, now that I understand your plan."

"My plan? Raam, I have no plan."

"Liar! You've been whoring yourself out, just like the rumours said. And when you found out that you were pregnant you slept with me to trap me into marrying you."

I gasped.

"How could you even think such a thing, Raam?"

"You must be a special kind of stupid, Amara. Because there's no way you could know that you're pregnant in just a day. It doesn't work that way. There's absolutely no way it could be mine. Not the slightest chance in hell."

He turned around and started to walk away.

"Raam! Wait!" I cried. He just kept walking.

"Raam! Don't go!" I felt it in me then. The anger that'd been threatening to raise its head for weeks. It burned bright and hard.

You've never brought me anything but suffering. Forced me into this life I never wanted. My mother's voice made its way into my mind.

You've been whoring yourself out, just like the rumours said. And when you found out that you were pregnant you slept with me to trap me into marrying you, Raam had spat.

It simmered in me, building pressure, making every part of me tense. I'd been angry before, at Daphne, at Aloysius, at my mother and father, but I hadn't known what the word *fury* truly meant until just that moment.

"Raam!" I called again. He had started making his way through the jungle and I followed him, pushing my way through the branches and shrubs, ignoring the cuts they left on my skin.

"Leave me alone, you stupid slut," he yelled over his shoulder, but I finally caught up to him.

I reached for his arm and grabbed it as he turned around, his own anger contorting his face.

"I'll teach you a lesson, you pregnant whore. Give it to you one last time, since you're begging me for it."

He pushed me down to the ground and lowered himself onto me.

"Raam! Stop it!"

He held both my arms down above my head and fumbled with his trousers.

"Raam!" The anger that bubbled inside me flooded from my chest to my hands. I clawed down at the forest floor, trying to manoeuvre myself out of his grip, my fingers clutching at the dried leaves on the ground.

"Stop!" I screamed, right from my gut. I felt the word erupt out of me like an explosion, with a sudden power I had never felt before. It felt like lightning was running through me. Everything was alight. The eruption was so intense that Raam was forced away from me, getting flung back and crashing onto a tree a few feet back.

I scrambled to my feet.

What just happened?

Raam looked at me fearfully, stunned.

"What did you do?" he asked, his voice just a whisper now. All his anger and bravado had evaporated.

But I didn't want to understand. I just wanted to get away from him.

Turning, I ran as fast as I could, deeper into the jungle. I ran and ran until I couldn't run anymore, and when I finally took a look around to see where I was, I realised that I was at the very edge of the jungle, close to the town. Close to where Heen Achchi's hut was.

But the small hut that rose before me wasn't hers, even though it was familiar, nonetheless.

I would recognise it anywhere. I had seen it many times before, though back then it was at the edge of the world. It stood, a small light flickering from within it, illuminating its red curtains.

How had it made its way out of my dreams and into the jungle? Did that mean the yakshaniya was here also?

My knees gave away under me, and I collapsed straight onto the damp jungle floor.

41

"DUWE? DUWE, NAGITINNA." *Daughter? Daughter, wake up.* The voice sounded like it was coming from underwater.

My head hurt. So did my limbs. I closed my eyes tighter, hoping to drift off again. I wanted, more than anything, to stay asleep.

"Duwe." The voice was persistent. I felt a cool hand on my shoulder, and then on my forehead. It stroked the hair off my face.

"Enna, duwe. Mehema kaley madha vatila inna baha, neh?" *Come, daughter, you can't just lie here in the middle of the jungle, no?*

I groaned, trying to bring myself back. What had happened to me?

I prised open one eye, and then the other. A wave of dark green leaves danced over me, blocking my view of the sky. I certainly was in the jungle; I didn't need the voice to tell me that. I knew from the smell of the mossy earth, from the sounds of the birds at a distance.

And then everything flooded back to me at once. What had happened with Raam. How I had hurt him. The horrified expression on his face as he looked at me. What he had said to me.

I pushed myself up onto my elbows.

Why he'd said those things to me. I felt my belly again. It felt the same—flat and unimposing. Was my mother mistaken? Had I jumped to conclusions and destroyed my relationship with Raam? But did I even want a relationship with him? How could I ever live my life with someone who thought of me that way? Who accused me of those horrible things?

"Ah, aharila." *Ah, you're awake,* the voice said, and it took me a moment to realise that it was Heen Achchi, her milky eyes gleaming.

The hut from my dreams rose behind her.

I pushed myself into a sitting position, even though I felt absolutely exhausted. I was sure I had just imagined it, but the hut stood in front of me just the same. Innocuous and solitary.

"Duwata amarudha?" *Are you in pain, daughter?*

The tenderness in her voice felt jarring. It wasn't her usual rasp.

I looked into her face, weathered with the crisscross of time. Her eyes, the very eyes that were supposed to see beyond this world and into others, were focused on me. She gave me a toothless smile, her gums a dark purple against her brown skin.

"Naah, Achchi." *No, Achchi,* I replied.

She gestured to my feet, which I could see now were covered in scratches and tiny wounds.

"Kaagenda diwwe?" *From who were you running?*

How could I even begin to tell her?

A tear slid down my face.

"Aney, duwe." *Oh, no, daughter.* She cupped her face in my hands. "Andanna epaa. Achchita kiyanna kavudha kiyala." *Don't cry. Tell me who it is.*

Her words only made me sob harder. Everything that Raam had

said washing over me, a wound as fresh as when it was first inflicted. How could he? How could Neha? I loved them both and they'd both betrayed me.

"Ara kolla, nedha? Monowadha keruwe? Achchita kiyanne." *It was that boy, no? What did he do? Tell me.*

But how could she ever understand? How could anyone?

I just shook my head, and Heen Achchi clicked her tongue.

"Okkoma ekaiy." *They are all the same.* She started to rise to her feet. "Enna math ekka. Mama kiyadennam karanna oney dhe." *Come with me. I'll teach you what you need to do.*

I barely had any strength in me. I just wanted to go home.

But then, did I even have a home I could return to, with Amma so angry at me? I'd have given anything to stay here, on the jungle floor, just a little while longer, but I knew it was no use. The real world wouldn't leave me alone. The best I could do was delay my reentry by following Heen Achchi, regardless of whether she was being ridiculous or not.

"Enna, enna, duwe." *Come, come, daughter.* She beckoned. And so I struggled to my feet and followed her. As always, she was deceptively nimble and confident in her movements.

We didn't travel far. She led me right towards the hut with the red curtains.

"Api monawadhe mehey karanney?" *What are we doing here?* I asked, but she ignored me.

Instead, Heen Achchi opened the small sack she was carrying. From it, she presented a lamp, some fruit, and a coconut.

"Heen Achchi, mey monawadhe?" *Heen Achchi, what's all this?* I asked, my voice coming out only as a small rasp.

She looked at me, then. Her milky eyes staring deep into my own, a look of understanding ebbing and flowing through her face.

"Mata therenawa. Mata duwage duka therenawa. Duka kiyana dhe pahasuwen nathi karaganna baha. Eth minisunge napurukam welata nam visidumak thiyanewa." *I understand. I understand your sadness. Sadness like yours can't be dissolved easily. But wickedness, on the other hand, there's a solution for that.*

I didn't understand, and so she kept going, all the while arranging the fruit and lighting the small lamp.

"Oyaghe duka withrak nemey, duwe, mata mey gamey gahanunge vedhanawa nonawathwa ahenawa. Magey penuma ehkaiy. Heen Achchita therenawa. Heen Achchita therenne naha wage inna baha. Ekaiy mama mehema keruwe." *It's not just your sadness, daughter. I feel the pain of so many women in this village. That is my sight. I can understand, and I can't pretend that I don't. That's why I did what I did.*

"Heen Achchi, monawadhe keruwe?" *Heen Achchi, what did you do?*

But she simply picked up the coconut and muttered something under her breath. And then, with a kind of strength I'd never have expected from her, she raised her arms and dashed the coconut against the jungle floor. The brown fruit slammed down with a crack, separating into two halves, the water within it spraying over us.

I held my breath. A soft wind whistled through the trees, delicate and fragile after the loud crack of the coconut. The light in the hut glowed brighter.

Heen Achchi was smiling.

"Mama maaniyangen udaw illuwa duwe. Duwa thani venney naha. Duwage andhura dakke daah-me mama illuwe duwage vedhanawa adu karanna kiyala. Anith gahanunwa andewwa pirimintath eh vageyma vedhanawa dhanenna kiyala." *I asked for a favour from the mother. You won't be abandoned, daughter. From the day I saw the darkness swirl around you, I asked for your pain to be lessened. And to all the men who made the women in this village cry, I asked for them to feel the very pain they inflicted.*

I gasped. Heen Achchi had been casting spells of her own. Here I was, asking her questions about my father, thinking she was a harmless old woman, but she'd been behind the whole thing—watching, waiting, biding her time. Would her spells work, though? Was she capable of really carrying out a hooniyama?

And that was when I saw the curtain in the hut inch open. I braced myself, ready for the yakshaniya from my dreams. Knowing that she had finally found her way to me, and me to her.

"Dan therey." *Now you'll understand,* Heen Achchi exclaimed, clapping her hands. I wanted to run. With every inch of my body I wanted to get away. But still my legs didn't move.

The trees around us shook. Their leaves broke free and rained down around us.

"Dakka dhe?" *Did you see?* Heen Achchi asked, pointing to the entrance.

There was something—no, some*one*—stepping out from behind the curtain. Closer and closer, she descended, her movements fluid and feline. My heart hammered so hard in my chest. I wanted to scream, but I could barely even breathe.

And then she stood in front of me, her eyes in line with mine.

"Bhagya?" I asked, exhaling.

But it also wasn't Bhagya at all. Her skin had taken on a bluish tinge, a light glow about her hair. She was dressed differently too—with numerous necklaces, and a sickle in one of her hands. And her eyes. The flames of a million fires danced just behind her eyes, with a type of rage I couldn't even begin to understand.

But Bhagya didn't reply. Instead, she eyed the coconut on the ground before picking up a piece of papaya that Heen Achchi had laid out and sniffing it deeply.

She looked gravely at the old woman.

"Thava kenek?" *Another one?*

Heen Achchi tilted her head in my direction, and a look of understanding washed over Bhagya. She nodded, and Heen Achchi took her leave, touching Bhagya's feet reverently before disappearing back into the jungle.

And then it was just the two of us.

"Who are you?" I asked, stupidly.

She smiled at me. "I think a part of you already knows."

"Kaali maani." *Kaali the mother.* The words escaped my lips on their own, like they had always floated there, waiting for the right moment to be set free. I had known she was special all along.

Her smile widened.

"Bhagya is not my real name. Well, it's a part of my name, I suppose, since I have so many. They called me Bhagavati in Kerala, where I was before I came to this island. But they usually call me Badrakaali, or, like you just did, Kaali for short."

Her stories have been told far and wide. There was a shrine for her made in the northeast of the island. Known throughout Hindu mythology, she takes many forms—from the ferocious Durga to the ultimate manifestation of Shakti, the mother of all living beings. She is worshipped and feared and venerated. Her kindness is gentle, her wrath powerful enough to send mountains tumbling down. She is many things, has many faces, and I could hardly believe I had witnessed one of them.

She smiled again. "But please continue to call me Bhagya."

"Do you live in this hut? I—I've had dreams about it." This couldn't be real. I must be still asleep on the jungle floor.

"I come to those who need me. And you needed me, Amara, many weeks ago when you lay here in this very hut. I heard your cries and I came. I tried reaching out to you, I stayed with you for weeks, but your father made you wear a powerful protection against me. A yanthraya, too powerful even for me. Thankfully, you removed it. I've been waiting until you were ready to learn the truth."

I'd only met Bhagya after Raam took the suray from me. Had that been the yanthraya all along?

But here she was, offering me what I wanted above anything else.

"The truth?" I asked. "Tell me, then, was I attacked? Did you attack me?"

"I've never attacked you, Amara. I'm here to help you discover your strength. I'm only trying to help you. And something tells me that things have taken a turn for the worse. Would you like to talk about it?"

If anyone was able to understand, it would be her, even if this was just some sort of dream. Bhagya motioned for me to take a seat at the foot of a tree, and I settled in, suddenly feeling like a castle made of sand on the shore, about to be washed away.

My eyes felt full of tears and I covered my face with my hands. Even if she was imaginary, even if I had just made her up in my head, I didn't want Bhagya to see me cry. I didn't want her to know about the mess I'd gotten myself into.

"Amara, it's okay." She moved close and wrapped her arms around me. This small gesture was all it took. It freed my tears and I started to sob. She didn't say anything. She just rubbed my back and let me weep. If she wasn't real, then how was she holding me now? Did I even care?

"I think I might be pregnant," I said, my voice trembling with uncertainty.

Bhagya simply nodded. There was no judgement. No disgust. No pity in her eyes.

"And when I told Raam he—" I felt a sob shudder out of me again, remembering the horrible things he'd called me. "He said it wasn't his. That I must have been with another man. That I was just trying to trick him into marrying me." I tried to keep my voice steady. I tried not to show her that my heart had been smashed into a million tiny pieces. My mother had never told me what to expect—not about my menses, not about men, not about how any of this was supposed to work. But Raam was the only man I'd loved.

"Oh, Amara. That's terrible. I'm so sorry."

"And that wasn't the worst of it. When he said those things, I got angry. Angrier than I had ever been. Furious. And then—" What could I tell her? Even I didn't understand.

"And then I pushed him back, and it was like I had all this power running through my body. Power I had never felt before. And Raam flew off me and crashed into a tree. I think. I don't know. I was so angry it was like I lost track of who I was. I know it sounds absolutely ridiculous, but I swear it happened. Only I don't know how. And—oh, goodness—what is happening to me?"

Bhagya's expression didn't change. She kept rubbing my back. If she thought I was losing my mind, she did a great job of not showing it.

"Never mind about Raam," she said. "What about you? And the baby?"

I sighed. "I don't even know for sure if there is a baby. I mean, Raam said that there was no way I could know so soon."

"Would you like to know?" Bhagya asked. There was something I couldn't understand in her eyes.

"Of course. But—"

"Amara, do you trust me?" She smiled.

The jungle seemed to pulse in time with her breath.

"I don't understand," I replied.

"You will. Now take a deep breath and relax." She reached her hands over my belly and I could feel it then, the comforting warmth that emanated out of me.

"Amara, look." I looked over to where her palms hovered over me. My stomach hummed, a soft light starting to dawn over it. It encased me, filling me with something remarkable. Filling me with love, and purpose—but I was still confused.

"Your body is trying to tell you something, Amara. It has many stories to share, if only you let it." I couldn't believe it. I was going to be a mother.

Bhagya smiled widely, flowers I had never noticed before blooming in her hair. A delicate vine snaked its way over her wrist. Even the air around her danced and shimmered.

But something nagged at me.

"And the way I attacked Raam?"

"You have more power within you than you'll ever understand, Amara. That is all. Whether it's coconuts falling on roofs at opportune times or girls falling sick with mysterious ailments when you can't take their bullying anymore."

Something slid around within me as she said that. I felt off-balance. Of course I had been angry. Both at Daphne and at Raam. But that didn't mean I wanted to hurt them. Did it?

"And what about what Heen Achchi said? About the other women in the village?"

The fire behind her eyes flashed once again.

"The women in this village need a saviour, Amara. Too long they have suffered in silence, being taken advantage of, used and cast aside like they are no more than mere rags. When Heen Achchi saw their pain, when she recognised the very same pain within so many of them, she came to me asking for help."

I understood, then. Why she'd suggested we learn more about the men who were attacked. What she wanted me to know about them.

"So it was you, then? You're the one who's been attacking the men in our village."

She looked at me defiantly. Daring me to tell her it was wrong.

But it *was* wrong.

"You attacked my father." My cheeks burned, wanting to tear at her face. I didn't care if she would attack me too. "He was a terrible husband, yes, but to hurt him like that? Hanging on for his life—"

"Please don't try to take his side," she spat. "See, this is the very problem. Women themselves excuse this behaviour. Do we hate ourselves so much that we are willing to side with men rather than hold them accountable for their actions? Or, well, maybe you don't even understand all that your father has really done?"

I remained silent, and so she continued.

"Don't you see, Amara? I'm about to give you a gift. To be in control of your own life, for once."

"I don't want it." The words shot out.

"You don't want a gift bestowed on you by a god?" Was it me, or did the light around her change colour? Did it flicker from a golden yellow to a bloody red?

"I don't want to hurt people. Even if they are terrible. Even if you think they do deserve it, that still doesn't make it alright to attack them. Not to me."

Her voice was still calm when she spoke to me.

"You won't be hurting them, Amara. You'll be stopping them from hurting anyone else. Wanting to be treated with respect is all most women want, yet we are bullied and abused and assaulted and everyone accepts it as the way things are. Don't you see? Things have to change. People need to be taught a lesson." Her voice rose as she spoke. The fireflies around her head vanished. The flowers in her hair started to wilt. She wasn't at peace with the jungle anymore. She was the storm that made trees shake. She was the tempest.

I stayed silent.

"I can see you don't agree with me. Maybe I was wrong. Maybe you are weaker than I thought. Here I was, thinking I could help you—" She shook her head, her lips pursed in disgust. "Forgive me, Amara, for thinking you were different. That you were special. I can see now that there's no place for me here. Go back to your life with your hateful boyfriend and a father who has forsaken you."

She stood up.

"Let's hope for your child's sake that it's a boy. The world doesn't need more women to chew up and spit out."

"Bhagya, wait!" I called out. There was one last question left.

She stopped and looked over her shoulder at me.

"You said you came to me when I was here in this hut. That's why you live there now. When was that? Why was I there?"

She gave me a sad smile.

"Why don't you ask your parents? Then you can decide who truly deserved to be attacked."

42

MY FEET FELT unsteady as I slowly made my way through the jungle. I should get home, I kept repeating to myself. I should get home. That was all I could focus on. To think of everything else, to think of anything else would—

It didn't matter. All that mattered now was that I got home.

Amma would be so angry if I got home after dark. The thought was comforting somehow. The only constant in my life was my mother's temper. It felt so normal. So mundane. When nothing that had happened to me in the last few hours felt real.

The trees started to thin. I was almost there. But still, even though I longed, more than anything, to make my way inside the little whitewashed hut and crawl onto my sleeping mat, I couldn't go further. Because regardless of Raam and Neha, or what Raam had said to me, or who Bhagya was, the fact still remained that I was pregnant, and that meant that my mother would be very, very upset. No matter how badly I wished things were different, this was a fact.

But how? Raam was so certain that it couldn't be his. And regardless of the filthy things he'd said, there was never anyone else.

Maybe—a ridiculous idea flung itself into my mind—maybe this was what happened to the Virgin Mary. Maybe the same thing was happening to me? But how? I was no devout. I barely studied the dhamma, let alone the Bible. I was simply caught midway between tradition and these new-world beliefs, trying to find balance, trying to find my faith, trying to find peace.

But still, I was not special enough to be chosen. I knew that. I've always known that. The baby must be Raam's. He must be mistaken.

If, in an occasion so rare that it existed only in the whispers of the village gossips, a girl got pregnant out of wedlock, then the only option was for her to get married. It didn't matter if it was love, or convenience, or whether you even liked the person anymore—the only option for a pregnant woman was to marry. And Raam—my Raam with the dimpled cheeks, who used to wrap his arms around me like he would never let go and swear to me that we were destined for each other—Raam had made it quite clear that marriage would be the last thing that would happen. Under most circumstances my father could convince him, I supposed. It was a matter of my honour, of my family's honour, after all. My father could go to Raam's family and explain the situation to them. And they'd most likely insist we marry at once.

The thought left me reeling. I remembered the way he looked at me when I told him. Like I was a disgusting slug he'd stepped on. The way he threw his head back and laughed like I'd said some sort of dirty joke. I had always thought Raam was like the moon, that he glowed, that he chased away the darkness in my life. But there was a side of the moon that we were never meant to see. And Raam had shown me that side of him today. I'd never even thought him capable of such thoughts, of such hurtful words. I'd never thought he was the type of boy who would lie to me about being engaged. That he would be intimate with me when he was betrothed to another. Or maybe I was so besotted by him that I had failed to see it before. And you can't unsee some things, not even if you desperately wanted to. I could never marry him.

And that meant that I couldn't stay.

My parents would never allow me to remain in their home, an unmarried mother bringing shame on them. They'd probably be run out of the village by the gossips. If I wouldn't marry Raam then they'd force me to marry someone else. And I couldn't allow that either. To be with another man like Siripala the fisherman, or Upali the toddy tapper. Men who hurt women. Who treated them like objects to use and throw away.

No, I couldn't stay. I would get as far away from my village as I could. I put my hand on my belly. It didn't murmur and glow like it did when I was with Bhagya, but I knew what was within me, just the same.

And I wasn't afraid.

Nervous, perhaps. And uncertain of the future. But how could I ever be afraid of something that was already a part of me?

The Virgin Mary had finally given me the strength I'd asked for, and not a moment too soon.

Everyone had let me down—my parents, my friends, the boy who I thought loved me. This child was all I had. For the first time in my life, I wasn't truly alone. I had someone to love. Who would love me back. I had a purpose. I wouldn't be like Amma, finding fault and nagging and complaining all the time. I would be my child's friend. I'd teach them to climb trees, and how to pick the best mangoes. I'd tell them the stories that lived in the jungle and hid in the stars.

The more I thought about it, the more my plan began to take shape. I'd run away. I'd convince one of the fishermen who sailed further north to give me passage. Some of them went as far as Colombo—I heard that Colombo was almost like another world. There was trade there. I could find work. I could read and write. I had been smarter than most of the girls in my class. I would find a way to make things alright. I would be the mother I wished I'd had. My child would know nothing but love and acceptance.

I took a deep breath, squaring my shoulders.

But the moment I stepped out from behind the trees, I knew something was wrong.

I was blinded by an orange light, and my nostrils burned with the smell.

Something was on fire.

Our house.

Our house was on fire.

I gasped, my hands over my mouth, trying to get closer. Were Amma and Thaththa inside? Were they alright?

I heard screaming. Angry chants.

"Get out, demon worshippers! Get out!" They screamed over and over again.

Aloysius was back, and he had brought his supporters with him. They were screaming in our garden as they threw coconut shells and stones at our hut.

"Get out, demon worshippers! Get out!"

The woven coconut fronds on our roof were ablaze, the flames dancing their way up to the sky.

I wanted to run into my garden. I wanted to chase them all away.

And I would have, if a small hand hadn't grabbed hold of mine.

"Amara Akki, I've been looking all over for you," Siyath Malli said, his eyes as large as saucers.

"What are you doing here? You'll get hurt."

"My parents sent me to search for you. To tell you to come to our house, where it's safe."

"I can't leave my parents in there, Malli," I rasped. I felt giddy with fear.

"No, no. Kumari Haminey must have known they were coming. We have your father with us also."

A sliver of relief from the horrific scene in front of me. But I wasn't going to run away. Not so that Aloysius could just get away with this.

"Malli, thank you. But I need you to run home now. I have to stop these men."

That only made him grip my hand tighter.

"No, Amara Akki. You have to come with me."

"Listen, Malli—" But Siyath Malli just gasped, looking at something behind me.

I started to look over my shoulder, but as I did, I felt fingers cover my face. My nostrils burned. It hurt to breathe. I was choking. I tried to scream, but my voice came out as just a whimper. I pushed away, trying to free myself, but my arms felt lifeless, like they were made of water. My knees betrayed me, flaying out, collapsing under my body.

And as darkness crept in from the corner of my eyes, I heard the yakshaniya's voice again. The demoness from my dreams had finally caught up to me.

"You were too late. I have you now."

43

THE DEMONESS GRASPED me by my hair, pulling me forward. I kept trying to cry out, but once again, no sound left my throat.

"Let me go," I tried, the words only in my mind. She looked back at me and smiled, unclenching her grasp on my hair as she flung me to the ground. Did it work? I wondered weakly.

She looked at me and smiled again, her black lips curling upwards. Her smell reached my nostrils—betel leaves—as I tried not to retch.

"What do you want from me?" Again, no sound, but she seemed to understand.

She got on her hands and knees and started crawling towards me, bringing her face just inches away from mine as I lay helpless on the ground.

"I want you to understand," she rasped, as something wet slid down her nose and landed on my face.

My body recoiled, but something in me hummed.

She was crying.

She might have been a monster, but she was sad.

"What's wrong?" I could finally speak.

She moved away from my face and lay down beside me. I could have gotten up, then. I could have run.

But something drew me to her. Something about her grief resonated in the empty space where my heart once lived.

She reached for my hand, her spindly, bony fingers wrapping around my wrist and pulling it over her stomach. It felt like touching raw meat wrapped in a spider's web—wet and clammy and too cold to ever have been human.

"They took it from me."

"Who did?"

"They did. They are all the same."

"What was it?" I asked. "What did they take from you?"

She turned her face towards mine. I could see worlds of pain and fury behind the pools of black in her eyes.

"Everything," she hissed, baring her teeth, and pressing my hand deeper into her belly.

As she did I felt it—the piercing, writhing, white-hot pain that started from behind my navel and travelled down between my legs.

"No!" I screamed. "No!"

"It's too late," she rasped. "Don't you understand? You've always been too late. You're mine. You've always been mine."

And with that, my world collapsed around me, blazing in heat, alight in fury.

44

I GASPED AWAKE, everything I'd just seen somersaulting through my mind, leaving me dazed and dizzy. I tried to take a calming breath, but an odd scent filled the air. I think it might have been camphor, and lamp oil, perhaps. These were not the smells from my home, nor the jungle. I opened my eyes and looked around. Where was I?

The room was small and dark, the only light emanating from a lamp on a shelf. Next to it were small glass bottles and vials, holding various liquids. There was a mortar and pestle as well. Medicines, I thought to myself.

There was a dull ache coursing through my body. Had I taken ill? I didn't feel completely focused—like my mind was trying to hold on to a corner of reality as it unwound from beneath my grasp. I took another jagged breath. I was lying on a small, stiff bed. Gingerly, I tried to sit up.

That was when I realised that my arms had been tied down. I was restrained.

"Help," I called out, stupidly. What else was I supposed to shout anyway? I struggled against my binds. They had been done up tight, and even if they weren't, my mind and my body were not acting in unison.

"Someone help me, please." My voice felt like it was a part of a dream. Like I was crying out while being engulfed by the sea. Maybe none of this was real? I tried to shift my weight on the bed, but it was difficult. And I felt so very tired.

"Help," I tried again, even weaker.

And just as I was losing my grasp on consciousness, a large figure entered the room.

It must be the woman again, I thought, wrestling to keep my eyelids open. It must be her.

But the form was too large, too bulky. And it wore shirt and trousers.

"Amara, you're awake," he said softly, a slight lisp to his voice. The birthmark on his eyelid stood out vividly against his scarred face.

"Jeevan Maama?" I called out, a wave of energy casting out some of my earlier drowsiness. And as I said his name his features swam into view. He was wearing what I thought were false teeth—a little too big for his mouth. But he was standing next to me. He had recovered.

"Amara, you have to be quiet," he said, his voice a murmur. Was it the flicker of the lamplight or was there an expression on his face that I'd never seen before?

"Jeevan Maama, what am I doing here? Why am I tied up?"

He sat next to me on the bed, wincing as he did, as if it hurt for him to move, and put a reassuring hand on my forehead.

"Please calm down, Amara. Everything is okay now. I had some of my men bring you to me. You're at my home, so you're safe now. The restraints are only for your own protection."

"What do you mean, my own protection? What do I need protecting from?" My questions fell out of me. Someone had grabbed me from outside my house. Pressed something to my mouth until I fainted. Nothing made any sense. My head swam, tumbling like driftwood.

"From yourself, Amara." He winced again as he shifted. He hadn't made a full recovery yet.

"What do you mean, Jeevan Maama? I still don't understand."

"I know you will, Amara. I know you will understand. You've always been so bright. Too bright for your own good, sometimes."

"So please tell me, Maama. Tell me why I'm here."

He sighed, his odd teeth glinting in the low light.

"Your parents—your father mostly—should have known better than to expose you to all this."

"To all what?"

"To all this demon worship."

I stayed quiet. I hated when anyone referred to it that way.

"No good could ever come of these things. Once you are on the wrong path the devil has a way of making his home in your heart. And that's my only explanation for what happened that day, Amara. That the devil found his way to me through you."

"I—what?" I faltered.

"You were possessed, Amara. I'd come to visit your mother like I often did, and was waiting down by the beach when you found me. You—" He hesitated. "You came to me. You were possessed, I could tell by the look on your face that you were not yourself."

Had I attacked him, then? Was that what he was saying? Were his wounds my fault? But I didn't understand. They told me he had been attacked in the jungle. Bhagya admitted to it herself. So what was Jeevan Maama talking about?

He took another breath and his eyes seemed to glaze over.

"There's no easy way to say this, Amara. But it's something you must know, all the same. You seduced me."

"I seduced you?" My voice was barely a whisper.

"Not you, of course, child. Not you, but the demon who was within you. The demon you were cursed with and the one your father exorcised."

"Thaththa?"

"Yes, he blamed me at first. Didn't want to admit that his dance with the devil was responsible for everything. Even so, I tried my best to help your family how I could."

I took a deep breath. The room around me had started to spin again.

"Everything was taken care of. But then your mother told me that you were pregnant. So you see, the devil always finds a way."

I tried to reach down to touch my stomach, but my hands were still bound.

Teasing me and making me wait, while you've already been with someone else. Raam's hurtful words found their way to me again. So he had been right. It wasn't his child. A sweat broke out all over me. He was right when he said I had been with other men. Even if I hadn't known.

But *had* I known?

My body gave me signs, I'd just chosen to ignore them. I hadn't trusted myself.

I have you now, you little bitch. It had been Jeevan Maama.

"I knew I had to protect you then, Amara. To take care of things."

It was the way he said it. The way his eyes swept over my body, landing just at my navel. The way he flinched, ever so slightly, the way his nostrils flared, the way he bit his lip.

Using every drop of strength I could muster, I lifted my head and looked down the bed. The thin white sheet that covered me was drenched in blood. I instinctively knew. The pain that seared through me in my dream wasn't just my imagination. The life inside me was no longer there. My uncle had snuffed it out.

"How could you do this?" I gasped.

"Don't you understand? I was only trying to help you."

The wail that came out of me wasn't mine. It belonged to an animal. A wild beast. A monster.

"How could you do this to me?" There was power in my voice now. Anger. My baby wasn't his to take away. It wasn't his decision to make—it was mine, and mine alone. It didn't matter if I'd been possessed. It didn't matter if a demon made me do it. So much had been taken from me already. And now he'd taken away even the faintest vestige of choice I had.

"Amara, you need to calm down. You've lost a lot of blood. You need to rest."

I pulled against my restraints, but it was no use.

"Let me go!" I screamed.

"You'll come to your senses when you calm down," he said, starting to stand up.

"No! Let me go now!"

He turned to leave.

"Help me! Someone! Anyone!" I couldn't see anymore. If he replied to me, I couldn't hear it. All I could feel was fire, angry and red, exploding out of me. I knew what I had to do.

"Bhagya!" I called out. "Bhagya, I need you." It was a ridiculous thing to shout, I knew. Even Jeevan Maama looked confused.

But still, she came.

She appeared next to me, glowing even brighter than I remembered.

"I'm here," she said, simply.

"You have to help me."

"Are you sure?" she asked. "There's no going back."

"I don't want to go back. I want to make him pay."

"Who are you talking to?" Jeevan Maama's voice rang through the room nervously. He couldn't see Bhagya, I realised. She was there just for me.

"Then let's give him hell," she said, climbing onto the bed and pressing her body against mine. I gasped, feeling her spirit enter me. But instead of pain and weakness, I just felt power. More strength than I'd ever felt in my life ran from my fingertips down to my toes. I pulled off the ropes binding me to the bed as if they were dregs of seaweed.

Energy radiating off me, I stood up, and in an instant, I had Jeevan Maama pressed against the wall. All his blood had drained away, leaving him pale and afraid as he cowered before me. Something inside me snapped as I launched myself at him, clawing and scratching and tearing into his face, his body. His screams bounced off the walls as he tried to protect himself, but it was in vain. He was a mere rag doll. He was nothing compared to the power that finally flowed through me.

I felt his skin and then his flesh and then his blood under my fingernails, running down my arms. My body moving on its own, moving in the way it felt it was always meant to, I bit at his face—the scar that stood pink against his cheek now gushing ruby-red blood. I pulled out his false teeth and crumbled them to dust between my fingers.

Eventually, he slumped down to the ground, as I stood over him, heaving. I couldn't believe what I had done. I couldn't believe this was me.

But while I felt disbelief, there wasn't even a drop of remorse.

He deserved it. He deserved it after what he had done to me. Done to my unborn child. Done to my family. A wave of grief rose up and I bent over, another howl escaping my lips.

What had I done?

I gasped as I sobbed.

What had I done?

That was when I noticed that there was someone else in the room.

My mother stood at the entryway, wide-eyed, clutching an ornamental wooden cross.

"Leave here, demon," she screamed. "The power of Christ compels you. Leave at once."

She looked so small. So afraid. So many worlds away from the stern lady who lost her temper if I was out too late. And yet, she knew everything. She knew what had happened to me. She'd *let* it happen to me.

I couldn't help it. I just threw my head back and roared.

"You think a silly wooden cross can stop me, Amma?"

"I've always known no good could ever have come from that man, with his demons and his spells and his witchcraft."

"But you loved that man, didn't you?"

"I never loved him," she spat. "A moment of weakness. A moment enough to ruin my entire life." She shuddered. "As a woman, what choice did I have? I was forced into this life I hated. Forced to marry a man I barely knew, who took everything away from me. To live a life so different from the one promised to me. Forced to raise his child. My mother wanted me to abort the pregnancy, and how I wished I had listened to her. My body was taken from me, and then my life too."

I almost started to pity her. Almost. But then she kept talking.

"The same demon that's inside you now must have been the one who made you seduce your uncle. Or who knows? Maybe it was just you. Maybe you're as sinful, just as adept in the art of seduction as your father. Either way, an abomination I was forced to birth."

The blast of rage that exploded out of me swept my mother off her feet. She flew backwards, hitting her head against the wall and crashing down onto the floor.

"You made your choice when you decided to keep me and marry Thaththa and still resented me for it. You never gave it a second thought when it was my turn," I spat.

"You *wanted* that thing that was inside you? Don't you understand, Amara, I was trying to save you! Give you the chance for a good life. A proper marriage to a noble family." Her voice was a whisper. I couldn't believe this was the woman who'd cooked me lunch every day. Who'd sewed me my school uniform. Who'd taught me how to make a fish curry. Had she hated me the whole time? Was I just a curse to her?

"You were trying to save your pathetic brother. He's the only person you cared about," I snarled.

"He's the only one who tried to protect me!"

"He raped me!" I screamed, my words exploding out of me with a gust of wind, pinning my mother back against the wall.

She held up her cross again, mumbling something to herself.

She's praying, I realised.

A laugh slithered out of me. It did not stop as I wrapped my fingers around the wooden cross and forced it up to her neck. It pressed deep into her skin, making her throat look as though it was about to burst.

"I know now that you've always hated me, Amma." I spat out the word *Mother.* It didn't feel right to call her that anymore. "But tell me, how did you force Thaththa to go along with your plan?"

A laugh, clipped and wicked, flew out of her, even as her face turned purple and she gasped for breath. "Stupid little girl. It was all his idea."

"Liar!" I screamed. The fire that burned within me was enough to scorch a million jungles. And with the kind of power I had only just begun to relish, I forced the cross into her throat, inch by inch, feeling the wood press, then puncture, then drive deep within her.

"Your father—" It was Bhagya's voice in my mind, as my mother spluttered and choked to death. Bhagya was still with me. Still able to talk to me. "Your father knows what really happened to you. Go find him."

She was right. I had to find out every morsel of truth, no matter how painful. There was no going back now.

45

PERHAPS IT WAS instinct, perhaps it was Bhagya's voice whispering in my ear, but my body moved on its own. Stepping out of this strange hut where I'd woken up, I knew I had to make my way down to the beach. My bare feet didn't even feel the ground beneath them. The stabbing pain in the lower part of my stomach and my lower back had withered away, replaced instead with an anger and bitterness that I could taste on my tongue—rancid and foul, permeating through me.

I was nearing home when I heard her.

"Amara!" Neha called, running towards me. Her hair was wild, and she had rips and dirt marks all over her lace dress.

"Amara! I've been so worried! I've been searching for you all night! I heard what Aloysius and his hooligans did to your home. My father is speaking to the Mudaliyar about it right now. I went to Siyath Malli's house and he said you were dragged away by some thugs. I've been trying to raise a search party for you. Oh, my goodness, tell me, are you alright?"

I looked at her—sweet, kind Neha, who'd never had to endure what I'd been through. Neha, who'd betrayed me once and begged for my forgiveness, only to rip my heart into shreds once again. She'd made her choice when she agreed to marry Raam.

"Why do you care, Neha? Won't it be easier for you if I'm gone?"

But Neha's eyes ran over my body, taking in the blood—mine and Jeevan Maama's and my unborn child's—that crusted all over me. Gasping, she tried to reach for my shoulders, but I stepped away.

"What happened to you, Amara? You can tell me. I can help. Whatever it is, we can deal with it together, you understand?"

And here she was, still acting like she cared about me.

"Stop pretending, Neha!" My voice came out an angry rasp. "How can you claim to be my friend after agreeing to marry Raam? You knew how much he meant to me! You knew how much I loved him!"

"Amara, I promise I didn't know. I hadn't spoken to you in a year. I thought he was just an infatuation when you were in school. My parents brought him as a proposal and insisted he was the best choice. I—I just went with it. We hadn't spoken in so long. I didn't know you were still seeing him."

"But you knew last night, at the perahera. You couldn't tell me then?"

"So much happened so quickly, Amara. We kept getting interrupted. I wanted to tell you, of course."

"Liar!"

"Amara, please," she pleaded. "Please forgive me. Please tell me what happened to you. Let me help."

Her eyes shone with tears. How could someone with a heart so full of poison manage to look so innocent?

"You know what, Neha? You should marry Raam. You both deserve each other."

"Amara." She sobbed, but what else was left to say?

"I must go now, Neha. One day you'll know pain as I have felt it. And then, perhaps, you will understand."

"No," she cried, tears shining bright on her face. "No, Amara, stay with me."

But there was too much evil in the world. Even in the places you would least expect. Even in the hearts of those who were supposed to love you.

I turned to leave.

"Amara!" Neha tried to grab my shoulder.

I reached out and pushed her, more gently than she deserved. Neha was lifted off her feet as she flew backwards, landing in a heap a few feet away from me. She wasn't hurt, but I needed her to go. There was no room for her in the vestiges of my own evil heart.

Neha stared at me, too shocked to even scream.

"Amara, don't do this," she whispered.

"I'm just finishing what you started, Neha. What you all started."

Someday, she might understand. But even if she didn't, that was alright. I didn't need understanding. I needed revenge.

46

IT WAS MORNING, just after dawn. The time of day I loved the most. The time of day when everything felt fresh and clean and new. When the world was ripe with second chances. But I didn't care about second chances. I certainly wasn't going to be giving any.

I walked past the smouldering ruins of our hut, unable to wring out even a drop of sadness. My life had been destroyed long before my home, I just hadn't known it.

My father was seated on a small bench, right where our garden met the golden sand. His face was still bandaged, the white fabric ashy as the wind blew debris and soot around him. He had his legs pulled up in front, covered in his sarong, his arms wrapped around himself. He rested his chin on his knees, like a small child, and was rocking himself back and forth.

"Amara," he rasped, when he saw me. He'd been crying. I could tell from his tearstained cheeks and bloodshot eyes. I'd never seen my father cry before. I should be sad—perhaps a part of me, a minuscule part that was buried beneath all this rage, took pity on him, but it was too late. Sadness was for the girl in my past. Someone I used to know. The innocent rabbit that was swept away by the mongoose. I wouldn't allow myself to be a victim anymore.

"Amara!" He tried to reach for me, but froze when his eyes travelled down the length of my body. My reddha was soaked in dried, hardened blood. Rivers of rust were left trailing down my legs. I hadn't bothered to wipe them away. They gave me comfort. They marked what was to come.

"What have they done?" He started to sob, shoulders shaking, gasping, wheezing for air. "What have they done to you?"

He knew.

I felt it in my bones.

My voice was steady. Composed. "You knew everything all along. You knew what Jeevan Maama did to me."

"I swear I didn't. I found you, that day on the beach. I carried you back myself. They told me you were possessed. I performed the exorcism myself."

"You know that's not true."

"We had to perform a complex charm on you, Amara. We—we had to alter your memory so you would forget the terrible thing you had done. It wasn't easy. Jayasiri suspected me of demonic rituals and we had to bribe him to keep him quiet. We couldn't even do the charm at our house for fear of a neighbour seeing you. We had to keep you at a small hut at the edge of the jungle until you recovered so we could keep it quiet."

The hut from my dreams. Where Bhagya said she'd found me.

"Stop. Lying. To. Me." The words spat out of me like venom from a snake. "You chose to blame this all on a demon when the truth was right under your nose. You'd rather let me, your daughter, take the blame for something a man did. Even one you hated. Is that how little you think of us? How little you think of me?"

"Amara, please . . ."

"I need to know what happened."

Instinctively, I reached down and grabbed a fistful of wet sand. Maybe I had lost my memory, but water always remembered. Within me, Bhagya thrummed. She would help me see the truth.

And suddenly, I was back on the beach, but at a different time. The sun had already traversed the sky and was about to set, throwing a mangosteen-coloured cape over the shore. I was trying to sneak back home when I saw Jeevan Maama on the beach. He was waiting to see my mother, but didn't want to come inside until my father had left to carry out a blessing.

"Good evening, Jeevan Maama," I said, hoping he wouldn't question why I was wandering around by myself.

"How's my favourite niece doing?" He'd never called me that before. He seemed to be in a good mood, I thought to myself. His teeth were red when he grinned. He'd been chewing betel with puwak again, and the smell wafted over to me.

There were two men with him. The same men who had come to my house after Jeevan Maama was attacked. They sat a few feet away, watching us. Jeevan Maama often brought one or two companions when he came to visit. He didn't want to risk travelling alone, he'd told me.

"Come, sit down with me a moment. You've grown up so much since the last time I saw you."

I didn't want to sit, but it would have been rude not to.

I'd taken a seat next to Jeevan Maama as he chatted and I listened, when I noticed a small bottle next to him on the sand.

"What's that?" I asked.

He grinned and held it up to his lips, drinking from it deeply.

"I'll give you a bit, if you like, but you have to promise not to tell your mother."

I held it up to my nose and sniffed. It reeked of fermentation.

"Is this toddy?" I asked.

"Shh!" he joked, holding a finger up to his lips. "Even better. It's brandy."

"I shouldn't."

"Oh, come on now. I thought you were fun," he said.

His eyes were on my face. Something passed over him—a cloud, perhaps, I thought. His smile turned direction.

He reached over then and tucked a strand of loose hair behind my ear. I frowned. It didn't feel right, him being so close to me like that, even if he was my uncle.

"Come on, then." His voice had turned harder, more insistent.

"No, it's alright. Thank you."

"Hasn't your mother taught you any manners? It's rude to turn down an invitation."

I didn't want to be rude. I reached for the bottle and took a delicate sip.

Jeevan Maama guffawed.

And then he lunged for me, grabbing my arms.

"I have you now, you little bitch."

My mother's voice cut through that memory—

I'll claw out your tongue if you tell. Of course she'd have wanted it hidden. All those voices I'd kept hearing, they were from that night.

I didn't need to remember any more. The echoes of what he'd done reverberated through me even now. Except this time, instead of extinguishing my light it only made it burn brighter. What had almost destroyed me then, now only gave me strength.

I turned this strength back to my father.

"What did you do after the exorcism?" I asked. I already knew, but I wanted him to say it. I wanted him to repent for his sins. For his part in all this.

"I wanted you to forget, duwa. The tonic was supposed to make sure your memories didn't come back. Same with the suray you promised me you would never take off. It altered your thoughts, and kept any spirits away." That was the spell I'd seen scribbled with his things. And while I had noticed Bhagya in town while I wore the suray, she couldn't come close to me. She only spoke to me after Raam took it off.

But Thaththa was wrong, it wasn't demons that I needed protection from. The people who hurt me were my own family. The very people who were supposed to love me and protect me.

The anger that was boiling and swirling within me was building momentum. I felt its pressure mount, needing release.

I looked over at the man who cowered before me. He could sense it too. That I had changed. That I had grown. That I wasn't at the mercy of those who harmed me any longer.

"You weren't possessed then," he whimpered. "In my heart I always knew it was that vermin Jeevan. But I chose to believe your mother. You must trust me. She told me that one of the demons from an exorcism had found its way into you."

How much longer did I have to endure weak men blaming women for their failures?

"Amara, I know you weren't possessed then, but you are with a demon now, aren't you?"

"I am. And I'm safer now, with a demon who cares about me, than I ever was with you."

"Amara, please listen to me. Yakku, they tell you what you want to hear. They help you get what you want, and then you are indebted to them. You understand? You'll never be able to escape. You'll be in their grasp forever."

"Stop trying to turn me against my only protector," I spat.

"You think they are protecting you, but they are not. They want your soul, Amara. They'll never let you go. Please, let me help you."

And with that, he reached out and splashed something on me.

I screamed as my flesh stung and sizzled. He had a small bottle of pirith pan—blessed water—in his fingers. With his other hand he grasped for his own suray and started muttering a prayer. For the first time since Bhagya entered me, I began to feel uneasy.

"No!" I cried, swiping at him, trying to pull the suray out of his hands.

He flung more pirith pan, and I yelped. A surge of power shot out of me, knocking him to the ground.

My heart twisted for the slightest moment seeing him like that. Thaththa, who'd taught me how to swim, who'd encouraged me to learn, who'd told me stories to make me laugh when I was sad about being bullied. The same man who had entrapped my mother. Who'd forced her into a life she didn't want, one in which all the blame was passed on to her. But that didn't matter either. None of it mattered. Because when I needed him the most, he had failed me. They had all failed me.

I knelt on the ground near him, snarling through the burning acid that continued to spray on my body. I mustered every inch of strength I could.

"Bhagya, I need you."

"I'm right here. But you don't need me. You've found your power."

She was right.

I reached over and wrapped my fingers around my father's throat.

"Amara, no!" he wheezed.

But it was too late. I pressed down on him, feeling the stubbly skin on his neck, forcing down on his Adam's apple.

"Amara, I'm sorry."

And there, on the very sand that had seen my life reduced to tatters, I felt his last breath.

I lay there with him. Was it for a minute or an hour? I'd never know. But after my anger subsided and a calm I had never felt before enveloped me, I stood up and waded into the ocean. The waves would soothe me. They would absorb my pain. I'd emerge reborn.

47

CLEANSED AND CLEAN, if only of the blood that had splattered my body, I waded back to shore. A reddha and hattey flapped innocently on our washing line, too near the beach to have been touched by the flames. I pulled them on and made my way inside the remains of our home. Everything was charred and dark, embers still glowing in the corners.

What remained of Amma's sewing machine stood in the corner. I pulled open the drawer and was in luck. Her hambiliya with the sewing money was safe. There wasn't much, but it would be enough for me to buy passage to Colombo. And once I was in Colombo I could start anew. I would be alone, but I wasn't afraid. There was nothing left for me to fear anymore.

My newfound confidence paid off. I was able to pay a fisherman who was sailing out at dusk. He looked quite taken aback that a young girl, unaccompanied, wanted to join his cargo, but his eyes glinted when I showed him my coins and he nodded his agreement. He even gave me some bread, and handed me a blanket.

"You can lie down there," he said, pointing down to a ladder leading belowdecks. "You look like you've seen death."

I hadn't just seen death, I wanted to tell him. I had wielded it like a sword.

But there was no need to alarm anyone. I simply mumbled my thanks, crawled down to the hull of the boat, nestled myself in the blanket, and felt the weight of a thousand sleeps overtake me.

I awoke to the gentle rocking of the waves. A bright stream of silver moonlight lit the opening that led to the deck, but otherwise I was in darkness. The hull smelled of fish, but I didn't mind it. I was free.

"Bhagya," I whispered. "Are you still here?"

And then she was. Not within me, like she was before, but sitting next to me, smiling from ear to ear.

"Amara, you did it."

"Because of you, and your help. Bhagya, I couldn't be more thankful to you."

"There's no need to mention it." She grinned. "It was my pleasure."

It was an odd choice of words. I'd killed three people, after all. It might have been necessary, but it certainly wasn't pleasurable.

"So, where are we going now?" she asked.

"Colombo. The main city."

"Perfect," she remarked. "I couldn't have picked a better place myself. There are plenty of men there who need to be shown the error of their ways. And now with you by my side, there won't be anyone stopping us."

My body felt like it had been drenched with cold water.

"What do you mean?"

"I had so many limitations before. I had to hide in the jungle most of the time, depending on offerings from Heen Achchi to keep me strong, and no one but you and her could actually see me. But when you let me possess you, I felt more powerful than I'd been in years. An invitation like that, well, let's just say there's no stopping us now. Imagine what we could do together? Imagine the justice we could seek?"

"Bhagya, I—I don't want to hurt anyone else. I already had my justice."

She took a moment to reply and when she did, her voice was low and angry.

"So it's just yourself that you care about, then? What about all the other women who have been treated unfairly? Don't you care about their plight?"

"I don't want to hurt anyone else, Bhagya. It's not justice when we are attacking men and they have no clue why. I don't want to become—"

"You don't want to become what?" Her voice had gone even deeper, and she'd lost her glow. "You don't want to become a demon like me?"

"That's not what I meant, Bhagya. I'm grateful to you, I really am. But—"

"That's not the way this works, Amara." She glared at me. "You can't just pick and choose when to use my powers. You can't suddenly decide to act innocent now that those who wronged you are gone. To pretend to be a puritan whenever it suits you."

"I won't harm anyone," I insisted. "I can't. It's not right."

"Was it right when you strangled your father on the beach? Or when you stabbed your mother with a wooden cross?"

"I—" But I had no words to say. Was I evil now too?

"Don't tell me that your father never taught you that. That a deal with a demon always comes with a price."

"I can't help you, Bhagya. I won't."

"I love how you think you have a choice. Tell me, Amara, have you looked in the mirror lately?"

There were no mirrors in the hull of the boat, but there was a shard of glass glinting on the floor. Bhagya picked it up and handed it to me.

"You might want to step into the light." There was a sneer in her voice, I noticed, as I held the glass in trembling hands. Something in me ached to not know. To go back to where this all started, weeks ago. But what would I have done differently? It was not my choices that had led me here, but my desperation. I didn't ask for any of what had happened to me.

It took me a moment to angle the glass just right. And when I saw what was reflected back at me, the shard slid from my fingers, shattering into pieces.

It was her. The yakshaniya from my dreams.

"It can't be," I gasped. Had I really become her?

"Didn't you think she looked familiar?" Bhagya asked. "I think it's all in the eyes."

"No!" I screamed. "I'm not her!" But to my horror, everything slid into place. The yakshaniya from my dreams had been me all along. She showed me that I would eventually kill Jeevan Maama, and Amma, and Thaththa. They weren't visions of the attacks that were taking place in the present. They were glimpses of my future. Of whom I would finally become. I killed my uncle, my mother, and my father.

But then, what about all those men who were dead in the paddy field? Aloysius and Raam and countless others?

"You're in my debt now, Amara. And this is how you'll repay me."

"No! There's no way. I won't let you."

I had to escape. I had to get away from her. I wouldn't live my life like this. I refused to become a monster. A paddy field of men wouldn't be dead because of me.

"Amara—"

"Get away from me!" I screamed. "You can't have me."

"Amara—"

But I started climbing the ladder to the deck. Bhagya was on my heels. I could feel her close behind me.

The sea breeze hit me as soon as I reached the top. A group of fishermen were at the far side of the boat, but they didn't notice me.

"Amara."

But I wouldn't give in to her. I couldn't. I had power. Bhagya had taught me that. I had a say in what happened to me. I had finally found my strength, and I wasn't about to let it go now.

There was only one thing left for me to do.

I took a deep breath, steeling myself. Then I placed one foot on the boat's railing, pulling myself over. I clung to the rusty metal for just a beat, but I wasn't afraid. I'd always loved the sea. I let go, dropping into the grey expanse of nothingness. The water was sharp and icy as it swirled around me. I could finally let go. I could finally have my release.

And as I choked on my very last breath, I heard her voice again.

"You're mine now."

EPILOGUE

RAAM WALKED HOME slowly. His back ached and his stomach growled. He'd been asked to work late, once again. His manager at the harbour, who'd once favoured him and given him the least amount of documents to file, was now cold and distant, assigning him more tasks than was fair. No one spoke of it directly, but Raam suspected that news of his broken engagement had managed to pervade his workplace, and along with it, the attitudes of the entire clerical department.

It wasn't his fault that Neha De'Almeida had had a change of heart. She had refused to even see him, insisting to her father that she couldn't go through with the engagement. Women were bitches like that.

Raam stopped for a moment to stretch. He was tempted to sit and rest by one of the trees. But the moon was high in the sky and he really should get back home, even though there was little comfort waiting for him.

His parents had also been curt with him since the betrothal was called off. He'd never thought they would fall victim to town gossip, but Amara's family dying and their house burning down had caused quite a stir. Every speck of the Capuwa's life had been picked apart by the townsfolk, with more than a few whispers insinuating that Raam had been involved with the Capuwa's daughter. He had been, of course, but it was irritating since he'd taken plenty of precautions to ensure that word never got out about it. No point raising eyebrows when she was just there for a good time—nothing more.

He had been paid his monthly salary today, and Raam had bundled it into a small pouch he kept hidden in his sarong. The sooner he could deposit it in the box he kept hidden in his clothes basket, the sooner he'd breathe easy. He used to know the jungle like the back of his hand, but it wasn't safe anymore. It hadn't been for over a year now.

The attacks, previously few and far between, were happening more regularly now—ironically, even after the death of the Capuwa. A demon is terrorising this village, the locals cried, though no one had been able to track down the true culprit yet.

The attacks were different now too. The first few had left the victims scarred, fearful, but alive. The more recent ones hadn't been so merciful. The casualties were clawed beyond recognition, their mangled, bloodied corpses left discarded on the jungle floor.

The latest one had been particularly gruesome, more so because the Mudaliyar's aide, Aloysius Peiris, had been quite a powerful man in the town. Loudly proclaiming that he feared no demon, he had marched into the jungle, clutching a Bible and a shotgun, hoping to put an end to this once and for all. His mutilated body had been discovered at dawn, but his head hadn't yet been found.

Raam wasn't foolish. The main road, while long, was the safest route, even though it was just him and the stars tonight. He felt for his pouch again, just in case. If he kept up a brisk pace, he should be home within the hour.

He was rounding the last bend, the one that cradled the tangle of trees that led to the jungle, when he spotted her. It took a moment for his eyes to adjust in the moonlight. She wore a flowing white dress that fluttered gently in the warm breeze, her long black hair untied and cascading down her back in thick waves. There was something about her that Raam thought familiar. Was it her? The Capuwa's daughter?

But surely, this beautiful woman couldn't be her? Amara had been barely a child. A sallow, fearful thing at that. This was a majestic lady, shining as bright as the moon. Raam was enraptured.

Something stirred in her arms. Perhaps a baby? he thought to himself. Was it the same baby she tried to entrap him with?

"Excuse me?" he called out, his voice cutting through the perfumed night air. "Excuse me, madam?"

He was nearing her now, and was certain that he had been mistaken. This was certainly not Amara. The beautiful woman before him fidgeted with her child, adjusting the bundle on her hip. She looked to be in distress.

"Madam?"

She turned her face towards him and indeed there were tears trailing down her cheeks.

"Can you help me, sir?" Her voice was low and melodious and unlike anything he'd heard before.

"Of course, madam. Has something happened? Why are you alone?"

She smiled the saddest smile he had ever seen.

"Yes, something terrible has happened. Please help me."

He felt something stirring in him—the specific type of gallantry that had been embedded in him since he was a little boy. Men are to protect women. And if he was lucky, he thought with a smile, perhaps he'd even be rewarded. A moonlight kiss with this beautiful creature would be well worth whatever it took to earn it. And if he was really lucky—Raam chuckled to himself, the pain in his back long forgotten.

"Of course, madam. How might I be of service?"

"Could you hold my baby for a moment? My arms are tired and she's growing heavy."

"Certainly." He reached out and took the bundle from her arms. He wasn't one to be smitten by infants, but was ready to do whatever she asked. The woman's fingers grazed his hand as she let go, and Raam felt a shiver run through him. That was strange, he thought to himself. It was a humid night, as it often was on the island.

"You know, you're quite lucky you met me tonight," he remarked.

She smiled softly, gazing up at him through heavy lashes.

"Is that so?"

"Yes. Most men wouldn't have the best of intentions for a woman they come across, alone at night, like this."

The woman smiled again and, turning gracefully, walked right into the jungle.

"Madam?" he called after her. Had she lost her faculties? Every person, child, and animal knew to avoid going into the jungle after dark. But he held her baby and had no choice but to follow her. Perhaps she was looking for someplace private, away from other travellers' eyes. The thought made his heart rise.

"Excuse me, madam?" he tried again.

She moved delicately, with the grace of a dancer, not once looking down as she made her way past the roots and leaves and undergrowth that made up the jungle floor. Raam struggled to keep pace, sweat starting to drip its way down his brow and sting his eyes.

"Wait!" he cried out, having had enough. Worried for his safety as well as for the safety of the child.

To his surprise, she heeded his request. Having reached a clearing, she paused and turned around. Was it him, or was time moving differently around her? The moonlight streamed through the branches, depositing dappled beams around them. One beam bounced off her face and he caught his breath.

She was so beautiful that he almost couldn't bear to look directly at her. And yet, he ached for her all the same—desire taking root deep within him.

"Thank you," she said, coming closer to him. "I can take her back now."

That was when Raam looked down into the bundle he held in his arms. He'd been too preoccupied with following the woman to focus on the child. The moon was smothered by a cloud just then, pushing the clearing into darkness. Raam adjusted the blanket, lifting it away from the baby so he could get a closer look.

And then he noticed the smell—like the stench that was left over on the beach when fishermen threw out the catch they couldn't sell at the market, rotten and salty and dying.

The moon uncloaked itself, breathing relief back into the jungle, and as Raam's eyes focused on the blanket he started to scream.

The child was dead. There was no doubt about it. Its little body was grey, blue veins pressing out against translucent skin. There was something about it that looked almost half-formed—perhaps the way its face was gnarled, perhaps because its umbilical cord was still attached to its stomach, oozing black. But worst was how its eyes were wide open, staring straight at him.

And then the woman was before them, smiling as if she enjoyed the look of fear on Raam's face.

"You looked like you wanted a kiss, Raam," she rasped. She wasn't beautiful anymore. All her softness had melted away. Different parts of her face were sewn onto her skull haphazardly, the stitches leaking red, the stench that emanated from her making him retch.

"No!" he screamed, terror flooding through him. He wanted to run away, but his feet stayed rooted to the spot. He was paralysed, powerless, beyond himself with fear.

"It's too late. You're mine now," she cooed. Her skeletal fingers brushed the side of his cheek, and she leaned in, pressing her rotting lips to his.

I WATCHED AS they found him two days later, right where I'd deposited him on the jungle floor. The smell of his decomposing body reached their noses first, causing them to retch. But that was nothing compared to the screams of terror when they saw him, his face twisted in abject fear, his entrails weeping out of him, his heart ripped straight out of his chest.

I chuckled as they clutched one another, wondering what demon was capable of such cruelty. *Demoness,* I wanted to correct them. As a woman, I was ridiculed and tormented and underestimated. As a yakshaniya, no more.

One of the young men peered up the tree where I crouched, licking my lips. He must have heard me laughing. Good. Let him search for me. Let him spend the rest of his years looking over his shoulder, wondering if the demon who prowled the jungle was just behind him. Let him be overcome with fear.

Maybe he'd even understand the bloodied corpse on the jungle floor for what it was—a warning. A warning for the men who take and hurt and destroy and then take some more. Let them be warned that I'm always watching. Let them know that I'm only biding my time.

ACKNOWLEDGMENTS

Some books come easy. You just sit down, start typing, and the words flow through you and onto the page like they were always supposed to be there. This was not one of those books. While I absolutely love where *Island Witch* ended up, the journey here was fraught with many doubts. The plot didn't come together until a much later draft, the historical element was different from the contemporary settings I was used to, and of course, imposter syndrome clouded every sentence I wrote.

If not for these amazing people, I can confidently say that this story would have simply stayed in the far corners of my mind. A huge thank-you to:

Melissa Danaczko, to simply call you my agent seems like a gross oversimplification of everything you are to me. Thank you for reading countless drafts, talking me through numerous mental breakdowns, and always, always encouraging me to stay true to the stories I want to tell.

The best editor in the world, Jen Monroe. I've always said that I knew from the very first time we spoke that I HAD to work with you. Thank you for always championing my dark stories and being an advocate for diverse voices. I'll never forget how you smiled when I told you my idea for *Island Witch*, and how much confidence that gave me.

The wonderful team at Berkley, none of this would be possible without you. To my publicists, Loren Jaggers and Stephanie Felty, I'm beyond thrilled and super thankful to work with you again. Elisha Katz and Jin Yu, thank you for doing such an amazing job at marketing my book.

A huge shout-out to the art team, especially Emily Osborne, who were so patient and kind, even when I asked for a million revisions to my stunning cover that I love so much!

My production editor, Jennifer Myers, and copyeditor, Sheila Moody, I know this must have been a difficult book, what with all the Sinhala phrases and cultural nuances. Thank you so much for being so considerate and respectful to my story and my characters' voices.

Candice Coote, who has consistently been so dependable, organised, and encouraging. I'm so grateful to have you as part of my team.

And to everyone at Berkley and Penguin Random House who helped bring *Island Witch* into the hands of readers! To simply say *thank you* feels so insignificant, but I truly appreciate all the hard work that has gone into getting this book out into the world.

The amazing team at Stuart Krichevsky Literary Agency—thank you for being so lovely!

A special thanks to Thilani Samarasinghe, my dear friend and historian extraordinaire, who patiently answered millions of my questions, lent me out-of-print books for research, and

WhatsApp-ed me countless images of historically accurate clothing. I am so very grateful to have you in my life, and still strongly believe that the world would be a better place if you simply ran it.

The authors Dandris De Silva Gooneratne, Bruce Kapferer, George Papiginy, and Miniwan P. Tillakaratne, whom I have never met, but whose writing on demonology, traditional religious practices, and Sri Lankan lore contributed greatly to the research required to write this book.

Sujee Maama, who generously helped me with a wealth of information, and who has always been such a support to both me and Chathura.

Abby Endler, better known as @CrimebytheBook—I don't think you realise how much your support has meant to me. I was a fan of your posts and book recs long before I was a published writer, and I'm so grateful to have gotten to know you!

My ever-supportive Berkletes, who have shown me so much love and cheered me on, even when I've gone MIA. It's bad form for a writer to be lost for words, but I don't think I'd ever be able to spell out how much you all mean to me.

My amazing friends and family, who patiently put up with my bad moods and bouts of silence—I know it was probably worse for this book than any other—I couldn't have done any of it without your love and support.

Hector and Harley, who force me to take writing breaks by coming into my office and howling until I play with them.

And, of course, to CJ. To list all the reasons why I am grateful for you would far surpass all the pages in this book. Thank you for filling every one of my days with laughter, love, and your exceptional cooking.